D1206978

BOOKS BY P. T. DEUTERMANN

P. T. DEUTERMANN

GHOSTS OF
BUNGO SUIDO

ST. MARTIN'S PRESS

NEW YORK

This is a work of fiction. All of the characters, organizations, and events portrayed in this novel are either products of the author's imagination or are used fictitiously.

GHOSTS OF BUNGO SUIDO. Copyright © 2013 by P. T. Deutermann. All rights reserved. Printed in the United States of America. For information, address St. Martin's Press, 175 Fifth Avenue, New York, N.Y. 10010.

www.stmartins.com

Library of Congress Cataloging-in-Publication Data

Deutermann, Peter T., 1941–
    The ghosts of Bungo Suido : a novel / P. T. Deutermann.—First U.S. Edition.
        p. cm
    ISBN 978-1-250-01802-1 (hardcover)
    ISBN 978-1-250-01803-8 (e-book)
    1. Bungo Channel (Japan)—Fiction.   I. Title.
    PS3554.E887G46 2013
    813'.54—dc23

                                                        2013009264

St. Martin's Press books may be purchased for educational, business, or promotional use. For information on bulk purchases, please contact Macmillan Corporate and Premium Sales Department at 1-800-221-7945, extension 5442, or write specialmarkets@macmillan.com.

First Edition: July 2013

10 9 8 7 6 5 4 3 2 1

This book is dedicated to the families of the 3,600 American submariners lost in the Pacific war, who, for the most part, will never know what happened to their loved ones other than that they remain on eternal patrol.

ACKNOWLEDGMENTS

Not being a former submariner, I consulted several sources in preparing for this story. Clay Blair's seminal work, *Silent Victory*, was my primary reference for the mechanics of the submarines, the personalities of the skippers, and the evolution of submarine tactics. In my opinion, Blair's book is the best one out there on the subject of the so-called Silent Service. Laura Hillenbrand's *Unbroken*, along with first-person depositions made after the war by ex-POWs, provided much of the information I needed to write about the POW experience in Japan. Don Keith's book, *Final Patrol*, tells the stories of some of the more famous boats and their equally famous skippers during World War II, and Joseph Enright's book, *Shinano*, tells the true and exciting story of how that giant carrier was actually sunk on her maiden voyage. I am indebted to the volunteers who maintain USS *Torsk* (SS-423) at the Baltimore harbor maritime museum, which I visited to get a feel for the physical aspects of a World War II diesel boat. As I did in *Pacific Glory*, I've taken some historical license with the timeline of events in this book in order to sustain the story.

Finally, I want to acknowledge the incredible bravery, fierce persistence, and professional stamina of those submariners who took the war to Japan while the rest of the navy was still picking up the pieces in Pearl Harbor and elsewhere. Their achievements were made at great cost, and their final resting places are, as the inscription reads at Arlington, known but to God.

Part I

LONE WOLF

ONE

"Make your depth three hundred feet."

The two planesmen turned their brass wheels together but in opposite directions. "Make my depth three hundred feet, aye, sir," said the diving officer.

Gar Hammond felt the deck tipping down smoothly, but his attention remained on those screwbeats echoing audibly right through the hull as the Jap destroyer kept coming. Steady course and speed. No acceleration. Even better, he wasn't echo ranging.

Yet.

He looked over at his exec, Lieutenant Commander Russ West, and watched him force himself to relax his grip on the console rail. "This is nuts," West muttered, then glanced hastily in Gar's direction, as if he'd thought it but not intended to actually say it out loud.

"Relax, XO," Gar said, laughing. "Two thermoclines, remember? He's deaf. As soon as he passes overhead he'll be totally deaf."

The exec managed a weak grin back, but the destroyer's screwbeats were getting louder, that unmistakable *pah-pah-pah* sound making every man in the crowded control room clench his teeth. Gar noticed that no one in Control was making eye contact with anyone else; they'd been on enough patrols to know that fear was contagious. He also knew that someone in the control room wanted to shout out, *If we can hear the destroyer's screwbeats, why can't the destroyer's sonar hear us?* Because, Gar thought, we're being quiet. The destroyer is not.

This was the most dangerous phase of the tactic, the one his crew called Asking for It, behind his back, of course. Get out in front of a Jap convoy, submerge deep, let the targets and the escorts pass overhead, then rise to periscope depth behind the last escort and fire a torpedo right into his stern while the destroyer's sonar was blinded by his own wake and propeller noises.

"Approaching three hundred feet," the diving officer announced. The hull was creaking under the increased pressure, but Gar had taken *Dragonfish* down to almost 500 feet before. More importantly, back up, too, a happy modulation on that old aviator rule: You want the number of safe landings always to equal the number of takeoffs.

It was almost time to sprint.

Pah-pah-pah-pah, louder now. The destroyer was almost directly overhead. If he'd detected them, this would be the moment when depth charges would start rolling off his fantail. He can't detect us if he's not pinging, Gar told himself. And even if he were pinging, those two thermoclines in the 300-foot water column above them should deflect his sonar beams. "Should" being the operative word.

Pah-pah-pah-pah.

Gar waited impatiently. They'd accelerate once he passed overhead, get right behind him, rise to periscope depth, take one firing observation, and shoot. He'd done this three times since taking command, and so far he'd never missed. He was, of course, fully aware of how nervous this made his whole crew. If that single torpedo did miss and the destroyer's lookouts saw its wake slicing alongside from astern, she'd immediately roll depth charges right into the *Dragonfish*'s face.

Pah-pah-pah-pah.

"*Down* Doppler, bearing zero five five," the soundman in the conning tower reported, the relief audible in his voice. The destroyer was headed away from them. Everyone strained his ears to detect any noises indicating the Jap had rolled depth charges, but all they could hear was those screwbeats, steady at about 12 knots, based on turn count, in the away direction.

Okay, Gar thought. Time to kill this hood.

"All ahead two-thirds," he ordered. "And come right to zero five five."

He saw the exec let out another deep breath. Eight knots was just about their top speed underwater, and they would entirely deplete the battery in less than one hour if they kept that up. Both of them scanned the array of instruments and gauges all around them in the control room. Gar felt the sudden surge of power as *Dragonfish* heeled into her turn. Control was, as usual, crowded and tense. The air was filled with the haze of diesel fumes and human sweat, mixed with a faint tinge of ozone as the batteries dumped amps.

"I'm going up," he told the exec. "Diving officer, bring her to periscope depth. Handsomely, please."

Once he'd climbed up into the conning tower he told the torpedo officer to make ready tubes one and two. The attack team seemed steady, especially now that the tin can above had gone past them without loosing a barrage of 500-pound depth bombs. The deck sloped upward as the Dragon rose to periscope depth. The conning tower was under red-light conditions, just like Control. It was dark outside, and Gar needed his eyes to be night-adapted once he raised the scope. Conn was even more crowded than Control.

"Passing two hundred feet," the diving officer reported from down below.

"All ahead *one*-third."

The helmsman acknowledged the order.

"Leveling at one hundred feet," called the diving officer.

It wasn't very hard for Gar to keep a picture of this tactical plot in his mind. Pausing the ascent was standard procedure. The last thing they wanted was for the boat to punch through periscope depth and broach in full view of the destroyer's after lookouts. He should be about 800 yards in front of us now, Gar thought, well within visual range even though it was past sunset. Assuming you had the time, it was always best to stabilize and trim her at 100 feet, then rise slowly to periscope depth.

"Sound, confirm bearing."

"Mushy bearing zero five niner, Cap'n. Plus or minus five degrees. I'm listening through his wake."

"Zero five niner, aye. Helmsman, come right to zero five niner. Indicate turns for three knots. Sound, watch that Doppler carefully."

"Sound, aye." The Doppler, or pitch of the audible screwbeats, was a critical indication. Down Doppler meant that the destroyer was going away from them; up Doppler meant the opposite. Steady Doppler meant he was broadside to them and thus probably turning around. They waited.

"Steady at periscope depth," the diving officer called.

"Indicating turns for three knots, and steady on zero five niner," the helmsman reported.

Gar went to the periscope well. "You ready?" he asked the attack team.

"We have a solution," the operations officer replied.

"Up scope," Gar ordered. "This will be a firing observation."

The electro-hydraulic motors down in Control whined as they sent the attack scope up to the surface, with Gar hunched over the eyepiece handles like a monkey as it rose, all elbows and knees. He could barely hear the torpedo data computer team comparing sound data to what their predicted firing solution plot was showing.

He trained the scope around to the last reported bearing of the destroyer so that he'd be looking right at him once the scope broke the surface. His eyes took a few seconds to adjust, and then he saw him, just a black blob in the darkness dead ahead of them, but with a phosphorescent wake pointing right at Gar's aim point.

"Bearing, *mark*! Range is one thousand yards. *Down* scope."

One second later he heard the magic words from the plotting team. "Bearing and plot agree. Torpedo running depth ten feet. Tube one ready. Plot *set*! Fire any time."

"Fire one!"

They felt the sudden impulse of pressurized air in the boat as the firing flask expelled the torpedo and then dumped its residual compressed air into the sub rather than releasing a huge bubble outside. Doctrine called for a second torpedo, but Gar disagreed: The torpedo's gyro was slaved to the ordered bearing. On a long-axis shot like this, if the first one missed, a second one would probably miss, too. One hit, however, would blow the after end of that bastard clean off, especially if the depth charges stacked on his fantail also exploded.

"Conn, Sound, fish is hot, straight, and normal."

"Run time, twenty-one seconds," said the ops boss, standing at the TDC—the torpedo data computer.

They all held their breath. Nothing happened for fifteen seconds.

"*Up* scope."

Gar could visualize the exec down in Control biting his lip. He and Russ had hashed this over many times before, with the exec arguing for leaving the scope down after firing when they were this close. The destroyer's after lookout *might* see the approaching torpedo wake, but he'd *surely* see both the wake and the periscope. Gar maintained that he needed to see what happened in order to take evasive measures if the fish missed and the tin can came about. *I can't wait for sound, XO, not when we're in the clinch.*

There—a soundless, bright red flash, down low on the visible horizon.

"Got him!" Gar called down. "*Down* scope!" A moment later the gut-punching thump of the warhead reached the boat, followed seconds later by several smaller explosions a half mile away. The Dragon whipsawed a bit as the underwater pressure waves enveloped her.

Got him good, Gar thought, as he listened to the depth charges detonating. "*Flood* negative and make your depth three hundred feet. Helm, all ahead two-thirds and come *left* to three two five."

The sound of smaller explosions drifted to starboard as they spiraled down and away from the sinking destroyer. The sound-powered phone talkers in the conning tower were mumbling into their phones, informing the rest of the crew that they'd killed another destroyer.

Gar, of course, felt relieved, although he knew they were just getting started. They'd counted two escorts, one ahead of what appeared to be a three-ship convoy, the other tailing astern. The second escort destroyer would be turning from the front of the convoy now, headed back to see what was going on. They couldn't yet hear echo ranging over all that noise from the mortally injured destroyer, but Gar knew they surely would.

"Passing two hundred feet," the diving officer called out as *Dragonfish* completed her turn to the northwest. This was the second, and most dangerous, phase of the tactic: fire from behind, go deep and 90 degrees off firing axis for 2,000 yards, then turn parallel to the convoy's course again, slow down, go quiet, and wait to see what the remaining escort would do. It was dangerous because while they turned their stern to the action, they were the ones who became deaf.

As they opened out to 2,000 yards, Gar talked to the plotting team about the convoy. The first lookout sighting had been two smoke columns over the horizon, just before sunset. They hadn't had to maneuver—the ships were coming right at them. Once the ships themselves hove into view, Gar had submerged and taken periscope observations. He was pretty sure he'd seen two tankers and a smaller something between them, plus one escort out front and the mast of another on the horizon. The exec, ever cautious, had wanted to confirm the convoy's composition with the radar before they set up on it, but Gar had become convinced that the Japs could detect submarine radar if they radiated for too long. His standing orders were to keep surface and air-search radars in the standby mode unless there was no other way to see what was out there, and then to use only one sweep or two.

He reviewed the next phase with the attack team: After sprinting away from the scene of the first attack, they'd stay deep and quiet. If the other escort did not seem to be having any success locating them, they'd open out some more and then surface in the darkness, light off the diesels, and do an end-around run on the convoy at 22 knots to get back out in front of them. This time they'd be going for the high-value targets, those two tankers. Success during this phase depended on their having an accurate count of the enemy escorts. If they'd missed one, it could get really exciting.

Gar did the math: By the three-minute rule they'd be in the off-axis position in just under eight minutes. He was ever conscious of the battery's limitations. Running submerged at full battery power was a chancy business for *Dragonfish*, although they'd done that many times, too, since he'd taken command. If they fully depleted the battery, they'd be forced to surface and duke it out with that remaining destroyer, which meant using their single deck gun against five of his, or even being rammed.

He leaned against the bulkhead near the periscopes and closed his eyes for a minute. The hatch to Control was right at his feet, and he could overhear the conversation below.

"Gotta hand it to him," the chief of the boat was saying. "Guy can shoot." The Dragon's senior chief petty officer, "Swede" Svenson, was almost too tall for submarine duty; he walked in a permanent hunch to keep from banging his head on the low overhead. He had a classic Scandinavian face, all angles and eyebrows, bright blue eyes, a prominent Viking nose, and a permanently ruddy complexion. Being chief of the boat, he was, of course, called "Cob."

"I'll give him that, Cob," the exec said quietly. "But this is still some crazy stuff. We should be shooting at tankers, not tin cans."

"Maybe this *is* how it's done, XO," Cob said. "The Dragon's sunk more Jap ships under Cap'n Hammond than she did in the two previous patrols."

Gar smiled. Cob had that part right. It was all about results these days. No results or even skimpy results, the brass found someone else to be in command, which in fact was how he'd come to command of *Dragonfish*. Under Captain Mason, who'd put her in commission, they'd had several shooting opportunities and scored on none of them. Mason was a pleasant man, compassionate, tactically very conservative, and always looking out for the welfare of his officers and crew. He'd apparently been a peach to serve under, but the boat's lack of results had resulted in his early relief.

Then the exec said something interesting. "I'm guess I'm just tired of being scared all the time, Cob."

"Crew's scared, too, XO, but they like all those Jap brag-rags on the conning tower just the same."

The plotting team interrupted his eavesdropping. "Plot recommends coming right to zero five five, speed three, and rigging for silent running."

"Make it so," he replied. "Sound, you got anything?"

"Sound, negative. No echo ranging. Yet."

"They may not suspect a sub, then," he said as he started down the ladder into Control. There were some sotto voce groans as the ventilation shut down for silent running. The temperature in the control room rose immediately.

The exec agreed with Gar's assessment. A tanker blowing up in a convoy always meant a sub; a destroyer going boom in the night might mean an operational accident, since subs supposedly gave destroyers a wide berth. So now they pointed the Dragon in the general direction of the convoy's movement and waited to see what, if anything, the other destroyer did.

"XO, take the conn," Gar said. "I need a sandwich. Have the crew stand easy on station, but let 'em know we'll be back at it in about a half hour."

He went forward to the tiny wardroom, where he took ten minutes to have a sandwich and a mug of coffee. The wardroom had a single table and room for six men at a time. There was a green bench on either side of the table in place of chairs. He put his mug into a dish drawer and then went to his cabin to flop for a few minutes. He needed to relax, and he also needed the crew to see that he was relaxed. What's the Old Man doing? He's taking a nap. Oh, okay, it must be safe, for the moment, anyway.

Thirty minutes later they called him, and he returned to the conning tower. Lieutenant Ray Gibson, the ops officer, announced, "Captain's in Conn," as Gar's head cleared the hatch. Gibson was no more than five-seven in his dress shoes. He wore oversized spectacles that made him look a lot like an owl. Given that and his last name, his nickname just had to be Hoot.

Gar asked Hoot what he had for him. Gibson recited the tactical solution, their course, depth, and speed, and where they were plotting the two tankers.

"Where's that second escort?"

"No data, Cap'n," Gibson said. "Nobody's echo ranging, either."

The exec shook his head. "Two tin cans, neither one of them echo ranging? That make any sense?"

"No, sir," Gibson said, "but there it is. Sound hasn't heard the first ping."

The exec eased through the crowd of people so that he could talk directly to the soundman. "Can you tune that thing, Popeye?"

"Have to take the whole system offline, XO," Popeye Waller said. He was the ship's senior sonar tech. "And you know what can happen then."

What could happen was that the sometimes-balky sonar system wouldn't come back up, and then they'd be in trouble. No sonar, no ears. The passive side of the sonar was preset into the frequency range of Japanese navy sonars. The exec wondered aloud if the Japs had changed freq.

"If he were pinging, couldn't we just hear it through the hull?" he asked.

Popeye, who'd pushed back his headphones, rubbed his ears. "If he were pinging directional, right at us, yes, we'd probably hear that. But if he's in omni mode, the same layer that's protecting us would deflect most of that energy."

"And if they've changed freq?"

"Then we'd never hear it until he was right on us and throwing bad shit in the water," Popeye said. He turned around in his seat. "You think they've switched?"

"It's possible," the exec said. "We never heard the first one either, and he was right on top."

"Okay," Gar said. "Enough. We'll loiter here for a little while longer, then go up and take a look. For the moment, though, I want to stay quiet until we *know* that second escort isn't hunting."

He was hoping the second escort was busy picking up survivors from the other destroyer. With their own speed limited to 3 knots, the convoy, going 9 knots faster than they were, was getting farther and farther away from them. He couldn't risk depleting the battery with another 8-knot sprint, so at some point he'd have to get up on the surface and on the diesels and chase down the convoy. They had to be damned sure they didn't surface into the loving arms of a vengeful Jap destroyer.

He wished he could close the hatch to the control room. All that hot, stinking air was doing what hot air always does: rise. Popeye had put his headphones back on and was steering the external sound heads around in a careful sector search. Nobody spoke. Everyone waited. The plotting team continued to update the tactical plot on the target convoy using dead-reckoning techniques, but they all knew it was only an estimate. They just had to wait it out. Gar told the exec to go below and start people back to their General Quarters stations.

After another half hour went by, he again asked Popeye what he was hearing.

"Ain't heard a peep, Cap'n," Popeye said. "Right now, it's just biologics and white noise."

"Well, that won't do," Gar said. "I really need to know where that second tin can is, and also what happened to the first one."

The exec had come back up into the conning tower. "By definition," he said, "the first one's right where you torpedoed him. He's either gone down, or he's a floating wreck. Two thousand plus yards, that way. Everyone's back at GQ, sir."

"Good. I'm getting a bad feeling about that other escort, XO. We're blind down here. What's he doing and where the hell is he?"

Pah-pah-pah-pah.

"You asked," the exec said softly.

Popeye clamped his headphones to his head and worked the sound-head controls. "No clear bearing, Cap'n. The layer's got us. But he has to be close."

"*Right* full rudder, all ahead *Bendix*," Gar ordered. "Control, make your depth four hundred feet, fifteen-degree down bubble."

The exec dropped into the control room as the *Dragonfish* heeled to port in her tight right turn, the bow tilting down dramatically.

Pah-pah-pah-pah.

The destroyer was close enough that they could distinguish a clear up Doppler, which meant this one was inbound with murder on his mind. They were all having to hold on as the planes bit into the Dragon's lunge for the safety of deep water. Then Gar remembered that spiraling wasn't the fastest way to achieve depth. He ordered the helmsman to meet her.

"Steadying on one niner zero," the helmsman called as he whirled the small wheel, his voice exhibiting some Doppler of its own.

Now the destroyer's screwbeats were close enough and loud enough to penetrate even the protective thermoclines, those invisible acoustic barriers formed by two layers of water at different temperatures.

Gar knew that everybody in the boat was screaming the same mental exhortation in his mind: *Go, Dragon, go.* The destroyer's propeller sounds were now just a steady thrashing of the water as he passed overhead.

"Pass the word to stand by for depth charges," the exec said.

No shit, replied the silent mental chorus.

Then they all heard it: a loud click as the first hydrostatic fuse fired.

A huge blast hammered them, followed by another and then another. A choking cloud of dust, humidity haze, and bits of cork insulation rained down. The Jap was right on the bearing, Gar thought, but their fast dive had saved them. The depth charges were going off at about two fifty, far enough above them to keep the Dragon from being imploded. Two more blasts, off to starboard. Still shallow, thank God. Gar found himself rubbing his magic charm, a chief petty officer's collar insignia he kept on his key chain.

"Passing through four hundred feet," the diving officer called. Gar's arms were rigid against the ladder rails behind the periscope well. Passing through? They'd gone down too fast, and now the boat was below ordered depth. Recover? Or keep going? Keep going.

"Ease your down bubble to five degrees, and make your depth *five* hundred feet," he ordered. "*Left* standard rudder."

The boat heeled back the other way as she executed the sudden spiral back to the left. Four more depth charges went off in succession, each one hammering the sub's hull in an ear-squeezing bang. He's setting them deeper now, Gar thought. The boat's steel hull was creaking and groaning, literally changing shape at these extreme depths, where even a small leak could sink them.

He looked over at the battery discharge meters. "All ahead Bendix" was slang for max power, regardless of what was left in the batteries, but those damned batteries kept score. They had maybe fifteen more minutes before the lights would go out.

Four more depth charges exploded, but this time, they were some distance away. He looked at the battery meters again.

Hell with this, he thought. I'm gonna go get this guy.

"Slow to four knots and come to periscope depth," he ordered, visibly shocking everyone in the conning tower. "Make ready tubes nine and ten."

The Dragon trembled as they came off full battery power to something more manageable and began the climb back to periscope depth, right through that protective thermocline layer that had *not* kept them safe this time. Why had they not detected pinging? This second destroyer had come right to them as if following a homing beacon.

Pah-pah-pah-pah. Slower now, as the tin can up above repositioned somewhere behind them for another run.

"Got him on zero seven five," Popeye called. "*Down* Doppler."

"Passing three hundred feet."

"Level straight to sixty feet," Gar said. No more fine-tuning. He was going to get up there, take a look, and take a shot. Right now this guy thought he was in charge. We'll see about that. They waited as the sub came up, tipping back and forth a bit as the diving officer fought to keep her in trim.

"Sixty feet, aye," called the diving officer.

Then they waited. The TDC team was entering sound bearings and assumed ranges, trying to coax the computer into a firing solution.

"Bearing zero eight zero, null Doppler. He's turning."

Coming in for another try. Gar hoped he would be set deep this time, while they would be back at sixty feet.

"Target's entering our baffles," Popeye announced.

Gar closed his eyes for a moment, visualizing the tactical picture. They had no idea of the range to their adversary, but he knew the tin can would steady up as he ran in to make another depth-charge run. That's when he would become the target.

"Bearing?"

"He's somewhere in the baffles," Popeye replied, impatiently. As in, I just told you I can't hear him anymore. "Dead astern."

"Passing two hundred feet."

He turned to the torpedo data computer team. "Set running depth to ten feet, torpedo gyro to three zero five, shoot nine and ten when ready."

Pah-pah-pah-pah-pah-pah. Closing rapidly. The external sonar heads were blinded by the Dragon's own propeller noises, but the destroyer was close enough now that the whole sub could hear him coming in. Three seconds passed, and then they heard and felt the first fish punch away from the stern tubes, followed a few seconds later by the second.

"*Right* standard rudder, make one full circle, then steady on two seven zero, periscope depth, and make ready tubes seven and eight."

"Hot, straight, and normal," Popeye reported.

"Run time unknown," said the TDC operator.

"No kidding?" Gar asked, and everyone grinned for a brief moment. He'd fired blind, but there was a decent chance the destroyer would be coming at them right on that bearing.

Then came a satisfying blast, followed by a second one. Gar saw the exec wince as the whole boat shook from end to end, then realize those weren't depth charges. The torpedoes had found their mark. Lucky, lucky, *lucky!* It sounded like the destroyer was disintegrating right on top of them. Time to stop that turn and get out from under.

"Steady as you go."

"Steadying on—one eight five."

"Passing one hundred feet. Coming to periscope depth."

"All ahead one-third, turns for three knots." He waited for a full minute for the speed to come off the boat. "*Up* scope."

A moment later they leveled off, mushing into the surface effect of topside waves as they slowed. Gar straightened up as the scope came up, the lenses still underwater.

"Passing eighty feet."

He held his breath. The scope might be dark, but there was no lack of sound effects. Two torpedoes had torn the approaching destroyer apart. The roar of an exploding boiler filled the conning tower, accompanied by the cacophony of rending steel as the destroyer's shattered hull collapsed into the mortal embrace of the ever-hungry sea. Thankfully the sounds were coming from astern of them now.

"Level at periscope depth," called the diving officer. His voice sounded more than a little bit strained.

These guys needed to buck up, Gar thought. It was one thing to lie in ambush for a fat merchant ship and blow its bottom out from a mile away. It was quite another to get in close with a Jap destroyer and go a couple of rounds—and then do it again.

He scrambled around the periscope well, completing a three-sixty quick-look. A steady rumbling noise filled the conning tower as the destroyer sank, her remaining boilers bellowing steam into the cold sea as her bulkheads collapsed in a series of loud bangs. Gar mentally pushed away images of her crew being boiled alive as they were dragged down into the depths.

Remember Pearl Harbor, you sonsabitches.

"Okay," he said. "That's that. Stand by to surface. Plot, give me a bearing to that first tin can datum. Radar, conduct two short-range sweeps as soon as you can."

Everyone in the conning tower seemed to exhale at the same time, and then they all jumped in unison when the sinking destroyer's depth charges started to go off as he plunged past their set points. The Japs always kept their ashcans armed. Any of the crew who had managed to get overboard alive were now having their insides squeezed up out of their throats.

Remember Pearl Harbor.

"Radar reports *no* contacts within five miles."

Got 'em both, he thought. The three-ship convoy must have kept going once their escorts started mixing it up with *Dragonfish*.

"One radar sweep, long range,"

He could hear a commotion below as the bridge crew assembled down in the control room. The chief of the boat was coaxing the planesmen, who were having trouble maintaining a level depth with everybody moving around in the boat. The radar mast motors whined as it slid up to full height to improve their radar picture.

"Conn, radar: one contact, zero six five, twenty-one thousand yards."

"Surface," he said.

The Klaxon sounded. "Surface, surface. Lookouts to the bridge."

There was a mad scramble down in the control room as the diving officer operated the ballast tank levers while Cob monitored the angle on the boat. The people in the conning tower had to flatten themselves against the bulkheads to admit the lookouts and the officer of the deck. Their ears popped as the first lookout opened the hatch. Everyone welcomed the cold, fresh air, even when it sprayed some seawater into the conning tower.

"XO, take the conn. Put three diesels on the line, and one for the can. Head to intercept that radar contact."

Gar remained in Control until the surface watch had been established and the boat's ballast tanks trimmed for surface running. He told the diving officer to make sure the negative tank remained full. If the Dragon had to submerge fast, the extra weight in the negative buoyancy tank would help get her under quickly. Satisfied, he nodded at the exec and went forward.

No radar contacts within 5 miles meant that both tin cans had been sunk, so now it was time to get back to the business at hand. They weren't necessarily home free, though. There was always the possibility that those destroyers had sent off a distress call to the Japanese air bases on Luzon. The intel people back in Pearl had reported that the Japs had some of their new, radar-equipped night bombers in the region. Plus, there was that third, intermittent radar contact they'd seen in the convoy. It could be one of those new patrol frigates the Japs had begun using. One-third the size of a destroyer, but lethal nonetheless.

There was another ear-squeezing pressure wave as the diesels were lit off. If the air in the boat were unusually foul, the crew would crack all the watertight doors in the boat. Then the engine room crew would start the diesels with compressed air and let them take suction within the boat through the open bridge hatch for a few seconds before opening the main induction valve topside. This would quickly suck all the accumulated gases out of the boat, replacing it with air coming in from the conning tower hatch. It also created a momentary tornado in the control room, where any pieces of paper not nailed down began to fly around.

Once the diesels were on the line and warmed up, the exec would order flank speed, about 20 knots. Gar calculated the pursuit time: The convoy had been making between 10 and 12 knots, so their overtaking speed was only about 10 knots. An hour or so, then, and they'd go back to their sanguinary work.

The word came down from the bridge to secure from battle stations. This meant that all the watertight compartment hatches could be fully opened, and Gar could make a quick inspection tour. Three of the ship's main diesels were feeding the propulsion motors; the fourth was recharging the starving batteries. He checked the hydrogen meters in the forward battery to make sure the heavy charge wasn't building up explosive gases. Then he grabbed another cup of coffee as he passed by the wardroom, where three of the junior officers were talking excitedly about the destroyers and the skipper's "amazing" torpedo work.

Gar knew better. That last shot had been a Hail Mary if ever there'd been one—firing two fish on a sound bearing from depth meant that the fish had had to launch, turn, stabilize their gyros, climb, and then stabilize again at ordered depth in under a minute before colliding with the destroyer's onrushing bow. Amazing, yes, but amazing luck, not amazing skill. He asked himself again why they hadn't detected pinging. This news would really interest Pearl. The Japs had been slow to realize that the American submarine force was becoming a much bigger threat to Japan's survival than the big American battle fleets. They were starting to improve their sonars, depth charges, and use of radar. Their torpedoes had always been the best in the world, unlike what the American submariners had struggled to deal with for the first two years.

He held on to the bulkheads now as he progressed forward; the boat was encountering the deep swell that was always present in the Luzon Strait. At flank speed, she pitched up and down in what felt like slow motion. Some of the guys he walked past already looked a little queasy. Being submerged a lot of the time, submariners were often lacking in the sea legs department.

In Forward Torpedo the sweating crew was just finishing the reload of tube one. The interior of the sub was still under red-light conditions, and the torpedomen looked like they had been slow-roasted during the previous hours. *Dragonfish* had sailed from Pearl with twenty-four torpedoes: fifteen steamers, seven electrics, and two Cuties, as the new homing torpedoes were called. After Torpedo carried eight fish, four in the tubes, and four reloads. The balance lived in Forward Torpedo. Gar was not a fan of the electrics, but they were the prescribed weapon for use against Jap ships that could shoot back. The merchies, on the other hand, could only watch in horror when the telltale trail of bubbles from a steamer appeared, poised to open up their engine room.

Tonight he'd fired steamers at both tin cans, which technically was a violation of approved doctrine. The main advantage of the electrics was that they left no telltale wake to show the escorts where the submarine was lurking. Gar, however, was no slave to doctrine, especially when it was emanating from big staffs, safe back in Pearl. The second tin can had already known where they were, and the first one wouldn't have been able to see the torpedo wake embedded in his own wake, bubbles or no bubbles. Besides, the steamers had a much bigger warhead. In any event, he was protected by the unwritten rule: Nobody in Pearl would be second-guessing his using steamers as long as the targets were on the bottom, where all Jap ships belonged. Except, he thought, the chief of staff at SubPac, Captain Mike Forrester, who was not one of Gar's fans.

He walked back aft through the boat, talking to the men and generally taking the crew's emotional temperature after the fight with the destroyers. The chief of the boat joined him on his way back to After Torpedo, where they'd finished reloading. As they headed back forward toward Control, he paused in the passageway and asked Cob if his predilection for engaging destroyers was truly scaring the crew.

"They love it when they sink a Jap ship," Svenson said. "But there is a pretty high pucker factor when you decide to go one-on-one with a tin can."

"Going after them is a better tactic than just going deep and spreading our legs," Gar said. "You go deep and just wait for it, you hand the initiative to them. You start shooting back, you raise *their* pucker factor and maybe throw 'em off the scent. I've seen escorts run for it when we shot at 'em. The best defense, and all that."

"Yes, sir, and I agree with you," Cob said. "I've never felt so damned helpless as when we're down below and getting hammered on. The guys'll get used to it."

"I hope so, Cob, 'cause this cat's not gonna change his stripes. We're out here to do a job of bloody work, and I'm just the guy, unfortunately, to take the fight to them for a change."

"They're good guys, Cap'n, but most of 'em are real young, remember?"

Gar knew Cob was right about that. The average age on board was probably twenty.

"Captain, please contact Conn," came over the announcing system.

Gar grabbed the nearest sound-powered phone handset, set the dial for Conn, and twirled the handle once, causing a squeaking noise at the other end. The exec picked up the phone.

"Whatcha got, XO?"

"Plot has these guys zigzagging. We're gonna be on 'em pretty quick—their true speed of advance is only six knots. I'm assuming a surfaced attack unless we discover another escort. I'd like to set battle stations, surface, in ten minutes."

"Make it so, XO. Keep the gun team below until we know for damned sure there aren't any more escorts. And Russ? I want you to conduct the next attacks. I'll be up there shortly, but I'm gonna sit back and watch the whole picture while you sink these tankers. Okay?"

"Absolutely," Russ said.

Gar hung up the phone and told Cob they'd be back at GQ in ten minutes. Cob hurried away to spread the word. Gar made his way to Forward Officers' Country for a quick head call.

One of the submarine force's superstars in terms of tonnage sunk, Commander Dudley "Mush" Morton, had introduced a different command-and-control approach to submarine attacks. Prior to Morton, the captain and only the captain conducted every attack. He manned the scope, supervised the TDC, approved the plot solution, chose the attack bearings and methods, and did everything but push the firing button. Morton, who became famous for conducting most of his attacks on the surface, realized that there was too much data coming at him during an attack, so he decided to step back from the minutiae of the actual attack in order to better grasp the big picture: where the target was, where the escorts were, where the next target was going to be, where the best escape routes lay, what the radar picture showed, and so on. Morton let his XO, another superstar named Richard O'Kane, execute the individual torpedo attacks, while he, Morton, made sure some other part of the tactical picture wasn't getting ready to bite them in the ass.

The result was a superbly trained exec who could go on to a command of his own already highly experienced in attacking Jap ships, as O'Kane had amply demonstrated. To do it required a very confident captain and an equally competent exec. Gar hadn't adopted this system yet, but, having removed the warships from this particular convoy, small as it was, he felt this was the time to let Russ have a shot and try out Morton's system. As in every other aspect of submarine command, until you actually tried it, you never knew.

He went back to Control, where the battle teams were already taking their places in the red glow of the night-lights. He told everybody there that the XO was going to run the attacks and that he was going sit back and criticize. There were grins all around, albeit nervous grins. He knew he was going to have to work on this problem. A scared crew was a dangerous crew—a man who's afraid will freeze faster than a man who's on the hunt with his blood up. Training, he reminded himself. We have to do more training.

"Set battle stations, surface."

He climbed the ladder into the dim red light of the conning tower to begin the dance. The stream of cold fresh air whistling through the hatch to the bridge was wonderful. The diesels were purring as only Fairbanks Morse engines could. The exec was getting ready to go up to the bridge, where he would conduct the torpedo attacks against the two tankers up ahead. Instead of the periscope he'd be using the target-bearing transmitters, or TBTs. These were simply a set of high-powered binoculars welded to a movable frame. The frame was connected electrically to the TDC weapons control computer. The firing officer would point the TBT at the target ship and squeeze a button. The target's bearing would be transmitted to the computer, and a firing solution would soon materialize. The computer would then continuously communicate the appropriate gyro and depth settings to the torpedo itself, which would be launched as soon as the attack team agreed that the computed solution looked right. The TBT was a bit crude, but very effective, because the firing officer didn't have to worry about up-scope/down-scope delays in getting the firing data into the computer. This time, Gar would stay down in the conning tower, directly below the bridge, and oversee the tactical plot and the TDC's outputs, watching out for errors or any indications that they weren't the only killer maneuvering out there in the dark.

The roar of the main engines subsided as the exec brought her down to 10 knots. The plotting team was back on station, and there were two target tracks unfolding on the plotting table, courtesy of some quick radar sweeps as they'd closed in. The exec could not yet see either of the two tankers, who should be running dark.

"Where's the third guy?" Gar asked the plotting officer.

"Haven't found him," replied Hoot, back on station. "TDC has a solution on the lead ship; we just need to get closer."

Gar studied the dials on the torpedo data computer. The range was 3,200 yards; they needed to get in to under 2,000 yards to ensure the torpedoes could reach the target.

"Go easy on the radar," he said. "I don't want it to become a beacon."

"Actually," Hoot said, "the exec says he thinks this guy is showing a light. He's using TBT bearings on that. We took one radar range ten minutes ago, and we plan to take another one before he shoots."

"Oh, my," Gar said. "A stern light. Talk about a fatal mistake."

"Yes, sir. Whoops, there's a zig."

Gar stepped back from the plot as the team tracked the target's movements with little penciled x's on the plotting sheet. From what he could see, the two ships were trying to zigzag in a loose column formation, which was probably why the lead ship had left a dim yellow light burning on his stern. The exec called down a course change to accommodate the targets' new course.

Gar itched to go topside to see what the exec was seeing, but Russ needed to learn how to do this without coaching. That said, nobody was using the periscopes. The plot was clear enough, the exec had a visual on the target, and the computer was happily crunching numbers, so he stepped over to the night scope, raised it, and took a look down the indicated bearing. He saw precisely nothing.

"Target's changed course to zero three zero," Hoot called. "Seems to be steady on that now."

"Give me a radar range," the exec called down. "One sweep."

The radar operator let the radar come up for a few seconds, then turned it off.

"Range is sixteen hundred yards, bearing one three five from us," the operator announced.

"Stand by to mark visual bearing. Stand by—mark!"

"Plot set!" Hoot reported. "Bearings and range match. Fire any time."

"Fire two!" called the exec, and the console operator mashed down on the mushroom-shaped firing button. Gar waited for him to fire a second fish, but the exec was apparently going to do it the captain's way. Gar smiled, set the scope onto the firing bearing, and waited.

Hoot was holding up a stopwatch. "Run time one minute thirty," he called.

"Hot, straight, and normal," announced Popeye, ever vigilant for a circular runner.

"Stand by to mark visual bearing on target two. Stand by . . . Mark! Estimate range at twelve hundred yards."

"Plot *not* ready," Hoot said. "Range and bearing *not* in agreement."

Gar left the scope and stepped quickly over to the plot, where he saw that the TDC's course and speed on target two were not agreeing with the exec's last visual bearing.

"He's still turning," the exec called down. "I'll get another bearing in one minute."

"Why the hell can't we use the radar?" Hoot grumbled.

"Because we don't know where that third target is, or, more importantly, *what* he is," Gar said. "Could be a tin can, just waiting for a radar signal to home in on."

A sudden glare of bright yellow light flooded down into the conning tower from the bridge, followed by a very loud boom. Gasoline tanker.

"Clear visual bearing on target two . . . Mark! Estimated range, one thousand yards."

"Bearing close, range agrees," called Hoot. "Solution!"

"Fire three," the exec ordered.

Gar went back to the periscope, dialed in a glare filter, and took a look. The first tanker was low in the water and burning from end to end, great gouts of flaming gasoline pouring off her port side. He came right with the scope and saw the second tanker, about a half mile behind the first. She was larger and now completely illuminated by the fire. As he watched she began a turn to the right, but then an enormous waterspout rose up just behind the pilothouse as the Dragon's torpedo struck home. Moments later, the dark ship began to sag in the middle as her keel gave way. This one wasn't burning, which meant an engine room hit. The XO was on a roll tonight.

He turned the scope back to the burning ship, which, if anything, was burning even harder now. Then he continued to the left, scanning the seas, whose small whitecaps created brilliant green lines in the light of all that burning gasoline. Twenty degrees to the left of the burning ship he saw something that made his heart stop.

"*Captain* has the conn," he shouted so that the exec could hear him topside. "All ahead flank, *emergency*," he yelled. "Come left with *full* rudder. Emergency dive, dive, *dive!*"

The helmsman responded instantly, although the rest of the men in the conning tower just gaped at him for a second before springing into action. The dive Klaxon sounded as the propellers bit into the sea and the sub began to heel to the right. There was a roar of escaping ballast tank air outside, followed by the first of the lookouts dropping down into the conning tower, with just the tips of their shoes barely touching the rungs as they literally fell down the ladder. Then came the OOD—officer of the deck—and finally the exec, who paused only long enough to secure the hatch, creating an immediate squeeze on everyone's ears as the main induction valve slammed shut and the diesels died away. In the space of ten seconds or so, they were back on the batteries.

Gar was still glued to the scope. "TDC, mark my bearing, prepare to emergency-fire tube number eight, running depth at twenty feet! Stand by . . . Mark!"

"Mark at three five zero, tube eight standing by."

"*Fire* eight, *shift* your rudder, make your depth three hundred feet, ten-degree down bubble."

The air in the sub pinched as the torpedo left tube eight.

"Pressure in the boat, green board," the diving officer called out belatedly from Control. It better be, Gar thought—we're under. "Make my depth three hundred feet, aye, sir."

"Hot, straight, and normal."

"Captain?" It was the exec.

Gar unstuck his eyes from the periscope as it went underwater, sent it down into its well, and refocused into the conning tower. The exec was staring at him with a what-the-hell expression on his face. His shirt was soaking wet from waves hitting the bridge as they'd executed the emergency dive.

"Periscope," Gar said. "Clear as day." He glanced at the compass indicator. "Ease your rudder to left standard."

"Target number three," the exec said, softly. "A goddamned I-boat."

"Torpedoes in the water," Sound announced. This stopped everyone in the conning tower cold. They should be safe, Gar thought, unless the Jap submarine skipper had guessed their course and intended depth once Gar had called the crash dive. *Should* be, unless the Japs had developed a homer.

"And *down* Doppler," Popeye announced. "They're going to miss astern."

A collective sigh of relief went up.

"Where's the layer?" Gar asked.

"Last layer was three hundred twenty."

Deep in the distance they heard torpedo eight explode, but whether it had hit the other sub or simply reached its end of run, they couldn't tell. The chances of their having hit the other sub were almost zero.

"Make your depth four hundred, rig the ship for silent running. Slow to four knots. We'll head east for a while."

Behind them they heard some breaking-up noises as the second tanker went down. Apparently the other one was still on the surface, trying to boil off the Pacific Ocean.

I need a drink, Gar thought. That had been too damned close for comfort. Instead, he told the XO he'd done good work. "Two for two, with single torpedoes. Who taught you that, anyway?"

TWO

On Monday morning Gar arrived at the SubPac headquarters building promptly at ten for his appointment with Captain Mike Forrester, chief of staff to Vice Admiral Charles Lockwood, who commanded all the submarine forces in the Pacific. Normally his division commander would be there with him, but he was on home leave back in the States. The yeoman asked him if he needed coffee and then indicated that he should take a seat in the outer office.

They'd gotten back from patrol three days ago to a generous pierside reception, which included Uncle Charlie, as Admiral Lockwood was known affectionately throughout the Pacific Fleet submarine force. Nimitz had chosen well in appointing him to three stars and command of the entire force. He was a demanding boss, but one who fought fiercely for his people when other commands proposed stupid things that affected the submarine force. Gar's being summoned for a one-on-one with the chief of staff wasn't that unusual. He'd handed in his personal commanding officer's patrol report on Friday afternoon, and Gar supposed Captain Forrester wanted to go over it with him.

The yeoman finally indicated that he could go into Forrester's office. The chief of staff was a tallish, spare man who was still showing the effects of injuries he'd sustained in an especially vicious depth-charging while skipper of *Albacore* back in late 1942. Most of the current skippers were convinced Forrester was in constant pain, which probably accounted for his acerbic disposition. Having brought home a full bag, Gar was not anticipating any criticism, and, at first, his expectations were rewarded. Forrester congratulated *Dragonfish* on a highly successful patrol and told Gar that radio intercepts had confirmed almost all their kills.

"Two tankers, two freighters, and two destroyers sunk; one tanker damaged," Forrester said. "That's a damned good haul."

"Thank you, sir."

He leaned back in his chair for a moment. "One thing got my attention," he said. "Those two destroyers in your bag. Prior to that you've downed three others. You're sinking almost as many tin cans as you are Marus. That's quite unusual. I was wondering if you were perchance hunting them deliberately."

Gar had to think about that for a moment. Their overall mission orders charged them to sink Japanese shipping, with an emphasis on ships carrying war matériel from the Southeast Asian part of the empire back to Japan. Everyone wanted to bag a carrier or a battleship, but the Pacific submarine warfare strategy was now firmly focused on strangling the empire's ability to wage war. Skippers were given a lot of latitude as to which kinds of targets they went after, with the only "crime" being to have a Jap ship in your sights and fail to attack.

"It's not a vendetta or a thirst for glory," Gar said finally. "I don't go looking for tin cans to attack, if that's what you mean. But I do think it makes sense to reduce the escort numbers around a convoy, if possible. There are, of course, situations when that isn't possible."

"Most skippers don't deliberately set up on the escorts," Forrester said. "They go for the high-value targets and then face the consequences if they have to."

"Sometimes I've done that," Gar said. "The problem is you give the initiative to the escort forces. They drive around topside with relative impunity, and they only have to get lucky once with a well-placed depth charge."

"So this is a matter of taking back the initiative? Putting the escorts on notice that they're targets, too? Back 'em off a little?"

"Yes, sir, exactly. Plus, if it's a small convoy, taking out the escorts just about guarantees we can make a surfaced attack, where we have the speed advantage."

"Unless you get a surprise, right?"

"Surprise?"

"Like the Jap sub that appeared in the middle of that 'defense-less' convoy."

"With all due respect, sir, what's that have to do with attacking escorts?"

"It means you didn't get them all, doesn't it?" he asked. "The escorts, I mean. That's the hole in your tactic, Captain. You have to get *all* the escorts or you can't surface to go chase the convoy ships, which, by the way, are moving away from you the whole time you're screwing around with the destroyers. It might work in a wolf pack, but not when you're all alone."

He had a point there. In retrospect, Gar knew he'd been lucky that the I-boat embedded in that convoy hadn't gone back to find them when that second destroyer did. If it hadn't been for the big gasoline fire, Gar would never have seen that periscope. He tried to turn the criticism into antipathy on the part of the chief of staff, but he damned well had a point.

"Think about it," Forrester said. "You were lucky this time, and the Dragon distinguished herself again. There'll be a medal in that for you and whomever you'd like to recommend."

"Thank you, sir."

"Now, you'll be going into dry dock later this week. The big job will be the installation of the new FM sonar. We're anticipating a week in dock, and then a couple weeks for training and R&R. And make sure you're at the weekly séance with your Uncle Charles to-night at the Palace, okay?"

Late that afternoon, Gar stood in the shower, eyes closed, his two hands splayed on the end wall, as he let an unlimited supply of hot water course over his body. He was pretty sure every submariner in the hotel indulged in this absolute luxury at least twice a day. That and a real, honest-to-God innerspring mattress. Even after three days, he could still detect *eau de diesel* on his skin, despite the best efforts of the Royal Hawaiian Hotel's excellent water heaters.

Early in the war, the submarine force commander had commandeered the top floors of the stately old hotel as a rest and recuperation center for the submarine skippers and their execs. It became standard procedure for a sub's crew, returning from a war patrol, to hand the boat over to an in-port relief crew upon arrival. This allowed them to decompress from the rigors of being sealed up in their iron coffin for as long as forty-five days at a time, all alone and often deep within the empire's territory. The wardroom officers, chiefs, and other enlisted decamped into R&R centers around the island, while the captains unwound among other commanding officers at the Pink Palace, safe from the inquisitive eyes of their ever-watchful subordinates. They could sleep, or get drunk if they felt like it; more importantly, they could talk candidly with other skippers about their experiences on patrol, forcewide equipment problems, navy politics, rumors and sea stories, and their execs. One floor down, the execs would be doing the same thing. Ladies were not permitted to be on any floor above the lobby, a regulation that Gar suspected was honored more in the breach than in the observance. There were marine guards in the lobby and concertina wire around the hotel's perimeter to keep away prying eyes and ears.

Once a week, Vice Admiral Charles Lockwood, ComSubPac himself, held court in the hospitality suite, where he could share his concerns about the force, and the skippers who happened to be in port could share their feelings about how things were going in the submarine war. Gar glanced at his watch. The admiral would be arriving in thirty minutes, and all the skippers were expected to be on deck before his lordship actually showed up. He went to the closet to get a fresh uniform.

After his meeting with the chief of staff he'd gone back to the ship to gen up a list of other maintenance items they could get done with the boat in dry dock. Gar suspected that one blade on the port propeller was dinged and making noise at even slow speeds. Two outer torpedo tube doors forward leaked excessively below 250 feet, and they had several lighting fixtures that were hanging by their wiring after that depth-charging. The relief crew had been inspecting the ship, and they were also making up a list of repairs and replacements. As they got closer to the actual docking day, most of the senior petty officers and all the wardroom officers would come back aboard to bird-dog maintenance and repair work in their departments. The first weekend back from patrol was a wonderful time to do nothing at all, but after that most of them would become bored with just sitting around.

Gar stood by the tall windows overlooking Waikiki Beach, sipping on a Scotch, trying to keep his mind in neutral. Some of the other skippers at the bar had given him quiet congratulations for the last patrol's box score, and he'd made appropriate noises back at them. There were an even dozen skippers at hand, but none of the SubPac superstars, who were either out on patrol or out on eternal patrol. The latter was a constant and depressing fact of life at these gatherings. At first no one had been willing to talk about the loss of a boat, but, as this war dragged on, the losses and their circumstances necessarily became part of the late-night tactical discussions around this very private bar.

"Excuse me," a voice said behind him. "Are you Gar Hammond?"

Gar turned around. A young-looking commander put out his hand and introduced himself as Chandler Scott, new skipper of *Batfish*.

"Welcome to the Pink Palace," Gar said.

"Heard about your latest trip," Scott said. "Guys are saying you hunt destroyers?"

Gar smiled. "Not exactly," he said. "I just don't subscribe to the notion that we have to sit down there and take it every time we get in the ring with them."

Scott nodded. "I like that idea, but every time I've tried to shoot one it's been so chaotic we never seem to hit anything."

"Once you've been detected and you're evading, it's tough, if not impossible. But—doesn't mean you can't shoot a steamer at him. If nothing else, he now knows you're gonna shoot back instead of just run and hide. The best way is to sneak up on 'em from behind and put one up the kilt. If nothing else, it upsets the rest of the escorts, *and* you create a hole in the screen."

"You the same Hammond who was brigade boxing champ back in '29?"

"Yup."

"That must color your thinking, then," Scott said.

Gar had graduated with the class of 1930 from the Naval Academy, where he'd excelled in intercollegiate boxing, lacrosse, and lightweight football. He'd stood 100th out of a class of 280, been commissioned into the battleship force, then volunteered for sub school in 1935. For the next seven years he served in two submarines. He'd done his XO tour in a fleet boat from July 1942 to November 1943. On a prospective commanding officer patrol with one of the older hands he discovered that he was not going to run his boat that way, assuming he got one. He'd taken command of *Dragonfish* in early 1944 as a fresh-caught CDR.

He knew he'd come up fast once the war started, making full commander in 1944. He believed he owed his rapid advance to a combination of his own ability and wartime attrition, in about equal measures. Chandler Scott had been two years behind him at the academy, and yet here he was, a skipper now, still remembering Gar as a boxer whose style was to walk directly across the ring to his opponent and beat the shit out of him.

"How do you mean?" Gar asked.

"From sub school on, they've hammered one rule into us: Never mess with a destroyer."

Gar finished his drink. "Look," he said. "I don't advocate setting up on a convoy and then breaking off from a fat tanker to see if I can sink an escort. The tanker *is* the mission. I'm just saying that if the opportunity presents itself, take the bastards out. If nothing else, it evens the odds up a bit. If we're talking patrol craft or depth-charged armed minesweepers, forget it. They're just too agile."

Scott was about to reply when someone called attention on deck.

Gar turned around from the window and stiffened into a half-hearted pose of attention, his drink incongruously at his side, while the rest of the skippers stood up. The admiral came in, waved them all at-ease, and, greeting everyone by his first name, got himself a beer. An overstuffed armchair had been reserved for him, and he sat down. Gar took a seat behind the main couch as the admiral launched into his informal briefing, relating the good news and the bad, and managing throughout to direct praise at each and every one of them.

It was a polished, sincerely meant performance, Gar thought. No wonder he got his third star. Better yet, they all knew that Admiral Lockwood cared passionately about their welfare, boats, weapons, and our enlisted people, unlike some of the flag officers out in the Australian forward bases. They also recognized that one purpose of these frequent, informal visits was for Lockwood to take *their* measure, both emotional and physical, quietly looking for signs that a skipper had been out there too many times and needed a prolonged rest ashore. He played the same game with the executive officers, and more than once an XO had come up to Lockwood privately to express his concerns about his own CO. Since returning from the last patrol, and despite the warm pierside welcome from the brass, Gar wondered if his own exec, a veteran of four war patrols, had been whispering in someone's ear. When one of the stewards handed him a discreet note from the chief of staff toward the end of the session, he felt that his suspicions were possibly confirmed. He'd been invited to dinner with the admiral. This wasn't unusual, except for the fact that he hadn't seen anyone else in the room getting notes. He put it in his pocket as the Q&A began and sat back to listen.

An hour later, the majordomo led Gar through the dining room to a corner table that was partially shielded by a three-piece Oriental screen and some strategically placed potted plants. The hotel's dining room was full, with both submariners and other naval officers. The admiral got up to greet him. He shook hands as if they were meeting for the very first time. Up close, he looked a lot older than the last time Gar had seen him, with pronounced dark pouches under his eyes that hadn't been so obvious upstairs. Maybe they came with that third star, he thought. The waiter brought drinks, took their dinner orders, and disappeared behind the screen. Once the drinks came, the admiral got down to business.

"So," he began. "How are you? How's command treating you?"

Gar wondered idly what would happen if he said he felt awful and wanted to be relieved that very evening. In fact, he felt fine. Physically tired, of course; any warship captain was always on duty, twenty-four hours a day. In a submarine command, that was true times ten. Unlike on a surface ship, where an entire team fought the ship and many of the fighting decisions could be made by decentralized subordinates, a submarine skipper had to make every decision himself, based on tactical data fed to him in the cramped confines of the conning tower, what he was seeing through hurried periscope observations, and how well he had formed the three-dimensional tactical picture in his mind.

"It suits me, Admiral," he said simply. "I've got very good people, lots of veterans, and the Dragon's a good, solid boat. When the time comes to go back out there, I'm personally ready to go."

"That was an outstanding patrol, Gar. You guys really rang the bell out there, killing an entire convoy, an I-boat, *and* three destroyers."

"It wasn't much of a convoy, Admiral," Gar said. "And it'd be a miracle if we actually hit that I-boat."

"It was pretty close to a miracle that you saw that guy's scope," the admiral said, then sipped his drink. Ah, here it comes, Gar thought. Forrester had put the knife in. "Do you have your exec on the scope during an attack, like Mush Morton did?"

"Usually I'm on the scope," Gar said. "But that night, once I thought I'd dealt with all the escorts, I put Russ West on the bridge for the attack on the tankers. I stayed down in the conning tower where I could watch the plot. I used the scope only after that first tanker blew up and I could actually see something."

"And I understand you stay off the radar as much as possible?"

"Yes, sir. I do use it, but sparingly. I think they can pick it up and home in on the reverse bearing."

"You let your XO conduct the high-value target attacks. You must think he's ready for his own command."

Gar hesitated. Say yes and he'd be breaking in a new exec. Say no and he'd be damaging Russ's career. When did you stop beating your wife . . .

"You're hesitating."

Gar smiled. The admiral had read his mind. "Russ is fully qualified to take command," he said. "And I enthusiastically recommend him for command."

"Okay, you've said the requisite words. But?"

"He's a thinker," Gar said. "For instance, he thinks that my going after destroyer escorts is tactically nuts."

"How do you know that?"

Gar smiled again. "He said it out loud," he said. "We were in Control, waiting for one of the escorts to go overhead. I don't think he meant to say it. He was just thinking it, and out it came."

"A moment ago, you hesitated," the admiral said. "Let me ask you something—does your hesitation have to do with what I'll call, for want of a better term, lack of killer instinct?"

"I feel like I'm being disloyal to my XO," Gar said, looking away for a moment. "Russ West is technically competent, experienced, respected by the wardroom and the crew, and rarely makes a mistake."

"You're avoiding my question."

He was right. Gar was avoiding his question. "It may just be a matter of style, Admiral," he said. "He would be a lot more cautious than I am, I think. He likes to wrap his brain around a tactical situation, think it through, and then do something. Me, I like to get to it. When in doubt, attack the bastards."

The admiral smiled. "The ideal skipper is one who can do both—absorb a tactical situation, think through the options, and then go for the throat. That said, I haven't met any ideal skippers yet. But I keep hoping."

"Lets me out, then. I never expected the third contact in that convoy to be an I-boat."

"But you were looking," he said. "You weren't down below, considering all your options. You were looking by the light of a burning tanker, and you'd already killed two destroyers. Yes, the XO was conducting the torpedo attacks, but you'd put that in motion. That's why you get the Navy Cross and he gets the Silver Star. You're the captain."

"For better or for worser," Gar said as the waiter approached.

"Exactly. Let's eat."

After dinner, the admiral ordered two more drinks and coffee. Gar could hear the voices of some of the other skippers in the dining room, but the screen was doing its job. The admiral ruminated about the course of the war and other generalities, and just when Gar thought that dinner with the boss was coming to a close, the admiral asked a surprising question.

"What do you know about Bungo Suido?"

"I know to stay the hell out of there," Gar replied promptly. "We've lost, what, five boats in or around there? Killer instinct won't save you in that patch of water."

"Even now?"

"Especially now," Gar said. "You're facing shallow water, mines on top of mines, shore-based radar, easy air cover, day and night, not to mention the whirlpools and hundreds of fishermen in boats and sampans out there, all with radios."

"But lots of important targets, including their remaining capital ships. The Inland Sea is kind of like their Pearl Harbor."

"As long as they're holed up in there, they don't threaten anybody. Given the minefields of Bungo Suido, I'd say stationary targets are Halsey meat. And if they do come out, they have to get through multiple submarine patrol areas. Coming or going."

The admiral nodded. He suddenly seemed distracted and then looked at his watch. Gar took the hint, stood up, and thanked him for dinner and the drinks. The admiral got up, too, thanked Gar for joining him, and then left the dining room. Gar sat back down, finished his drink, and then made his way toward the beachside doors. He didn't know if any of the other skippers in the dining room had seen them talking, but he didn't want anyone making a big deal about his three-star dinner date.

He hoped he hadn't damaged Russ's chances for his own command. He was a good solid exec, and Gar had meant what he'd said about differences in command style. The first two years of the submarine war had been very frustrating, what with defective torpedoes, the lack of a clear submarine warfare strategy, and the residual effects of three decades of peacetime navy. The so-called superstars, officers like Sam Dealey, Mush Morton, and Dick O'Kane, were so-called because they quickly broke the peacetime mold, came up with new and far more aggressive tactics, and started to sink lots of enemy ships. Increased aggressiveness was the primary feature of their command style, and that question was always lurking in the minds of the admirals when they assigned an officer to command: Was he a scrapper or a thinker? If you were a scrapper, how far did you take it? Like Gar's going after destroyers—was that going too far? Gar knew that some of his contemporaries thought so; now he surmised that his own exec probably agreed with them.

Oh, well, he thought. That's why the decision on who goes to command gets made at the three-star, not three-stripe, level.

He stepped out onto the expansive lanai overlooking the hotel's private section of Waikiki. Music and the sound of women's voices drifted up from the beach pavilions, which were in silhouette against a setting sun. "Now that's more like it," he said to himself and headed down toward the water. As always he was struck by the incongruity of the dreamlike scene along Waikiki Beach when contrasted with the realities of submarine warfare, where professional success meant you bathed your submarine in the body-filled debris field of another ship, and failure meant you rode your own tomb down to the abyss and an instant death when the submarine collapsed, creating the same conditions inside the sub that occurred in the cylinder in a diesel engine at the instant of ignition.

He'd come a long, long way from Somerset County in southwestern Pennsylvania's coal country. His father, now dead, had been a miner, and his family had lived on a small place in the country some nine miles from the mine. The place was still there, but his mother, who had begun a descent into dementia, now lived with her younger sister. His younger brother had gone into the mine at eighteen but had been killed in a car accident three years later. Gar had wanted nothing to do with the mines and had used his talents as a football player and a boxer to finagle a scholarship to Penn State for one year and from there an appointment to the Naval Academy.

His reverie was interrupted by the sight of a very inebriated woman coming toward the hotel. Either that or she was executing a serious zigzag plan to confuse lurking submarines. When she staggered into a palm tree not far from where he was standing, he hurried to rescue her. She was backing away from the offending tree, cursing it roundly as Gar materialized in front of her. She looked up at him, focused intently, and announced that she had to pee.

"Looking for the ladies' room, right?" he asked.

"Damn right," she said. "Who're you, anyway?"

"The guy who knows where the ladies' room is," he said, taking her by the arm. "Follow me."

"You gotta pee, too?" she asked, leaning into him. He hadn't quite seen her face, but the rest of her was most definitely female. Her hairdo was one of those waterfall numbers, dense straight blond hair that draped over half her face. She reeked of rum and was decidedly unsteady on her feet, due in part to the loss of a shoe somewhere back on the beach. She was wearing a buttoned-up sleeveless blouse and tan slacks. He put his arm around her back and steered her gently toward the hotel.

"You sure you know where we're going?" she mumbled, clinging to his arm.

"Right through here," he said. "Down the hall by the dining room, and there's the ladies' room. I'll see you to the door. Did you get into mai-tais?"

"Jesus," she said, then hiccupped loudly. "Some kinda rum drink. Lots of pineapple juice. Oh, shit, I think I'm gonna—"

Gar put the rudder over just in time to steer her into the darkness beyond the lanai and let nature take its course. Good thing about pineapple, he remembered. Tastes about the same coming back up as it does going down.

Once the gastric excitement subsided, he helped her back onto the sidewalk, where she exhaled forcefully, probably killing many innocent insects. He handed her a handkerchief.

"C'mon," he said gently. "You still have to pee."

"Still gotta pee," she echoed. "Sorry about that. My name's—my name's—shit."

"I doubt that very much," Gar said with a grin as she sagged again.

He managed to get her to the door of the ladies' room without any further drama but then faced a command decision. She was legless, as the Brits liked to say. She'd undoubtedly slide down to the carpeted floor if he let go.

"Here we are," he said hopefully.

"Here we are," she said, trying hard to focus on the door. He finally got a look at her face. She had pretty eyes except for the fact that they were so bloodshot. Her lipstick was smeared, and her cheeks were pale. He realized that, although she was amply proportioned, her forehead came up to about his breastbone. She'd looked bigger outside, but he guessed it was that mop of blond hair. She was actually rather petite.

At that moment the door opened, and an older woman stopped short. Gar had seen her before at the hotel but didn't know who she was—one of the managers, perhaps.

"Um," he said. "Can you possibly—"

The woman gave him a wilting look, asked him if he was proud of himself, and then took his drunken waif back with her into the ladies' room.

Gar stared at the door for a moment and then decided that the evening's portents had turned against him. Too bad, he thought. Cleaned up, she was probably a beautiful girl. He wondered if he should wait.

Nope, he thought. Gotta pee.

THREE

Gar watched from the bridge as the *Dragonfish* rose out of the water in the clutches of the floating dry dock. Russ West, the exec, and the ship's diminutive ops boss, Lieutenant Hoot Gibson, stood alongside him. A second sub was being dry-docked right alongside the Dragon, and her XO was perched on the so-called cigarette deck, smoking a cigar and reading his morning message traffic. The Dragon was being docked for a new screw, work on three ballast tank valves, replacement of two torpedo tube doors, and the installation of a fourth periscope mast, which also had a radar embedded, and the new frequency-modulated sonar. The underwater hull would also be cleaned of marine growth, which was extensive enough to reduce the ship's top speed by 2 knots.

"Does this new sonar system really see mines?" Gibson asked.

"The guys who've used it call it Hell's Bells," the exec said. "That's what the mines sound like when the gear finds 'em."

"Seems to me like the right answer to a mine contact is right full rudder."

"Unless you're trying to get *through* a channel where there are known minefields. This thing would let you skirt the edges—the Japs always plant mines in lines."

"How in the world do they know where the Japs have planted minefields?"

"Somebody goes boom in the night?" the exec suggested. "Pac-Fleet intel says they've changed the type of their fields this year, from antisurface to mainly antisubmarine. That means deeper." He peered over the side. "Looks like we're about there."

"Where's the new sonar going?"

"Bottom of the bow. It looks out and up and reportedly sees out to five, maybe six hundred yards. Enough warning to maneuver. Skipper'll get a brief next week once it's installed."

The walls of the dry dock were now completely dry, and water was spilling off the ends as the platform deck surfaced. Hardhats were already walking around in rubber boots down on the platform deck, kicking dying fish back into the water. The pungent aroma of all the marine life that had been sucked into the strainers around the Dragon's hull over the past year filled the dry dock. Gar could see the captain of the other sub and their own ship's superintendent walking down the zigzag ladder on the wing-wall.

"Any word on when we're going back out, Cap'n?" Gibson asked Gar, making a face at the smell.

"I've no idea," he replied. "XO, let's go down in the dock. You won't get to see the Dragon naked very often."

After the ship had been safely dry-docked, Gar took a shuttle bus over to the officers' club for lunch. There he ran into Lieutenant Commander Marty McVeigh, a classmate and friend who'd gone into the naval intelligence business right after graduation. Being in the staff corps instead of the line, he was a grade behind Gar in rank and was assigned to the ever-growing staff up in Makalapa Crater working for Admiral of the Fleet Chester Nimitz. They had lunch together and shot the breeze on the course of the war, who'd been getting promoted, who'd been fired, and all the usual navy gossip. Then Marty gave Gar the first indication that their lives on *Dragonfish* were about to get really interesting.

"There's scuttlebutt coming out of Nimitz's office that he wants a submarine to penetrate into the Inland Sea," Marty said.

"That would mean trying to get through Bungo Suido," Gar said. "We're talking death wish there. Any idea why?"

"Word is that the Japs have a brand-new, really big aircraft carrier about ready to come out. Much bigger than anything we have.

With the Philippines invasion under way, Nimitz does not want that thing joining the fray."

"So why don't we bomb the damned thing?" Gar asked. "We've got the Marianas now—Guam, Tinian. If you listen to all the army air force guys, there's not much the B-29 *can't* reach from there."

Marty lit up a cigarette and perversely waved away the resulting cloud of blue smoke. "Those zoomies are great on propaganda," he said, "not so great at long-range bombing, apparently. Yes, they could reach it, but the word is they can't hit anything with precision. It's too far for fighters to go with them, so they're dropping from thirty thousand feet and mostly blowing up rice paddies. Anyway, the Joint Chiefs have told the army that the B-29s are to work Japanese cities. Japanese ships are the navy's problem. You know how it is—interservice politics *über alles*."

Gar could only shake his head. Next thing we know, he thought, the flyboys will want their own service.

"How soon before we invade the main island in the Philippines?" he asked.

"Next sixty days or so; they're still trying to decide where to go in, if you can believe it. MacArthur has his ideas; Nimitz has his. Same old shit."

"And they want a sub to force Bungo Suido for one carrier? I mean, hell, I'd love to get a carrier, but why not wait for him to come out? We've got boats all along that coast now."

"The word I'm hearing is that she can carry as many as three hundred planes. If she did a Wounded Bear on us, that could be serious."

Wounded Bear, Gar thought. Every PacFleet submariner remembered that fiasco, where the big Jap carrier *Shokaku*, damaged at the Battle of the Coral Sea, had run the gauntlet of *eight* waiting U.S. submarines to make it back to the Inland Sea without a scratch. He told Marty that he still thought Bungo Suido would be almost a suicide mission. Marty said he'd heard that Uncle Charlie had said the same thing to Nimitz. "You know what Nimitz supposedly said? Get a volunteer."

"The kindly old gentleman, showing his fangs," Gar said. Then he remembered his conversation with Admiral Lockwood. The one where he asked what Gar thought about trying Bungo Suido.

"What's the betting on when we'll have to invade Japan itself?" he asked, subconsciously wanting to get off the subject of those deadly straits with all those sunken submarines.

"Late '45, early '46," he said. "Lots of planning already going on. More and more visiting firemen from Washington coming to Makalapa. MacArthur's got himself a ministaff up there, making sure he doesn't get cut out of the big show."

"I believe that."

"We're seeing more generals, too. Just two days ago, some two-star named Leslie Groves showed up at the morning intel briefing—big, kinda fat guy, looked like he could be a screamer. Anyway, as soon as the general appeared, Nimitz's aide whispered in the boss's ear, and next thing I knew, Nimitz leaves the briefing with this guy in tow."

"Must be one of MacArthur's acolytes," Gar said. "I've heard they're nothing if not terribly important."

"Still," Marty said. "It was kinda unusual for a two-star's arrival to make a four-star get up and leave the briefing."

"Maybe he's a messenger from the Joint Chiefs," Gar said. "Way above my pay grade, anyway. My main concern these days is getting my Dragon ready for the next patrol and wondering where that's gonna be."

"Maybe they'll pick you guys for the Inland Sea mission."

"Hope to Christ they don't," Gar said, and he meant every word.

Gar went from the O-club to the headquarters building of the 14th Naval District, where he was met at the entrance by an armed marine guard. He checked Gar's ID against the expected visitors list and then handed him off to a second marine to take him upstairs. Gar wondered why there were still marine guards at what was essentially an admin headquarters, three years after the Pearl Harbor attack. Surely they no longer anticipated an invasion. The nearest Japanese were thousands of miles away and being driven back into their Home Islands, albeit one bloody inch at a time.

He was there for a briefing on the new mine-detecting sonar system. *Dragonfish*'s weapons officer, Lieutenant Tom Walsh, and soundman Popeye Waller were waiting. The marine delivered Gar, Walsh, and Waller to a room that looked a lot like a classroom. There were two engineering duty officers standing next to a long table. Seated at the head of the table behind a viewgraph machine was a four-striper. A lieutenant commander who identified himself as a staffer from the Pacific Fleet headquarters up on Makalapa Crater came in behind him. He introduced Gar to the others, letting everybody know that he was the captain of *Dragonfish*. He in turn introduced the four-striper as Captain Westfall, program manager for the new sonar system.

Gar shook hands with the EDOs and the captain and introduced his guys. The four-striper told them to sit.

"Captain Hammond," he said. "I'm David Westfall, head honcho at BuShips for the frequency-modulated mine-detection system. This system was designed and produced for minesweepers, not submarines. We're here because Admiral Lockwood interceded with Admiral King to divert some of these systems to his boats here in PacFleet."

The captain didn't sound too pleased. "Was BuShips happy with these, um, diversions?" Gar asked innocently. Like most sub skippers, Gar was no fan of the navy's Washington bureaus.

The captain grunted. "No, not that it matters. But I want you to know that there have been some difficulties in adapting this system to a submarine version."

"As in, it doesn't work?"

"It hasn't worked very well so far," he said. "We had one test on a dummy minefield using a sub, and the first time out the thing just quit. The second time it worked like a charm. The third time it worked half-ass. Like that."

"Not reliable, then."

He shrugged. "It's a new electronic system. The frequency-modulation aspect means that, when it works, you can see mines underwater. See them very well, in fact. The tweaking and peaking, the subsurface environment, the ability of the operator, the

quality of the power supply, the flexibility of the technicians—
these are the important variables. Let's have an overview."

He produced a portfolio of view-graphs and proceeded to give a
system technical overview briefing on the new sonar. When he'd
finished he asked if there were any questions.

"You said the sub version looks up at an angle," Tom Walsh said.
"Can it see straight ahead, or down?"

Westfall fished through the slides and put up the one showing
the ray path of ensonification. "It has to look up because, for the
sub version, the transducer is mounted on the stem, under a sharply
raked bow," he said. "The assumption being that you would be
running at depth, two fifty to three hundred feet. Our design parameters were that the Japanese-moored mines are planted from
the surface down to two hundred fifty feet."

"So if there's one at three hundred feet, the sonar won't see it,"
Gar said.

"If you trimmed the bow at a down ten-degree angle, it probably
could."

"Probably."

Westfall sat back and sighed. "The detection performance for
all sonars is based on a probability analysis, Captain. The original
idea was to give you warning so that you could *avoid* a minefield.
Are you talking about deliberately penetrating one?"

"Not exactly," Gar said, equivocating while trying not to think
about Bungo Suido. "I'm talking about finding myself in a minefield we didn't know about and trying to get out."

Westfall seemed to accept that at face value. "The system would
allow you to know the average depth of the mines around you, assuming that they're all planted at or near the same depth. If it's a
random disposition, no straight lines, random ambush depths—"

"In other words, an antisubmarine field."

"Yes."

"Then you're screwed," said the captain.

The two EDOs were taken aback, but Gar laughed, grateful for
the captain's honesty.

"As I said before," Westfall continued, "this system was designed for minesweepers on the surface looking down into the sea. You'll be deep in the sea and looking up. It's designed to keep you *out* of a minefield. I wouldn't bother running it in depths over a hundred, hundred fifty fathoms. Otherwise, turn it on, and leave it on. If you hear Hell's Bells, back down hard, see what you got, and find some other place to go if you can."

"Okay," Gar said. "Now, most of our underwater sound work is passive, so as not to give listening Jap destroyers a beacon on us. This is an active system—can they hear it?"

"We *think* not," Westfall said. "Detection probabilities are based on a cone of five to six hundred yards. It's FM, so we're trading power for enhanced discrimination, and one of the available options is to change frequency within a narrow band. We recommend that the operator do that frequently, because water conditions can affect performance without your knowing it."

"Right," Gar said. "Where's the display going to be?"

One of the EDOs from the shipyard told him that it would be next to the sound display in the conning tower. "It's being installed today, in fact," he said.

It was Gar's turn to sigh. More stuff in the conning tower. Surface search radar, air search radar, passive sonar, periscope, the plot, the TDC, and now active sonar. Maybe it *was* time to adopt Mush Morton's method of having the XO conduct the attack with the CO standing back and absorbing all this information.

"It's the technical wave of the future," the captain said, as if reading Gar's mind. "We're turning increasingly to electronics to define the battle space. Even surface ships as small as destroyers have to dedicate an entire compartment to displaying their tactical situation these days. They call it CIC, Combat Information Center."

"We call it the conning tower," Gar said, "and it's already crammed full of stuff. Could I shoot at something using this FM sonar? Like at another submarine?"

"We've looked into that," Westfall said. "Right now the display shows little pear-shaped blobs wherever the sonar sees mines. Another sub would appear as a much bigger blob, depending on his aspect. If he's broadside to you, and at your depth, the whole screen will go green on you. If he's end on, it'll look like a slightly bigger blob. Then there's only one way to answer the question."

Gar raised his eyebrows at him.

"Fire one!" Westfall shouted, then dramatically lowered his voice. "Then go really deep."

Everyone's a comedian, Gar thought, as the EDOs chuckled.

That night he was having a drink up in the skippers' lounge with two other captains when Captain Forrester showed up. He came over to the Royal frequently in the evenings and even had a room down on the fifth floor. He was always welcomed into the evening BS sessions, first because he was Lockwood's chief of staff and thereby privy to a lot of inside dope about what was going on in the war, and, second, he'd been a skipper himself. Normally commanding officers wouldn't have much contact with the chief of staff; their direct bosses were division commanders, four-stripers who'd distinguished themselves in command. Both Lockwood and Forrester, however, made a point of keeping close to the COs, mostly because of the sorry history of American submarine torpedoes at the beginning of the war.

After a half hour or so, Forrester gave Gar the high sign, and they went to one corner of the lounge, where he produced a brown envelope. He withdrew a pair of glossy black-and-white photographs and handed one over to Gar. It showed a large, dark building, shaped like a shoebox, with what looked like a dry dock on one side and a pier on the other.

"Okay, I'll bite," Gar said. "Looks like an aerial photograph of a dockyard building, maybe in a shipyard?"

"Correct," Forrester said. "There's a scale on the bottom. White lettering, bottom right. That building is fifteen hundred feet long."

"Yes, I can see that. The dockside cranes look wrong, though. Too small. Is that a distortion of the camera?"

"No. If you look closely, they're the same size as the cranes on the adjacent pier. It's the building that's really big."

"Where was this shot?"

"Near Hiroshima, on the Inland Sea. Actually, it's the Japanese naval arsenal at Kure. A reconnaissance B-29 flying out of China took it while he was doing a target survey."

"Did he bomb it?"

"No, when this was taken they couldn't reach the Home Islands with a load of bombs. This was a photo-recce plane, so it has longer range than a fully loaded bomber. That picture was taken two months ago."

Okay, Gar thought. Big, fat building in a Jap shipyard. Even from 30,000 feet, the B-29s out of Tinian should be able to hit that. So why was he getting an oh-oh feeling about this little meeting? He looked over at Forrester, who handed him the second picture.

"This is what they were hiding under that building," he said.

The second picture showed almost the same scene, this time with a few wispy white clouds framing the image. Where the building had been there was now the unmistakable shape of an aircraft carrier under construction. This must be the ship Marty had been talking about, Gar thought.

"That thing's huge," Gar said. "Same scale?"

"Same scale. Taken two weeks ago. She's slightly over a thousand feet long. The army photo interpreters saw this, went back and found the previous shot, and then realized this needed to get back here to Pearl."

"Well, if the B-29s can't handle this, sounds like a job for a carrier strike force, Captain. Halsey needs to take the Big Blue Fleet in there."

"We're talking the Home Islands, Gar," Forrester said. "With all due respect to Admiral Halsey, a carrier task force would get its ass kicked pretty hard, they venture into Home Island waters. Actually, Admiral Nimitz thinks this a job for a submarine."

Oh, shit, Gar thought. Here it comes. They want a sub to get this thing, and that means Bungo Suido—and this was coming from Nimitz himself? Gar made the argument about Tinian that he'd made to Marty.

"The airfield on Tinian won't be fully operational for another two, maybe three months," Forrester said. "Besides, those cranes and all that stuff on her flight deck aren't construction materials,

Gar. She's just about completed. Admiral Nimitz says that we cannot afford to let a carrier of that size get loose in the Pacific right now, especially with the invasion of Luzon imminent. The Japs are already moving large fleet forces south."

Gar tried to ignore that sinking feeling in his gut. "She'll have to come out sometime," he said. "And then we'll let one of the boats on empire patrol take her down. What's the big deal?"

Forrester cleared his throat. "Remember the Wounded Bear, Gar?"

That was just what Marty had said. At their "chance" encounter in the O-club. First it had been Uncle Charlie casually inquiring about Bungo Suido. Then Marty. Now the chief of staff. Plus the brand-new and improved FM sonar. Oh, boy, he thought.

He tried again. "Right now we all have standing orders to stay the hell out of all the Home Island straits, especially Bungo Suido. We've lost five boats in and around those waters. Mines everywhere, their best destroyer forces, a zillion fishing boats and sampans to provide early warning, constant local air patrols, no really good charts of the area—"

Forrester interrupted him as if he'd heard that all before. "Nimitz proposes that we send a boat into the Inland Sea to keep that carrier from ever leaving Japan. It's a tall order, I know, but *if* it can be done, they'd never expect it."

"With good damn reason," Gar said, realizing that all his objections had already been surfaced and overruled at PacFleet headquarters. "That would be like trying to get a sub into the Chesapeake Bay, right past all the Norfolk navy bases."

Forrester said nothing.

"And then? Suppose we do get a boat in? He's going to drive up to the Kure arsenal in, what, fifty, sixty feet of water? Unable to submerge? And torpedo a carrier at the pier?"

Gar had raised his voice enough to attract the attention of the other skippers in the lounge.

Forrester leaned closer and gave him a meaningful look. "Not just any boat, Gar."

FOUR

The next day Gar spent cloistered with the hydrographic office at SubPac headquarters, studying the charts they did have of the Seto, as the Inland Sea was known in Japan. Captain Forrester had told him the entire mission was extremely close-hold, even within the already highly restricted world of sub skippers. Gar was not to discuss it with anyone yet until given specific permission. "If it makes you feel any better," he said, "the admiral is going to have one more try at turning this brain fart off. But I have to tell you: Nimitz almost never changes his mind once he's made a decision." Gar had wanted to say, *Nimitz was a sub skipper—if he really wants a sub to get into the Inland Sea, let him try it, then.* Sadly, he was brave but not that brave.

He spent the afternoon on board the Dragon, checking on the progress of the repairs and the installation of the new sonar system. *Dragonfish* was a Balao class, new construction in early 1944, with the stronger hull and better everything inside. Captain Westfall was right about electronics beginning to take over warship design. The Dragon had been commissioned with two periscopes; now she would have four. She'd started out with one HF radio set; now she had six different radios *and* an underwater telephone system. At the beginning of the war they'd computed fire-control problems using a handheld calculator called the Is-Was and plotted the tactical picture on a copy of a chart. Now they had the torpedo data computer and a lighted plotting table that showed their position in real-time motion across a geographic plot, called a DRT. If they added one more piece of gear to the conning tower, they were all going to become very good friends every time they went to GQ, and nobody had better smile, either.

It had been difficult not to pull the exec aside and tell him about the mission that was coming their way. The closest he had come was when Russ commented on all the new gear up in the conning tower. "We're gonna need it," Gar had said mysteriously.

That evening Gar went down to the dining room. He didn't bother to change from work khakis. The place was full for a change because of some big conference going on up at Makalapa. He had to settle for a deuce out on the lanai, which wasn't all bad. Even though it was hotter than usual, the lanai was dark enough that he could avoid making eye contact with other skippers if he wanted to, and tonight he wanted to. He had a low tolerance for people in general, and having to listen to shipyard workers, the FM sonar engineers, the exec's litany of daily problems, and some staffies from SubPac all afternoon hadn't improved his disposition. He told the waitress when she finally showed up to start with a double Scotch rocks, and he'd decide after that whether or not to eat or drink this evening.

A few minutes later she brought his drink, and then the maître'd came though the lanai doors with the same woman he'd semirescued a few nights ago. This time she was definitely sober and actually quite attractive. Somewhat to his surprise she was wearing the uniform of a WAVE lieutenant commander. The pair were scanning the crowded room for a table, and there weren't any. The maître'd saw that Gar was in uniform and gave him a discreet eyebrow. Gar nodded. He brought her over, and Gar stood up to greet her. She thanked him for letting her join him and introduced herself.

"I'm Sharon DeVeers," she said.

"Gar Hammond," he replied. She had a firm handshake and grayish green eyes that were no longer bloodshot. She still wore her luxuriant blond hair in a wave across one side of her forehead. "Are you one of the visiting firemen?"

"No, I'm assigned to CincPacFleet legal; I'm one of the lawyers up there."

He signaled a passing waitress for Sharon, who ordered a ginger ale. When the waitress left he made a comment about expecting her to have a real drink. She smiled and said that she was still recovering from the hangover of the last time she'd been here.

"I can understand that—you were pretty hammered."

She stared at him for a moment and then put a hand to her mouth. "That was you?"

"The one and only. And I believe you got ambushed by something called a mai-tai."

"I am so sorry," she said. "I have never been so drunk in my life. And the next day—God!"

"Lemme guess, a bunch of the guys from the office demanded that you just had to try one. Or three."

"Bingo," she said. "After the first one I thought it was just the best fruit concoction I had ever had, especially because it had very little liquor in it. Silly me."

"Yup, that about describes it. I'm a Scotch man myself—straight up or on the rocks."

"M-mmm, I like Scotch, but I save it for when I'm having a drink with a really close friend," she said, with a definite twinkle in her eye. Gar tried to gauge how old she was. "Where are you stationed?" she asked.

"That's a deep secret," Gar said solemnly. "The entire war effort would grind to a halt if that were revealed."

"Un-hunh," she said. "Those are submariner dolphins, and you're a commander, so I'd guess you're one of those special people they have locked up on the top floors."

"Listen," he said.

She pretended to listen.

"Hear the grinding?"

"Nope."

"*Damn*," he said. "Most women are so impressed with that."

"You don't have to impress me, Captain," she said. "You were a complete gentleman the other night, so please let me spring for dinner tonight as a small measure of my appreciation."

"Okay," he said immediately, and she laughed. She had a very nice laugh, for a lawyer. The waitress sailed by, depositing Sharon's ginger ale on the fly. They toasted each other.

"You have a family back in the world?" she asked.

"Nope," Gar said. "I'm just a fleet-average sea dog. I go from sea duty to sea duty, so I never saw the need for a wife, etc. And you?"

"I was almost married once," she said. "Right after law school. He was brilliant and unfaithful, in about equal measure. After that I decided I'd make it all about me and never looked back."

"So," he said. "What does CincPacFleet need with a herd of lawyers?"

"Oh, you'd be surprised at our case load. Courts-martial, courts of inquiry, like when a ship is lost. International law issues—such as when one of our subs sinks a hospital ship. The Law of the Sea. Atrocity cases. Geneva Convention. Special missions."

"Wow," he said. "I had no idea. Bet you never did a court of inquiry on the loss of a submarine, though."

Her expression said, *Why not?*

"Nobody comes back to answer the questions."

"Good point."

"What is your role in all this lawyering, if I may ask."

"If it's a court-martial, I'm usually the military judge."

"You don't look old enough to be a judge," he said. He wasn't being gallant—she really didn't.

"I was a judge in real life," she said. "Before this awful war. State court. And as to age, I'm forty-one last month."

This time Gar was being gallant. "Going on thirty-five," he said. "How do you manage that?"

She smiled again, and that smile lit up the table. "Lots of illusion there, Captain," she said, "and dieting, and makeup, and a really special Filipina hairdresser down on Broad Street."

She was four years older than he was. He was entranced. A small dance combo opened up and he asked her if she'd like to dance. She asked if he had ordered yet. He said no.

"Why don't you and I blow this pop stand, then, and just go upstairs?" she asked, while rubbing a stockinged foot against his right leg.

"The marines don't allow ladies above the third deck," he said, trying not to whimper.

"There are no marines on *my* floor," she said. "If that helps."

As it turned out, Miss Ginger Ale had a bottle of truly lovely single malt, which they dutifully sampled. The windows were open, and the music from the lanai drifted into the room.

"Now I'd like to dance," she said, and so they did. She moved right in, a glass of Scotch in one hand and Gar in the other. One thing led to another, followed by a prolonged hot shower. Gar had learned a long time ago, via the good offices of older and sometimes married women in and around various navy towns, that when a woman in the mood knows what she wants, all that's required is what one does every great navy day: follow orders willingly and to the best of one's abilities. If the lady likes to subdue her natural inhibitions with a wee dram or three first, God love her.

They got dressed and went back down to the dining room for a late supper, and then out to the lanai, which by now had pretty much emptied out. It was another gorgeous evening in Hawaii. He asked her how she'd come to be here.

"Wanted to do my bit," she said. "With an entire generation of young men absent at war, my work as a state court judge was pretty dull. I was single, turning forty, tired of hearing mostly frivolous lawsuits, and wanting a change of pace."

"Get what you wished for?"

She nodded and then smiled. "Certainly did tonight, kind sir."

"I'm very glad," he said. "Being the male part of the equation, I felt lucky that you even looked my way."

"I have to be careful," she said. "Up there at headquarters, I mean. Everyone's a bachelor, even the ones with the wife and kiddies' pictures on their desks. The four-stripers are the worst offenders."

"Comes with that fourth stripe," Gar said. "The one that proclaims for all to see that you're officially old and on a bold course for imminent pasture."

She laughed at that. "A lot of them seem to think they're going to be admirals pretty soon," she said, signaling the waiter for another drink.

"One, maybe two," Gar said. "Back in '42 the chances were better, but now? I think this thing's going to be over in a year or so, and then most of those admirals *and* their strikers will be getting Dear John letters from BuPers."

"And you?"

"You mean after my command tour? Honestly, I have no idea. I might have to get out and find a real job somewhere. I try not to think about it."

Sharon asked whether he would ever get married.

"Marriage?" he echoed. "As in a family, kids, a house in the suburbs? Like I said, just never felt the need, I guess. I've been on sea duty for my entire career except for sub school and a year at postgraduate school. My more politically savvy classmates have done tours on staffs, shore stations, Washington, but I'm a haze-gray and underway guy. Once I got into the boats my career objective was to get a sub command; the war was a bonus."

That seemed to surprise her. "My, my," she said. "The war was a *bonus*? That's a little stark, isn't it?"

"What's that old British Army toast? To a long and bloody war? It originated in the fact that advancement in the British Army was strictly by seniority and length of service. If you were going to be promoted, somebody literally had to die."

"From what little I've heard about losses in the Pacific submarine force, promotions ought to be rolling right along."

He'd forgotten she was a headquarters maven, and the one thing he'd learned about staffs, especially big staffs, was that they loved to gossip. Submarine losses were closely held, mostly because the Japs were pretty quick to claim a kill every time they tangled with an American boat. It was to PacFleet's advantage to let them think they were wiping the American submarine force off the map when in fact they were not. There was, however, just one little fly in the ointment when it came to applying British regimental logic to his own situation.

"Look," he told her. "What we do is murder. We lie in wait,

mostly invisible, until some big fat tanker or freighter drives into my field of view. Then I fire a half-ton warhead into his guts from about a half mile away, and whoever doesn't die in that explosion gets burned to death in the resulting fire, dragged down by the wreckage, or eaten by sharks. If there are escorts, and they're any good at their job, we in turn catch hell for the next several hours. We go deep and get depth-bombed. It only takes one, close enough to the hull, to send us down to oblivion right behind the ship we just sank. If that happens, nobody knows what happened to us except the Japs. We disappear without a trace except maybe a diesel oil slick that dissipates the first time the wind comes up. As to promotions, there's just one problem. In the army, if the colonel of the regiment gets killed, his regiment needs a new colonel. In submarines, unfortunately, the commander always goes down with the command."

"So it's not about promotions or advancement, then."

"Correct," he said. "It's about command itself. See, in submarines, the captain *is* the boat. The officers, the chiefs, the enlisted, they're a vital part of the equation, but the captain *is* the boat. For better or for worse, he makes all the decisions when the time comes to fight. Plus, we're a results-oriented outfit. I got command because I was qualified, one of many, and because the guy I replaced wasn't getting results."

"He wasn't any good at murder."

"One way of putting it, I suppose. I am good at it. I sense that the other skippers don't like me much, but the brass loves my statistics, all that Jap tonnage on the bottom. That's what I meant about the bonus. I'm getting to do what I've been trained for during all those years of peacetime, and I'm good at it."

"That sounds a bit cocky to me, kind sir."

He shrugged. "I'm not bragging," he said. "Just stating a fact. *Dragonfish* is getting the job done. The captain *is* the boat. I happen to be captain."

"And after the war's over? I mean, we all know this can't go on, that the Japs can't keep doing this."

"I try not to think about that," he said.

"That bad, hunh?"

He laughed. "Unimaginable," he said. "And you? I see no wedding ring. If I may ask?"

"After my near-miss, I never felt the need," she said with a perfectly straight face. He laughed out loud.

"No, I mean that," she said. "I was the only female in my law school class. That's all changed now, especially with most of the men being in the service, but back then all the guys wanted to know what the hell I was doing there. Getting a JD, just like you, sport. I had the great fortune to go to work for the government as an assistant DA before the Depression really bit down. No money in it, of course, but that's one thing about a depression or a recession—lawyers, especially prosecutors, are in demand. Everyone wants someone to blame. I got the judgeship because of the war, again, because the men who were better qualified than I was had joined up in one form or another."

"How do all those JAG guys treat you now that you've joined up?"

"Well, it was kind of back to law school for a while: What are you doing here? I gave them the same answer as before: Same thing you're doing here. Of course it's competitive in the JAG offices—lawyers are competitive by nature, even if what they're doing is temporary. I finally remembered that I was in the navy now. I've succeeded up there because I'm good at what I do, and because my competition focuses on the blond hair and as much leg as I'm willing to display and forgets all about my years as a prosecutor and then my time on the bench. Essentially, when it comes to the courtroom, they never see me coming."

"We're alike, then," Gar said. "The Japs never see me coming either, except when they do. That's what keeps it interesting."

"As to marriage, well, I'm pretty happy with being a one-woman band. If I'd had kids at home and a husband, I probably could never have done any of this. Like tonight, for instance."

"Speaking of tonight, can I see you again, before—um."

She grinned. "Before you have to go back to your secret submarine and then set sail on an even more secret mission, departing at a secret time?"

"Can't tell you, remember? It's a secret."

"I'll bet my hairdresser knows not only when you're leaving but where you're going."

Gar shook his head. "Probably," he said. At this point, Honolulu was definitely a company town. "But back to the question?"

She took his hand discreetly. "The answer is that it's never going to be as good as it was earlier this evening, not unless we happen to fall desperately in love and are willing to just *die* if we can't be together day and night forever and ever."

"That a no?" he asked with as straight a face as he could muster.

She smiled again and finished her drink. "You know I'm right about these things."

Gar noticed she was slurring her words just a bit and decided to quit trying. "We are two of kind, after all," he said. "I agree with you. I'd still love to prove you wrong about certain parts of your theory, but this has been a delightful interlude. It's like we're adhering to one of Murphy's laws—the one that says you fool with a thing long enough, you inevitably break it."

"There you go," she said. "Now, if you ever need a lawyer while I'm out here, I'm your shyster."

They said their good nights and parted company, she to her room, presumably, and Gar to his, the one that was guarded by marines. He lay in bed thinking about the evening's delightful interlude, as he'd termed their encounter.

There were times when he questioned his decision to forgo the wife-and-family scene. Tonight wasn't one of them. Sharon DeVeers was definitely a sport model. Gar's first ship after graduation had been a battleship, USS *New York*. The Depression had landed with both feet and he was sending money home to his parents like most other junior officers, except of course the married ones. Demand for just about everything faltered badly, and when the mills closed up, so did the mines. Being on sea duty he really didn't need much in the way of money, so he felt pretty good about being able to support the folks—and grateful that he hadn't tied the knot as a fair number of his academy classmates had. Then the ship was reassigned to the Pacific Fleet and the so-called China station, where being a bachelor was the best of all possible worlds.

Sharon had it right, he thought. A one-night stand was part and parcel of their respective attitudes. He really liked her, of course, but there was no future in that sort of thing during wartime, and she knew it, too. Besides, he told himself, if you want to fancy yourself a lone wolf, don't hang around the pack.

He grinned in the dark. He had almost convinced himself. Bad sign, Gar Hammond, he thought. You're starting to believe your own bullshit.

FIVE

By the end of the week *Dragonfish* was out of the dry dock and back alongside a finger pier. Gar asked the exec to assemble all the officers in the wardroom. When Russ came down to Gar's cabin to let him know they were ready for him, Gar told him to step in and pull the curtain.

"We're going back out early," he told him. "Special mission."

Russ groaned. "Aviator rescue station?" The subs were increasingly being used to take up stations around the carrier battle fleet's next strike target. It was vital duty but lousy hunting.

"Nope," Gar said. "Empire, but with a catch."

He saw the exec's hopes rise. Empire patrol areas, those close to the Home Islands of Japan, meant much better hunting prospects. Then he focused on that last word.

"Catch?"

"They want us to penetrate Bungo Suido."

The exec stared at him. "You're kidding," he said finally.

Gar just looked at him.

"You're *not* kidding." The exec sighed. "Five submarines not enough? They want to make it an even number?"

Gar had no answer for that. The exec was clearly stunned. The submarine force couldn't prove that they'd lost five subs in and around Bungo Suido since early 1942, but they were pretty sure. The straits of the Japanese main islands had been proscribed since *Wahoo* failed to return from a patrol. The legendary Mush Morton had managed to penetrate one minefield into the Sea of Japan, and he'd done some real damage, reported that he was coming out, and that was it. *Wahoo* simply disappeared. The best guess was that she had hit a mine in La Pérouse Strait on the way out, but a guess was all they had when a sub didn't come back. All SubPac could do was put a black flag on the status board in the general area of Japan. For the most part, they had no real idea of what had happened to any of them. They simply failed to come home.

"Do we know why?" the exec asked.

"Not officially," Gar said. "We'll receive sealed orders just before we sail."

"And unofficially?"

"It involves a carrier. That's all I think I should say at this juncture, and that's between you and me."

The exec tried to put a good face on it, but he was struggling. "I guess we'll have a target smorgasbord in there, assuming we make it through."

"This new sonar should make a big difference," Gar said. "I've been to a briefing with the head scientist for that project. We have an updated version of it, and hopefully updated means better. It supposedly can tell you that there's a mine within five, six hundred yards of you, and roughly where it is. It doesn't tell you what to do next."

"Back the hell out of there?"

"But in which direction?" Gar asked. "The Japs aren't stupid, other than when they started this war. Originally they mined all the choke points to keep their battle fleet and their bases safe against battleships. The mines were all set shallow, and big. Now they're aiming almost exclusively at submarines."

"A good portion of their battle fleet being on the bottom."

"Exactly. They're finally realizing what the real threat is, so now the moored mines are planted at various depths, down to two hundred fifty feet in some cases. It used to be theoretically possible to go deep and drive under the minefield and hope like hell you didn't catch a cable and pull one down onto the boat. Now it's a true 3-D problem, hence the new sonar. In the meantime . . . is everybody in the wardroom?"

"Yes, sir. What will you tell them?"

"Simply that we're going out early on a special mission."

"Bungo Suido?"

"No. I'm keeping that close-hold, too."

The exec nodded. Gar knew what he was thinking: If word got out that the Dragon was headed for Bungo Suido, there would definitely be some transfer requests surfacing. Submarining was a volunteer sport. If someone asked to get off a sub, it was understood in the force that he could go to other duty on surface ships with no questions asked.

"Is that fair, sir?" the exec asked.

"Fair, XO? As in, what's 'fair' got to do with anything?"

"What I meant was—"

"I know what you meant," Gar said. "All submariners are volunteers. We owe it to the men to tell them when we're going on a particularly dangerous mission. This time I can't do it. My excuse is going to be that I don't know what the actual mission is yet, and won't until I open the orders."

"Transfer requests will be moot at that point, Captain."

"Yup. Now that *you* sort of know, you want off?"

"Are we being frank, here, Captain? Because if we are, hell, yes. Bungo Suido? Any sane man would want off. But that's different from my asking to get off. That I won't do."

"Good answer, Russ, and I'm expecting the same thing from the officers and crew. Nobody wants to mess with Bungo Suido. All we can hope is that the Japs will think the same way and won't be looking too hard. They simply won't expect it."

"For many damned good reasons," the exec said, echoing Gar's own sentiments, as he pulled back the curtain. "The officers are assembled, sir," he declared formally.

"Ducky," Gar said.

It was their last night in port. Gar luxuriated in a final hot shower at the Pink Palace and then dressed and went downstairs for a drink and some supper. The all-officers meeting had been a bit strained. The wardroom recognized that they weren't being told a whole lot other than that they were off on a special mission. Gar's reluctance to answer any questions, plus the exec's grim face, apparently spoke volumes. The officers knew better than to push it, Gar realized, but he felt that he'd been disloyal to them in one sense. He rationalized it by telling them, and himself, that the mission was the mission. Submarines were offensive weapons, and he firmly believed in the notion that they deliberately drove in harm's way. The fact that some of his officers were married with wives and children worrying back in the States was something he had to coldly ignore. They very well might not come back from this one, but there was a war on, and the submarine force was at the tip of the spear.

He took a table out on the lanai as was his custom, ordered a double Scotch, and then sat back to enjoy the whisky and not think too much. He'd avoided the sixth-floor hospitality suite. He did not want to see or talk to any of his brethren this evening.

Where you bound this patrol?

Can't say.

Oh, come on—we're all in this together.

Can't say. Hell, won't say. Besides, it's no big deal, although, if you knew, you'd say I was nuts. Truth to tell, you'd be right. I think the whole fucking thing is nuts. Bungo Suido, for God's sake.

New sonar or no new sonar, the four-striper's words hung in his memory. Works some of the time, but not all the time. Wasn't designed for submarines, you know? Wonderful: a sonar that would let you see there was a whole minefield right in front of you, help you steer into it, for the love of Mike, and then, what— quit?

The wave of fear ambushed him. He'd felt fear before, when the depth charges were clicking and booming out there in the black depths, but this was different. This was helplessness compounded by his decision not to tell his people what the brass wanted the Dragon to do. It was the kind of helplessness you'd feel when you were out in a river and you first heard the thunder of a waterfall around the next bend. What's the matter, there, Captain Lone Wolf: This is how you've played it all along, yes? What's the problem now?

He blew out a long breath and finished his Scotch. The waitress slid by, saw the empty glass, and raised an eyebrow. Gar nodded. Yes, ma'am, hit it again, harder, please. The double had begun to work its magic, even though a part of his brain remained entirely too sober. Getting boiled tonight was not going to change anything.

"Hey there, sailor," a familiar voice said.

He cranked his head around and saw Sharon's face.

"Thank you, God," he said, and she grinned and sat down. Her face was a bit flushed, and she was carrying the remains of a Scotch of her own.

"You look a bit stressed," she said.

"I'm think I'm going quietly insane," he said. "We've got a special mission, and we're probably not coming back."

Her face clouded. "What?"

"Can't tell you," he said. "But I'm scared. For the first time in my entire naval career, I'm scared. I think I know how my crew has felt during some of the last few patrols."

She just looked at him, as if trying to figure out if this was bachelor bullshit or something much more real. Studying his face, she decided it wasn't bullshit.

"The 'bonus' going a bit sour, is it?"

"Jesus Christ, lady. Your memory is annoying."

"Lawyer memory, Captain. It's how we get ya."

He shook his head. "They're sending us to Bungo Suido," he said. "Five of our boats are already dead in that part of the sea. Five skippers and their execs whom I knew personally, three hundred or so crewmen. All with goddamned fish swimming in and out of their mouths. All—"

"*Stop it*, Gar Hammond," she said. "Just stop it. And enough of that stuff, too." She took his refill away from him and parked it on her side of the table.

He gave her a look that said, *You are going to lecture* me *on drinking too much?* She understood immediately.

"I'm a professional boozer, Gar," she said quietly. "You're just pretending. So, yeah, you're officially eighty-six. You should be sober when you discover that you're human, just like the rest of us."

Gar closed his eyes. He didn't need this. He was already embarrassed at revealing that finally, the big bad submarine captain was tasting real fear. She reached across the table and took his hand. "Why don't we go upstairs?" she asked. "Now that you're done drinking."

He sighed. He didn't want sex. He didn't want any more booze, either—she was right about that. He wanted—hell, he didn't know what he wanted.

"C'mon," she said, pushing back her chair.

He looked around the dark lanai, as if not wanting anyone to see them, then recognized how ridiculous that was. He signed his bar chit and followed her through the dining room to the elevators.

Once in her room he sat on the edge of the bed. There were two chairs in the room, but they were covered in clothes and books, so there was nowhere else to sit. Sharon went into the bathroom. When she came back out she was wearing a full-length white slip and nothing else.

"Oh-oh," Gar said.

She smiled at him and crossed the room, doing something with her hairdo that made it suddenly fall down.

"Up," she said.

"Up, aye," he said, trying to think of something really clever to say.

She took his clothes off and then pushed him back onto the bed with one finger. He did as he was ordered, and she joined him, sitting across his hips while she continued to run her fingers through her hair. Gar recognized who was in charge and simply lay back to enjoy the show, Bungo Suido and all its drowned ghosts suddenly forgotten. Sharon proceeded to bend down and apply her lips to his, and after that, to present all the other best parts for similar attention from him.

"Don't make me whimper," he said, after a while.

"No whimper, no joy," she whispered.

He whimpered.

"Atta boy," she said.

SIX

On the afternoon prior to *Dragonfish*'s departure, Gar was summoned to SubPac headquarters for a final briefing. The summons included the exec, Russ West. They arrived at the headquarters building, with its three-star flag fluttering on an antique yardarm outside, and were ushered into the admiral's office ten minutes later. Gar was surprised to see that the admiral wasn't there; the chief of staff, Captain Forrester, was. He was even more surprised to find two Japanese men sitting at the admiral's conference table. One was wearing the uniform of a U.S. Navy lieutenant commander. The other, much older, was dressed in a long-sleeved white cotton shirt and khaki trousers. Captain Forrester made the introductions.

"Captain Hammond," he said, "this is Lieutenant Commander Bobby Tanaka from the CincPacFleet intelligence division. Next to him is Mr. Minoru Hashimoto, who has been interned in a POW camp here on Oahu since late 1943." He turned to the other two. "Gentlemen, this is Commander Hammond and Lieutenant Commander West, the captain and executive officer of USS *Dragonfish*, which is one of our submarines."

Both of them rose at the same time. Bobby Tanaka shook hands with Gar and West. The older man bowed to them individually but said nothing. Gar tried to estimate his age but found it difficult. He was of medium height and very slim. His hair was almost white and his face severely weather-beaten. His hands and forearms, which he kept rigidly to his sides, indicated that he'd spent many years in manual labor of some kind, probably commercial fishing. Standing next to Hashimoto, Lieutenant Commander Tanaka looked positively elegant.

Gar had met Tanaka before. He was a native-born American whose parents lived in New York City. He had an Ivy League education and, being fluent in Japanese, had probably made some significant, if necessarily classified, contributions to naval intelligence efforts. He'd briefed the sub skippers a couple of times at the Pink Palace, and each time the appearance of a Japanese face in those precincts had caused quite a stir.

Forrester asked everyone to sit down and then took the seat at the head of the table. "Commander Tanaka, would you explain to Captain Hammond why Mr. Hashimoto is going to go out on *Dragonfish*'s next war patrol?"

What? Gar thought. A passenger? On *this* mission? A POW? Were they nuts?

"Yes, sir," Tanaka said. "Captain, Mr. Hashimoto was born and raised in a small fishing village just outside of Kure, near Hiroshima City, on the island of Honshu. He started out as a fisherman's apprentice, eventually owned his own boat and then a small fishing fleet. He lost all that to a typhoon and then set up a small boatyard near the village, where they repaired hulls and engines. Hashimoto-san's village and boatyard were seized by the army in 1928 to accommodate the expansion of the Kure naval arsenal. The villagers were basically thrown out of their homes and livelihoods without compensation, and if they complained, the provincial governor simply put them in jail.

"When the war began, all of the local fishermen and anyone else connected with the fishing industry were put under the authority of the army military district commander at Hiroshima City. You may not realize this, but Hiroshima is an army city. It contains the Japanese Second General Army headquarters, which controls fourteen divisions in Korea and on Kyushu, as well as the Fifteenth Area Army, which has eight divisions in western Honshu and Shikoku Island. Hashimoto-san was one of thousands of civilians who were suddenly under the control of the Japanese army, not known to be a kind and loving institution. He was captured by the *Albacore* at the end of '43 off the coast of Shikoku when they shot up a trawler fleet. He was brought to Oahu a month later. He has relatives back on the mainland, who'd left Japan back in 1928 and settled in California. They, of course, are now in one of the internment camps. He's fifty-nine years old, a widower, and despises what Tojo and the militarists have done to Japan. He's been cooperative, and looks forward to the day when America defeats the lunatics and can bring sanity back to Japan."

"That's all very interesting," Gar said. "But why on earth do you want to put a civilian on board for a mission like this?"

"Your mission involves a penetration into the Inland Sea of Japan, specifically the straits of Bungo Suido. Hashimoto-san knows those waters like the back of his hand. He's going to guide you through them. In return, you will at some point put him ashore."

Gar thought about that for a moment. Then he turned to the old man. "Do you speak English, Mr. Hashimoto?" he asked.

Hashimoto looked over at Tanaka for guidance. Tanaka nodded his head once. "Some," he said, in the familiar polyglot accent of the local Hawaiians. "Got pretty good pidgin now."

"Hashimoto-san has been given English lessons in the compound," Tanaka said. "All the Japanese POWs are learning English. It's part of, let us say, our conversion program. He understands English better than he speaks it. You've heard the Hawaiian locals, Captain. He can communicate as well as they can, once you get used to the dialect. He does, of course, speak fluent Japanese, albeit with a provincial accent. Someone from Tokyo would probably make fun of him. He's brought along something I think you'll find to be very useful."

He nodded at Hashimoto, who reached under the conference table and produced what looked like a rolled-up poster. He stood up, laid this out on the table, and unrolled it, revealing a hand-drawn nautical chart of the western end of the Inland Sea. He slid the chart across the table toward Gar with a short bow of his head.

A treasure indeed, Gar thought, as he examined the chart. Even though he couldn't begin to read the Japanese kanji characters, he realized that a local fisherman would know things about that area that not even the Japanese naval hydrographers would know.

"Captain Hammond," Tanaka said, "you need to know that the orders to take Hashimoto-san back to Japan come from the top. It was Admiral Nimitz's office who asked my boss if there were any POWs here in the Islands who knew Bungo Suido and who'd be willing to help the U.S. Navy."

"You raise an interesting question, Mister Tanaka," Gar said. "The question of divided loyalties."

"Yes, sir," Tanaka said. "I know, especially when you consider how most Japanese army troops react to the notion of surrender. But Hashimoto-san was a civilian, and he has a very different perspective. All I can say is that when I discuss this with him, he speaks fervently about the coming destruction of his homeland and curses the militarists who have betrayed the Japanese people. The people in the Seto provinces—Seto refers to the Inland Sea—are very traditional, and they're being treated like medieval slaves. You go ashore anywhere along the Inland Sea and you're going way back in time."

"Yet the reason the *Albacore* destroyed Mister Hashimoto's trawler fleet was because most fishing boats out there are carrying radios and reporting to the military authorities," Gar said. "They see a periscope, we lose a boat. Excuse me," he said, glancing at Forrester. "*Another* boat."

"That's because they're required to have a soldier on board any time they go to sea beyond the Seto, even for just a day. The army's secret police, the Kempeitai, are watching them as much as they are watching the shoreline for intruders and spies. This war has been a disaster for the ordinary people in the countryside, and I think they know it's going to get worse and that, ultimately, there will be an invasion."

"That's very interesting, Commander Tanaka," Captain Forrester interjected. "But what the captain's getting at is, can he trust Mr. Hashimoto not to lead them directly into a minefield?"

"Well, first of all, he wouldn't have had any detailed information about minefields. When they'd go out, they'd be led out by a Japanese navy minesweeper, and brought back in the same way. Hashimoto was no longer going to sea once the war started, and only went back to fishing when they confiscated his boatyard. What he does know is the hydrography of Bungo Suido and its approaches, from both directions. He knows where the deep reefs and ledges are, the deep holes, where mines can and cannot not be planted. Things like that."

Hashimoto said something in Japanese to Tanaka.

Tanaka rattled off some lightning-fast Japanese of his own. Even Gar could tell the difference in their accents. Hashimoto listened carefully, nodded twice, said the word *hai*, and then asked Tanaka another question.

"He's asking why your ship is going into the Seto."

Gar glanced over at Forrester for a cue as to what he could reveal, but the chief of staff's face was a professional blank. Understood.

"Well, Commander," Gar said to Tanaka, "I'm supposed to open sealed orders after we leave Guam. All I've been told unofficially is that we are to try to penetrate Bungo Suido and, assuming we succeed in getting through, conduct a special mission. Hell, you work at CincPacFleet—perhaps you can enlighten all of us?"

"Sorry, sir," Tanaka said.

"Cannot or may not?"

"*May* not, sir. Truth is, I *thought* I knew what you were going to be tasked to do, but once this passenger business emerged, all of us snuffies on the intel staff were cut out of the loop. Anyone asking questions gets his head bitten off."

"Well, then, *you* answer Mr. Hashimoto's question, because I sure as hell can't."

Tanaka said something in Japanese to the old man, who grunted.

"What'd you tell him?" Gar asked.

"It's a secret," Tanaka said.

Got that right, Gar thought. He got up from the table and went to the windows overlooking the sub-base finger piers. A secret

mission within a secret mission. The carrier was the ostensible objective, although he had no idea of how they would manage that.
Either way, he wasn't going to talk about that in front of a Japanese
civilian, and a POW to boot. What upset him even more was that
all these clever staffies didn't trust him, the commanding officer,
enough to tell him what the hell was going on here. Besides hurting
his pride they were possibly compromising the mission: If he knew
what they were really doing, he might be able to do some planning
that would enhance their chances for success, preferably before
they cut all ties with Pearl and went west. Taking a foreign national, an *enemy* foreign national, along for the most dangerous run
of their lives was outrageous. They could get his chart translated if
they had to, but there was no reason to let a Japanese, even one who
now professed loyalty to the American side, come along.

He made a decision. "No," he said. "I won't do this." He turned
to the chief of staff. "I'm the commanding officer of *Dragonfish*,
and obviously I don't really know what this whole mission is about.
I don't think you do, either. The intel officer here says *he* doesn't
know. On top of that, I'm being asked to take a Japanese POW on
board on what is an obviously either a highly classified mission or a
harebrained idea that nobody wants to own up to. I think you need
to get somebody else."

Captain Forrester stared at him in shock. "Are you asking to be
relieved of command?" he asked finally.

"I say again: If my superiors don't trust me enough to tell me
what's really going on here, then yes, I'm asking to be relieved of
command."

"Think about what you just said, Captain, " Forrester said.
"Think hard."

Gar laughed out loud. "You think I don't know what people say
about me? That I'm some kind of nutcase because I hunt destroyers?
You like the results well enough, as I recall, but I've seen the looks
from the other COs at the Royal. Great score, man, but damn!
Well, here it is: You want me to take the Dragon through Bungo
Suido? With a Japanese national as my navigator? Then somebody
better tell me why."

He signaled to Russ, nodded to Tanaka and Hashimoto as politely as he could, gathered up his cap, and left the conference room. Forrester looked as if he'd just been slapped with a wet fish.

Gar finished his dinner at the Royal that night and asked for a Scotch and some coffee. Needless to say, he'd been thinking all day about what he'd said at the meeting with the chief of staff, and wondering if he'd really screwed up. Rising to command of a fleet submarine in wartime was more than likely going to be the pinnacle of his otherwise pretty undistinguished naval career, as he had explained to Sharon DeVeers. *Dragonfish*'s reason for being was to destroy the Japanese Empire's ability to wage war, and that was as simple a proposition as he could imagine. Okay, some of his own tactics at sea were unconventional, but the results spoke for themselves. High-value hulls on the bottom. Destroyers blown to pieces, their crews going into the sea while their own depth charges rearranged their innards. A cruel game, but there it was. And every tin can Gar put down meant one less his boat and all the others had to fear.

The Japs had come to Pearl Harbor and started all this shit, not the other way around. *Remember Pearl Harbor* wasn't just a bond-drive slogan to career naval officers. America was going to kick their asses all the way back to Tokyo, and then burn Tokyo and the rest of Japan to the ground. Old Bull Halsey had had it right from the get-go: Kill Japs, kill Japs, kill *more* Japs. He'd heard Japan was a very pretty country. It would be even prettier once all those bloodthirsty, death-worshiping, samurai-sword-toting bastards had joined their ancestors, preferably disguised as well-done chop suey.

The waiter brought him his Scotch and coffee as he forced himself to calm down. The chief of staff had been visibly upset today, and Gar had this sneaking suspicion that Forrester might be all too ready to relieve him. For some strange reason, though, he didn't really expect to be relieved of command. He wondered how Uncle Charlie would have handled his outburst, or whether he'd have done such a thing in the presence of the three-star. Either way, he'd drawn one of those famous lines in the sand. The Dragon was supposed to sail at 1000 tomorrow. Unless somebody in authority came to see him to explain this crazy business before tomorrow morning, he'd shut down the engines, double up the lines, and tell the crew to stand down. If another three-striper with a big grin on his face showed up on the pier as his relief, then so be it. God knows there were enough prospective commanding officers hanging around, secretly hoping for someone like Gar to make a mistake.

He and West had walked back to the boat after Gar's sudden declaration. Once back aboard, he asked the exec to join him up on the bow, away from the chain of sweating sailors who were busy passing boxes of stores aboard back aft.

"Okay," Gar said. "Say something."

"I think I'm not ready to be a CO," Russ said. "I would not have had the balls to say what you did in there."

"Sure you would, XO," Gar said. "Especially if you were being asked to own this bizarre trip."

Russ had stared down at the water under the pier for a long moment. "Thing is . . ."

"Yeah?"

"The thing is, we were always taught not to question the orders of our lawful superiors, because there would be times when they knew something we did not or could not know. I'm just wondering . . ."

He had him there, Gar realized. "Yeah, me, too, of course," he said. "But the whole deal goes off the tracks when you realize your own bosses don't know what the hell's going on. I think Captain Forrester's as much in the dark as we are, and that means Uncle Charlie is, too. Especially when it comes to putting all our asses on the line while we depend on some old Jap guy to act as some kind of Injun guide. Remember Custer?"

"As I remember," the exec pointed out delicately, "Custer ignored what his Injun guides were telling him about the lebenty-million Sioux who were right over the next hill."

"Details, XO," Gar said with a snort. "I'm the CO, and if I have to trust them, then they have to trust me."

"Yes, sir," the exec had said, even as Gar began to realize that now it was the exec who was probably indulging him, the captain.

What he was really saying was, since when did a three-star have to explain his orders to a three-striper? Yes, they knew the one objective, but Gar still had this niggling suspicion that there was a whole lot more to this business of putting an elderly Japanese man ashore in the Inland Sea. Forrester had shown him the pictures of this mysterious carrier, but then he'd ducked all of Gar's questions about how they were even supposed to get at it.

That old refrain kept ringing in Gar's ears: WTF, over?

He became aware of a small commotion in the dining room behind him, the sound of chairs moving and people standing up, and then a voice behind him asked, "Are you Commander Hammond?"

Gar looked up, then hurriedly pushed back his own chair and stood up at rigid attention. "Admiral *Nimitz*?"

"May I join you, sir?"

"Yes, sir, uh, yes, of course, sir."

Nimitz sat down, waited one beat, and then indicated that he wanted Gar to sit down as well. Gar pulled his chair back under himself and sat down at semiattention. Nimitz's face looked like it had been carved out of stone. Gar had seen pictures and thought them posed. Not so. Nimitz fixed those famous ice blue eyes on Gar for a long moment.

"I am told," he said finally, "that you want to know why we want you to go into Bungo Suido with the help of a Japanese POW."

Gar took a deep breath. It was one thing to posture in front of the SubPac chief of staff. It was an entirely different proposition to defy Admiral Chester Nimitz, face-to-face, but—what the hell, he thought. "Yes, sir, I do. To go into Bungo Suido is to step across the bones of five submarines. So, yes, sir, I do want to know why."

Nimitz nodded. "Because I say so," he said quietly.

Gar blinked. That was clear enough. "Yes, sir."

"I am responsible for the execution of our entire war effort in the Pacific Ocean area. Our objective remains the total and utter destruction of the Japanese war machine, and the total and utter destruction of the Japanese nation's will to conduct this war."

Gar sat back in his chair. "Yes, sir," I said. "I understand that. But Bungo Suido—"

Nimitz held up his hand. "Bungo Suido is a technical problem, Captain," he said. "If you truly think it's beyond your capabilities, I will get someone else. There is no lack of submariners waiting for command, as I'm sure you know. That would, however, be quite disruptive a day before your scheduled departure."

"Yes, sir."

"You have a fine boat and crew, and you personally have done very well in damaging the Japanese war effort. But above and beyond that, you need to understand that there are forces at work in this war that *dwarf* the *Dragonfish* and all its efforts. You may, in time, understand what I'm talking about, *if* you survive this mission. But for now, this is all I'm going to tell you: Your orders are not the result of whimsy."

"Yes, sir."

"I want you to sail tomorrow morning. Take the Japanese Hashimoto with you. He will get you through Bungo Suido and, more importantly, to your objective. What happens after that will be up to you and your crew. Am I making myself clear, Captain?"

Gar knew when he'd been outmatched. "We'll do our best, Admiral."

"We're counting on that, Captain. More than you could ever imagine." He paused for a moment and gave Gar another dose of that icy stare. "Do not ever challenge me again, young man."

"Aye, aye, sir."

Gar became aware that Admiral Lockwood and Captain Forrester were watching from across the dining room. Everyone else in the dining room had sat back down and was pretending not to watch. Nimitz stood up, wished Gar good luck, and then left to rejoin Admiral Lockwood, who gave Gar a wry smile and a sympathetic shake of his head over his shoulder as he followed his boss out of the hotel.

Well, I showed him, didn't I, Gar thought as he tried to avoid the puzzled looks from the rest of the diners. Six yes-sirs and an aye-aye. He took some small comfort in the fact that he wasn't the first naval officer to be steamrollered by Chester W. Nimitz. The Japs didn't stand a chance.

We don't, either, he thought.

His coffee had gone cold, much like the pit in his stomach. He wondered if Sharon DeVeers would have been impressed.

Probably not, he thought, but then she'd just order another Scotch and make bogeymen like Chester Nimitz go away. He saw the waiter and raised a finger for a refill. As the waiter approached, he changed his mind. Recalling the previous evening, he decided to at least pretend he was still in control of his fate, but as he remembered the image of Sharon poised above him on the bed he had to smile. His life was becoming one interesting ride after another.

SEVEN

The northern Philippine Sea

Gar studied the sharp, bare pinnacle of granite shimmering in his periscope. "Lot's Wife, bearing two niner five," he reported. "Down scope."

"That's a pretty good match with our estimated position, Captain. A range would help."

Gar told the exec he could calibrate the surface-search radar on Lot's Wife, a 300-foot-high volcanic crag sticking up out of the ocean, using the attack periscope. They knew its precise height above the sea, and thus could focus the radar's range gate using the periscope's stadimeter. The pinnacle's Japanese name was Sofu Gan, and it lay 400 miles south of Tokyo, at the very northern extremes of the Philippine Sea. American subs entering empire patrol areas always used it as a navigational reference point, as did, apparently, Japanese warships headed south into their ever-shrinking Greater East Asia Co-Prosperity Sphere. Or at least they used to, before SubPac saturated the area with submarines. "When finished, make your depth two hundred fifty feet, then put us on a course to our rendezvous point at five knots. We'll surface after dark to get back on planned track."

"Three three five looks good."

"Okay. I want all department heads in the wardroom once you're confident in the track. We'll need the Bungo Suido charts and Hashimoto-san's chart."

"Aye, aye, sir."

Gar went down the ladder into the control room and then forward to his cabin. It was two hours until full dark. They were twelve hours behind their projected track due to some bad weather out of Guam. Gar wanted to make up some of that time to avoid spending an entire day submerged at the entrance to Bungo Suido. He planned to surface an hour after dark if the area was clear and run on the diesels toward their objective.

He flopped down on his rack, automatically checked the course and depth indicators by his feet, and then closed his eyes. So far, so good. They'd left Pearl on time with everyone on board, including the elderly Japanese gentleman. That novelty had made for some interesting reactions among the crew, but the exec had done a good job of prebriefing everybody, emphasizing that Hashimoto-san hated the Japanese military for seizing his livelihood and drawing Japan into a war with the Americans. Lieutenant Commander Tanaka had come down to the pier to say good-bye to the old man. Standing there in his navy uniform, he'd lent some credence to what the exec had been telling them. He'd brought a departure gift for the old man, a cylindrical box wrapped tightly in tissue paper. Hashimoto-san was berthed in the chiefs' quarters, and, after three weeks of transit across the North Pacific, he seemed to have been accepted pretty well by the denizens of the goat locker.

He'd proved his worth when No. 2 main engine tripped off the line. The motor mechs had been climbing over the Fairbanks Morse engine, trying to find the problem, when Hashimoto-san showed up. He'd watched the snipes for a few minutes and then, with a combination of Hawaiian pidgin and sign language, asked if they needed help. It turned out that the old man was a wizard with diesel engines, and in no time flat he was tearing into the fuel pump assembly, finally identifying a broken linkage as the root of the problem. After that, he was welcomed in both engine rooms and kept himself busy tweaking and peaking all sorts of machinery. He'd taught the boat's mechanics some lessons about the Japanese way with machinery, which took "fastidious" to extreme limits. Every nut, washer, bolt, and gasket—anything that came out of or off a machine—was carefully cleaned, oiled, measured, and then rein-stalled with a calibrated torque wrench, as opposed to the old-navy "give it a two-fart twist and send it home" technique. Some of the pumps ran so smoothly once Hashimoto-san got hold of them that the chief engineer had to put his hand on them to make sure they *were* running.

Dragonfish had been escorted all the way to Guam by a destroyer, which allowed them to run on the surface the entire time except for daily training dives. The threat from Pearl to Guam hadn't been Japanese but trigger-happy American planes, which tended to bomb any submarine on the surface and then ask questions later. One army air force B-29 had made a low pass two days out from Guam, but they'd been mostly rubbernecking. The tin can had fired off some flares as the lumbering bomber approached, just in case. They'd also got some valuable training with their captive destroyer, making submerged approaches from all angles. The destroyer's sonarmen had kept themselves up to date by using *Dragonfish* for some sonar training in return. They'd refueled in Guam, detached their escort, and headed for empire waters, a mere 1,600 miles distant.

Gar had opened the sealed orders pouch upon departure from Guam as instructed. Inside he found three things: another sealed envelope; a two-page operations order, signed by Admiral Rennsalear, the deputy chief of staff for operations at the Pacific Fleet headquarters; and a single black-and-white picture of the mysterious supercarrier. Unlike many operations orders, this one was quite succinct:

Open the second envelope once inside the Inland Sea, but not before. Otherwise, *Dragonfish* is to penetrate the straits of Bungo Suido, proceed submerged to the vicinity of the Kure Arsenal, and attack an unnamed aircraft carrier. Attack no other shipping en route to or once within the Inland Sea. Your sole objective is the aircraft carrier, either fitting out at the Kure naval arsenal, or wherever encountered. Upon completion of the attack, escape back to sea and report, but otherwise, maintain radio silence until clear of the Inland Sea.

Then one interesting technical note: Set torpedo running depth for 10 feet when attacking this carrier.

That made no sense at all to Gar. An aircraft carrier drew between 30 and 40 feet of water. If he'd ever encountered the Wounded Bear, IJN *Shokaku*, he'd have set his fish for 25 feet running depth. Ten feet? Somebody knew more than he was telling about this mysterious ship.

The picture wasn't particularly good as a recognition photo because it was an overhead shot. Fine for dive-bombers, but their view of this ship, assuming they found her, would be from about a foot above the water. The good news was that if they succeeded in bagging this big guy, they'd accomplish in one attack a tonnage score to equal even the most famous of the PacFleet sub skippers.

Big if, though.

The sole attachment to the operations order, besides the picture, was a map of the *known* minefields in the Inland Sea approaches, with the clear inference that there were probably *un*known minefields.

That was it. No mention of the old man, although Gar had had his orders on that score from Nimitz himself. The second envelope looked like nothing more than a letter, but it was heavily taped and labeled *For Commanding Officer's Eyes Only, upon arrival* inside *the Inland Sea*.

He sighed and looked at his watch again. They were supposed to rendezvous later tonight with the *Archer-fish*, through whose patrol area they were going to transit. The skipper of that boat, a seasoned veteran named Joe Enright, would brief them on what they'd been seeing in the op area and give them any recent information on Jap patrols, radar usage, and aircraft surveillance. *Archer-fish* would have already made an intrusion into the approaches to Bungo Suido to confirm water and sonar conditions so that *Dragonfish* could optimize the setup of her new sonar before they got there. While they were surfaced for the *Archer-fish* join-up, Gar's guys would be rigging the defensive cables that would shoulder away any mine mooring chains they happened to scrape up against. Gar made a mental note to remind the XO to get evening stars; an accurate fix was vital for a submarine rendezvous.

He'd met several times with his tactical team after reading the

sealed orders. Everyone was interested in the carrier, and Gar had
even expected some amplifying information from SubPac while
they'd been making the transit. They'd heard nothing. In fact, there
had not been a single message addressed to *Dragonfish* since they'd
left. This whole patrol was one big mystery, Gar decided. Or they'd
already been written off.

He'd also spent a lot of time with the exec and Hashimoto-san,
whose English was better than he had first let on. They worked on
making a composite of the U.S. Navy charts for Bungo Suido and
the Inland Sea and the old man's personal charts. Everything on
his charts was annotated in kanji characters, and they'd labored
mightily to translate depth and obstruction marks into characters
that both of them could recognize. Hashimoto-san had, of course,
no knowledge of minefields, but he did show them interesting hydrographic features that would make the placement of mines almost impossible. They'd slowly managed to develop a plan of attack
for the penetration of Bungo Suido, and that was going to be the
subject of the department head meeting this evening.

ComSubPac Headquarters, Pearl Harbor

"And, last but hardly least," Captain Forrester said, "Guam reports
Dragonfish has departed for empire waters. No mechanical problems,
traded in one sick fish, one emergency leave case, but otherwise
she's off to the races."

"The original reluctant dragon," Admiral Lockwood said, and
Forrester grunted his agreement.

"That night Chester Nimitz went down to 'share his thinking'
with Gar Hammond, I would have given a lot to hear what he said."

"I'll bet it didn't take very long," Forrester said.

Lockwood smiled. "A half-dozen yes-sirs is what it looked like.
Maybe ninety seconds. Everybody in the dining room pretending
not to notice. Wonderful."

"Hammond has his moments," Forrester said. "And a disrespectful tongue, too."

"The real killers are that way, Mike. He's never been married, been at sea for almost his entire career, and goes for the throat when he finds Japs. It's just too bad he didn't come to our attention until now."

"If a guy like that had been out there in '42, he probably wouldn't still be with us," Forrester said. "Mush Morton, Sam Dealey, they were hotshots, too, but they never gave me the impression that they were out of control like Hammond sometimes does."

"And where are they, now, Mike, hmm?" Lockwood asked, knowing all too well the answer. "I wouldn't want Gar Hammond for a staff officer, but for this harebrained mission, he's perfect."

"He asked me why we didn't just go in and bomb the damned carrier, especially if she's still in dry dock. I deflected him, but it seemed like a reasonable question."

"Nimitz has his reasons, and, as I witnessed personally, one does not go asking Himself to explain why he wants something done. Anything else? I need a drink."

"No, sir, other than to remind you that we won't hear from *Dragonfish* until she gets in *and* back out of the Inland Sea."

"If she gets back," Lockwood said.

"Don't go jinxing it, now, Admiral. They'll get back."

The rendezvous with *Archer-fish* was scheduled for 0130, and *Dragonfish*, courtesy of an 1830 four-line star fix, was in position at the appointed time. Gar took a long look around with the night scope. They were lying surfaced and motionless in a flat, calm sea on what appeared to be a clear, starlit night. He'd kept her at what they called radar depth, the boat's decks awash in order to make as small a radar target as possible should any Jap planes be patrolling. Gar had their own radars in standby, and he was hesitant to put either one into radiate. They were a good 60 miles from the Japanese coast, but a radar signal could be intercepted farther than the radar itself could see. There was no one topside in case an emergency dive had to be made, and they were back to running on the battery, in deference to any prowling Jap subs.

"Like two scorpions looking for each other in the dark," he muttered, continuing to train the periscope in a slow, continuous circle.

"Especially if one of 'em is a Jap I-boat," the exec said. "Who makes the first move?"

"We're the ones passing through *Archer-fish*'s patrol area," Gar said. "We came to the rendezvous point on the surface and on the diesels, and then we went quiet. If he was anywhere around, he'd have heard us on the diesels, and should be looking at us right now."

"Asking the same questions we're asking?"

"Yeah, probably. Radar, put the SJ on short time constant, radiate for one revolution."

"Radar, aye," said the operator at the other end of the conning tower. "One rev, STC on. Stand by."

They waited.

"One contact, very small, one five zero at two thousand yards."

Should be him, Gar thought, as he spun the periscope to 150. He couldn't see anything, so he keyed the signal light embedded in the periscope head three times in accordance with this day's recognition code sheet. If the radar had caught *Archer-fish*'s shears or periscope, he should answer with two flashes.

"Got him," Gar announced. "What's the second signal?"

"The letter Dog. Then the letter Tare. He should answer with the letter Fox."

Gar keyed the light: long, short, short. Pause. One long. *DT.*

The reply was immediate: two short, one long, one short. *F.* This should be *Archer-fish*. Since he had initiated the light sequence, Gar now spelled out a course and speed to *Archer-fish* and ordered Control to trim the boat up to the normal surfaced depth.

"Station the bridge watch," he ordered. "Four lookouts. Come to course three three zero, switch to main engines, speed ten." He turned to Russ. "XO, stay on the scope. Once he gets alongside we'll need a light-line party forward to get a sound-powered phone circuit up. Do a one-sweep air-search radar transmission every six minutes, and a ten-mile surface search sweep every other ten minutes."

"Aye, aye, sir," the exec said and handed Gar his jacket and binoculars. It was November in the North Pacific, and the tropical heat of the Luzon Strait was a distant memory.

Fifteen minutes later the two subs were running alongside each other at a distance of 75 feet, and Gar was on the sound-powered bridge-to-bridge phone line with Commander Enright.

"How's the hunting?" he asked.

"Not worth a shit," Enright said. "We've been out here a month, had a couple of scares, but zero worthwhile targets. Where you guys going that you need my BT logs?"

"Big secret," Gar said. "But I'll give you a hint: From here it's three four zero."

"You do that, you'll run right into the minefields at Bungo Suido."

"Fancy that," Gar said.

"You out of your gourd?" Enright asked.

"Somebody is," Gar said. "From our perspective, though, it looks a lot like a direct order."

"The Inland Sea? Can't be done, Gar. Hell, from twenty miles out you're looking at pretty much constant air cover, and when they take somebody through, we've seen as many as a dozen escorts."

"So there is a channel through the minefields?"

"Must be," Enright said. "Their big ships come through there from time to time. But where the channel is, where it starts, and how far offshore? Only the Japs know that. You got one of those new FM sonars?"

Gar told him about the upgraded mine-hunting sonar. Enright said he hoped it worked.

"Do you have some BT logs for me?" Gar asked.

"That's affirm. Last thirty days, inshore waters, or as close as we could get without somebody jumping our asses. Water's getting colder, layer's getting thicker, but there won't be any layers in Bungo Suido—the tides are too big and the currents too fast."

"That's what we were told, too. You need any spare parts?"

"Nope, we're good right now. We'll trade movies if you want to, but so far, nothing's broken down. Yet. I've included some pass-down notes with the BT data about their air search patterns and when they seem to quit for the night."

"These radar-equipped planes?"

"We think so—the two times we've been jumped they came straight in on us."

"You have your radar on the air when they did?"

"Once yes, once no. We only come up at night, and preferably in dirty weather. They don't seem to like flying when it's low viz. May be different if something big's coming in or out. If the merchies *are* running, they're way inshore under all that air cover, or over in the SOJ."

"We have anybody there?"

"Not that I know of. Ever since we lost *Wahoo*, I don't think anybody's made it through either Shimonoseki or La Pérouse Strait."

They talked for another few minutes, mainly about the currents running closer inshore and any communications frequencies they'd been able to monitor. There were four other American subs patrolling in the empire areas, and none of them were having much luck, either. Enright wished Gar good luck with whatever craziness they were up to, and that was it.

Gar checked with the forecastle crew to make sure the bathythermograph logs and pass-down notes had made it on board, waited for the IC-electrician to send across and then receive some movies, and then ordered the light-line to be retrieved. Five minutes later, *Archer-fish* rumbled off into the darkness, headed back out into her patrol area. The three-man line-handling party came to the bridge with the small waterproof bag sent over from *Archer-fish* and took it below to the control room. Gar decided to stay on the surface to top off the batteries as long as the radar didn't indicate any snoopers; he told the OOD and the bridge crew to listen as well as look.

Back down in the conning tower he checked the track, adjusted the ship's speed to make the planned entry point at the straits two hours before dawn, then went below to see what Enright had sent over. Normally he would have sent off a position report, but the orders were clear: radio silence. *Archer-fish* would report the rendezvous, so Pearl would know the Dragon had made it this far. Considering what they were about to attempt, that might be the last time anything was ever heard about the *Dragonfish*. Everyone on board except perhaps Hashimoto-san knew they might very well end up on that dreaded "missing, presumed lost in Empire Patrol Area" list, like *Pickerel, Runner, Pompano, Wahoo,* and *Golet.*

Gar tried to banish that thought. Getting through the minefields of Bungo Suido was going to be a one-man, one-sonar show, and he did not need the distraction of a bunch of drowned ghosts, wherever they were now sleeping.

EIGHT

"This is the captain speaking."

That announcement produced the usual quiet throughout the boat. They were submerged at 300 feet and basically standing still as the boat pointed into an east-running current coming at them out of the entrance to Bungo Suido.

"We're about to do something that is unusually dangerous. We're going to penetrate the straits of Bungo Suido and go into the Inland Sea of Japan. We're on the hunt for a very large aircraft carrier that has been spotted by army air force reconnaissance planes at the Kure naval arsenal. Our mission is to torpedo this ship, wherever we find her."

Gar paused for a moment to gather his thoughts. He rarely got on the 1MC to address the entire crew. Up to now, he'd always kept his cards pretty close, but he'd finally concluded that the danger of what they were about to do justified letting his people in on the secret mission orders.

"Many of you know that our boats have been told to stay out of Bungo Suido and the other straits of the Home Islands for over a year now. We've lost five boats in this area, and when we go in tonight, we may be driving over their remains. Or not. Nobody knows where they actually went down. But the Japs have this place covered with destroyers, patrol frigates, land-based air, minefields, miniature submarines, and shore-based radar stations. The fishing boats that operate along this coast each have a soldier on board, a soldier with a radio. They know we'd love to get into this protected area, and they're determined to prevent it.

"Now, we've had boats *outside* Bungo Suido, and the northern entrance, Kii Suido, for over two years. They know we're here, and when their fleet units do come out, they come out at high speed and with lots of cover. We've been able to sink the occasional merchie, but rarely a major warship. One of the things we're counting on is that they will have become complacent about the possibility that we'd try to force the straits and actually go into the Inland Sea.

"We have an upgraded version of the new FM sonar. This sonar can see mines. If we can see them, we can avoid them. That said, if we can get through the minefields, we'll still face lots of challenges that we don't normally have to worry about. The Inland Sea is small, and it's relatively shallow. Lots of small islands and reefs. Thanks to Hashimoto-san, we have much better charts than what the Hydrographic Office could give us. But—we have to also get through the Hoyo Strait, where the tide causes large whirlpools. Then we have to get within torpedo range of a major Japanese naval base. We can probably do that, because the last thing they'll expect is an American submarine hunkering down right off their piers."

He paused again, because this was the hard part.

"If we succeed in putting a spread of torpedoes into a brand-new aircraft carrier moored to a pier, we then have to find our way *out* of the Inland Sea and back to the safety of deep water. How we do that is going to depend on a lot of things, and all I can say now is that we'll surely be winging it when the time comes. Some of you might think this is some kind of suicide mission, but I can assure you that it is not. I intend to get in and get back out, and to hurt them bad in the process, but for the next twenty-four to thirty-six hours, I need everybody, absolutely everybody, to play heads-up ball.

"Okay. The tide out of the straits is coming up on the end of the ebb. We'll have about an hour or so of slack water, and then the flood begins. If all goes well, we should be through Bungo Suido and then the Hoyo Strait in two hours' time, after which we'll have to see where we are and what we're looking at. Keep the chatter on the sound-powered phones to a minimum, please. We'll be at GQ stations, buttoned up but not at silent running, which means we'll be able to breathe. Man your GQ stations in fifteen minutes. That is all."

He hung up the 1MC microphone and left the control room. He knew the people in Control would want to comment to each other on what he'd said, and they couldn't do that if the captain was still standing there.

Once he got to his cabin, he called the exec and asked for the chief of the boat to come see him. Cob must have been expecting it, because he was there in under a minute.

"Swede," Gar said, "this one's gonna be a level bitch."

"Piece'a cake, Skipper," the chief said.

"Yeah, right, but look: What I'll need you to do is float. The first time we drag a mine's mooring chain down the paravane wire, guys are going to piss their pants. I need you to buck 'em up. Keep 'em focused. Keep 'em quiet. All sorts of shit can go wrong here, and we're going to be jumping through our asses just to stay alive. Savvy?"

"Piece'a cake," the chief said again. "Just lemme get some diapers on."

Gar laughed then. "Bring a set for me," he said.

Dragonfish headed into the straits at slack water, running at periscope depth so they could do their piloting with the radar. They were trimmed bow-down 5 degrees and with the radar mast up. The night was still clear and calm, with no visible moon. On his last periscope observation, Gar had seen small patches of fog and mist here and there. He would have preferred a heavy fog, but he knew he couldn't have everything. They had taped down the old man's annotated chart on top of the new dead-reckoning tracer plotting table. The DRT would allow the conning team as well as the officers in Control to do radar navigation.

Hashimoto-san had told them to keep to the middle of the Bungo channel and to the left, or west, side of the Hoyo channel. They expected Bungo to be mined but had no information on Hoyo. Hashimoto-san said the water on the west side of Hoyo was very deep, and the tidal whirlpools there would make mooring mines almost impossible. There was one ledge they'd have to watch out for, but otherwise, once through Hoyo, they should have a straight shot to Hiroshima Bay.

"Gotta love this DRT," Russ said. The plotting table had a glass top, under which a small light projected a compass rose onto the chart from below. Whichever way the submarine turned, the light, driven by a series of gears and servomotors slaved to the sub's main gyro, turned with it, giving them a real-time view of where they were and where they were headed.

"It's the radar fixes we believe, XO," Gar said. "Everything else is an approximation." He didn't mind having the new plotting table to look at, but the downside was that it required two more plotters in the already crowded conning tower. "Speaking of which, let's get a round of bearings."

The radar operator called out ranges to preplotted points on the shore, and the DRT plotters penciled in the results. So far, they were right on track, moving into the not-so-loving arms of the straits at 5 knots. Because it was slack water, that was 5 knots over the ground. It also wasn't suffocatingly hot in the conning tower for a change. The outside water temperature was a chilly 55 degrees, a far cry from the stultifying tropical waters of the South Pacific. Gar had to thread his way through the various operators to stand behind the FM sonar display. Popeye Waller was on the stack, as the operators called the display. He wore headphones and was constantly adjusting the intensity and brightness of the scope.

Gar would have preferred being down at depth so that the new sonar could look *up* into the minefield. The problem was they couldn't navigate if they ran deep. He'd ordered the boat trimmed down 5 degrees to give the sonar a more level look ahead of them,

but even so, the sonar would probably not see any mines right below them. He was counting on encountering only contact mines; if
they had planted magnetics, the Dragon would be in deep trouble.

A gonging sound came out of the sonar speaker. Hell's Bells.

"Relative bearing, thirty port," Popeye said. "Drifting left, no
threat."

It was almost a relief to "see" their first mine. Gar kept one eye
on the DRT and the other on the sonar scope. There was an amber
smudge to one side of the scope. The smudge kept changing shape
like some kind of ghost as it passed down their port side and then
disappeared.

"DRT, plot every one of these contacts."

"DRT, aye."

It wouldn't be a very accurate plot, but it would be better than
nothing when they came back out. *If* they came back out.

Another gong, then a second.

The Dragon was in the minefield. The muted conversation in
the conning tower went silent.

"Two contacts, relative bearing twenty port, twenty-five starboard."

"Split the bearings," Gar ordered.

"Recommend three three zero true to split the bearings," Popeye
said.

"Helmsman, make it so."

As long as there was no current, the mooring chains that anchored the mines to the bottom should be standing straight up and
down. They were traveling at keel depth of 60 feet. The mines
were somewhere between 250 and 20 feet below the surface, each
with a mooring chain leading down to the bottom. The bad news
was that they were in a minefield. The good news was that no Jap
destroyer could come in there after them. But a plane could, Gar
reminded himself.

Gong.

"Dead ahead, range five hundred yards," Popeye announced, his
voice no longer quite so calm.

Gong. Gong.

"Two more, relative bearing twenty port, thirty port."

"Come right to three five *five*," Gar ordered. "Sound, confirm bearing drift when you get it."

Gong.

"Relative bearing starboard twenty."

"Mark your head, helmsman."

"Three four two, Captain."

"Steady, three *four* five."

"Three four five, aye, sir, shifting my rudder."

Gong.

"New one, dead ahead," Popeye called out. "Range six hundred yards."

"All stop!" Gar ordered, thanking God they weren't heading into the big, 6-knot tidal current that ran through here. That didn't mean there was no current, however.

"We have bearing drift port and starboard," Popeye said. "Should clear."

"*Should* clear?" Gar echoed. "That's nice."

No one laughed, and Gar realized how frightened everyone in the conning tower was.

"Range to the one dead ahead is four five oh, no drift."

"Sing out when the beam contacts are at ninety."

"Range dead ahead is now three five oh."

Gar felt the boat slowing down as its forward momentum came off. He couldn't wait much longer to turn or the diving planes would lose effectiveness.

"Two five oh, and we're just about abeam on the side contacts."

"All ahead one-third, turns for five knots, come right to zero one zero with *full* rudder."

"Zero one zero with right *full* rudder aye, sir."

"Range is two five oh, and entering the sea return. Captain, I can't see it anymore."

Gar watched the gyro repeater above his head, mentally shouting at it to begin turning, but the boat had so little way on that she wasn't responding.

"Starboard stop, starboard back Bendix," he ordered. He could hear the first threads of panic in his own voice. Steady on, he told himself. Steady on.

Then they felt the starboard propeller bite in, going astern, yanking the bow to the right. As soon as Gar saw the gyro repeater indicating that they were turning, he stopped the starboard engine and then ordered both to go ahead together at 5 knots.

Clank.

Gar felt the hair rising on his neck.

Clank. Clank. Clank.

They were hearing the mooring cable of a mine scraping down the port side of the submarine, riding that steel paravane cable strung between the bullnose, the forward portside diving plane, and the after portside diving plane. As long as it didn't catch on anything, they'd be safe.

Gong. Gong.

"Two more, starboard twenty, starboard thirty. We need to come left."

"Steady as you go, helmsman."

"Aye, sir, shifting my rudder and steadying on—zero zero seven."

The clanking sound stopped as the boat's stern swung to the right, away from the deadly caress of the mine's anchor chain. Gar waited for a full minute to make sure they were clear.

"Starboard contacts will clear; good bearing drift."

Gar exhaled quietly, as did everyone else in the conning tower.

Gong.

"One more, port ten, maybe less. Contact is in and out. Probably deep."

Gong. Gong.

"Two more, one dead ahead, one starboard ten."

"All stop. All back full. Ranges?"

"Nearest mine is four five oh and closing."

Gar waited until he felt the propellers going solidly astern, then stopped engines and shifted to bare steerageway ahead. He wanted the boat to drift forward with enough speed to maintain control, but not so fast as to run up on the mines ahead. He also had to make sure they didn't back into the ones they'd just passed. He tried not to make eye contact with anyone else in the conning tower. They were deep in a box of spiders and everyone knew it. His brain was racing to find a way out. He had to keep a 3-D picture of all the mines they knew about, and the new ones ahead, too.

Gar realized he needed help.

The exec leaned in toward him. "Put a twist on?" he asked quietly. "See if there's a hole somewhere?"

Gar nodded. Good thinking. "You got the bubble?"

In this case, "bubble" was slang for the tactical picture. Having the bubble meant you thought things were under control. Losing the bubble meant you'd become confused. Russ said yes.

"Okay, take the conn, twist us through an arc of sixty degrees, each way, and try not to make forward progress."

"Got it," he said.

"XO has the conn, " Gar announced. "Sound, report all around."

He stepped back from the FM sonar stack and went to the DRT table. As the exec gave quiet maneuvering orders, he ordered the radar operator and the plotters to get a fix.

The radar mast went up and on. A quick round of ranges was taken, and then the mast came down. The resulting fix, plotted on the DRT, was sloppy but showed they were off track to the north. There *was* a current.

"Conn, Sound."

"Conn, aye."

"I have echo ranging, bearing one five zero. Faint up Doppler."

This wasn't Popeye reporting, but the secondary sonar operator, who was listening passively on a broader spectrum of frequencies. Gar studied the chart. One five zero was behind them. A Jap destroyer was coming up the right, or northern, side of the Bungo channel.

The sub was trembling slightly as the opposed screws twisted her to port. She didn't twist like a destroyer—she was heavy and distinctly logy. She also had to be making a fair amount of noise. To Gar's right he could hear the exec and Popeye exchanging information on the mine picture.

"Any luck, XO?" Gar asked. The plotters were laying down a

line of passive bearings to the echo ranger. It could be anything from a small patrol craft to a full-sized destroyer.

"Not yet, sir," Russ said. "We're going to twist back to starboard, see if there's a hole out there." He turned to the helmsman. "All stop, starboard back one-third, port ahead one-third. Shift your rudder."

Gar stood back from the plot to organize his thoughts. They had mines all around them, with no apparent escape route. Now they also had a warship of some kind coming up from astern, type and range unknown. As long as they were in the minefield, the warship could not roll in on them with depth charges in the event he gained sonar contact. The Dragon, on the other hand, could fire a torpedo at the warship from the "safety" of the minefield, but for that, they needed a range. He ordered the radar mast up again for a single sweep, range display set to 10 miles.

"Radar contact, one four five, range sixteen thousand yards."

Then he remembered their orders: Make no attacks until the carrier had been dealt with and whatever other tasking was in that envelope had been taken care of. He instructed the attack team to set up a solution on the warship, with another single-sweep radar range mark in five minutes. He'd be prepared to shoot at this guy, but only if he made trouble. Meanwhile, they needed to get out of their spider box.

"Anything, XO?" he asked.

"We're passing our original track heading now, Captain. I'll twist sixty starboard. We may need to submerge below periscope depth and see what's what, say at two hundred feet."

Gar closed his eyes to envision the 3-D picture. Then he realized that they couldn't do that. There might be one or more mines right below them right now.

"Continuing up Doppler on the echo ranger," Sound announced. "But not like he's coming right at us. Estimating he's transiting, not attacking."

"If he's transiting, then he'll know where the safe channel is, Captain," the exec said. "If we could get behind him . . ."

"Popeye, can you tell the depth of the mines you're seeing on that thing?"

"The transducer is at periscope depth, Captain," Popeye said. "It looks up at five degrees. Everything I'm seeing is fifty, sixty feet below the surface. These are all aimed at submarines running at periscope depth."

Gar thought fast. The boat was trimmed bow down 5 degrees to compensate for the sonar's 5-degree up-look. If he leveled the boat to an even keel, and some of those mines around them "disappeared," then they had a way out—on or close to the surface. First he needed another range on that Jap ship, and another navigation fix.

He ordered the radar plotters to double up, one for the ship contact, one for the navigation ranges. He couldn't afford to make two sweeps if that warship coming up behind them was equipped with passive radar sensors. As it was, the Japs had already been given one chance to detect their presence.

"Doppler steady on the echo ranger," Sound announced. "He's probably at CPA."

"Radar team ready?"

They nodded, grease pencils poised over the radar repeater's scope. The last range to the destroyer had been at 8 miles, so there shouldn't be a problem with the Jap's lookouts seeing the radar mast. Gar waited for him to get past CPA, his closest point of approach.

"Do it."

As the mast went up for its radar snapshot, he felt the trembling of the screws subside. He checked the gyro repeater. The bow was still swinging lazily to starboard. He could hear the trim pumps whining down in Control as the diving officer fiddled with the ship's trim. Without way on, *Dragonfish* was essentially trying to hover, with no help from the dive planes. He asked the exec if there was a hole to starboard at sixty feet. The exec shook his head. They were still boxed in.

Gar explained what he planned to do: Wait for that destroyer to go by, come all the way up to the surface, and then get behind the tin can or whatever it was and follow him through the Bungo and Hoyo channels into the safety of the Inland Sea.

"We won't move until Popeye thinks there are no antisurface ship mines riding just under the surface."

"And if there are?"

"We look for another goddamned hole, XO. Nav team, you get a fix?"

"We got two ranges and bearings, Captain. Not great, but they confirm a set to the east-northeast, two knots. The tide's still slackwater, so this is probably the base current."

Gar turned to the TDC. "What you got?"

The weapons officer, Tom Walsh, was operating the torpedo data computer. "We have a fair solution on that guy, Captain. We have Cuties in five and six."

"How fast is he going, Plot?"

"Twelve, maybe thirteen knots, Captain."

"Forget the Cuties. They're too slow. If we have to, we'll use electrics."

"How can we surface safely without knowing if there's a floater right above us?" the exec asked.

My straight man, Gar thought. "Great question, XO. But we just twisted in place a hundred twenty degrees. I didn't hear any chains scraping the hull during the twist. Control, bring us up to decks awash."

"Control, aye."

They were still pointed in the direction of that surface ship's wake. As Control blew ballast tanks and the sub began to rise, Gar decided to get the boat back under control by putting on some forward motion. "XO, go all ahead one third, make turns for four knots."

As the exec had pointed out, they were taking a big chance. Popeye still couldn't verify that there weren't antiship mines lurking just below the surface. He wouldn't be able to do that until the FM sonar could see into that depth layer, but Gar knew they had to get some way on if they were ever going to keep up with that surface ship and trail him into the relative safety of the Inland Sea.

"There's nothing showing up in front of us, Captain," Popeye said.

"That a guarantee, Popeye?"

"Negative, sir. Anything hanging just below that five-degree up-look is *not* visible."

That produced a strained silence in the conning tower. What the hell, Gar thought, in for a penny, in for a pound. Besides, if something was lurking right above them, where was its chain?

"XO, once we get behind that ship, we'll turn to his strongest sound bearing, and then we'll go on the diesels. We'll never keep up on the battery."

"Aye, aye, sir."

He was beginning to like this command-and-control setup. He could stand back, take in the whole picture, and make decisions without being mired in the minutiae of steering the boat, order by order. Mush Morton had been right. On the other hand, Mush Morton and his beloved *Wahoo* were now dead and lying probably not too far away from here, either.

"Come left to three four zero," the exec ordered.

"Conn, Control, we are on the surface, decks awash. Main induction is clear."

Gar went to the night periscope for a look-around. It took a moment for his eyes to adapt, but he saw absolutely nothing.

"How far behind that guy are we?"

"By the plot, he should be at least ten thousand yards. Radar?"

"Negative."

Five miles, he thought. Would he hear the submarine's diesels lighting off? He sighed. They had no choice. If that guy turned to conform to the cleared channel and they missed it, they'd drive right back into the minefield. He reached for the bitch-box.

"Maneuvering, Conn, open main induction and light 'em off. Put some amps in the can, but gimme three so I can stay with this tin can."

He turned to the exec. "XO, take a radar range from time to time, single sweep. See if we can close up on him so we don't miss any important turns. We'll let him do the navigating for the next hour. And open the hatch—let's get some fresh air in here."

"Lookouts?"

"Negative. One plane and we're back in the soup. I don't want to leave someone out there."

NINE

The destroyer led them through a series of dogleg turns for the next forty-five minutes, maintaining a steady 12 knots through the darkness. The nav team made periodic radar-fix sweeps until Gar realized that there were operational navigation lights on the shore. He got Hashimoto up to the conning tower to see if he could identify the lights using the periscope and then mark them on the chart, after which they began to get much more precise navigation fixes. The mine-hunting sonar indicated that they were running on the north side of the minefields and that there were no mines above 40 feet depth, and no mines at all once they reached and passed through the Hoyo channel. The tide was just beginning to flood back in, so the famous whirlpools were not in evidence.

By midnight they were inside the Inland Sea. Gar slowed down to let their tour-guide destroyer draw away toward Hiroshima Bay, secured the diesels, and, after one final visual fix, submerged. The water depth shown on Hashimoto's chart was 450 feet, which agreed with the boat's own fathometer. Gar ordered the boat down to 250 feet, where they'd be protected acoustically by a distinct thermal layer hovering at 200 feet.

The exec sent the crew to midnight rations and then set a modified battle stations watch throughout the boat. He told people to get some sleep on station while they could. Gar met in the wardroom with the ops officer and the navigator to go over the consolidated chart, the U.S. Navy's version as marked up by Hashimoto. The Inland Sea was like a bathtub, with steep sides and depths ranging from 700 to as little as 40. The islands surrounding it were the tops of drowned mountains, and there were plenty of pinnacles rising from the sea floor to just below the surface to make the navigation even more interesting. Hashimoto knew where each of them lay because that's where the best fishing was, and he had marked the chart accordingly. It was important for them to know where the fishing boats would and would not typically go, because they were going to have to hide for most of their tenure inside this basin.

Radio had copied the fleet broadcast while on the surface, which contained a December weather forecast for the Inland Sea area aimed right at *Dragonfish*. A cold front was predicted to move across the Sea of Japan, bringing rain, snow, and fog over the southern Japanese islands by late morning; lousy weather for navigation, but great for hiding right under the noses of the Imperial Japanese Navy. Come the dawn, Gar expected, there'd be all sorts of traffic up on the surface—interisland ferries, tugs, cargo ships, fishing boats, not to mention harbor patrol craft, mine tenders, and even transiting naval shipping. Tomorrow they'd lie low; tomorrow night they'd make their move under the cover of all that predicted slop and try to get close to the Kure naval arsenal, and then, oh by the way, locate, identify, and attack the world's biggest aircraft carrier—at its moorings.

Piece'a cake, as the Cob would say.

Then Gar remembered that he had one more envelope to open, but first they needed a lair. He climbed back up into the conning tower with the chart. With the navigator's help, he drew a box enclosing the deepest parts of the Seto's western basin on the DRT chart, clearly marking two pinnacles that rose from the bottom to within 50 feet of the surface.

"Stay in this box at two knots," he told the nav team. "Keep the boat quiet and under the layer at all times, and be alert for set and drift as the flood tide builds back in. Use the FM sonar to locate these pinnacles, and use them as navigation reference points."

Then he called for the exec and went to his cabin. When Russ got there, he got the second envelope out of his safe. Inside they found two pages. One contained two paragraphs addressed to CO

Dragonfish, CO's eyes only. The other was a diagrammatic set of instructions for some kind of device. Gar read the two paragraphs aloud to the exec.

"Upon safely reaching the interior waters of the Inland Sea, and *before* prosecuting any attack on the target aircraft carrier, proceed to the vicinity of the fishing village of Akitsu (34°19'0" North, 132° 49'18" East). Once there, put Minoru Hashimoto safely ashore by best means available. Ensure that he takes with him the contents of the small box given to him by LCDR Tanaka at Pearl, and that he understands and agrees to the operating instructions contained on the following page.

"This part of your mission takes precedence over the attack on the carrier, which shall be conducted as soon as possible thereafter. In that regard, a mobility kill is sufficient to accomplish your objective. Maintain radio silence until *Dragonfish* is either safely out of the Inland Sea or the strong probability exists that your escape from the Inland Sea is in doubt."

"In other words, Spartans, come back *with* your shield or *on* it," Russ said.

"Lovely," Gar said, looking at the second piece of paper. "What is this thing?"

The exec looked over his shoulder at the instruction sheet. The diagram showed a device shaped like a small thermos bottle, about ten inches tall. On the bottom was a butterfly switch, and on the top a thin, telescoping antenna. The instructions were pretty simple: Hashimoto was to go to the gardens surrounding the Hiroshima Prefectural Industrial Promotion Hall, on the eastern side of the Motoyasu River in Hiroshima City itself. Once there, and without being observed, he was to turn the butterfly switch to the right to the on position, pull up the antenna, and hide the device somewhere in the gardens where it would not be visible. He was to do this on the day when paper rained from the skies over Hiroshima City.

"Paper rain?"

"Beats me," Gar said. "Intel-speak. Get him up here, let's see if he knows."

In the event, Hashimoto did not know. Paper rain sounded like some kind of haiku to him. He'd brought the cardboard box containing the small thermos bottle. The switch was clearly marked OFF and ON, and the antenna could be pulled out to nearly 2 feet in length. The device weighed perhaps 3 pounds.

"This, apparently, is the price of our bringing you home," Gar told the old man.

"Is this weapon?" Hashimoto asked.

"If it is, it's a pretty small weapon," Gar said. "We don't know what it is. We are supposed to put you ashore at Akitsu and then leave the area. Do you know that place?"

"Yes," Hashimoto said. "I have family there."

"Do you have papers? ID card? Money?"

"Tanaka-san give me these things," he said and pulled out some papers from a small pouch. "For police."

"If you just show up in Akitsu, will someone report you to the police?"

"No," he snorted. "Everyone hates police. They steal. Beat people. Family there. Safe."

"How will you get to Hiroshima when the time comes?"

"Walk. Bicycle. Bus, maybe. No problem."

Gar rubbed the side of his face for a moment. "I wish I could tell you what this is all about, Hashimoto-san, but I have no idea."

"Like Tanaka-san said, secret stuff," Hashimoto said. "I do it."

"Okay," Gar said. "Let's go look at a chart. If you're ready, we'll get you ashore tonight."

ComSubPac Headquarters, Pearl Harbor

Captain Forrester gave the usual perfunctory knock on Admiral Lockwood's office door and then walked in. Lockwood was reading an after-action patrol report and making some notes for his next happy hour with the skippers up at the Palace.

"Whatcha got, Mike?" he asked without looking up.

"Possibly another *Awa Maru*, I'm afraid."

Lockwood looked up over his reading glasses. "You're shitting me, right?"

"No, sir, unfortunately not. This just came down from State via CincPacFleet. A damaged Jap freighter made it into Taipei and reported that a second ship, the *Hoshen Maru*, had been torpedoed and sunk, and that it had been carrying four-hundred-plus British POWs. Japs claim it was marked as a hospital ship *and* lit up."

"Was she precleared, like the *Awa Maru*?"

"No, sir, and this is the first we've heard about it. PacFleet thinks it's a propaganda ploy by the Japs. Problem is that the Brits verify that there probably were some of their POWs on that ship."

"God*dammit*," Lockwood said. "Any idea which boat?"

"We're checking on that, sir. We need the sinking location and, of course, time and date. Ops is researching sinking reports and who's where out there."

"*Awa Maru* was cleared through diplomatic back channels as a marked and lighted hospital ship, and we put that out to all the boats. This sounds different, but still—four hundred POWs? God."

"Yes, sir. CincPacFleet is sending down a JAG officer. If the Japs are going to make a claim, then we'll need talking points."

"Okay, keep me advised. You meet with the JAG. Tell him—"

"Her."

"What?"

"Her—Lieutenant Commander DeVeers. WAVE officer. Connie White said she was the resident international lawyer."

"Then you definitely meet with her, Mike. Lady lawyers make me nervous."

An hour later Sharon was escorted into Forrester's office by one of the yeomen. He stood up to greet her and offered coffee, which she declined. She was wearing whites because there had been an awards ceremony earlier that morning up at Makalapa.

"Miss DeVeers—is that correct?" Forrester asked. "*Miss* De-Veers? I'd address a lieutenant commander as mister, but, um . . ."

"That's fine, Captain," Sharon said, amused at his sudden discomfort as she sat down in front of his desk. The white uniform skirt highlighted some of her best features, and the good captain was having trouble keeping his eyes in the boat. "Did you get our memorandum?"

"Yes, we did. Admiral Lockwood and I are horrified at the thought that one of our boats may have killed POWs. That said, there's no way our skippers can know what some of their targets are carrying."

"Yes, sir, we understand that. This is *not* another *Awa Maru*, but the feeling at Makalapa is that the Japanese are going to try to make it into a major international propaganda incident just the same."

Forrester well remembered the *Awa Maru* case. Through a diplomatic channel opened by the International Red Cross in Switzerland, the United States and Japan had made a deal: If the Japanese agreed to transport 2,000 tons of Red Cross relief supplies for starving Allied prisoners of war being held in Southeast Asia, the Americans would guarantee safe passage for whichever ship carried out the voyage. The Japanese were required to mark the ship as a hospital ship with large white crosses on her sides and special lighting, all of which they did. The ship went to Singapore without incident and delivered the supplies. The Japanese then took advantage of the safe-passage deal to fill her with 2,004 important passengers and thousands of tons of tin and rubber. Because of a communications foul-up, one American submarine failed to get the word and sent the 12,000-ton ship to the bottom during the return voyage. There was but one survivor, the captain's personal steward, who was picked up by the submarine, who only then learned the name of the ship.

The uproar within U.S. Navy flag channels had been immense when the sub reported the sinking. The sub's captain had been relieved of command at Guam and court-martialed immediately on orders of Admiral King himself. When Admiral Nimitz reviewed the court-martial proceedings, he was not satisfied with the relatively light punishment awarded to the sub's captain, so he issued letters of reprimand to all the members of the court-martial.

"Merry Christmas," Forrester muttered. "What are the next steps?"

Sharon consulted her notes. "We need to know which boat was the likely culprit, and whether or not any special warnings were sent out by SubPac regarding this ship."

"*Culprit?*" Forrester asked. "We only have the Japs' word that she was marked as a hospital ship or even *was* a hospital ship. They've been shipping POWs back to Japan for months now, usually on something called a hell ship, not a hospital ship."

"Captain," Sharon said, "please forgive my poor choice of words. We need facts, is what I should have said. Which boat was responsible, if that can be determined. When. Where. What the attack party saw when they fired."

Forrester's face showed surprise. "Boat? Attack party—who've you been talking to, Miss DeVeers?"

"I spent some time with one of your skippers," she said. "A Commander Hammond? I believe he's on patrol right now."

"That's classified information, Miss DeVeers. He should not have told you that."

"He didn't reveal anything, Captain. They were going back out. It's what most boats do, isn't it? He said there was a special mission, but he didn't offer details and I didn't ask. We had better things to do with our time."

Forrester colored a little at that last remark but then quickly changed the subject. "Look here, Miss DeVeers. There's something I need to know. Is CincPacFleet coming at this incident looking for scalps or looking for a way to pee on this fire?"

"They're looking for the facts, Captain," Sharon repeated. "What Admiral Nimitz will do with those facts is beyond your pay grade and mine, I suspect. It's early days, but this is on the front burner right now, so we'd appreciate any information as quickly as possible."

"Right," he said. "We'll get right on it."

Sharon stood up to go. Forrester was staring again.

"Will you be my point of contact for this matter, then?" he asked.

Sharon smoothed down her uniform skirt. "If you wish, sir," she said.

TEN

Two hours later, the Dragon came up to decks-awash. Gar ordered Control to trim the boat down by the stern, which exposed the forward hatch long enough to allow a small team to get a rubber raft out on deck. There was a light fog hanging over the water, and once they opened the hatch they could smell the distinctive odors of rural Asia: charcoal smoke, fish, and a whiff of sewage. There were no lights visible in the fishing village ashore, but Hashimoto had been able to steer them in toward the beach using just the fathometer. He said there was a long reef extending out from the point of land where the town's main pier was. Once he found that, he knew where they were. Gar thought that it was too bad they had to put him ashore before they made the attempt on Kure.

Tanaka had explained some things about Hashimoto before they left Pearl. The Japanese army's treatment of POWs was atrocious beyond belief. This stemmed from two things. First, the Japanese had never expected or planned to capture entire armies at the beginning of the war. Second, surrendering to an enemy was an extreme cultural offense in the eyes of the Japanese army. They were expected to fight to the death, because an honorable death in combat was the acme of a Japanese warrior's entire life. They expected their enemies to match their own martial fervor. To surrender was to forfeit your personal honor and even your identity, as well as to besmirch your family's honor forever. It was because of how they viewed surrender that they were wholly unprepared to deal with American and British POWs, who had, by surrendering, sunk to the status of pariah dogs. The POWs came to the camps believing that their war was over; in fact, it was just beginning.

Tanaka said that American interrogators, led by a civilian named Otis Cary, had devised a very different strategy to first neutralize the shame and depression of being captured, and then to turn Japanese prisoners into assets by convincing them that, once the war was over, they could play a vital role in rebuilding their nation. This was accompanied by humane, even kind treatment, respect for their cultural rules and mores, and, above all, education. It hadn't been easy, especially for the few military Japanese POWs captured so far.

Hashimoto's case was different. It helped that he wasn't an army man—he'd been a civilian, owner of a successful business until the army requisitioned everything and put him back to work in a fishing boat. His relatives who'd gone to the United States and who'd tried often to convince him to join them before the war were an asset in this argument. He'd agreed readily to the mission of carrying what looked like a thermos bottle into the city of Hiroshima in return for being able to get back to his family again and, possibly, to help mitigate the reportedly awful conditions in the countryside. Gar had initially believed Hashimoto might be playing the Americans, but after a while he'd come to trust the old man's motives.

As the boat was being readied, Gar took him aside. "Conditions in Japan are going to get much worse," he told him. "The big bombers are coming, and life will become very hard."

Hashimoto nodded. He'd made some friends in the crew, especially among the chiefs, and already knew a lot about what was shaping up for his homeland.

"I've been thinking about this thing you're supposed to plant in downtown Hiroshima City. I think it's a weather instrument, not a weapon. I don't know what paper rain is all about, but when the bombers come, weather will be important."

Hashimoto looked at him. "You tell me not to do it?" he asked finally.

Gar shook his head. "No, because I'm probably all wrong about what this thing is. All I'm saying is, once you hide it, get out of the city. Cities in Japan will become terrible places very soon."

Hashimoto blinked and then nodded again. The word came up that the raft was ready, and Gar offered his hand and wished the old man good luck. Hashimoto shook his hand, stepped back, bowed respectfully, and then climbed up the ladder to the conning tower hatch, his ditty bag in hand.

It took forty-five minutes for the shore party to take Hashimoto in to the beach and get back out again. During that time a thicker fog bank rolled in from the south, and they had to use the radar twice to make sure the current wasn't taking them toward that reef. This close to shore there was only 100 feet under the keel, which would not offer them much protection if a patrol boat surprised them. Gar was already uneasy about the fact that they'd neither seen nor heard *any* patrol craft; perhaps the Japs thought they were safe this far up into the Seto. The transit into Akitsu had taken them within hailing distance of several small islands, but they hadn't seen a soul. Gar stayed on the bridge during the boat evolution. The shoreline was visible in the darkness as a deeper shadow, but there wasn't a single light anywhere. Curfew, he thought. They're all in the house for the night.

He checked his watch; nautical twilight would be upon them in about ninety minutes. The exec had the conn down in the conning tower. They'd stayed on the battery to avoid detection, but the ventilation system had been sucking in some much-welcomed fresh air while they loitered close inshore. After what seemed forever, the rubber raft materialized out of the darkness and made fast to the port side forward. Gar scanned the shore through the TBT binocs while they got the raft back aboard, deflated it, and humped it down the ladder. Then he heard the clunk of the forward hatch.

"Everybody's back, and the forward hatch is secured," Control announced.

"Okay, XO, let's get out of here," Gar said. "Once we get five miles off the beach, light off the mains and take us back out to the wait-box. We'll submerge at dawn, find a layer, and get under it for the day."

"Aye, aye, sir," the exec said. "Coming to two zero zero."

Gar stayed up on the bridge as they moved out through the

gathering fog. Periodically the radar mast would go high for a brief transmission. Once they got submerged offshore, they'd have about ten hours to wait for darkness and plan their next move. He'd been assuming they'd make their approach to Kure submerged, but the more they'd studied the charts with Hashimoto, the more it looked like they'd have to be running on the surface, if only because of the navigation problem. There were two very narrow channels into Hiroshima Bay, and the water depths off the naval arsenal were such that even periscope depth would be risking running aground. That meant they needed a really dark night and some lousy weather to pull this thing off. They'd also have to calculate how and when to get some charge back into the batteries before they had to submerge again to get out of Hiroshima Bay alive.

Gar finally went down below into Control, where he met with the boat officer, Ensign Brown. "How'd it go?" he asked.

"No probs, Skipper," Brown said. "Hashimoto told us where to make a landing, which was around a point of rocks from the town. Darker'n a well-digger's ass out there, so we just paddled until we ran aground on some gravel."

"I take it no guard towers and searchlights?"

Brown shook his head. "We didn't see a soul or a light. We could smell the place, though. Eye-watering. Hashimoto said they dried their fish on racks in the open air, and that's what the stink was. I can't imagine anyone actually eating that shit."

"They're an alien culture, Mister Brown," Gar said. "We keep sinking all their merchies, they'll be eating stone soup pretty quick. No sentries, boats, or anything moving out there?"

"Not a thing, Skipper. Dark, and totally quiet. We could see the loom of city lights to the north, probably Hiroshima, but there wasn't a sound coming from that town, not even a barking dog."

"Probably ate 'em all," the Cob offered.

"Okay, good job. He took his secret box with him, right?"

"Yes, sir, he did. It was starting a light drizzle when we put him ashore, and he was trying hard to keep it dry."

"Wasn't raining paper, was it?" Gar asked.

"Sir?"

ELEVEN

It took three days, not one, before they could make their move. Three long, hot, stultifying days submerged out in the middle of the Inland Sea, the boat turning in a 2-degree, 5-mile-wide circle at 250 feet, trying to conserve the battery while they waited for the weather. At night they came up to recharge the eternally thirsty batteries, running just two of the mains and keeping watch all night for scout planes or the odd itinerant patrol boat. Then back down an hour before dawn to the dreaded wait-box.

The men kept busy doing light maintenance, training, and sleeping. Gar and his department heads went over their plan for the umpteenth time in daily meetings. It was simple enough: If the Inland Sea could be visualized as a bathtub, then Hiroshima Bay was like a sink attached to one side of the bathtub, and Kure was like a soap dish attached to the sink. There were two channels up into Hiroshima Bay from the larger Inland Sea, and then one long, narrow channel down between some islands and along the east coast of Hiroshima Bay to the Kure naval arsenal. The water depths ranged from fairly deep in the first two channels to around 80 or 90 feet in the bay itself to downright hopeless right outside the Kure harbor, where there was only about 60 feet. They'd have to time the tides, too, because there was a big, 6-knot current coming through those two approach channels at ebb tide. They could submerge, barely, going through either channel to avoid detection from the shore, but if they entered the bay at the ebb, they'd only be making a net of 2 miles an hour at best over the ground against such a current.

The biggest discussion item was whether to submerge at all. They could do the thing in two stages: Transit at night well up into Hiroshima Bay, then find a hole, submerge, and wait out the following day. Then they'd make the attack the next night after about a one-hour run on the surface down to Kure. After that, well, much would depend on whether the Japs figured out they had an American sub in their inner precincts. Either way they could probably get out of the Kure area and back into Hiroshima Bay for yet another day of lying quietly near the bottom. Even if they actually sat on the bottom, which itself was a dangerous proposition, there'd only be 30 feet or so of water above the periscopes. Airplane pilots were able to see down that deep out in the open ocean, and the clarity of the water in Hiroshima Bay was just one more unknown.

The other option was to accomplish the entire mission in one night. Leave the wait-box right after sundown on the surface and drive all the way through the night to Kure. Stay on the surface and thus employ the diesels, recharging as they went, and using lousy weather to shield them from visual detection in those narrow channels. Get to Kure at around one in the morning, make the attack, and then run like hell, with the tenuous option of submerging in Hiroshima Bay if the hue and cry became too pressing. They had some good charts now, thanks to Hashimoto, and a couple of candidate hidey-holes up in Hiroshima Bay if they had to go to ground. Otherwise, shoot the place up, turn tail, and make best speed back up into the bay and then back down, through one of those two channels, and out to the safety of the relatively deep Inland Sea. By the second day of twiddling their thumbs in the wait-box, Gar had made a command decision. They'd do the whole thing on the surface. If they were detected on the way up, they'd regroup and do something different.

There was another way out of the Kure Harbor area, which was to the south of the naval base. The channel was narrow—only 500 feet wide, with a bridge 36 feet overhead and a limiting depth of 18 feet at mean low water. The Dragon drew 16 feet in her normal surfaced condition. If they had to, really *had* to, they could squeeze through there, but anyone with even a high-powered rifle could make serious trouble for them. Checking the tide tables, they saw that high water would occur while they were raising hell up in Kure. That gave them another 6 feet under the keel, but by the time they got to that choke point, the ebb current would be running, making navigation and maneuvering both difficult and dangerous. Gar and the nav team plotted the thing out anyway; there was always a chance that their preferred escape route could fill up with patrol craft and destroyers after the Dragon started tearing things up at the naval base.

They also considered painting some fake side numbers and a red meatball on the shears just to confuse shore-watchers who might catch a glimpse of them heading into Hiroshima Bay. The problem was that they looked nothing like a Jap submarine, which had large structures up on the bow and stern to support aerials, not to mention a completely different hull line. They then considered painting a swastika on each side of the sail to make a shore station think the Dragon was a German U-boat. They were allies, after all. Gar knew there had to be shore stations all around the bay and especially at the entrance channel to the Kure base. Presumably they'd have advance notice of naval unit movements, and even recognition signals and codes. The key to all these complications was going to be the weather. They needed a dark, rainy, even foggy night, and that's what they finally got on the third night.

"Nasake-jima should be coming up on the port hand in about fifteen minutes," the navigator announced. "Moro-shima to starboard. How's the visibility?"

"Shitty and gritty," the exec reported from the bridge. The air flowing down the open hatch was indeed wet and cold, but still a wonderful change from the day's worth of breathing their own exhalations. "No lights, that I can see," Russ added.

Gar was down in the conning tower, continuing his Mush Morton command-and-control approach of letting the exec drive the ship while he drove the tactical problem. They were taking surface-search radar observations once every five minutes, and the steep-sided Japanese islands were giving them a good nav picture. They were operating two of their four engines to reduce noise in a channel that was just 1 mile across. Gar had the boat settled as low in the water as they could get and still keep the main induction pipe dry in order to diminish their own radar signature. He wished they had had one of those radar signal detectors, but he was counting on the choppy sea and passing rainsqualls to obscure their passage through the channel. Gar knew there was a certain element of self-delusion in that thought, but they certainly should have the element of surprise here. No American sub in its right mind, etc., etc.

About halfway through the passage the exec sang out that they were getting their first visual challenge. He reported a flashing amber light from the Nasake-jima side. The island itself was just a dark blur in the night, but the light was coming from low down, practically on the water's edge, right where you'd expect a coastal fortification to be. Somebody had seen or heard them.

The exec gave Gar a bearing, and he put the acquisition periscope on it. After a minute he realized they weren't sending Morse code. He had two options: send something back that was nonsense, or keep the light off entirely. It seemed to him that they could barely see the Dragon, if at all, even if one of their coastal radars had detected something in the channel. If he used their own mast-mounted signal light, they'd then have a precise bearing for the second half of the challenge: a 6-inch coastal artillery gun.

"We'll stay dark," he told the exec. "Clear the bridge in case we have to dive."

The two lookouts came sliding down the ladder, followed by the exec. He started to close the hatch, but Gar told him to leave it open. He mostly wanted the people off the bridge in case the shore station fired and rained shrapnel on the bridge. He kept his periscope on the blinking light, but it was losing strength. He hoped that they were pointing it out into the channel without having any idea of where those rumbling diesels were. After a minute, he couldn't see the signal light anymore, and there was no gunfire.

They were through their first gate. The easy one, he reminded himself.

He ordered the bridge crew back up topside and told Maneuvering to bring the other two diesels on the line. What they needed now was speed. At 20 knots, they could be at the innermost part of Hiroshima Bay in just under an hour. Then they'd turn northeast through two more tight channels and finally southeast to go down the north side of Etajima island, which happened to be home to the Japanese Naval Academy. The weather was cooperating nicely, with windy rainsqualls and even a little snow for effect. According to the weather forecasts from Pearl, this system would blow through the Seto by tomorrow night, to be followed by cold and clear. By then they had to be back in the wait-box. If this thing went as planned, they could be there before dawn. After all, he asked himself with a grin, what could go wrong?

TWELVE

They reached the next bottleneck at just after midnight. By then it was blowing snow, and they were navigating by both fathometer and surface-search radar. The water was only about 80 feet deep, so now they were pretty much committed to a surface approach on Kure. If they'd been trying visual coastal navigation under these conditions they'd have been totally lost, but Hashimoto's chart, the rocky island cliffs, and the occasional protruding pinnacle made for great radar nav. There were still no lights showing ashore, and even Hiroshima City seemed to have been blacked out. Gar had given up trying to be sparing with the radar; it was all they had. He could only hope that the normally attentive Japanese wouldn't be scanning for an American sub radar right here in their backyard.

By 0115 they were creeping around the headland above the naval base. The diesels were secured and they were running all-electric now. The dry-dock notches and the long flat bulkhead piers made for a distinctive radar signature, and for the first time they saw lights ashore through the snow. Electric arc welding was creating splotches of bluish white lightning along the piers, and there were some even bigger lights way up in the air, probably on the booms of harbor cranes. The city might be blacked out, but this shipyard was going full blast. Gar instructed the exec and the radar nav team to get in to about 800 yards and 40 feet of water and hold there. Gar stayed on the periscope down in the conning tower to examine the waterfront through the tumbling clouds of light snow.

Okay, he thought, as he turned the scope from left to right a degree at a time, where's this giant aircraft carrier? There was a band of lights along the harbor's edge, then darkened warehouses and steel-yard buildings silhouetted in the background. Spaces between the buildings were either finger piers or dry docks. He spotted two destroyers moored bow to bow along the main bulkhead pier, which put them in silhouette against the welding arcs. It looked like there were other ships inside the dry docks, either moored there or up on blocks behind a caisson wall at the head of a dry dock.

Nothing that was obviously a big carrier. Had the damned thing already sailed? Were they sitting here in the lion's mouth, on his tongue, actually, and all for nothing?

The industrial lights and welding arcs had put the background buildings into impenetrable shadow. Even with a filter, every time he focused on something in the periscope an arc welder blinded him. It was probably blinding them, too. Then he saw two fat barges tied up to the left of the leftmost destroyer. They looked a lot like the ammunition barges tied out in the West Loch of Pearl Harbor. It was customary in the U.S. Navy to remove all ammunition before a ship went into dry dock. If a ship was going into the yards for a six-month overhaul, she would drive over to an ammunition depot and do a complete off-load. If it was going to be a quick one-or two-week repair, then barges like these would be brought alongside, the ammo off-loaded, and the barges anchored nearby. If that's what those two fat boxes were, Gar now had a way to light the target area up.

"Open all forward outer doors," he said softly. Then he got on the ship's announcing system.

"This is the captain speaking," he began. "We are in position, eight hundred yards off one of Japan's major naval shipyards. It's snowing outside, and the shipyard is barely visible in front of us. Once we start shooting, things will happen very quickly. Right now we appear to have the element of surprise. It's one in the morning, the night shift is going at it over there, and the rest of the base appears to be darkened-ship. Once we ID the carrier, I'm going to fire every fish we have in the tubes, so a first priority will be reloads as quickly as possible. We're gonna shoot this place up and then run like hell back to the deep part of the Inland Sea. We will be pursued, but as long as this weather lasts, we won't have to deal with aircraft. Stand by to stand by, and remember Pearl Harbor."

He called the radioman up to the conning tower. "When you hear the first fish let go, go out on the HF with that message we precanned."

The radioman nodded and dropped back down into Control. Gar and the exec had encoded an encrypted message to Pearl that said they were presently attacking the naval arsenal at Kure. That would be the first indication at SubPac that they'd actually made it through Bungo Suido and all the way to Kure. The Japanese had an excellent high-frequency direction-finding network, which was why they'd stayed off the air so far. Once Gar started shooting, there'd be no need for them to detect the Dragon through direction finding, so he wanted to get one message off to Pearl in case they never made it back out to the open sea.

Gar took a moment to think through his tactical problem. The TDC setup would be different this time. There'd be no course and speed inputs since he'd be shooting on direct bearings at a moored target. Where the hell was that carrier? There was simply nothing there big enough to be an aircraft carrier, or if there was, he might be looking at it end on and just not recognizing what he was seeing. For that, he needed more light. He told the exec to stay up on the bridge and to look for that carrier.

First, those two destroyers. He assumed they were tied up at a shipyard for a reason and were thus probably *not* ready for a quick underway response, but assumptions were not in order just now. They could also be sitting there with boilers lit off and the crew ready for a five-minute jump-start, or at least able to man all those guns and start shooting back. So, business before pleasure.

"Initial firing bearing is zero eight five, range eight hundred yards. Torpedo running depth ten feet. Target is a destroyer moored to the bulkhead pier. I will then switch eight degrees to the right to shoot at a second destroyer, also moored. One fish per destroyer.

Then I'm going to come back left to bearing zero five five and shoot one fish at a pair of moored ammo barges. If we get a circular runner, we will *back* full emergency—there's no more useful water ahead of us. Got it?"

There was a murmur of acknowledgment.

Gar took a deep breath. "Tube one," he said.

"Tube one is ready. Plot set."

"Fire one."

They all felt the familiar thump, and Gar thought he could see the steam-bubble trail unfolding in his periscope.

"Shifting targets, firing bearing is zero niner three, range eight hundred yards, tube two."

"Tube two is ready. Plot set."

"Fire two."

Thump.

"Both fish hot, straight, and normal."

Gar swung back to the first destroyer just in time to see a huge waterspout erupt amidships, breaking him into two pieces. The explosion sound reached them a few seconds later as his midships sagged into the harbor in a boil of water and smoke.

"First destroyer is down," Gar reported. He swung right in time to see another waterspout, this one forward of center on the second destroyer. There was a red glow at the base of the water column, and then her forward magazines went off.

Okay, he thought, I was wrong about their off-loading ammo. The boom of the warhead was followed by the sound of a much larger explosion that seemed to go on forever as six hundred rounds of 5-inch ammo cooked off alongside the pier. Bet they stop welding over there now, he thought.

Lots of light, but still not quite enough.

"XO, you see any carriers?"

"That's a negative, Cap'n," Russ called back. "There's something in the big dry dock to the right, but it looks more like a building than a ship."

Gar swung around for one more confirmation bearing on the two barges and then fired a third torpedo into the outboard barge.

The barges were a little bit farther out, but this time he'd guessed right about what was on board. The whole world lit up as a monstrous fireball rose into the air, followed by an ear-squeezing pressure wave. It made the second destroyer look like a campfire in comparison. They'd see that one all the way up in Hiroshima City, he thought. Two more hash marks for his destroyer score sheet. Then the second barge exploded.

"Captain," Russ called. "Bearing zero niner niner—go high mag."

Gar quickly swung the periscope around to the right onto 099 and took a look under high magnification. He began to hear debris hitting the water around the boat as pieces of those barges came down. They were still blowing up like a Fourth of July fountain, creating a virtual parade of booming explosions.

In the scope, the shipyard was illuminated now with garish colors of red and orange in clear detail. On the bearing was a large black building with two protrusions canted out at 30 degrees from the upper stories. Gar looked and looked, trying to make it into something recognizable. Some kind of magnesium round went off on the ammo barges, and then he saw something down low, almost on the water, which gave it away. He realized he was looking at a dry-dock caisson, the huge floating wall that is sunk in the notched end of a dry dock once the ship is inside and positioned over the blocks.

That wasn't a building. That was their target.

The bastard was completely out of reach—he was in dry dock!

A hail of metal began to fall on the hull outside, and the exec and his two lookouts came scrambling down into the conning tower. There were some smaller explosions out in the water, which Gar hoped weren't aimed shell fire.

"Is that it?" the exec asked.

Gar nodded, wondering what they could do now. They didn't have much time before they'd have to get the hell out of here. The Japs would be in shock at what had just happened, but then they'd react. All the same, they hadn't made this trip to be defeated by a goddamned caisson wall.

Gar had three fish left forward, four aft. He wanted to save the four stern-tube torpedoes to use against pursuing Japs if he had to.

Something large hit the deck forward, then rolled over the side, sounding for all the world like a depth charge. He took another look. The first destroyer had capsized; the second one was just gone.

Gar told the exec to get on the other scope and use both radars to start looking for incoming trouble. Those two destroyers were history, but there should be at least a couple of the new Hiburi-class escorts nearby somewhere, and, being diesel powered, they could get under way in a hurry. Then the second ammo barge blew up again, pulsing a fireball hundreds of feet into the night air.

"Start backing out, XO," Gar said, as yet another large object landed close aboard the port side. It must be raining absolute death and destruction over on those piers, he thought.

He turned back to stare at the huge carrier in dry dock. Even with all the fireworks, her back end still looked like a building, and she seemed to have two hangar decks instead of just one. There were some guns mounted on the stern parapets, and now that he knew what he was looking at, he could make out the support girders for the overhanging flight deck.

"Bearing!" he called out "Mark! Make ready tube four. Range—estimate one thousand yards. Set running depth at twenty feet."

"Four ready, plot set."

"Fire four! Make ready five, same parameters."

Torpedo number four left the tube with a solid thump, followed a minute later by number five. Sound reported a normal run.

Gar couldn't tell through the periscope whether that huge ship was afloat inside the dry-dock basin or resting on her keel blocks. The caisson being closed, it was more likely that she was on the blocks. He hoped to blast away the caisson with three torpedoes and, if nothing else, upset the ship as the water rushed into the dock.

"Make ready tube six," he ordered, and then torpedo four hit the caisson. A satisfying waterspout erupted above the caisson and then fell back into the harbor, but they couldn't hear the warhead explosion over the cacophony of the exploding ammo barges.

Torpedo five hit just to the right of four, raising another big water blast. The caisson was now obscured by a dense cloud of dust, smoke, and debris, but he wondered if they'd done any real damage. A dry-dock caisson was just a big, hollow barrier with ballast tanks in the bottom half. To put a ship in dock you flooded the dry dock, and then a tug pulled the caisson out of the way. The ship would be pulled in, lined up over its blocks, and held in position by mooring lines. Then you pushed the caisson wall back into position at the harbor end of the dock and flooded down its ballast tanks. The caisson would settle into a notch at the end of the dry dock. Then you pumped out the dock. The pressure of the harbor water on one side of the caisson would seal it into position as the dock emptied. As the water was pumped out, the ship would settle onto her blocks, and work on the now-exposed underwater hull could begin.

He'd hit the caisson with two large warheads, but nothing seemed to have happened. He needed to dislodge it, not just damage it. He swung the scope around to put the vertical crosshair on the left edge of the caisson.

"Tube six: Bearing: Mark! Range one thousand yards. Set running depth fifteen feet."

"Cap'n, we have two radar contacts heading this way from Etajima," the exec called out.

"Set up a solution on them after I get this one off," Gar said. "Where are we, Plot?"

"Tube six ready, depth fifteen feet, plot is *set*."

"Fire six!"

Thump. This time he could definitely see the torpedo's wake as it planed up to 10 feet and then settled back down to 15 and headed for the dry dock. Sound again reported a normal hot run. Gar could hear the exec in the background calling out ranges and bearings to the TDC operators on the two inbound contacts. They were probably Hiburi-class patrol frigates; small but lethal. Time to run.

THIRTEEN

Gar took the conn, ordered up the diesels, and then made a hard right turn to the south. They no longer had the option of getting out the way they'd come in. They were going to have to run the Hayase Seto notch. He swung the scope back toward the dry dock in time to see torpedo six explode. He couldn't tell if he'd hit the caisson or the stone sidewall, because an instant later a large warehouse on the drydock's southern side obscured his line of sight.

Oh, well, he thought, effort made. It'd take them some time to replace that caisson, so, if nothing else, he'd put their largest dry dock out of commission. If he *had* managed to dislodge the caisson, a 42-foot-high wall of water would have thundered down into the empty dry dock, lifted the ship off her blocks and sent her careening into the stone sidewalls of the dry dock. With luck her screws and rudders would be damaged, and if there were any large access holes cut into her sides and bottom, there'd be some serious flooding of her engineering spaces.

Luck. Would. Could. Shit!

He swung the scope back to the left, where the ammo barges had been, but there was nothing there except a towering cloud of flickering smoke. The lights were going out all over Kure. Maybe they thought it was an air raid. Now all they had to do was outrun two angry patrol craft making 30 knots in their direction.

"Gun team battle stations, and make ready tubes seven and eight," Gar called out. He began to look for targets as they bolted south and west out of the Kure harbor at 20 knots. While they maneuvered to clear the harbor, Gar called down to Radio to put out a second message to Pearl about the attack and the frustrating news that the big carrier had been moored behind a dry dock caisson. Gar wanted to say that they thought they'd damaged her, but he knew in his heart she was probably untouched. The exec spoke up from the plotting table.

"Confirming two high-speed surface contacts, bearing three four zero, closing, range is now thirteen miles."

The Japs could start shooting at a range of about 8 miles, *if* they had radar gun control, which they probably did since they were heading right for the fleeing Dragon. The notch was 2 miles ahead of them, and while he was pretty sure destroyers could not go through there, smaller patrol craft certainly could. On the other hand, Gar wasn't sure the Dragon would make it through, either, with only 18 feet of water depth over the rock bottom at mean low water.

Time for me to go to the bridge, he thought. He told the exec to take the conn and drive them through on the radar, while he dealt with whatever was waiting for them in the notch itself.

He called down to Control to tell him what the state of the tide was right now, then ordered all scopes and radar masts down except for radar observations. The road bridge over the notch was charted at 36 feet; the Dragon's sail structure was 25 feet above the water. The notch itself was less than 300 wide, with a sharp turn required to avoid a shoal right after going under the bridge. The tide was key: Mean low water and they'd have only 2 feet under the keel; higher tide would give them a few more feet under the keel but also might have them taking the periscopes off on the bridge trusses. There was no alternative now, though—not with those two tin cans in hot pursuit. A quartermaster helped Gar into an exposure jumpsuit and an inflatable aviation-style life jacket, then handed him his binoculars. Then he went topside.

The snow was still coming down, and the fire-and-light show back in the Kure harbor was diminishing into muttered thunder. There was no wind other than the relative breeze created by their own passage. The diesels were roaring, and the gun crew forward was loading up the 5-inch gun and waiting for orders. The Dragon had a pair of twin-barreled 20 mm antiaircraft guns mounted back on the so-called cigarette deck behind the bridge. Gar ordered them manned as well. There would be at least a surveillance station on one or both sides of the notch, if not shore guns of some kind. The 20 mm would be more effective in close quarters than the 5-inch. He looked out into the gray swirl of snow ahead and tried to think. They'd have to slow down in the actual strait to keep from causing bottom suction effect—the high power being transmitted into the water by the props could create a semivacuum in close proximity to the bottom and actually suck the hull down into a grounding. The bitch-box spoke.

"Bridge, Nav. We'll have eleven feet of water under the keel and eight feet of clearance under that bridge."

Tight, very tight, he thought. He could hear the 20 mm crew breaking into the watertight ammo boxes and pushing shells down into the slide magazines. Up forward the gun crew was huddled behind the gun itself against the cold. He couldn't see much of anything, then remembered to take off the red-lens night-vision protection goggles that everyone wore down in the conning tower. Much better, but he still couldn't see anything but flying snow-flakes.

Time to think. So, first, slow down; there was no way they could go through that tiny strait at 20 knots and then do the zigzag turn around the shoals on the other side. He told the exec to slow to 10 knots. Then he tried to assemble the tactical picture, but realized immediately that he had to be down below in the conning tower for that. He hesitated. The captain's place in a fight was on the bridge, except he was blind up here. He could just see the gun crew forward. Otherwise, they might as well have been out on the open ocean. He called down to the exec to come to the ladder.

"Get suited up and take the bridge. I need to be where I can see that radar. Your job will be to work the guns as we go through if they start shooting."

Three minutes later Russ clunked up onto the bridge, and Gar went below, red goggles back on. There he had the DRT picture, the chart, radar, and the mine-hunting sonar scope right in front of him. He announced that he had the conn and slowed further to 8 knots. The notch was directly ahead at less than a mile. Then they heard distant gunfire coming down the hatch. Not their guns—shore batteries. Before Gar could react, the exec called down from the bridge.

"Shore batteries, port and starboard," he shouted. "But it sounds like they're shooting over us, way over us."

"Don't shoot back," Gar ordered. "I'll tell you when."

"Captain, those destroyers are changing course. Heading east now. There's some trash on the scope around them."

Then it dawned on him. The shore batteries were shooting at their own destroyers. Gar heard more thumping booms, a steady cannon fire in the night, but there were no shell bursts rising anywhere near the Dragon.

"I think they're shooting at their own ships," Gar said to the plotting team. "Focus now on the nav problem. We go through, we turn hard left just past the lower channel buoy, then hard right to split the next two buoys. Then southwest for deeper water."

The navigator pointed to a fish weir just past that first buoy. "We may hit that, sir," he said.

Gar nodded. "If we do, we do," he said. "Better that than actual pilings. Range to the notch?"

"Eight hundred yards," he said. "Should be a reflector buoy coming up on our starboard hand."

Gar passed that to the exec and asked if he saw anything. Negative. Just more snow. A long minute passed. The shore batteries were still blasting away up into the Kure harbor approaches. The two radar contacts were maneuvering in all directions.

"I can hear the beach to starboard," the exec called down. The diesels were echoing off the steeply terraced sides of the island.

"Can you see the bridge beacon?" Gar called up.

"Negative," he said. "Just more—wait! Wait! Affirmative. We need to come left two degrees to head right for it."

"Finally," Gar said. "Navigator, make it so, and you take the conn."

The chart showed that the bridge across the strait had a lighted reference beacon right in the middle of the structure to help ships and boats come through. A minute later they sailed under the bridge, which is when the Japs heard them.

A flare of white light lit up the hatch above as shore searchlights snapped on from just below the bridge structure.

"Shoot 'em out, XO," Gar shouted. "Use the twenties."

Instantly the 20 mm guns began to bark topside, and empty shell casings clanged down on the overhead of the conning tower.

"Unlighted buoy abeam on the port hand," the exec yelled over the racket of the 20s.

"Coming left to one three zero," the navigator called out.

Their second 20 mm got into it now, and the noise down in the conning tower became deafening. Suddenly the white glare from above went out and the shore guns stopped firing.

"Come right with full rudder to two zero zero!" the navigator shouted.

Gar felt the boat heel as they made the sharp turn, and then there was a scraping and rumbling sound along the port side as they wiped out the thin pilings of the fish weir. Gar held his breath, wondering if they should have stopped the port screw, and then came the deeper rumble of that propeller entangling itself in something. Gar wanted to stop it, but they needed that prop to push them through the tight starboard turn. The rumbling became heavier, and then subsided as the engineers took it into their own hands to shut it down and lock the shaft.

"Steady two zero five," the navigator called. "Captain, what speed now?"

Not the 20 knots we needed, he thought. "Go to full power on the starboard screw," he said. "Head for Moroshima. Control, get me damage reports."

Gar climbed back up to the bridge, where the gun crews were kicking 20 mm brass over the side. The snow was still falling as the boat accelerated out into the lower reaches of Hiroshima Bay.

"Anybody hurt?" he asked.

"Cookie burned his hand on the port twenty barrel," the exec said, "but the Japs never fired a round at us. I think they were all getting flat once the twenties started in. What'd we hit?"

"That damned fish trap, I think," Gar said. "We'll have to stop and send a diver over, but first we need to get to deeper water." He looked at his watch. They had three, maybe four hours left until daylight, and there would most definitely be a search on by then. On one screw they could make about 15 knots, and it was only 12 miles down to the Moroshima Strait, where the water was 300 feet deep. Once through Moroshima they'd be in the deep part of the Seto, where they could go to ground and plan the next steps.

"We need to stay on the surface, then," the exec said.

"Yup. I don't expect aircraft out in this weather, but they definitely know which way we're headed. What they don't know is which strait we'll take to get back out to deep water."

"Moroshima's the closest," Russ said. "If I had any patrol boats out, that's where I'd tell them to converge."

"Me, too," Gar said. "Keep the radar off until we get right to the straits. Secure all the guns, and get these people below. We run into bad guys, we're going downstairs in a hurry."

"You think Moroshima's mined?"

Gar hadn't actually considered that. He was more tired than he realized. "The only way we'll *know* is to go through submerged, with Hell's Bells on," he said, thinking out loud. "You're right. That's what we should do. Okay. Stay up here while I go below to see what the snipes think."

Gar went down the ladder, checked the nav plot, and told Cob to let people stand easy on station, get some chow and coffee while they transited. He told the sonar team they'd be submerging at the entrance to Moroshima and possibly going through another mine-field. Everyone in the conning tower looked positively delighted at that prospect. He went in search of coffee. The cooks came through—there was hot soup, sandwiches, and coffee in all the right places. Gar had one of the mess cooks take chow and coffee up to the bridge. Then he went back to Maneuvering.

The chief engineer, Billy Bangor, must have heard he was coming because he was there before Gar arrived.

"Whaddaya think?" Gar asked him.

"We tried to keep it on the line, but the vibration was just too bad," Billy said. "I think we need to stop, send a guy over the side with a battle lantern and take a look."

"This is a tough place to do that, Billy."

"Yes, sir, I know. But if that prop is as badly damaged as I think it is, we gotta get rid of it. It'll be too noisy otherwise, even if we're just dragging it."

"Blow it off?"

"Yes, sir. Primacord."

"Who's gonna set that?"

"That would be me, Cap'n," he said with a grin. "I'm a certified diver, and I've been to school on Primacord."

"You an *experienced* diver?"

"No, sir, not at all," he said brightly. "But I've got this really super certificate from the dive school. And a secret Primacord decoder ring."

It was Gar's turn to grin. "Ask Cob if we have anybody in the crew who's maybe done this before."

"Aye, aye, sir."

"We're going to submerge just before going through the next strait. That way we'll be able to see mines if there happen to be any. I'll be able to give you maybe thirty minutes to look, decide, and then blow the damned thing off. Got it?"

"Yes, sir. Piece'a cake."

Cob was obviously infectious. The more unreasonable the request, the more likely everybody would be mentioning cake.

The coffee wasn't doing anything but pressurizing Gar's bladder. He went forward, talking to people, telling them what they'd done and where they were bound next. He checked in with Radio, and they said they'd gotten the second message out. Finally he hit the head, and then his rack. They were transiting across the Inland Sea of Japan. By now the entire Jap navy was probably looking for them. In a snowstorm, admittedly, but in an area where they just about had to be after transiting that notch. They'd sunk two destroyers and two ammo barges, torn up the Kure dockyard, maybe hurt their new carrier, maybe not, and then got clean away while the shore batteries fired at their own approaching ships. The Dragon was down to one screw and 15 knots tops, on the surface. Underwater, maybe 5, and, more importantly, no ability to duplicate that twisting maneuver which had extracted them from their little spider box in the Bungo Suido minefield.

He looked at his watch. Forty-five minutes to get to Moroshima. He picked up the sound-powered phone.

"Conn."

"This is the captain. When we get five miles out from Moroshima, take a radar sweep. If we're clean, stop the boat and let the engineers take a look at the port prop. Show no lights. When the snipes are done with what they have to do, we'll submerge for the passage through Moroshima. Tell the XO."

"Got it, Cap'n."

"Good," he said. "I'm gonna take a nap."

That word would get around the boat in about two minutes. He lay back on his bunk. "Piece'a cake," he mumbled before passing right out.

FOURTEEN

Admiral Lockwood was listening to the morning briefing when a messenger came in from Communications and handed a piece of paper to Captain Forrester. He scanned it and passed it to Lockwood. The briefer, seeing there was something going on, stopped talking while Lockwood read the message and then nodded his head.

"Gar Hammond made it in," he said and then looked up, realizing no one knew what he was talking about.

"The *Dragonfish*. They got through Bungo Suido and made it into the Inland Sea *and* they've attacked the Kure naval arsenal. How 'bout that shit, eh?"

There was a murmur of approval as well as surprise among the gathering of staff officers, many of whom had had no knowledge that one of their boats was even going to try to get through Bungo Suido, much less attack a Jap naval base. Then another messenger came in with a second piece of paper. Lockwood read it and then shook his head.

"Amazing," he said. "They got to Kure but the damned carrier was in dry dock, so Hammond attacked the dry dock! And sank two moored destroyers plus a couple of ammo barges."

"Hammond and his destroyer obsession," muttered Forrester. "Did they damage the carrier?"

Lockwood shrugged. "Who the hell knows, but if he sent torpedoes against the caisson wall and it collapsed, they certainly did some damage. Can you imagine an aircraft carrier coming off the blocks and then colliding with the stone sides of the dock? The Japs must be out of their minds about now."

"Now comes the really hard part," Forrester said. "The getaway."

"God, yes. If there ever was a hornets' nest stirred up, Brother Hammond has taken the cake. Get word to PacFleet, and see if they can get some air force recce assets over that base."

"Aye, aye, sir," Forrester said as Lockwood motioned to the briefer to continue with the rest of the morning brief.

He was headed upstairs to make the call to Makalapa when the assistant operations officer intercepted him with a file folder.

"This is the information you requested on the *Hoshen Maru* sinking," he said. "Looks like it was the *Gar* that did the deed."

"The *Gar*?" Forrester repeated. "It would have to be the *Gar*, wouldn't it."

"Sir?"

"Never mind."

"Do you want me to get a copy up to PacFleet JAG?"

"No," Forrester said. "Let me take care of that."

He went to his office, quickly scanned the folder, and then asked his yeoman to put in a call to PacFleet JAG and ask Lieutenant Commander DeVeers to come see him.

Sharon arrived at SubPac headquarters an hour later. She was wearing her blues this time, in deference more to the month of the year than any colder temperatures. Forrester gave her the folder and then asked her to read through it to see if that was what they needed. Sharon did so while Forrester looked out the tall windows at the subs moored down at the finger piers.

"Yes, Captain, I think this will do," she said.

"Have the Japs starting beating the drums about this incident?"

"Not to my knowledge, Captain," Sharon said. "But State doesn't necessarily share what they know with us."

"Are you familiar with the operating areas discussed in the report?" he asked.

"No, sir, not really. I can figure out what 'empire' means, but—"

"Perhaps I can help you," he said. "Let me give you a quick tour of the operations briefing room. We have a large graphical chart for the areas."

Sharon wasn't quite sure what that had to do with the price of rice, but she agreed. Forrester made a call and then took her downstairs to the ops briefing room. When they came in she saw that the three walls were covered in huge maps, some of which had curtains drawn across them. Forrester took her to the largest map, which displayed the entire Pacific theater of operations. She was aware of the watch-standers all staring at her as if they'd never seen a woman in uniform. Captain Forrester was standing quite close as he explained the various area dispositions, almost like a proud teenager with the prettiest girl at the prom.

She sighed mentally. Another amorous captain, complete with wedding ring and family pictures on the desk. Next would be an invitation to lunch in the flag mess for an in-depth discussion of submarine warfare. Then an invite to a reception somewhere, followed by some lush tropical drinking and finally a hands-on experience on the dance floor. She thought back to her brief time with Gar Hammond and realized she missed him, lone wolf BS and all. Forrester was wrapping up his description.

"So you see, Miss DeVeers, this is a really big operation."

"Wow," she said, playing her part. "I had no idea. Where's Gar Hammond in all of this?"

Forrester cleared his throat and then told her that that was, of course, highly restricted information. Some of the enlisted plotters appeared to be suppressing grins when she asked about Hammond by his first name. Her question seemed to be the signal to terminate the grand tour.

As they left the briefing room, Admiral Lockwood appeared on the stairway to the second deck. Forrester made introductions, and the admiral asked her how the *Hoshen Maru* case was shaping up. She told him what little she knew and ended by saying that Captain Forrester had just given her the *most* interesting tour of the operations center.

"Is that right," Lockwood said, also seeming to suppress a grin.

"I'm sure that was very interesting indeed. Keep me informed, will you? If Washington is going to get all spun up over this, I'd appreciate a heads-up."

"I'll pass any information we get on to Captain Forrester," she replied. "As he requested."

Lockwood gave Forrester a quick why-you-old-dog look and went into the operations center. Sharon smiled sweetly at the discomfited captain, then took her leave and the folder back to Makalapa.

The Inland Sea of Japan

One squeak on the phone brought Gar back awake. "Captain."

"Cap'n, snipes say they gotta blow it. Primacord is set. Request permission to—"

"Tell them to blow it and get back inside as soon as possible. Anything on the radar?"

"No, sir. We're clean. The strait's dead ahead, and it's still snowing to beat the band."

"What's the fathometer showing?" Gar looked at his watch. He'd been down for an hour. It felt like a big mistake. He needed another twelve or so to get even. Had to make sure the XO got some time down, too, he reminded himself. Gar needed that brain of his.

"Two hundred eighty feet."

He heard the sharp bang of the Primacord going off back aft. They'd wrapped it around the tail shaft just forward of the propeller. If they'd done it right, the Primacord would have cut the entire screw off the tail shaft.

"I'll be up."

He sloshed some water on his fuzzy face and then went aft to the control room.

"How many people we got topside?" he asked.

"Ten," the diving officer said. "Two in the water, eight tenders all around."

"Who did the dive?"

"Billy Bangs and Cob," he said.

Good man, he thought. I bet he didn't have to ask Cob, either.

"Control, Maneuvering."

"Control.

"They got it off. Diving party's coming in."

Gar nodded at the phone talker. "Captain says well done."

He repeated Gar's message, and then Gar climbed up into the conning tower. He'd finally come to realize that this was indeed where he needed to be, not on the bridge. Here lived the tactical picture. The nav chart, with a real-time depiction of where they were on that chart. The radar. The sonars. The TDC. This was the nerve center. What had that captain said the surface guys called it? CIC? The captain on the bridge was a tradition, but only if he could see.

"Gimme the bubble," he said.

FIFTEEN

They submerged and started into the Moroshima Strait. They stayed shallow, running at 150 feet. Gar wanted the mine-hunting sonar to tell him if there were mines ahead, but he also needed to be able to get back up quickly and shine the radar for a sweep or two, in order to see where they were and where they were going.

He'd sent the exec below with orders to get an hour of sleep.

"Just one?" Russ had asked with a weak smile.

"We'll call you," Gar said. "Trust me on that."

Russ went below. Gar told the team to take them on into Moroshima.

For five minutes they waited. Then: *Gong.*

Fuck.

They began the dance, but this time with only one screw, which made the Dragon sluggish in tight spaces. Just to help things along, Maneuvering reported that the port stern tube was leaking, probably caused by the Primacord blast so close to the stern tube seal.

"All stop," Gar ordered. All one engine, he thought.

"Popeye, what does the whiz-bang see?"

"Two ahead," Popeye answered. "One to port, one to starboard. Can't tell depth."

The ops boss spoke up from the TDC. "The tide's going out, so the chains oughta be straining southwest. The mines are probably deeper than they normally ride."

Gar waited while Popeye analyzed the scope picture.

"Both have bearing drift. We can pass between them."

Between those two, Gar thought—but what if there were a whole gaggle of the damned things down at, say 200 feet? This sonar looked *up*. On the other hand, he couldn't just point down into the depths now. He realized that once they committed to a depth within a minefield, they were stuck there.

"Nothing above us?" he asked. He was conscious of the rest of the conning tower listening to this quiet conversation about 1,000-pound mines in the water all around them. He stood at his periscope observation stand, not to use it but to keep out of the way of all the plotters, phone talkers, and TDC operators jammed together in the conning tower.

"Not yet," said Popeye helpfully. Good deal, Gar thought.

"All ahead one-third," he ordered. If the sonar looked up at 5 degrees, then this was probably a surface field, aimed at ships not subs. Unless, of course, they'd planted two layers. He told the diving officer down in Control to see what the bottom looked like according to Hashimoto's chart.

They crept ahead, navigating on a dead-reckoning track. There was a 5-knot current through there at maximum ebb tide, but they were two hours from the max ebb. Still, they were sweeping over the ground partly on their own power and partly in the grip of that current.

Gong.

"Two more, both to port. Should clear."

Gar studied the chart on the DRT tabletop. The current streamed right through the strait on a course of 190, just to the right of due south. The water depth in the strait was 180 feet, but there was a hole just outside the strait where the water depth went to almost 400 feet, then back to 180 again. He told the fathometer operator to watch for that hole. They should cross right over it, and if they did, they'd know where they were without having to take a radar peek.

Gong. Gong.

"Two more dead ahead. Recommend we come right ten degrees."

"Make it so, helmsman."

The fathometer operator raised his hand. "Depth beneath the keel is two hundred. Two fifty. Three hundred. We've just crossed over a ledge. Four hundred feet."

They were clear of the strait.

Gong.

Not clear of the goddamned minefield.

"Depth beneath the keel is now back to one eighty."

Gar studied the chart again. To the left of their track was shallower water. Easier to moor mines over there.

"Come right to two one zero," he ordered.

"Two one zero will clear the mine ahead," Popeye said.

"Once we pass this one we'll come to periscope depth and stop. Popeye, look hard as we come up."

"Cap'n," the ops officer called, "if we want to stop forward motion over the ground, we'll have to back down."

Gar nodded. He should have caught that. Backing down on one screw would probably not overcome the force of a 6-knot current. Except now that they were out of the strait, the current shouldn't be quite that strong.

Gong.

Time to try.

The off-center pull of the single propeller began to fight the helm to the point where the helmsman couldn't maintain directional control. That turned out to be a good thing. As the bow fell off to starboard, the gonging stopped.

"Starboard stop, starboard ahead two-thirds," Gar ordered. He watched Popeye as he frantically scanned the screen. Then he watched the pit log, which finally came off the zero peg and showed forward motion. He slowed to one-third ahead and waited.

"Clear ahead," Popeye said.

They waited some more. Gar wanted ten minutes of clear sailing before coming up for a radar fix. He looked at the clock on the forward bulkhead. It was 0440 local time. They had maybe an hour and a half until first light, at which point they'd have to submerge for the day.

Gar was very tired. They all were. The thought of going down to 350 feet somewhere out in the middle of the Seto and taking the rest of the day off was wonderful even if it did mean the end of fresh air.

While they waited, the radioman brought up some messages. He'd been copying the fleet broadcast the whole time they'd been tearing stuff up in Kure. Apparently, Pearl was very pleased that they'd managed to get into the Seto. Gar looked for a message acknowledging his second report—that they hadn't been able to get at the carrier. Nothing there. Probably observing that old rule: If you can't say something nice, don't say anything at all.

"Conn, Sonar."

"Go ahead."

"I have a noise spoke, weak and intermittent, two seven zero. No classification."

Gar grabbed the 1MC microphone. "Rig for silent running."

The vent system shut down immediately, but it wasn't so bad with that cold water outside the skin. "Start a plot. Open outer doors forward."

A noise spoke could mean anything from a hunting destroyer to an enemy submarine to a fishing trawler.

"Bearing drift?"

"No bearing drift."

That meant whatever it was, it was coming straight at them. Gar remembered the destroyers back in the Luzon Strait whose sonars they could not hear. The problem with a single sound bearing was that there was no way to know how far away he was, not without a few hours of fancy plotting.

"Say the fathometer."

"Two five five beneath the keel."

"How many fish we got forward?"

"Tubes one and two reloaded; three in progress. All steamers."

"Control, make your depth two hundred feet. Three-degree down bubble. Popeye, keep watching. I don't want to descend into another minefield."

"Clear so far, Cap'n."

"Say the layer."

"No layer, so far."

If there was going to be a protective layer, it was deeper than they were now. No layer, they were going to be fair game.

"Conn, Sonar, amplitude *in*creasing slightly. Still no classification. Bearing drifting slightly right."

"Passing two hundred feet. Trimming up."

Gar tried to think of something brilliant, then realized he was too fatigued to think.

"Call the XO," he said. He'd had his hour, maybe even a little more. Gar knew he needed another brain up here.

"Steady at two hundred feet."

"A thin five-degree layer at one ninety, sir."

Not much protection. The larger the temperature differential between one layer of seawater and another, the more sonar waves bounced off, thus masking them. The noise spoke on the screen was at 270, drifting slightly right. They needed to come left, to increase that bearing drift and make the Jap pass astern of them, but not so far left that they reengaged the minefield. Plus, there was a pinnacle to the east of the Moroshima Strait's southern exit. Nine feet of shoal water.

Gar's plan had been to surface and get a radar fix, but now . . . well, now they didn't know exactly where they were.

"Come left to one eight zero," he said.

"One eight zero, aye."

"Does the fathometer depth agree with the charted depth?"

"No, sir. Based on our dead-reckoning position, depth should be three hundred feet, but shoaling ahead to two forty."

Gar's ultimate objective was to get back to the safety of their wait-box, where the water depth had been 600 feet. The route to the wait-box was just not deep enough for them to be safe from a serious antisubmarine search, which would surely be coming in the morning.

There was nothing else they could do, he finally decided. They had to surface and run as fast as they could before daylight drove them down again.

"Popeye, anything?"

"No, sir. Clear on my scope."

"Sonar?"

"Noise spoke is still there, Cap'n. Bearing two niner five now; passing astern. I make it out to be a diesel."

Diesel. That could be anything, a fisherman, an I-boat on the surface. Coming from the southwest, headed home?

"Come to periscope depth," Gar ordered. "Stand by for visual observation."

They came up to periscope depth. Gar put up one of the periscopes, walked around the compass circle, and saw precisely nothing. He checked the depth meter to make sure his scope was indeed above the water. It was.

Still nothing.

"Down scope. Radar, get a fix."

The surface-search radar mast went up for about one minute, then back down. The scope operators had drawn what they'd seen in yellow grease pencil on the scope: the edges of three islands. They then measured the ranges out to those edges and drew arcs on the chart. Their position on the chart was right where those arcs intersected. You hoped for a point intersection but usually got a small triangle. It was good enough to show Gar where they had to go to achieve a good hidey-hole out in deep water. The question now was, surface and go 12 or 13 knots, or submerge again to 100 feet and go 6? The daylight problem drove the answer. They simply had to surface if they wanted to be in deep water by the time the antisubmarine forces came out in force to hunt them down.

"See that noise spoke contact anywhere?" Gar asked the radar team.

"Negative, sir. No surface contacts."

"Sonar, is that possible?"

"Yes, sir. There may be a sound channel. He could be close aboard or twenty miles away."

Gar looked at his watch. Time to decide. His eyes burned, and he felt his sinuses contracting. The exec climbed up into the conning tower.

"Stand by to surface. Nav, plot us a course at fifteen knots to the deep hole. XO, here's what we got."

He briefed the exec on the situation and then asked him to take the conn.

Gar got the chief cook on the horn and told him to prepare a hot meal while they were running on the surface. They'd be down for ten hours once they went into hiding; the sub's atmosphere would be bad enough without the smell of cooking food. He told Maneuvering to pack the battery tight over the next ninety minutes. They acknowledged and requested permission to work on that leaking shaft seal before they went deep again. Gar had forgotten all about that, but those guys who were looking it in the eye knew what would happen to a small leak once the sub headed for deep water: It would become a big leak.

They came up fifteen minutes later. It was still pitch black and snowing outside. Another sweep of the radar revealed no surface contacts. Even the nearby islands were a little fuzzy on the scope. Don't quit on me now, Gar prayed, looking at those indistinct images. If they lost radar, they'd be here forever.

The diesels lit off with a satisfactory roar, and they plowed south and east to find safer water. The exec stayed in the conning tower, while one officer and three lookouts went topside. The flow of cold, clean air was a welcome relief, as always. Mixed in it somewhere Gar thought he smelled frying chicken. Now that they were on the surface, the sonar had no contacts. He thought about taking a peek with the air-search radar, but the current conditions should make that moot. Should.

Gar wedged himself into a corner of the conning tower and closed his eyes. Once daylight came, he expected a full court press from the Japanese. They had to have detected the Dragon's two HF radio transmissions. That meant they knew there was a U.S. submarine in the Inland Sea, and they wouldn't rest until they found it. The Dragon might not have accomplished her mission of damaging that carrier, but she'd certainly embarrassed whatever admiral owned the Inland Sea. An American submarine torpedoing dry-dock caissons and moored destroyers right in front of one of their most important naval arsenals? Somebody would be on the hara-kiri list for that one.

He tried to project what he'd do next. Hide for a day in that hole, where the water was 600 feet deep. Then—what? They'd have to surface to recharge the batteries before attempting Bungo Suido again. They could, if they had to, stay down for thirty-six hours, after which the CO_2 levels would begin to overwhelm the scrubbers. If I were the Jap commander, he thought, I'd look hard at the chart of the Seto and then station four destroyers right above the Hoyo Strait. They could sit there at idle for a couple of weeks. The Dragon would either have to shoot her way out of there or die trying. They'd draw a line between the Moroshima Strait and Bungo Suido and just wait for their prey to make a move.

Okay, but there was another way out of the Seto. The Kii Suido. The northern exit. What if they laid low for as long as they could and then went back northeast *into* the Seto? They had food for four more weeks, and some torpedoes left. Maybe go back to Kure. Damned Japs would never expect that. The water here was shallow, only 165 feet in most places, but the winter was setting in, with its shitty weather, low visibility, snow squalls, short days, and ink black nights.

We could, he thought. We could retrace our steps back into Hiroshima Bay and do it all again. Then run for the *northern* exit from the Seto—Kii Suido. He tried to imagine what the exec would think of that and smiled. An image of Cob's face rose in his mind. Don't say it, he told his weary brain.

SIXTEEN

They got to the hole at daybreak, or what passed for daybreak. The snow was still flying, and the radar showed nobody operating within 20 miles of them. Gar stayed on the surface for as long as possible to max out the batteries; then they dived and leveled off at 350 feet, 50 feet deeper than a much more generous thermocline layer. They were finally down where they belonged, in the deep, black, cold embrace of the Seto.

Then they slept. Gar had the watch officers put a 2-degree port rudder on at 2 knots, and they commenced executing a continuous circle in the black depths of the sea. They set four-hour minimal-manning watches in Engineering and Control. The rest of the crew hit their racks or slept on station in corners, on top of torpedoes, in storage cubbyholes, on mess-deck benches, in the wardroom, wherever they could find 6 horizontal feet and some quiet. Everyone was exhausted. Besides, men sleeping burned up less oxygen and produced less CO_2.

Gar got some chow, hit the head to pump personal bilges, and then lay down in his own rack for eight straight hours. Bliss.

Until that port shaft seal let go.

The sound-powered phone squealed.

"Captain."

"Major flooding in two engine room, Cap'n," the exec said. "We need to come up."

Gar squinted at the depth gauge—350 feet.

"Any echo ranging?"

"None heard, sir."

"I'll be up."

By the time he got to Control, the diving officer was having trouble keeping the trim on the boat. She was getting stern heavy, and they were urgently transferring water through the ballast system, trying to keep her on an even keel. Gar went back to Maneuvering, where the chief engineer was on the phone with the damage control team.

"Can we come up?" the engineer asked. "It's pretty bad back there, and the pumps aren't keeping up."

"The layer's at three hundred feet," Gar said. "Above that, if they're up there, they'll hear us."

"Even fifty feet would help, Skipper," Billy said.

Gar called Control and told them to make their depth 300 feet. The diving officer said he'd try but was worried about the up-angle getting out of control. He said they'd pulled the people out of After Torpedo. The exec showed up in Maneuvering. He'd been back to the port shaft alley, and his khakis were soaked.

"We have to get up to periscope depth," he said. "That seal is blowing like Yellowstone."

"We might be walking into something worse," Gar said.

He threw up his hands. "There'll be seawater getting into After Battery very soon," he said. "After that . . ."

After that, the electrolyte in the battery would begin generating chlorine gas, and that would be the end of them.

"Stay on things here," Gar said. "I'm going to the conning tower."

"As soon as we can, Cap'n," he said. "They're getting nowhere back there."

Gar didn't need reminding. The sub would get so heavy aft that she'd begin to stand on her hind end as they tried to get closer to the surface. With only one shaft operational, there was the distinct possibility that they'd start sliding backward into the depths. The deep water that had been protecting them would then consume them.

When Gar got to Control, he ordered all the watertight doors closed and the men to action stations torpedo. They'd be in a torpedo fight right away if they came up into a hornet's nest of Jap escorts, and Gar's best antidestroyer torpedoes, the slow but deadly electric homers, were all in After Torpedo.

Which had been evacuated. *Dammit!*

"Come to periscope depth," he ordered. "Power us up, but don't blow unless you have to."

"We'll have to," the diving officer said. "We're too heavy to drive up on one shaft."

Gar had to think fast. The batteries were depleted after a day at depth. He only had one propeller left. Ordinarily with a flooding situation, he'd have blown all ballast tanks and be driving the boat up with both screws going full bore, and even that would have been dicey.

"Do what you have to do," Gar said. "A fight's better than that really deep dive."

He climbed up into the conning tower, where their trusty battle stations crew was already on station. The boat was pointed up at about a 10-degree angle, and they could all feel the throbbing of the starboard screw trying to drive them toward the surface. Then a ballast tank rumbled as it filled with compressed air. The depth gauge showed 265, but their ascent was perilously slow. The good news was that for every foot of depth they gained, the torrent of water pouring into their nether parts would be slowing down. The bad news was that they were making a hell of a lot of noise.

A second ballast tank rumbled, and the ascent angle eased off to 8 degrees. They were now passing through 245 feet.

"Sound, anything?"

"Ballast tanks," Popeye said grimly. His gear was deaf until all that compressed air bubbling out of them got out of the way.

"Passing two hundred feet," Control reported.

"Hold her at one hundred feet, if you can," Gar replied, eyeing the Plexiglas status board that showed sunset happening at 1745 local time. The clock above the board showed 1730. Darkness was their friend; snow, sleet, hail, and fog would be even better.

"Passing one fifty feet."

Gar called the exec in Maneuvering. "This helping?" he asked.

"Yes, sir, and now the pumps are effective."

"Get people back into After Torpedo as soon as possible," Gar said. He didn't have to tell him why. He was glad torpedoes were waterproof.

"Leveling at one-ten feet," Control reported. Gar didn't say anything. The diving officer had his hands full trying to get a proper trim on the boat. They still were carrying a big slug of sea-water aft. Gar could feel it. His big problem now was that they'd lost their protective layer and made far too much noise. He had no idea of what might be up there, waiting for them.

"Control, can you bring her to periscope depth without broaching?"

"Not yet, Cap'n. Trim's way off, and the bubble is dancing."

"When you're stable, bring her up."

Gar had taught all the officers who stood diving officer watch to be absolutely frank about the boat's stability at any given moment. Trimming a submerged submarine is an art, and sometimes officers were unwilling to admit that they were having a hard time achieving trim. A submerged submarine is continuously fooling the ocean into not swallowing it whole. A diving officer had to have no illusions about how good he was. If the boat was out of trim, they were all at risk. Gar could hear the trim pumps working as the diving team worked to balance water loads in their tanks with their own buoyancy. It was a little like trying to hover a fixed-wing aircraft. He wondered who else could hear all that motor noise.

"Coming up to periscope depth now," Control reported.

"Up scope," Gar ordered, even though they weren't quite there yet. He wanted to be on the eyepiece when the tip broached the surface. As soon as it broke, he did the circular duckwalk for a quick look. It appeared to be dark, with a stiff breeze blowing whitecaps soundlessly across the water. That was a good thing; whitecaps hid periscopes. Gar held the scope to just 1 foot above the water for the first look, then brought it up to 3 feet.

No company visible. Sound confirmed a quiet environment—no diesels, pinging, or aircraft sounds. Gar ordered the periscope down and the surface radar mast up for a single-sweep observation.

"Conn, Radar. I have no picture."

"You mean no contacts, or no video on your scope?"

"No nothing, sir," the operator said, disgustedly. "I think this goddamned thing's broke-dick."

Gar ordered the mast down immediately. This was a real problem. The radar techs were already tearing into the equipment cabinet. They *had* to have that radar. He couldn't surface or even bring the diesels on the line without knowing what was lurking out there in the snowy darkness. For that matter, they couldn't even get a navigation fix. After circling aimlessly all day at depth and subject to whatever currents had been at play down there, they really couldn't know where they were other than by matching the observed water depths with the charted depth. That made for a pretty loose fix.

Gar went down the ladder from the conning tower to meet the chief engineer, who reported that the repair team needed to get back topside to pack that shaft seal from the outside, so that pressure at depth would squeeze the packing *in* instead of trying to push the inner seals out into the shaft alley. That, of course, meant they had to surface.

"The battery is at thirty percent," Gar said. "Not to mention the air inside the boat becoming a diesel fog. We'll have to surface any way we look at it. ETR on the radar?"

"They're just getting into it," called the exec from the conning tower. "Pray that we have the part."

"XO, what do you recommend?"

"Battle surface guns," he said promptly. "Go up there expecting trouble and ready to shoot. Keep the TDC team in place for a torpedo shot. If nobody shows up, light off a single diesel for battery charge and fix the seal. Anything after that is gravy."

"I concur," Gar said. "Make it so."

Russ nodded and disappeared from the hatch to take charge. He was getting good at that, Gar realized, and he'd have to be once he got his own command. Gar's reservations about him going to command had vanished. He reminded himself to tell Russ that.

Gar watched the periscope go back up as the exec took a look for himself. One of the radar techs came down the ladder with two vacuum tubes.

"Those the guilty bastards?" Gar asked.

The tech said he hoped so and went aft to one of the storerooms. Gar hoped they weren't Easter-egging. He told Cob to get the word out that they were going to battle surface as a precaution and then fix the seal. Then he went to the wardroom. Normally for a battle-surface evolution Gar would be in the conning tower, or at least in Control, but he wanted the exec to run this one without his being right there, looking over his shoulder.

Gar could hear the bridge team assembling at the base of the ladder going topside, and the 5-inch gun team headed forward to their hatch. The Dragon's crew was now a well-oiled machine, to the point where the GQ alarm really wasn't necessary. Each man knew what he had to do to bring the boat up on the surface, man all the guns, get a diving team out onto the fantail and over the side with seal packing, light off the diesel engine, purge the foul air out of the boat, complete the trim pumping to lift the stern up so the divers had an easier job of it, set and maintain a tight visual watch all around, and, oh by the way, fix the damned radar. Gar was superfluous, for the moment. If a destroyer came barreling out of the dark, *then* he'd have a job.

"Surface! Surface! Man gun stations."

The Dragon came up, still tail heavy and making more noise than Gar wanted to hear as the ballast tanks were emptied. Keep negative flooded, he thought, in case we need to get back down chop-chop.

"Flood negative *and* safety," the exec ordered. Atta boy, Gar thought.

Mooky the cook came in with a tray of fried-egg sandwiches. Gar grabbed one and then told Control he'd be in his cabin. He knew they'd pass that word up to the exec, and he'd recognize it for the vote of confidence that it was. Gar felt the hatch open topside and waited for the blast of fresh air that was forthcoming. Oxygen was good stuff. He went forward.

What about that sound contact? He thought about that for a good nine seconds before the sleep monster pulled him down.

Two hours later he awoke to the squeak of his personal devil, the sound-powered phone that hung next to his head.

"Captain."

"Repairs complete on the seal, Cap'n," the exec said. "Radar team's still digging around in the equipment cabinets. No visual or sonar contacts. Cooks're getting a hot meal together. I've pointed us south toward the straits. I've got the gun teams standing easy on station."

"What's the weather?"

"Dark, no precip right now, no moon. Just dark."

"Very well," Gar said. "I'll be up."

He got a cup of coffee on the way through Control and climbed up into the conning tower. The exec was on the scope as he arrived, walking the eyepiece around in the familiar circle.

"Who's topside?" Gar asked.

"OOD, two lookouts, the twenty-millimeter team, the five-inch team. Battery's almost at eighty percent. Surface radar still not up. Sonar is cold. Best we can tell, no contacts."

Gar went over to the DRT table to see the plot. They were out in the middle of the Inland Sea. The night before, they'd been surfaced in front of the Kure naval arsenal sinking two destroyers, setting off the ammo explosion from hell, and blasting the dry-dock caisson holding the biggest carrier they'd ever seen.

No contacts?

Gar felt a tingle at the base of his spine. If the Japs had figured out what they were doing, they'd have put a line of escorts across the escape route, down by the Hoyo channel. Then they'd follow the boat down until they could get her in a mousetrap.

"Bring everybody inside," Gar said quietly. "Secure the gun crews, the lookouts, everybody. Once they're safely in the house, light off the FM sonar."

"You think they're out there?"

"I'd be very suspicious if they're *not* out there. Any Jap commander who knows these waters knows this is where we have to be if we're still in the Inland Sea."

"If they're out there, what are they waiting for?"

"Aircraft," Gar said. "Radar, equipped night bombers."

"We could take a look," he said. "The air-search radar is up."

"I think that would create a beacon," Gar said. "Let's try the FM sonar first."

It took fifteen minutes to get the various gun crews and lookouts back down. If there was nothing out there in the darkness, they'd stay on the surface for the night and work their way down toward Bungo Suido. They still had their rough plot of the minefield and the access channel they'd followed coming in. Gar wanted the battery topped off, the crew fed and rested, and the surface-search radar working before they made their run through Bungo Suido. They'd missed their carrier, but they hadn't done all that bad.

Gong.

That sound made everyone in the conning tower freeze.

Were they in a minefield? Way out here, in the middle of nowhere?

Gong. Gong.

Gar stared at Popeye, who was wiping his forehead with his sleeve.

"Popeye," Gar said, "we're on the surface, for Chrissakes. What's that thing picking up?"

"Objects on the surface?" he asked. "It looks *up*, remember, Cap'n?"

"How far?"

"A thousand yards, tops. Three of them, forty degrees apart."

Gar's blood ran cold. "You're telling me we have three contacts within a thousand yards of us?"

Popeye raised his hands in frustration. "They're not mines," he said. "At least I don't think so. This thing's looking into the surface layer, zero to forty feet. They're not big, but they're absolutely out there."

How long have we been sitting here, Gar thought, confident there was no enemy anywhere near us? Dear God. How I wish we had the means to detect the enemy's radars. The Japs certainly could.

The hatch to the bridge was still open, if nothing else for the fresh air. The two guys working on the surface-search radar were muttering to one another, oblivious of what the FM sonar had come up with. The lone diesel was rumbling happily away, making amps without a care in the world.

The exec was looking at Gar with one of those what-now-boss looks.

"I have to see," Gar said.

They'd been wearing their red goggles in the conning tower to preserve some semblance of night vision.

"It's pitch black out there, Cap'n," the exec said. "Three contacts at a thousand yards are waiting for something. We need to sub-merge."

Waiting for something. What, for Chrissakes?

Aircraft, he remembered. They were waiting for a radar-equipped bomber to come out to catch the stupid Americans sitting almost motionless on the surface.

"I *have* to see," Gar said again.

The exec nodded and handed him the exposure suit and his life vest. Gar heard one of the radar techs swear. Still no joy in fixing the bearing radar. He took his binoculars and went topside to the target-transmitter mount. He locked the binocs into the frame and then asked for a bearing to the nearest FM sonar contact.

The night was cold and as dark as Gar had seen it on this trip. He popped the goggles up onto his head and stared out into the darkness down the indicated bearing. The boat was making 2 knots in a southerly direction, but there was almost no wake, only the deep throbbing pulse of the sole diesel engine on the line.

They didn't have to stay on the surface. The battery was nearly full. On the other hand, if they wanted to reach Bungo Suido by daybreak, they needed to run on the surface. Hoyo channel was not mined, or, if it was, they knew the clear channel through. Bungo Suido was different. They knew the safe way in, but after that, they'd have to do the minefield dance to get back out. That would take time and lots of amps in the can.

"Raise the air-search mast, take two sweeps," Gar ordered. "Prepare to emergency dive. Switch to battery power and secure the diesel."

The exec acknowledged. Gar heard the radar mast coming up while he stared hard into the darkness.

It was hopeless. There was nothing to be seen out there. The diesel engine shut down, and he heard the main induction valve at the base of the sail slam shut. Then the radar operator in the conning tower erupted:

"Single bogey, two seven zero, *inbound*! Range, five miles and closing fast!"

As Gar digested that bad news the sea lit up with the white blaze of three searchlights, each one pinned right on them. Gar stood up to say something but was interrupted by the howl of a shell coming overhead and exploding right in front of the boat.

"Dive, dive, *dive*!" he yelled down the hatch as a second shell and then a third landed close aboard, flaying the sail and the bridge with shrapnel. "Take her *down*!"

He was headed toward the hatch into the conning tower when a fourth shell hit close aboard, ricocheted across the water, and smacked into the bridge, the impact knocking him sideways. He was thrown into a heap in one corner of the bridge even as he heard the rumble of air leaving the ballast tanks and felt the boat tilt down, accelerating as she went.

The hatch. The hatch was still open. They were waiting for him.

He rolled toward it but was defeated by yet another shell, which exploded over the bridge with a white blast of energy that knocked him flat again, gasping for air and deafened.

He looked forward at the sea rushing up, an angry black curl of water surging around his feet as the deck plates tilted down so steeply that he couldn't gain his footing. He rolled toward the hatch as the water swirled around him, his lower body already underwater, and did what he had to do. He tripped the latch and then slammed the hatch down and spun the wheel as best he could before the advancing wave swept him right off the bridge and into the cold waters of the Inland Sea.

Part II

CAST AWAY

SEVENTEEN

Gar popped up a moment later, suddenly conscious of the boat's thrumming starboard propeller going by much too close for comfort. Pursued by more shell splashes, the Dragon disappeared in a roil of white water. A moment after that, as he surfaced in the tumult of her submergence, he heard the roar of aircraft engines and then the whistle of falling bombs. He literally didn't know what to do next, but then there was a tremendous punch from below. It felt as if his innards were being strained through his rib cage, and then he was airborne, his arms and legs windmilling in the night air. The last thing he remembered was pulling the CO_2 lanyard on his life vest just before hitting the sea.

When he came to, he was lying on a wet wooden deck. He was on his belly, his head turned to one side, his arms extended alongside his body with palms up, and his legs stretched straight out behind him. His ears were still ringing, but he could hear the excited gabbling of Japanese and feel the deck heeling as whatever kind of ship he was on made a hard turn. His left ear was supported by the bulge of his still-inflated life jacket. He blinked the saltwater out of his stinging eyes and focused on the searchlights stabbing out into the darkness around him. One came from behind; another, dazzlingly bright, came from the wing of an aircraft that was buzzing overhead. In the light he saw a Japanese minesweeper boring in and dropping depth charges over an already disturbed area of the sea.

Gar was cold, wet, and concussed, but he was able to work out what was happening. They'd been jumped by minesweepers, not destroyers. Wooden hulled and diesel powered, not quite 200 feet long, but armed with depth-charge racks and a mine-hunting sonar. He watched in growing dismay as the spotlighted boat made its run, then turned out of the cone of light and away from her erupting depth charges; he felt the deck heel sharply as his sweeper followed its partner in to the target area. The plane flew around the action at low level, keeping the whole area lit up as they tried to find and kill Gar's submarine. Unable to raise his head, he closed his eyes and stopped watching.

Had they made it down soon enough? Deep enough? Those bombs had gone off pretty close to the surface, so maybe, maybe . . . but there was something ominous about that large patch of foaming sea, reflecting an occasional sheen of oil. He heard orders being shouted behind him, then felt the thump of depth-charge projectors going off amidships. He could feel the wooden hull trembling as the diesels pushed the sweeper in at full power.

Go, Dragon, go, he thought. Dive, turn, dive some more, turn the other way, all on one lone shaft, while two FM sonars and a radar-equipped plane extended electronic talons deep into the sea, hungrily grasping for one little blip.

The searchlight above and behind Gar went out, and then came the underwater explosions on either side as his sweeper's depth charges exploded.

Shallow, he thought. Much too shallow. These guys were excited; they'd failed to think it through. The blasts raised tremendous waterspouts into the darkness, confirming the shallow settings. They were spectacular, but the ones that did the business had to get down to 300 feet if you wanted to see debris, bodies, dead fish, and fuel oil erupting to the surface. He felt the sweeper slowing down as they waited to see what happened next.

Something kicked his right shoe, and he heard some more rapid-fire Japanese. It sounded like two men were arguing, probably over whether to keep his inert body on board or just pitch it over the side.

A third voice joined in, an older, deeper voice, ringing with authority. He heard two almost simultaneous *"Hai!"* Argument settled, orders given. He continued to play dead, although he wasn't sure that he really wanted to go back into the cold water. As he felt hands grasping at his wet trousers and shirt, a powerful explosion went off *under* the sweeper and split it into two pieces. A Cutie? The shock knocked the men who'd been grabbing at his clothes off their feet and, he was pretty sure, right over the side. Gar wasn't hurt because they'd just lifted him a few inches off the deck when the Dragon's farewell gift swam silently in from behind and killed the sweeper.

One thought stuck in his mind as he tumbled back into the sea: They'd made it. They'd evaded, then sent up the acoustic homer to go find some Japanese iron. Or, in this case, wood. Then another thought occurred to him: Or had his sweeper hit a mine? He looked up over his shoulder as the front half of the sweeper leaned over and subsided into the sea with the rest of them.

The rest of them.

There were several Japanese swimming away from the wreck in the darkness. Gar couldn't see them, but he could definitely hear them. It sounded like officers were telling their people to get out of there, and then he remembered why. There were depth charges on board, and once they left port, the Japs always carried them armed.

He tried to swim away, too, but discovered that his muscles were not going to cooperate very much. His life jacket, still partially inflated, got in the way. The best he could manage was a miserable dog paddle into the dark, away from the sinking ship, the pooling diesel fuel, and all those Japs. He'd been on the bow when the explosion hit, so any remaining depth charges ought to be in the other direction. He turned to his right and paddled harder, trying to quash the nausea rising in his stomach from the fumes. His legs felt like cold rubber, and he was having trouble concentrating. A couple of times he forgot why he was swimming away from the wreckage, where there ought to be pieces to hang on to. It had been a minesweeper. There'd be wood. Of course, the Japs would figure that out, too, and he'd have to expect a fairly hostile welcome if he tried that.

He felt rather than saw or heard a distant underwater explosion.

Not a depth charge, but something else, similar to what they felt when one of their own torpedoes went off in the guts of a Jap ship a mile away. There was a second explosion, muted, as if deeper. Had the Dragon hit a mine? Gar didn't want to think about that. Except there shouldn't have been mines there. Too deep.

Suddenly a white light flooded the area. Between that and the saltwater in his eyes, he couldn't see a thing. He felt the pressure of a bow wave coming, and soon another wooden hull was bumping along beside him. Once again he heard jabbering topside, and then a bowline dropped down in front of him. Instinctively he slipped into it and was unceremoniously hauled aboard like a stinky fish, which he probably resembled at that point. Once he flopped down on the deck he heard several hissing intakes of breath. He didn't help matters by rolling over on his side and puking all over their nice wooden deck. By then there were more shouts from alongside, and they went back to work; one guy who looked like a sumo wrestler sat on his haunches, staring at Gar like he was considering the best way to turn him into chum.

They worked at picking up more survivors from the other minesweeper while Gar lay curled up on the deck in his own effluent. Unless the Dragon was still in the area, setting up for another homing torpedo attack, they were all probably safe for the moment. As his mind cleared in the cold night air, he realized he had real problems here. If they figured out that they'd caught the commanding officer of a U.S. submarine, Gar was bound for a torture chamber somewhere in Tokyo. He was pretty sure his jumpsuit had no indications of rank on it, but he was wearing a khaki uniform shirt underneath, complete with shiny silver oak leaves. The minesweeper crew might not know that meant he was a commander, USN, but someone ashore probably would.

He opened his eyes to see if the sumo was still staring at him. He was gone. As surreptitiously as possible he got the oak leaves unsnapped and quietly disposed of over the side, but that still left a clear indication that there had been rank insignia on his shirt. Then he remembered his lucky charm, his CPO insignia.

He curled up into an even tighter ball over in the shadows of the bow while the crew looked for more people in the water. It took him a few minutes to get the CPO insignia off his penknife chain and onto one collar of his shirt.

It might work, he thought. He was the right age to be a chief petty officer. Then he remembered his dolphins, pinned above his left shirt pocket flap. They were gold. A chief's would have been silver. Would they know that? They weren't polished and, in fact, were pretty tarnished. Still, it was a lingering detail.

Suddenly hands were jerking him off the deck and into a semi-standing position, followed by a blast from a fire hose to wash the diesel fuel and his own various secretions off. His face must have been really foul, because they spent some time blasting him in the face with that hose. When that was over, a diminutive officer wearing white gloves and carrying a 5-foot-long bamboo stick that Gar thought was longer than the Jap was tall walked up to him and began a methodical beating the likes of which Gar had never had in the boxing ring. He later found out that the ends of the bamboo had been split into six segments to add to the effect. He screamed the whole time at Gar, who ended up curled back into a quivering ball with his whole hide on fire. It would have been far worse had Gar not been wearing his exposure jumpsuit.

When that was finally over, they threw him literally down the hatch into the bosun's locker up in the bow of the minesweeper, where he landed on coils of marline, hemp, mooring line, rags, cans of paint, manila mats and fenders, and bales of canvas. The hatch slammed down, and Gar was blissfully unattended. He passed out, almost gratefully.

Reveille came some unknown hours later in the form of a bucket of cold seawater. Gar couldn't move—every muscle in his body was black and blue from that bamboo massage. The big sumo guy came down the ladder, grabbed him by his jumpsuit, and threw him *up* the ladder and out onto the deck. That should have hurt a lot, but Gar couldn't tell the difference. There stood his good friend, the bamboo man, who did it all again, accompanied by loud screaming and chantlike noises each time he swung his magic stick, which was often. Gar did notice it was late daylight and snowing, and they were coming into a harbor of some kind. Actually, he recognized it. He was back at Kure. Physically, but not for much longer mentally.

The next time he came to he was in what he thought was a ship's steel compartment. It also felt like there were other people there, but he couldn't see them. His eyes had been beaten shut. He tried to open them, but it wasn't happening beyond the aching slit stage. He could see a little bit out of his right eye, but not his left. His nose was so full of clotted blood that he had to breathe through his mouth, and that hurt his teeth. He didn't know how much time had passed since he'd been picked up and beaten half to death on the minesweeper.

"Easy, mate," an Aussie or possibly British voice said next to him. "Easy, now."

Gar managed a subdued grunt.

"Beat you fair and proper, they did," the voice said. "Yank, right?"

Gar grunted again.

"Saw those dolphins on yer shirt," the voice said. "Know where you are, then, mate?"

Two grunts.

"Yer on the bloody great *Shinano*, you are. Can I make a suggestion?"

One grunt.

Gar felt the man's fingers relieving him of the gold-plated dolphins.

"These here'll get you a samurai chop, they will. Yer submarines are fair killing them, in more ways than one. There was one here the other night, by God. Sank two destroyers. Peppered the whole shipyard with a barge-worth of ammo. Blew up the caisson, this whole bloody ship we're on went off its blocks, banged in the bow, chipped a screw, flooded out a machinery room. These are gold, ain't they?"

One grunt.

"Was that you lot, then?"

One grunt.

"Brilliant," he said, obviously impressed. Then his accent changed. "Look at me," he said quietly.

Gar tried. His right eye was the only working option. He focused, but nothing happened. Then it did.

A smiling Japanese face was staring right at him. "Fair dinkum," it said, in a perfect New South Wales accent.

Gar knew he was fucked.

"Captain, isn't it?" it said.

Truly fucked.

The Jap read Gar's mind and, with a vicious smile, nodded his agreement with Gar's all too obvious assessment.

EIGHTEEN

ComSubPac Headquarters, Pearl Harbor

Admiral Lockwood stood behind his desk with a pained expression on his face, a message clutched in his hand. This was potentially a real disaster. *Dragonfish* had reported in after getting clear of Bungo Suido and the minesweeper trap. She'd been damaged by the aircraft attack and was limping back to Guam. That wasn't the big news. The big news was that Gar Hammond had been lost overboard in the process of an emergency dive. That led to an even bigger question: Had he been killed or had he been captured? If he'd been captured, and they made him talk as only the Japs could do, the entire war effort might be in great jeopardy, because submarine captains were privy to the fact that navy cryptographers were reading the Japanese navy's message traffic.

"We have to assume he's been captured," he said. "You know, always assume the worst."

Forrester nodded. "Have we informed PacFleet?"

Lockwood shook his head. "I'm gonna have to go up to Makalapa and do this one personally with Chester Nimitz. Christ on a goddamned crutch. If they find out about ULTRA . . ."

Forrester got up and started pacing around Lockwood's spacious office.

"Nimitz will remember Hammond, won't he," he said. "Of all the skippers . . ."

Lockwood turned toward him. "You really don't like Hammond, do you, Mike?"

"No, sir, I do not. Much too much ego, insubordinate, disrespectful, and generally a pain in the ass. With all the quality people we have waiting in the wings, it would just *have* to be a guy like that who's now got the most important secret of the war in his hands. *Jesus!*"

"Yet he managed to get a boat into the Inland Sea," Lockwood pointed out, "through the graveyard of Bungo Suido, and then all the way to the piers at Kure. And back out again, almost, anyway. That's no small accomplishment."

"When they start pulling his teeth out one at a time with red-hot rusty pliers, we'll see about that," Forrester said.

Lockwood, somewhat surprised by the intensity of Forrester's animus toward Hammond, shook his head. "I've never, ever, hoped and prayed for someone's death, but just now . . . okay, call my driver. I've got to go up the hill."

"I'll get a message off to *Dragonfish*," Forrester said. "Get more details on what happened, and their thoughts on survivability. It is December, and Japan's a cold goddamned place in the winter."

Lockwood, his lips compressed into a thin, flat line, reached for his brass hat.

The Inland Sea of Japan

As it turned out, it was something so trivial it was almost heart-breaking that had given him away: the two letters CO stenciled on the back of Gar's exposure suit. The gold dolphins hadn't helped, because Gar's name was engraved on the back. The Japanese officer who happily explained all this to him spoke colloquial English, in various dialects, and boasted of having seven other languages besides. He was a perfect mimic and proud of it. He was also an officer in the Kempeitai, which was ostensibly the gendarmerie, or MPs, of the Imperial Japanese Army. According to SubPac briefings, however, they were really a Japanese version of the German Gestapo. This one was in his late thirties, wearing an army uniform with prominent black stripes, and he appeared to be quite fit.

Gar tried to look around. There were several other prisoners, each sitting with his back to a bulkhead, hands tied behind him, and each blindfolded with a dirty rag. His captor lit up a cigarette for himself and offered Gar one. Gar shook his head, gingerly. He didn't want it falling off.

"Know where you are, Captain?" the Jap asked.

Gar recalled him saying Shin-something, but that meant nothing to him. Unh-unh, he grunted.

"You are onboard His Imperial Majesty's newest aircraft carrier, *Shinano*!" he said, crying out the last word with great pride. "The largest carrier in the entire world. Was that why your submarine was sent here? To sink *Shinano*? Can't be done, you know. Not by a single submarine, anyway. Especially with your puny torpedoes. You did frighten everyone, I'll give you that. But sink this ship? Never!"

Gar said nothing.

"Listen carefully, Captain. There are, of course, things we need to know, but we will not pursue those things here and now. Later, in Tokyo. You are going to Ofuna, our navy's special information center. Ofuna has, how shall I put this, experts in information retrieval. Especially when it comes to submarine officers, of which we see so few. I have been assigned to escort you to them. This ship is preparing to sail soon, to go from Kure to the Yokosuka naval arsenal for final fitting out. This is also how you will journey to Ofuna. Okay?"

Gar nodded, wincing at the way his neck bones creaked. Stick to grunting, he thought. The Jap shifted to his version of a British accent. Showing off.

"Excellent, my good man. Look here, I have a proposal for you. We shall treat each other with respect, as officers of similar rank. We are not friends, of course. We are enemies. But for now, for this voyage, we can have a truce, if you agree. I will not interrogate you or subject you to any more, um, physical stimulation. You will not attempt to escape or to inflict sabotage. In fact, I will give you a tour of this great ship. I want you to understand that Japan is *not* defeated, that we are *much* stronger than you Americans think we are. Do you agree to behave? Will you give me your word, then, as an officer?"

Why the hell not, Gar thought. This was probably some clever Asian ploy to gain his confidence, bind Gar to his protector, and then suck up some intelligence on the sly. Fair enough. That was his job. Gar's job was to give name, rank, and serial number, and otherwise keep from getting killed if at all possible. The fact that they knew he'd been the captain of the sub that had savaged Kure was probably what was keeping him alive right now. They had to wonder how that had happened. Captains knew things, and there was plenty of time afterward for reprisals.

"I give you my word," Gar said, muffling his sibilants through wobbly teeth.

"What is your name, rank, and serial number, please?"

Gar recited.

His captor called in Japanese to two soldiers standing nearby. They came, lifted Gar up, and helped him limp out of the compartment and into a long passageway. Both eyes were working again, sort of, anyway, which was a relief. The deck was not tiled, as was the case with USN ships. It was shiny steel. Gar also noticed that there were no watertight doors where he would have expected hatches, but then he realized they might be well above the waterline, where hatches would be superfluous.

He was delivered to what looked like an unoccupied officer's stateroom. It was barely furnished, with a single two-tiered bunk bed, a desk, a chair, a washbasin, and a locker. The room was perhaps 6 feet wide and 10 long. There was a ventilation duct in the overhead, and a telephone handset was mounted on the wall. They sat him down in the chair. Gar put his stinging hands in his lap and waited for whatever was coming next.

Moments later a steward showed up, or at least that's how he was dressed—white cotton trousers under a white tunic, wooden sandals on his feet. He was extremely deferential in the presence of the Kempeitai officer, never once raising his eyes off the deck. He proffered a wooden tray with some rice balls, a cup of what Gar assumed was tea, and a small stack of hot, damp white cloths. Gar's captor indicated for him to put the tray on the desk. The steward then backed out of the stateroom, bowing repeatedly as he went.

"I will leave now," Gar's escort said. "Clean yourself, eat something, rest. I will return in two hours."

"What is your name, please?" Gar asked.

The man hesitated. "That is strictly forbidden," he said finally. "Wait, I know. You may call me Charlie Chan."

Gar looked at him through puffy eyes. "Charlie Chan is a *Chinese* master detective," he said.

"True," he said. "But we have conquered them, too, yes? And you're next, of course."

He stepped out into the passageway, then closed and quietly locked the door. Gar sat there for a moment, taking stock. All this civility, now food and hot cloths, a stateroom—so why did he feel like a steer in a Nebraska feedlot? Go ahead, eat up. Eat as much as you want. We insist. Really, we do.

On that famous other hand, he could be tied in chains down in the bilges somewhere, subsisting on whatever water dripped down through the gratings from a leaky steam line. He knew this was a game of some kind, but he also knew his responsibilities here: maintain strength if possible, tell them nothing of value, and escape if he could. So he gratefully used all the hot cloths, drank the tea, and gobbled the sticky rice balls. Then he lay down in the rack, a maneuver that took a few minutes. The two beatings had been expertly administered to inflict as much bruising as possible. The food and tea helped but were no substitute for a handful of APCs. He forced himself to ignore the pain and to go to sleep immediately, wondering if they were at sea already. If this thing was as big as she'd looked through the snow the other night, one might never know.

He awoke not two but eight hours later, according to his watch. He was surprised they hadn't taken it. The stateroom was dark, with the only light coming from the passageway outside, streaming through a tiny ventilation grate above the door. He tried to move but couldn't. A moment of panic—had they tied him up? Then he realized it was his muscles that were tied up, having been well and truly tenderized by that furious banshee on the minesweeper.

Eventually he did manage to get up and find a light switch and the basin. He tried to make some water come out of the single tap, but there was only the hiss of air going the other way. The water line wasn't activated. He wondered how much more of this behemoth wasn't finished yet. The passageway outside the door was quiet, but there were things, industrial things, going on throughout the ship. He tried to feel whether they were moving, but concluded they were still parked alongside the pier.

Fifteen minutes later he heard the lock click in the door, and then Charlie Chan was back. He'd changed uniform and was wearing a light jacket this time. The two guards were right behind him, standing at loose attention out in the passageway.

"What ho, Captain," he chirped. "I say, you do look a frightful mess."

British Charlie Chan. Gar tried to think of something witty but ended up just staring at him.

"It's time we had a tour, you and I. First, the jakes, eh, what? Then a tour of His Imperial Majesty's most amazing new ship."

He spat out something in Japanese, and one of the goons came in and slipped a pair of handcuffs on Gar. They were steel rings but with what felt like a silk cloth between them, long enough that he could have put his hands in his pockets if he'd wanted to. They then attached what looked like a white leash to his left hand and handed the other end to Charlie Chan.

"A few rules," Charlie said. "First, you must walk behind me, no closer than two feet. You must keep your eyes cast down except when I show you something I specifically want you to observe. If one of the crew or the shipyard workers says something to you, you are to keep silent and not look him in the face. And otherwise, do not speak. Okay?"

He stepped out of the stateroom and tugged on the leash. Gar followed him down to the head, where he was unleashed to make morning ablutions. Gar pretended not to notice that his urine was red. Before they left the head, he was handed a loose white garment resembling the top half of a kimono. There were Japanese characters emblazoned on the back. Then they headed what felt like forward because the deck was sloping gently upward. There were others in the passageway, and Gar thought he heard soft hisses and giggles as they went by, the Kempeitai officer with his American dog in attendance. Gar did as he had been told and kept his eyes down and his trap shut. He was much taller than everyone around him but felt considerably smaller. One goon led the procession, the other stayed behind Gar, carrying a heavy wooden baton. Gar could just imagine what those characters on the silk jacket said.

They climbed three ladders and then went through a hatch into what had to be the hangar bay. Charlie Chan stopped and told Gar to look around. It was pretty amazing. They were at the back end of the hangar bay, which stretched ahead of them for at least three football fields in length. There were no planes, but the hangar was filed with industrial gear—small tractors, welding machines, cable reels—and a cast of thousands, sailors and shipyard workers, milling about in seeming confusion. There were two large squares of light in the overhead, 50 feet on a side, embedded in what had to be the flight deck some 60 feet above where they were standing. Gar assumed these were elevator access holes, although he didn't see the elevators themselves.

"Three hundred planes," Charlie boasted. "And more on the flight deck. All along here, machine shops, repair facilities, elevators to the rooms below with ammunition and spare parts. Much bigger than your Essex class, yes?"

Gar nodded. He'd been aboard one Essex-class carrier in Pearl, and he'd thought that was pretty damn big, but this was overwhelming. He looked up at the sky through those two big squares and was surprised to see the clouds moving aft. His surprise must have shown.

"Ah, yes, Captain, we are at sea. Still inside the Seto, but soon we leave for Tokyo and your new place of residence. Amazing, isn't it? You cannot feel her move, she is so big."

Of course, the Inland Sea was perfectly flat. It would be interesting to feel her movements once out in the greater North Pacific Ocean, Gar thought. Or once she had to conduct evasive maneuvers while trying to get by all the waiting subs. Maybe even *Dragon-*

fish, assuming she hadn't joined all those other boats asleep in the deeps of Bungo Suido.

They proceeded up four flights of stairs, or ladders, in navy parlance. That brought them out onto the flight deck and into a wintry breeze and cold gray sunlight. They were definitely still in the Inland Sea, surrounded by small green islands. Even in winter, it was gorgeous. The ship was steaming into the wind, with thin trails of boiler smoke coming out of two oddly canted funnels that leaned out to starboard, away from the flight deck. There were a few hundred men working on the flight deck, welding in tie-downs, installing safety nets, and bolting on HF antennas out on the deck edges. As they walked past the after elevator aperture, Gar could see that the flight deck was armored—it looked like 4 inches of solid steel. Charlie Chan saw him looking. "Yes, Captain, armored steel flight deck. Stop a one-thousand-pound bomb."

"That must make her very top-heavy," Gar said.

"So I was told, " Charlie said. "Supposed to be two hangar decks, but she would not have been stable in that configuration. *Shinano* is a conversion."

"Really?"

"Yes. She is sister to *Musashi* and *Yamato*. Do you know those ships?"

Gar smiled at him. The Japanese had kept those two battleships secret right into 1943. They were the biggest battlewagons ever built, 70,000 tons and 18-inch guns. *Shinano* had probably started building as a third in the class and then, after their disaster at Midway, the Japanese had opted to finish her as a carrier.

"Yes, we know about those ships," Gar said. "Also very big." He decided not to mention that one of them, *Musashi*, had been sunk. Charlie seemed highly edified that he even knew about them by name. No reason to spoil his good mood.

They continued their walk up the starboard side of the flight deck, heads bent into the rising wind, while the shipyard workers and ship's officers gawked at the spectacle of the policeman leading a captive with a leash for a tour around the ship's expansive upper works. By now Gar really wanted to know what had been embroidered on the back of his *hopi* coat, because there was derisive laughter after they passed by the groups of workers.

They walked to the very forward end of the flight deck, admiring the beautiful scenery ashore, which looked more like a painting than an actual countryside. A few small fishing boats darted right in front of the big ship's bow in order to cut off pursuing devils. Gar wondered if Hashimoto was out on one of them, patiently waiting for the paper rain. He also remembered Hashimoto describing the Kempeitai police as hated and treacherous dogs. Gar was under no illusions about Charlie Chan becoming his best buddy. He was counting coup, parading the captured skipper of an American sub as his poodle.

"No catapults?" Gar asked him over the buffeting of the wind. His flimsy coat was not built for warmth.

"No need," Charlie said, indicating the thousand feet or so of flight deck behind them. With a stiff wind over the bow from the ship's own speed, even a loaded dive-bomber could probably make a takeoff run with ease. Gar saw Charlie looking up at the windows of the bridge on the island structure amidships. Someone was waving to him in the peculiar fashion of the Far East, fingers down in a come-here motion.

"Ah," Charlie said. "Let us meet Captain Abe, captain of *Shinano*. He will be very much interested in meeting you."

Gar was already pretty tired and cold. It felt as if damned near every muscle in his body was in spasm, and he was having a tough time walking and climbing all those ladders. Nevertheless, up they went.

Captain Abe was of average height for a Japanese and looked to be about fifty years old. He was gray and grizzled and had a face that fairly shouted *no nonsense*. He was wearing blues, his dress cap, and white gloves. Several officers were standing around on the bridge, while a navigation team was quietly doing the piloting as the great ship threaded its way through all the small islands and channels. Quartermasters manned both bridge wings and called in bearings to known points ashore every three minutes.

Gar stood the required two steps behind Charlie as he explained to Abe who, and presumably what, he had on the other end of the leash. He heard the word "Ofuna" again and watched the officers smile. Apparently Ofuna had itself a reputation, Gar thought. He was very conscious of his leash, but he kept his eyes down. He kept telling himself that this was still better than being in the bowels of the ship with the other slaves.

"Captain Abe requests to know the name of your submarine," Charlie said.

At this point Gar had a decision to make. Stick with the name, rank, and serial number, or answer innocuous questions like this and then begin to feed them some misinformation when the right opportunity presented itself.

"*Dragonfish*," he said, and Charlie translated. Abe said something in Japanese.

"Balao class," Charlie translated. Now it was Abe showing off. Gar nodded but was careful not to look directly at him. Abe spoke again.

"How many submarines will we face on the way to Yokosuka?" Charlie translated.

"Ten," Gar said without hesitation. "The waters this side of the Japanese Islands have been divided into ten patrol areas. Some have one submarine, some a wolf pack. It will be an interesting journey."

Charlie looked at him for a long moment before translating. Abe laughed and grunted out a short comment. The other officers also laughed.

"He says, nice try," Charlie reported. Gar continued to stare down at the deck.

Abe went over to a small desk next to the bridge's captain's chair. He opened the desk and withdrew a pistol, which he brought over to where they were standing. Then he asked Charlie a question. Charlie translated.

"Captain Abe wishes to know if you would like to kill yourself now. You are totally dishonored. He will grant you that privilege because you were a commanding officer. You can even use his pistol. Out there, on the bridge wing, where there are drains."

The bridge went quiet. They were all staring at Gar now, with his leash and multihued, battered face. Gar took care with his words.

"Tell Captain Abe that for us, capture is an unfortunate but temporary circumstance. There is no dishonor in being captured."

Abe snorted after hearing Charlie's translation, and some other officers laughed their contempt. Then he spoke again.

"You have no concept of honor, American dog. You are correct about your position being temporary. Since you will not kill yourself, we will have to do it for you. Temporary, yes. This I know."

"May I speak?" Gar asked Charlie. Abe gestured that he could with a contemptuous wave of his gloved hand.

Charlie translated as Gar made his reply.

"This is what *I* know," he said. "In 1942, Japan was supreme in the western Pacific. Now, what's left of your overseas armies are starving in Malaya, destroyed in New Guinea, and expelled from the Solomon Islands, which even you renamed the Starvation Islands. Rabaul is lost. Tarawa is lost. Kwajalein is lost. Guam and Tinian are lost. The Philippines have been invaded. Okinawa has been bombed. Here in Japan, the flow of oil and food and rubber and tin and coal has been cut to ten percent of what you had coming in 1942.

"You have this one magnificent carrier, and it is very impressive, but it is one carrier. Admiral Halsey has forty-two Essex carriers and thirty-five smaller ones. He is coming with a fleet of five hundred ships. The American navy has more than ten *thousand* ships. Soon Japan itself will be lost. And yes, Captain, you *will* run a gauntlet of American submarines if you try to get to Yokosuka."

Charlie Chan had been slowing down a bit as Gar recited the Japs' real strategic circumstances. Gar still was not looking Abe in the face; he had a gun in his hand and, Gar suspected, a thunderous expression. No point in giving him an excuse. When Charlie stopped speaking, Abe exploded into a torrent of angry Japanese.

"None of this is true," Charlie translated. "None of it. Tokyo has told us repeatedly of great victories, of hundreds of American ships sunk, *your* armies dying in the jungles like insects, your airplanes littering the Pacific Ocean. What you say is lies, all lies."

"Do you go to Tokyo with a full load of fuel, Captain?" Gar asked. "Is there plenty of food aboard? Dozens of airplanes?"

Charlie hesitated. Abe saw that and pressed him, then hissed in annoyance. He gave a short, sharp order and turned away.

"That is none of your business, prisoner," Charlie said, but looking nervous for the first time. "You are correct. There is much to be done. He has ordered me to put you to work."

He passed the leash to one of the goons, who pulled Gar forcefully off the bridge and toward a succession of ladders pointing down into the depths of the ship. The last sight Gar had of Captain Abe was of him slapping the barrel of that pistol into his open palm, as if trying to decide what to do with it.

Oh, well, nice while it lasted, he thought.

NINETEEN

They went down seven sets of ladders, which meant they were nine decks below the carrier's bridge. They ended up on a mezzanine deck somewhere under the hangar bay. The main engineering spaces were right below them, and this deck contained auxiliary machinery, ventilation fan rooms, motor generator rooms, and a host of other smaller spaces arranged along a passageway on the starboard side of the ship. There Gar joined the rest of the prisoners, who numbered about fifty. They were divided into groups of five, with a Japanese marine in charge of each group.

Gar's personal goon pointed him at a group of four. When he joined them he was handed a wooden mallet, a blunted chisel, and a basket of oakum fiber. Their job was plain to see: stuff the oakum into every bulkhead penetration in front of them, and then hammer it tight around the cable, pipe, or wire bundle coming through the hole in the vertical bulkhead. As in warships the world over, there were hundreds of penetrations through the bulkheads between adjacent spaces. None of these appeared to have the simple metal device the U.S. Navy used to ensure watertight integrity, called a stuffing tube. On this ship there was just a drilled hole, and they were stuffing it with oakum, as had been done in the seventeenth century. If the space ahead of where they were working ever flooded for any reason, the water would soon be pouring into this space. In damage control parlance, that was called progressive flooding, and it always had one, inevitable result. Oakum was a joke, a bad joke.

They stood on small stools to reach the cableway penetrations that ran along the overhead. Gar wondered why they were bothering. A stuffing tube anchors the caulking material between two metal collars that are permanently attached to the bulkhead. Water pressure on one side pressed the collar into the other side, sealing it. Hammering oakum into the holes gave the impression of sealing them, but he knew that with the first hint of real pressure all that oakum would pop right out, no matter how hard they hammered it. They were kidding themselves, especially if this compartment was below the waterline.

They were not allowed to speak to or even look at each other. Anyone caught looking around got whacked on the head by the ever-ready bamboo baton. Still, Gar could see that most of the prisoners were Allied soldiers or sailors, dressed in the tattered remnants of various uniforms. They were all considerably thinner than he was and bore the many scars of the Japanese army's hostile indifference toward POWs. In retrospect Gar realized that the captain's offer to let him shoot himself should not have come as a surprise. Wait until the B-29s come, he thought.

His thoughts were interrupted by sharp commands from the guards. They picked up their baskets and went single file into the next compartment, where they set to work hammering oakum into the other side of their previous efforts. The senior guard finally spotted Gar's wristwatch and then quickly relieved him of it.

Hours later they were all herded back up several ladders and out into the cavernous hangar bay. From there they were marched to the very back end of the hangar bay, through a long passageway, and out onto the fantail of the carrier. The flight deck extended overhead, supported by crisscrossed I-beams rising out of the steel of the main deck. There they were made to sit in ranks against the final bulkhead, their backs to the cold steel, and their hands in their laps. One of the goons came along the line of sitting men and inspected their hands to make sure they were empty. They showed him palms up, palms down, and then dropped their hands back into their laps. If one didn't do it fast enough, the guard would reward him with a smack on the elbow from his baton.

Once the hand inspection was complete, the guards clapped handcuffs on each man and passed a steel wire through all the handcuffs, which was then shackled to the deck at each end. After a while two mess cooks came out onto the fantail area, each carrying a wooden tray. The men were allowed to take two rice balls apiece, each impregnated with a single drop of soy sauce. Once the rice had been distributed, the team came back with a black pot and a large copper dipper. They each got to drink one dipper of water.

From the looks on the goon squad's faces, the POWs were being positively pampered, even though they were outside on a weather deck, sitting against cold steel with no coats or jackets. The sun was going down, illuminating nearby islands and the distant shore with a cold, metallic light. They could see two destroyers plowing along in the carrier's expansive wake. It looked to Gar like they were making 20 knots. The props below them vibrated more than Gar would have expected for a brand-new ship. An occasional puff of stack gas whipped across the fantail, making their eyes water. The goons stood against the lifelines stretched across the very back of the fantail area, four of them, dressed out in padded vests, woolen trousers, Japanese army caps, and black gloves and carrying their ever-present batons.

As full darkness came, Gar felt movement along the line, as everybody began pressing into the center of the line of sitting men for mutual warmth. A small red light came on above them; it was mounted under the flight deck so as not to show beyond the edges of the deck. The smell of cooking food wafted back along the deck, and the guards, after a final check of the wire, went into a small guardroom just forward of the fantail area. They left the hatch open so they could keep an eye on their charges.

Gar was sore, cold, dead tired, and depressed, and this was just his first day in captivity. Some of these guys were wearing what looked like British uniforms, which meant that they could have been shipped back to the Home Islands from Singapore. That city had fallen almost three years ago. That was not an encouraging thought, nor were his prospects once they got to Tokyo. The Japs had to know the U.S. submarines were strangling them. A captured skipper would be made to sing in detail, and then he would be beheaded. Or maybe just beheaded. On that happy note, he fell asleep.

SubPac Headquarters, Pearl Harbor

It was almost seven thirty before Admiral Lockwood got back to his headquarters.

"How'd the boss take the news?" Forrester asked.

"I think he aged a year right in front of me," Lockwood said. "But after we'd kicked it around for a while, we decided there was nothing to be done. If they break him, they'll either change their codes or they won't. If they do, we'll break 'em again."

"That's easier said than done, I suspect," Forrester said. "Why wouldn't they change their codes? Disinformation?"

"Sure. They're Japs. You know, clever Oriental bastards. If they find out we're reading their message traffic, then they could start throwing in some bullshit, like a fake transit route of the next carrier deployment. Get us to deploy subs—right into a minefield we didn't know about."

"Oh, boy."

"As Nimitz pointed out, we don't even know if he's been captured," Lockwood said. "The waters out there, off Japan? In December? How long would someone floating around survive? An hour? It's not like he's going to swim to the nearest Jap destroyer."

Forrester thought the admiral was starting to whistle past the graveyard. "There's no way in hell to predict what he'll tell them, if anything," he said. "Knowing Hammond, he'll probably sing like a canary and baffle them with so much bullshit they won't know what to believe."

"One can always hope," the admiral said. "Any word on what happened to that carrier?"

"Weather's prevented the air force from getting any aerial photography. Snow, low cloud cover, the usual excuses."

"Oh, c'mon, now, Mike, what good's a camera when it's snowing, right? They'll get out there. Tell me about the deployments for the Lingayen Gulf landings."

"Uh, yes, sir," Forrester said, glancing at his watch. "I can get a briefer up here, but it's almost twenty hundred . . . ?"

"Jesus, is it? Okay, tomorrow will do." He went to the small mahogany cabinet in the corner of his office and retrieved a bottle of bourbon. He offered a glass to Forrester, who declined. Whiskey made his liver hurt.

"Is this goddamned war ever going to end?" Lockwood asked, looking out the windows at the muted lights around the Pearl Harbor lagoon. "Talk about time on the cross."

"Think how it must be for the POWs out there in Asia," Forrester said. "We know this has to end sometime, but they have no idea."

Lockwood raised his glass. "Here's to Gar Hammond, then. Let's hope and pray he holds."

TWENTY

The next day began at predawn. Each man was forced to get up and walk to the lifelines at the back of the fantail. Below the lifelines were woven-steel safety nets, installed to catch anyone falling or being blown off the flight deck above by prop wash or a gust of wind. They were then made to get down into the nets in groups of three.

Welcome to the POW head.

When everyone had had a chance to relieve himself, three prisoners were detailed to man a fire hose and wash down the netting. Gar noticed that the fire-main pressure wasn't very impressive. U.S. Navy fire mains ran at least at 100 psi; these looked far more anemic. Once again he wondered how much work remained to be done before this ship would be truly ready for sea. He could guess why they were moving her: B-29 photo-recce birds, and then a submarine attack. The naval bases near Tokyo were probably much better defended than these beautiful islands. He jumped when a baton landed between his shoulders. No looking around. Yes, boss, got it.

Breakfast was a repeat of dinner. Two rice balls, with no soy this time, and a single ladle of warm tea. Then a long hike back down belowdecks to continue caulking the cable penetrations. During the night he'd managed to get some information from the guys on either side of him. The prisoners were a collection of army guys from the Southeast Asian theater. They'd been brought from camps in Malaya, Borneo, the Dutch Indonesian islands, and even China.

Gar was apparently the only American, and they already knew that he had been the skipper of a submarine. How they knew that he couldn't fathom. He was surprised to learn that they thought they were getting better treatment here on board this ship than in the camps from which they had been sent.

They spent the day back down in the bowels of the ship, still hammering oakum. There was no midday meal, only a ladle of water every three hours. Then back to the fantail for another night in the cold. One of the prisoners had developed a vicious hacking cough. Three guards took him away before everyone else went on the wire, and they never saw him again. They doubted the guards took him to sick bay. The other guys had been working at a copper mine before this job. They said that anyone who got seriously ill was usually thrown down one of the abandoned shafts. The other prisoners would then be made to shovel ore into the shaft until they could no longer hear the man screaming.

"They're not human," Gar commented to his wire mate.

"Neither are we, sunshine. Not anymore."

When they woke the next morning, the carrier was anchored off the Kure naval arsenal and already surrounded by a dozen barges bringing supplies, fuel, more oakum, in bales this time, and what looked like a variety of electric motors, pumps, and refrigeration machinery. In peacetime a ship as large as an aircraft carrier would take up to two years to fit out, which was the process of installing the tons and tons of equipment needed to turn her into a warship. It was apparent to Gar that they were in a hell of hurry to get her out of here, and the POWs joined the lines of sailors hauling stuff on board from all the barges into the hangar bay for the rest of the day. Gar noticed the one thing they did not bring aboard was any sort of fresh food.

That evening as they were assembled for the wire, Charlie Chan appeared on the fantail and gave orders to the goons. Gar was rousted out of the line before the rice balls came, which hurt his feelings. One goon ahead, one astern, Charlie and Gar in the middle, and with Gar back on his familiar leash, they went forward into the hangar bay and then climbed what seemed like an endless series of ladders. Charlie said nothing to him this time until they reached the bridge, which was full of people. It was obvious the ship was getting ready to heave up the anchor and get under way again. They perched Gar on a binocular storage box out on the port bridge wing, with stereo goons in attendance. Charlie reported to Captain Abe, who looked over at him and made an annoyed face. He said something in Japanese to Charlie, who bowed several times and backed away as if he'd been caught crapping on the deck.

"What did you do?" Gar asked when Charlie came out onto the bridge wing.

"I did what he told me to," he said. "He told me to bring you up here."

"Seems to be in a bad mood today."

"He is very angry, but not at you. You are a distraction. He says the ship is not ready to go to sea, but that Tokyo is insisting. There was another B-29 today. They fear a major bombing raid."

Gar thought of several clever things to say but kept his mouth shut. Charlie noticed.

"Did they feed you tonight?"

Gar shook his head.

Charlie bowed slightly. "I am sorry. No one has eaten. There is no electricity in the main galleys. Something happened."

"In my navy, we'd say they are working on it."

He nodded. "Yes, they are. If there is no food soon, some engineers will be shot."

That oughta do it, Gar thought. He could just imagine what his snipes would think of that logic. On the other hand, there probably would be food. Gar must have smiled, because Charlie asked him what he was thinking. Gar told him.

Charlie didn't smile, but his face did soften. He dismissed the goons and then just stood there, looking out over the bullrail. The sun was going down, and they could hear the clattering of the anchor chain from under the extended bow, nearly 500 feet away. Despite his perfect military bearing, Charlie looked apprehensive.

"What is your name, please?" Gar asked.

Charlie looked down and began to repeat that that was forbidden. Gar held up his hand, and Charlie stopped.

"We're going out to sea tonight, aren't we?" Gar asked.

Charlie nodded.

"We're going to die, then," Gar said. "I was telling the truth the other day. There are at least ten submarines waiting for us. Only one has to get lucky. This ship will never see Tokyo Bay. So: I would like to know your name."

"So you say," Charlie replied. "Captain Abe sent for you. He wants you to watch as we outrun all these imaginary submarines. If they do shoot torpedoes at us, they will bounce off. This ship began life as a battleship. Belowdecks there is heavy, heavy armor. Our Type 97 torpedoes could do some damage. But yours? I am told that half of them do not even explode."

He's got me there, Gar thought. The Bureau of Ordnance had finally admitted there was a problem with their fish and fixed them—but only after two *years* of complaints from the submarine force, with the bureau blaming all the problems on the submarine skippers. Apparently, the Japs weren't the only ones with a hidebound headquarters bureaucracy.

The wind freshened as the ship turned toward the west to go around Etajima and then head southeast for Bungo Suido. The city lights had been doused in Hiroshima, probably due to that B-29 recce flight, which reinforced Gar's notion that the Japs knew exactly what was coming one of these days in the form of an aluminum overcast. Captain Abe came out onto the bridge wing to study some navigation features. He looked Gar up and down as he sat forlornly on the binocular box, then snapped something at Charlie Chan.

"He says he is glad you will get to watch tonight. That once we leave Bungo Suido, your personal defeat and dishonor will be complete, as we outrun all those *hundreds* of submarines outside."

"Ask him what about the other submarine that came into the Seto with us. Does he know where she is hiding—and waiting?"

Charlie translated, and Abe did a double take. Gar didn't think that possibility had even crossed the captain's mind. Then he barked out a loud *Ha!* He said something in Japanese to the other officers. They all laughed in unison. Abe gave Gar a dismissive wave and went back into the pilothouse. Thirty minutes later they steamed around the western end of Etajima and were met by four destroyers. For all their scorn, it seemed they weren't letting *Shinano* sail anywhere all by herself. Two of the tin cans fell in ahead of the carrier, two astern. They picked up speed as they headed down toward the straits. The night was clear, but the islands they passed were all darkened, with no navigation aids illuminated. It was getting colder, and Gar was starting to shiver. Charlie went into the pilothouse and came back out with a quilted Chinese-style jacket for him. Gar put it on but was unable to button it up. His wrists stuck out of the sleeves a good eight inches. Charlie pretended not to notice. Gar knew he looked ridiculous, but he was very grateful for the coat. The lookouts, who were stationed up on the level above them, were wearing similar coats.

"Major Yamashita," Charlie said, suddenly. "My name is Yamashita. My uncle is a lieutenant general in the Imperial Army. He rules the Philippines."

Gar nodded. "Thank you," he said. He won't rule them for much longer, he thought. Dugout Doug MacArthur was on the move, at long last.

They passed through the Hoyo Strait without incident and then headed down into Bungo Suido. Three minesweepers were in line-abreast formation ahead of them now, and *Shinano* slowed to 5 knots so that they could follow in the sweepers' wakes. The after lookouts on the small wooden ships must have been apprehensive at the sheer size of the carrier following them through. The swept channel appeared to be right down the middle with two sharp turns halfway through. Gar could hear the navigation team gabbling away inside the pilothouse and lots of sharp *Hai*s and *Dozo*s from the bearing takers, who were manning alidades on the next level up. He couldn't see the bow of this ship; the flight deck extended over the forecastle area just as it spread over the fantail back aft. The two giant square holes in the flight deck gave the whole structure a weird appearance.

Gar wondered if his Dragon was lurking out ahead, waiting for them to come out. Or had those two distant booms been her death knell as she darted into a minefield they didn't know about? Gar had trouble picturing himself as the sole survivor. Major Yamashita had gone back into the pilothouse to watch the navigation through the minefields. It wasn't as if he had to guard him. It was a good 50 feet down to the armored steel flight deck, and nearly 80 more to the water if he decided to go over the starboard side. Besides, if they were going to run the torpedo gauntlet that Gar knew was out there, he'd much rather be up here than ten decks below.

Charlie came back out to the bridge wing bearing two flat boxes, the shape and size of cigar boxes.

"Eat," he said.

Gar had no idea of what he was eating, but it was surprisingly good, if distinctly fishy, and he finished every scrap, eating with his caulk-stained fingers.

"Thank you very much," he said. "You are very considerate."

Charlie—he had to quit calling him that—Major Yamashita seemed a bit embarrassed by that. "It will take all night to reach the approaches to Tokio-wan," he said. "I think Captain Abe wants you here for the whole trip."

"Fine by me," Gar said. "This is not a night to be belowdecks."

The major gave him an exasperated look. "Nothing will happen, Captain," he declared, but his tone of voice had a certain whistling-past-the-graveyard edge to it. That was reinforced by a sudden commotion inside the pilothouse. Major Yamashita eased closer to the door to see what the fuss was about. Then he sucked in a great quantity of air through his teeth.

"Radar," he said. "The radio room has detected submarine radar."

"Just one?" Gar asked innocently.

Yamashita grimaced. He was an army major out at sea on what had to be the most valuable submarine target of the war, and now he knew there was at least one American boat out there in the darkness with meat on its mind. The minesweepers fell off to one side as the carrier increased speed, followed by a broad turn to port. She'd begun a zigzag plan, and the tin cans up ahead generally were matching her movements. Just to add to the fun, a crescent moon appeared out of the cloud layer and lit up the sea. My kind of night, Gar thought. He tried to gauge her speed, but the ship was so big he really couldn't tell. That vibration was back, though. He could feel it trembling through the binocular box.

We did that, he thought. Damaged a propeller, blunted the bow. Maybe it'll slow her down. If she could run at full speed, and for a ship of this length that would be 30 knots or faster, none of their subs could ever end-around her. She'd have to run right over one to be in danger. That's what the Wounded Bear, IJN *Shokaku*, had done, run at 30 knots all the way home. By the time each of the American subs had detected her, she was already out of range and disappearing over the horizon.

Shinano leaned to port in a ponderous turn as she executed the preprogrammed zigzag plan. If the chase became a horse race, a zigzag plan was a double-edged sword. It could screw up a firing solution if the target made a wide course change just as the torpedoes were approaching. The truth was, however, that ships were usually going from Point A to Point B when they went to sea. Through some clever plotting techniques, American subs could determine the base course underlying the zigzag plan and prepare their own torpedo approach on that. Your target could twist and turn, but she would always end up making that base course over the ground, and effectively lose some speed of advance doing it. Drive up ahead of her if you could on that base course, and she'd eventually come right into the loving arms of your TDC and its lethal progeny, six hungry steamers.

Then there was more commotion in the pilothouse, with lots of excited reports coming up on their version of the bitch-box. At the same time, Gar heard some of the carrier's forced-draft blowers spooling down out on those Leaning Towers of Pisa that were her oversized stacks. The major was frowning as he listened. Gar guessed something had gone wrong down in one of the boiler rooms, because the ship was definitely slowing down. Gar pretended not to notice. They were two hours out of Bungo Suido, and this was prime hunting territory. *Archer-fish*, for instance. Gar knew that there were two, not ten, more patrol areas north of this area. If *Archer-fish* made a sighting but could not catch this big boy, she'd certainly flash the word by radio to the other two, but not before Joe Enright had taken at least one shot.

Gar was getting sleepy. He suspected he was the only one on the bridge that night who was. The unexpected food was probably to blame. He wanted to stay awake. This was probably the most unusual vantage point of the war—Japan's biggest carrier steaming into genuine Injun Country with a U.S. sub skipper in a box seat. Gar wondered what Captain Abe was thinking right now; he hoped not about throwing the resident Jonah over the side. Gar wouldn't have blamed him.

It was also interesting to watch Major Yamashita as the excitement level rose in the pilothouse. Gone was the cocky military police officer. He was an army guy in a navy setting, and Gar thought he was starting to pucker up a little. In an army fight you could dig in or bug out if you thought you were facing something overwhelming. At sea you had no choice but to face it. Gar's offhand but dire predictions hadn't helped, and even as the ship's captain scoffed, Yamashita seemed to be much less willing to go into the pilothouse to find out what was going on. A case of not wanting to know, perhaps.

The carrier was still executing her zigzag plan, making bold turns to the right and then, five or six minutes later, back to the left to foil any incipient torpedo data computer solutions being generated somewhere out there in the darkness. Gar couldn't see the escorting destroyers, as they were all running darken-ship, but occasionally red flashing-light messages came from ahead, where the destroyer division commander was riding one of the tin cans. Gar hadn't seen any radar screen consoles in the pilothouse, and he couldn't remember seeing radar antennas up on the mast. All that could have been planned for the eventual fitting-out period up in Yokosuka. He was thus really surprised when the carrier's red truck lights, which were mounted way up on the mast, started signaling vigorously. Gar could read Morse code, but these were Japanese signals. Use of the truck lights instead of directional signal lights meant that the carrier was sending an urgent visual signal to *all* the destroyers simultaneously. It also meant that if there *was* a sub out there setting up for a shot, he now had an invaluable visual bearing to add to the computer's relentless thirst for target data.

The major was definitely getting worried now as the noise level among the bridge officers continued to rise. Something was going on, and Captain Abe's temper was deteriorating audibly. Gar continued to make himself small in the dark corner of the bridge wing. The major muttered something in Japanese, and Gar gave him an inquiring look.

"*Two* submarine radars," he said quietly. He wouldn't look at Gar as he was saying it, and Gar wasn't going to provoke him or anybody else up there with any I-told-you-so noise. Then there was a rash of radio chatter inside the pilothouse.

"Ha!" the major said with a triumphant grin. "The destroyers have driven the submarines away. No more radar!"

Or there was a sub out there who'd been running dark and fast on the surface, trying to overtake this beast, and a zig or a zag on the part of the carrier had allowed the boat to submerge and set up a shot. The absence of radar did not necessarily imply the absence of danger.

The wind had increased, streaming across that distant square bow in gusts up to 30 knots. There were hundreds of shipyard workers down on the flight deck below, milling around, staring at the dark ocean racing by or huddling in small groups drinking tea. Gar tried to imagine the excitement in the conning tower of whoever was shadowing them. Big, big target. No identification, because she'd never been seen at sea. Going fast, but then she slowed down for some reason. Four destroyers in the screen, but sticking in close to the target, not ranging out ahead and on the beams, looking for intruders. Now Abe was signaling to all four at once. That was an emergency move.

Gar felt rather than heard the first torpedo hit, way back on the stern.

TWENTY-ONE

It was a nasty, off-axis thump on the starboard quarter, followed by the dull boom of an explosion pushing up a substantial water column behind the ship. It must have scared the hell out of all the POWs chained to the counter back there, not to mention maybe breaking some bones. Gar counted down the seconds, and then came a second hit, farther forward. This one was more muffled, as if deeper, and there was not much of a water column. The third one hit just aft of the carrier's island structure and packed a real wallop that he felt the full length of his spine. He decided to rise up on his tiptoes, because he knew whoever was doing this had probably fired a full spread of six, given the size of this ship. A fourth explosion blasted into the air just forward of the island, sending up a huge column of water, the spray from which was blown back across the bridge, obscuring the windows in sheets of seawater and causing the carrier to whipsaw a couple of times. The pilothouse was a good 130 feet above the ocean's surface, so this had been a shallow hit indeed.

As the panic spread inside the pilothouse, Gar waited for five and six, but nothing more came out of the night. Missed ahead, he thought, but four good hits down the same side were going to cause some serious damage. With any luck she'd capsize. There was now pandemonium in the pilothouse, with everybody trying to talk at once until the captain shouted something and they all fell silent. Reports started coming up via the bitch-box. In contrast to the excitement on the bridge, these voices sounded calmer. Gar glanced over at the major, who was holding a fist to his mouth. To Gar's astonishment, the ship wasn't slowing down. They were still plowing through the night sea at about 18 knots. He heard gunfire out ahead of them from one or more destroyers, but he was pretty sure that the sub had done her firing submerged. That flashing main truck light, visible in all directions for 10 miles, had been a serious error.

Two junior officers appeared in the pilothouse door and started yelling at Gar. The major jumped, then grabbed his arm. "Captain wants you," he said.

Oh, shit, Gar thought as the major practically dragged him into the pilothouse and across to the captain's chair. Abe had a triumphant look on his face as he started yelling at Gar. The major translated while trying to make himself invisible. The bitch-box was going full blast, and there were three officers taking notes and consulting some damage control plates on the chart table.

"He wants to know if you see what is happening. After four torpedo hits, *Shinano* presses on. She has shrugged off your submarine's best efforts as the bites of a flea!"

More along that line followed, which quieted the pilothouse as the other officers listened in. When he was finished, Abe looked at him as if expecting some kind of reply. That's when the ceramic mug sitting on the window ledge by his chair began to move. It slid slowly to the right, all by itself, making a thin scraping noise. Every eye on the bridge focused on that mug as it traveled across the ledge and came to a stop with a tiny clink against a window frame. None of them had noticed, but *Shinano* was developing a distinct list to starboard. One of the junior officers made a sharp bow toward the captain, then pointed at the centerline, where an inclinometer was mounted in the overhead above the pelorus. It showed a 5-degree list to starboard. Only two minutes after being torpedoed, she was listing.

The major took this opportunity to yell at Gar in Japanese, slap him in the face, and then drag him back out to the port-side bridge wing, as the noise level roared back up inside. Gar was surprised but offered no resistance; he realized Yamashita was getting Gar, and himself, out of Captain Abe's line of fire—but why, he wondered. Once outside, the major started rubbing the sides of his own face, exhibiting the first signs of genuine fear. Gar gave him a nod of thanks, and Yamashita nodded back.

"It can't be that bad," Gar said. "The ship is still going forward at the same speed. If she were in real danger, they would slow down."

Even as he said that, he noticed that his perch on the binocular box now required the use of his lower legs. It occurred to him that their blind faith in the unsinkability of this carrier might be leading them toward an avoidable disaster. With the ship still going ahead at 18 knots, there would be tremendous hydraulic pressure on the hull ruptures, and Gar knew probably better than anyone on the bridge about the state of below-deck watertight integrity.

"Do we have to stay here?" Gar asked the major.

"We have not been dismissed," he replied in a shaking voice.

"Don't you think they're a little busy in there right now? I think we should go down to the flight deck, where all those people are."

Yamashita looked over the port bullrail as if surprised to see several hundred men down on the flight deck, most of them milling around in growing disorder. Some of them appeared to be looking through the stacked pallets of materials. Many were wearing hard hats, which told him they were civilian shipyard workers, but there were more than a few ship's company out there on deck as well.

"We must have permission," the major said. "It was the captain who demanded you be brought to the bridge."

At that moment there was a deep rumbling sound forward of the island, and the bitch-box inside lit off with a panicked call. A roar of steam came out of the forward stack. From Gar's days as a new ensign on a battleship, he knew that volume of steam meant someone had deliberately lifted the safety valves on a boiler. That meant flooding had reached a main machinery space. A moment later, the volume of steam increased. Gar looked back at the major, who was clearly terrified of what he was seeing. He saw Gar looking at him.

"I cannot swim," he said. Gar couldn't hear him over the roar of the escaping steam, so he said it again.

Now Gar knew why the major was so scared and, more importantly, why he'd bullied Gar out of the pilothouse. The initiative had passed to him, the prisoner.

"Not a problem," he said, shouting over the roar of the steam. "I can swim. We need to find the life jacket lockers. There'll be some on the flight deck, and probably more down on the hangar deck. Come on, let's go look."

Yamashita took one more look at the panicked scene inside the pilothouse and said, "Yes, we go."

They took the exterior ladders down the port side of the island structure. As they went down they saw one of the destroyers closing in on the port side from astern. The flight deck crowd was growing, and so was the starboard list. Gar had to keep one hand on the bulkhead as they scrambled down the ladders. There were no lights showing anywhere on the flight deck, and the civilians were clearly panicked. Gar saw no one wearing a life jacket. Surely they hadn't gone to sea with no life jackets, he thought. The thunder of escaping steam was beginning to diminish as the boilers bled out five decks below. They were still making way, however, so she had propulsion power available.

When they reached the flight deck, Gar told the major to go find life jackets. He sat down against the island bulkhead, next to a row of pallets filled with tubing and valves. No one seemed to notice him. The white padded jacket helped, and he kept his head down. Then he remembered the prisoners clipped to that wire down on the fantail. He could find his way back there, he thought, and cut them loose somehow, but only if the goons had abandoned them. The major returned empty-handed and more than a little white-eyed. He had to catch himself against the bulkhead to stop his forward motion.

"No one knows where the life jackets are, and there are no boats or rafts. *Goddamn* navy."

Gar almost grinned but caught himself. There were hundreds of pallets stacked all over the flight deck; if nothing else they could upend one and use it as a float when the time came, and he was getting more and more convinced that the time *was* coming. There was a sudden outbreak of yelling as one of the electric trucks they used to move stuff around the flight deck went rolling straight over the starboard side, pausing momentarily in a catwalk before upending and disappearing into the sea. Two sailors trying to catch and stop it went over the side with it. The list was becoming steep enough that some of the pallets themselves were starting to slide.

The escaping-steam noise stopped suddenly as if someone had put a stopper in the escape piping. Perhaps the sea had done that, Gar thought. The ship felt different now, heavier, and the period of her normally ponderous sea roll was increasing. That, together with the fact that she was hanging for a moment at the end of each roll, meant that her stability was being rapidly compromised. She was no longer plunging ahead at 18 knots, either. Gar grabbed the major's arm.

"The prisoners down on the fantail," he said. "They are clipped to a wire. I want to go back there and save them."

Yamashita was beside himself with indecision. His entire world depended on permission, tradition, or actual orders. All of these things were disappearing before his eyes, and this giant ship was leaning over to take a look down into the 3,000 feet of water beckoning beneath her keel.

"You're an officer," Gar said. "If you order the guards to release the prisoners, they will do it. Then we can make preparations for going into the water. But we must hurry."

"You can swim?"

"Yes, I can swim. I will help you, but it would be better to go from the stern than from way up here, yes?"

One of the loaded pallets positioned between them and the rest of the flight deck made a noise and then started sliding toward them. They had to move fast to avoid being pinned against the bulkhead. Other pallets followed their leader. Gar took the lead once they were moving aft, easing his way through the increasingly noisy crowd of frightened shipyard workers on the flight deck. There were some chief petty officers out on the deck now, trying to restore order. They were quickly surrounded by a throng of shouting workers, probably wanting to know where the life jackets were.

They continued aft, away from the increasingly agitated crowd swarming out of the ship and onto the flight deck. The list had stabilized for the moment, but they were still over between 10 and 15 degrees. Gar could feel what was happening, and with that thick armored flight deck, *Shinano* was already top-heavy. Add to that the tons of stacked pallets and a thousand or so human beings, and the damage control officer had his hands full. Gar found a wool watch cap on the deck, which he pulled down over his head. With that and the padded jacket he was less obviously one of the POWs.

He didn't know how to get back to the fantail except by going down to the hangar bay. The major balked at that, especially since they were on the downhill side. Going down *into* the ship was not his idea of safety just then. Gar explained that he needed him to deal with the guards, and that *he* needed Gar to keep him afloat. They would go down, get those guys freed, and then come back up to the flight deck if Yamashita insisted. The major sputtered about it not being allowed, but then relented as Gar started down an interior passageway ladder on the starboard side. When they came out onto the hangar bay, Gar smelled something that gave him the chills: bilge water. He knew it as a unique smell, a mélange of salt-water, fuel oil, dead marine life, rust, and oil-soaked pipe lagging, all overlaid with a warm, humid blanket of condensed steam. It meant only one thing: The main engineering spaces were flooding.

They made their way aft some 400 feet along one side of the hangar bay. They saw at least three damage control parties furiously working gasoline-powered pumps and another one operating a bucket brigade. For God's sake, Gar thought. A bucket brigade for a 70,000-ton ship. The dozens of lights embedded along the overhead of the hangar bay were flickering, and Gar could hear the roar of diesel generators in the emergency service rooms on the margins of the bay. The list seemed less extreme down there, closer to the waterline, which made sense. They were probably counter-flooding, much the way a sub trimmed its attitude underwater. There was a wet mist visibly gathering along the hangar bay's over-head, though, which Gar hoped to God wasn't gasoline vapor.

The final passageway was blocked by overturned pallets of

supplies, so they ended up clambering over the mess to get out to the fantail. It was much darker back here, and Gar saw buckled deck plates on the starboard quarter. Two of the diagonal braces for the flight deck had been bent by the blast of the first torpedo. The vibration from the screws was much more pronounced than before, especially the ones on the port side. He wondered if their tips were coming out of the water because of the list. Why the hell hadn't they stopped the ship? From the size of the wake, it looked like they were still making 10 knots or so.

The good news was that the goons had fled. The bad news was that all the POWs were still attached to that wire, and Gar saw no way to cut it or the lock that attached it to a padeye on the bulkhead. The black water of the Pacific Ocean looked awfully close as he stared at the damage to the starboard quarter of the ship. Then he jumped as a dark gray shape came out of the gloom, passing very close aboard. It was one of the destroyers, and half her crew was topside, holding ropes and nets, obviously bent on taking people off the carrier. The major saw that, and for a moment Gar thought he was going to jump for it, but then the tin can disappeared around the corner of the fantail.

Then one of the POWs recognized Gar and gestured excitedly, pointing at a firefighting ax mounted to one of the flight-deck support beams. He climbed up the sloping, buckled deck and took it down. As he headed for the end of the wire, one of the goons stepped out on the fantail and started yelling at him, brandishing his baton indignantly. The major went at the man in his best imperial army voice, bracing him up against the front bulkhead and shouting the harshest Japanese Gar had ever heard. Gar went behind the major and got to the padeye, stuck the pick end of the ax into the hasp, positioned the ax head for leverage, and pulled with all his much-diminished strength. He did it four times before he felt something happening, cheered on the whole time by the trapped POWs. Then he heard what sounded like a warning shout and instinctively ducked as the goon's baton whistled over his head and smacked the bulkhead.

Gar didn't hesitate—he thrust backward with the ax handle and connected with the guard's groin. He went down with a gasping whimper, curling up into a writhing ball of pain. Before Gar could do anything else, the major calmly came up behind the disabled guard and hit him on the head with a chain stanchion he'd found somewhere. The guard's eyes rolled up into his head and he lay still.

Gar took the ax back to the padlock and finally broke it apart. The wire went whipping out of that padeye at the speed of heat as the POWs all tried to stand up at once. Then the whole line fell down in a heap due to the list of the ship. While they sorted themselves out, he and the major looked at each other and then dragged the inert body of the guard over to the starboard lifeline and pushed it over the side. It should have taken a few seconds for the splash, but it didn't. It had been at least 25 feet to the waterline on the night they left Kure. Now it was more like 10 feet. That fact even registered with the major, who made one of those hissing sounds as he stared over the side. The starboard-side screws weren't turning anymore. A passing swell broke green water over the edge of the buckled deck, as if to make it clear that time was fleeting.

The POWs didn't wait to thank them or even talk to them. They headed en masse for that passageway and disappeared into the gloom.

Gloom?

The lights had gone out in the hangar bay, except for some emergency battery lanterns mounted along the bulkheads. The POWs were all assholes and elbows disappearing over the clutter in the passageway. The major's eyes were almost as round as Gar's as the significance of what he'd done sunk in. He was, after all, a military policeman. Gar grabbed his elbow and told him it would be okay, that he would never say anything, and those POWs certainly wouldn't, either. Now he had to get him back topside before he completely lost it—but then Gar realized they'd waited too long.

TWENTY-TWO

A rumbling sound began deep in the hull. Gar immediately recognized it, having heard it before as a submarine skipper: the sound of collapsing bulkheads deep in the ship, the bang of huge sheets of steel giving way under the relentless pressure of the ocean, the pinging of rivets blasting around inside compartments. The two remaining screws on the port side slowed to a stop. There was a loud bang, followed by a horrific rending sound, and then they could feel the stern sag down into the sea. She was listing to starboard and settling by the stern at the same time. Gar slid across the wet deck to the lifelines and saw that the water was only a few feet down, if that. The major just stood at the entrance to the passageway, transfixed.

Gar spun him around, and they both pushed into that dark passageway where all the pallets were upended. Gar motioned for the major to grab one while he pulled another out from the mess. Another loud bang, and the ship gave a soft but scary 70,000-ton lurch. Gar could hear foam rising over the fantail. He found a coil of rope in the heap of materials and wrestled it and his pallet—*his* pallet!—out onto the fantail, the major right behind him. Gar opened the coil of rope and tied the major's pallet to his, leaving a bight on each end so they could hold on to the pallet once they went over the side.

They actually didn't have to go over the side. The side came to them in a foamy rush of cold water that swept across the fantail in a hissing series of increasingly larger waves. From up on the flight deck

they heard the beginnings of an avalanche of stuff that was now sliding backward along the flight deck. The major was trying to say
something, but no words were coming out. The noise got louder and
louder—deep rumblings, banging steel inside the ship, and the
whoosh of enormous bubbles beginning to pour out of the hull all
around them. She was going, and soon.

Gar clambered up on his pallet and wrapped the bitter end of the
rope around his forearm. The major did what Gar did. In a moment
they were surfing on a wave of water that was making a waterfall off
the fantail as the ship's stern lifted for a moment. Then she settled
back again, and they found themselves being pushed away from her
by the sheer volume of water being displaced. Their pallets were
flipped several times in the process, but they obligingly popped right
back to the surface each time. Soon they were a hundred feet or so
away from the ship. The major's face was white as a flounder's bottom, but he was still hanging on. At that precise moment the moon
appeared from behind a bank of clouds, revealing the full scope of
the disaster.

My God, what a sight, Gar thought. They could see down the
entire length of the flight deck as she settled by the stern, heeling
over to starboard by at least a 25-degree angle. Those two outward-
leaning stacks seemed intent on pulling her over. The two destroyers
alongside were backing away to avoid being hit by the stacks. That
maneuver sent up a collective wail from the flight deck, where at
least a thousand men were sliding across the deck toward the starboard deck-edge catwalks. Gar lay on his belly across the pallet and
motioned for the major to begin kicking with his feet to get away
from what was coming. A ship that size going down would suck
anything within 500 feet right down with her. The major apparently understood and started flailing away, his eyes screwed shut.
They had to really work at it because, once the flight deck dipped
far enough for the water to reach one of those elevator openings,
she'd go down like stone.

Gar saw one of the destroyers ease back alongside, her bow
crunching against the carrier's side forward of the island structure.

The carrier was heeling faster now, and one edge of the flight deck was perilously close to the destroyer's mast. Some of the officers up on the carrier's bridge had made it down to the flight deck and were crawling up the inclined flight deck toward the bow. A bright white column of steam erupted from the forward stack, drowning out the cries of the shipyard workers who were trying to get to that destroyer, but it was no use. The destroyer backed away suddenly, and he could see why. The ship was low enough in the water back aft that the after elevator hole was about to start filling. Two more destroyers edged closer to the sinking carrier up at the bow, which was now lifting out of the sea.

"Harder," Gar yelled at the major. It wasn't easy to move the pallets. Both of them were hanging over one edge and kicking themselves forward. The major was kicking as hard as he could, but without knowing how to swim, he wasn't very effective and began to hold Gar back. There wasn't a thing Gar could do about that. Then he heard a sound like Niagara Falls behind them. He didn't look back but kept kicking, hoping like hell they hadn't been going in a big circle. One of the destroyers began sounding the danger signal on her steam whistle. Gar finally ran out of energy and stopped kicking. He looked back to see the front third of the carrier's flight deck lifting high into the air, the deck's white directional lines clearly visible in the dull moonlight. He couldn't see any more scrambling, tiny figures on the flight deck, but a growing cloud of steam, air, and dust boiled out of the front elevator hole, until it, too, began to fill. A moment later, with a weird groaning noise, *Shinano* disappeared, sliding stern first into 500 fathoms of water. She left an enormous whirlpool, around which Gar could barely make out the hundreds of heads of the men who'd gone over the side as they followed her down into the depths. A minute later all that remained was that cloud of steam and dust, spreading out over the water, as if looking for its source. Gar was overwhelmed. What a colossal waste.

The fourth destroyer emerged from that cloud and nearly collided with one of the others. She backed down furiously and then came to a stop as the other three tin cans began pulling people out of the water. The major had said that *Shinano* had sailed with nearly three thousand people on board. There was nowhere near that number of heads visible as the four destroyers hauled them out like herring. Gar and the major were perhaps 500 yards away from the rescue operation by this time. Gar was torn—rescue would be tantamount to a death sentence for him. If nothing else, the survivors would equate Gar with the submarine that had just killed their ship and he'd be torn to pieces on whatever deck they hauled him onto, and who could blame them. On the other hand, his chances for survival out there on a small wooden freight pallet in the cold waters of the North Pacific were those famous two.

Gar felt the rope tighten and then relax, followed by a frantic, gurgling cry behind him. He looked around for the major, but he was nowhere in sight. There was a slight chop forming on the sea as dawn approached. The skies were clearing enough for him to see a few stars in the western part of the night sky. He was exhausted, thirsty, and, he realized, dangling shark bait right beneath his pallet. He hauled himself up onto the wooden boards, got it off center, and flipped right back into the water. The other pallet was still attached. Gar pulled it to him, tied the two pallets together to make a bigger raft, and tried again. This time he succeeded by doing the old spread-eagle. He lashed himself to the pallet. He put his head down on the rough-sawn boards and closed his eyes for a minute or so. He was out of the frigid water, so now he at least had a chance.

Within five minutes he was shivering in the light breeze. The air temperature was lower than the sea temperature, so the occasional wave slapping over the semisubmerged pallet actually felt good. He was trying to decide whether he'd survive longer *in* the sea than on top of it when the pallet bumped into something. He opened one eye and promptly got saltwater in it. Another bump. Then he realized the pallet wasn't doing the bumping.

He opened both eyes and was face-to-face with the maw of a large shark. The beast had its head out of the water and was looking at Gar with one of its dead eyes. There was a long strip of what looked like a khaki uniform shirt hanging out of the back of the shark's mouth.

Gar stared for a second, his heart starting to hammer, and then raised his arm and smacked the shark across the face. It was like hitting a piece of sandpaper, but the shark blinked once and then submerged. Gar waited for it to mount a full attack, but nothing happened. His hand stung, and he opened and closed it to restore circulation. He scrunched up onto the pallet, to make sure none of his arms or legs was hanging out, and waited to see what would happen.

A few minutes later came another bump. Gar opened his eyes, unaware that he had closed them. It was darker, but the breeze had dropped. He could smell fuel oil, and he was really cold now, past the shivering stage and entering the early warm-feeling stages of hypothermia. There was something in front of his pallet. He stared into the darkness, trying to make it into a shark, but it wasn't. It was a human head.

A body, he thought.

He considered what to do, but his brain was very sluggish.

A body.

A clothed body?

He crawled a few inches forward on his pallet raft and reached for the head, hoping it was still attached to more than a single bone.

It was, and he turned it around. The face was Japanese. He felt below the body's chin and grabbed the collar of a sodden coat.

It took him ten minutes to get that coat off before the body bobbed away from his grasp. He almost lost the coat, too. Once he got it onto the pallet he rolled himself into it. The edges where a zipper would be didn't close across his front, but the extra layer of fabric, even wet, felt like a greatcoat. He went back to sleep, praying that it was just sleep and not the end of everything.

He awoke to full, warm sunlight and the sounds of excited Japanese. As he tried to gather his wits he smelled the pungent odor of dead fish. He opened one eye and saw a small fishing boat about 10 feet away with four elderly Japanese men staring at him and gabbling. He opened both eyes, blinked, and looked again. Standing wide-eyed at the helm of the 40-foot boat was none other than Hashimoto-san.

TWENTY-THREE

Gar was almost too exhausted to think. He was desperately thirsty. His forehead felt sunburned, and his feet felt like wet rubber. He realized that he had better not "recognize" Hashimoto until he knew where he stood with the rest of the fishing-boat crew.

Moments later he was being hauled aboard like some big fish and deposited on the wooden deck. He heard several hissing intakes of breath and the word *gaijin* several times. The wooden deck was warm and invited him to go back to sleep, but then a bucket of cold seawater hit him in the face, ending that idea. Then came noise. Someone was yelling at him again, someone who wasn't happy. Best he could tell, all Japs were seriously into yelling and were absolutely never happy.

Just shoot me, he thought. I am so tired of this shit. Why, oh why, did you bastards come to Pearl Harbor?

A moment later a light fishnet was thrown over his body, and then he was rolling on the deck as they wrapped him up. Sunlight. Wooden deck. Sunlight. Wooden deck. After three rolls they felt secure and he felt like that famous bug in a rug.

Another bucket of seawater, and then a face was in his face. He struggled to focus. It was Hashimoto. He was the one doing the yelling, but from the look in his eye, the look the others couldn't see, he was trying to tell Gar something. As in, keep still, play along, we'll talk later. Gar closed his eyes, which brought him a swift kick in the ass. Then they dragged him to the back of the boat and tied him to the cleats on the stern. There was a chock through which he could see dozens of small boats combing the sea. Then he could smell bunker oil. The Japs must have called out every fishing boat from the Kure district to search for survivors from *Shinano*. He didn't see any destroyers, but they could have been out of his visual range. He wasn't any less exhausted from being wrapped in the fishnet, so he went back under.

When next he woke, somebody was gently slapping his face. He opened one eye and discovered Hashimoto kneeling next to him. He thrust a glass bottle of water into his mouth and Gar drank greedily. He pulled it out so Gar could take a breath and then put it back in, as if feeding a baby, looking over his shoulder the whole time. Gar felt the boat's small diesel chugging away underneath him and realized it was dark.

"I must hide you," he said. "They must think you go overboard."

"Um," was all Gar could manage.

"I cut this off," he said, indicating the fishnet, "and then put you in the net hole. You stay quiet."

"Um."

He quickly cut through the netting and then propped Gar upright. With Hashimoto helping, Gar crawled into a small cubbyhole at the back of the boat. It almost wasn't big enough for his American-sized body. Hashimoto positioned a wooden hatch, thrust another bottle of water into the cubbyhole, and then closed the hatch with his foot.

"I come for you, by'n'by," he said. "No noise."

The cubbyhole stank of fish, and there wasn't much air. The diesel kept putt-putting away as Gar heard him walk forward. He drank some more water, then wedged the bottle, which had no top, into a corner. The diesel wasn't running very well, and its exhaust smelled like popcorn. Gar wondered about that for a good ten seconds before falling asleep again.

He woke to the sounds of an altercation between the crew of the fishing boat and some nasty-sounding people who were on either another boat or a pier. Gar turned as soundlessly as he could in his hidey-hole and peeked through a crack in the side. The boat was alongside a pier, and the tide must have been out, because the deck of the pier was a good 8 feet above the boat's gunwales. Three soldiers were standing on the pier. One of them was blistering the air while the other two, their rifles at port arms, looked bored. From over his head he recognized Hashimoto's voice answering back.

The noisy one on the pier listened for a few seconds and then said something to his two cohorts. They shifted their rifles into a hip-shot firing position, and everything got quiet. Then a rope snaked up from the deck to the guy in charge. He held the end of it and waited, while the soldiers kept their rifles pointed down at the boat. Gar couldn't see who else was on the pier, but he suspected any bystanders had left quickly once the rifles were unlimbered. Then the man on the pier began to pull on the rope, and a basket spun its way up. The riflemen put down their weapons and dumped the contents of the basket, a bunch of fish, into a much bigger basket. They repeated this procedure three times until Hashimoto started protesting again. The guy in charge started looking for a way to get down into the boat but couldn't find one. He pointed his finger down at the boat and scolded some more. Then all three of them hoisted the big basket of fish and backed out of Gar's sightline.

An argument broke out on deck as soon as the soldiers had left. Gar relaxed as best he could and waited. It was early in the morning, and the skies were gray again. He hoped the tide was coming back in soon. Even if it was, it was going to be several hours before Hashimoto could let him out of the hole. That basket of raw fish was going to look pretty good to Gar about then.

By three hours after dark that night, Gar was ensconced in yet another boat. Hashimoto had rescued him an hour after sunset and taken him out onto the pier and then to a ladder that led down under it. They stepped off the ladder into mud that was at least a foot deep, and suddenly Gar couldn't move. Hashimoto showed him how to use the framing of the pier to pull each foot out, place it ahead of him, and then let it sink back into the ooze again. The mud smelled of dead fish and sewage in about equal proportions. It was truly eye-watering, and each step was a huge effort.

Then he saw where they were going. Stashed under the pier was the carcass of a fishing boat. There was no engine, screws, rudder, or even a cabin. There was just the hull, covered by a wooden deck that had a rectangular hole where the forward cabin and pilothouse had once been. They climbed aboard the derelict boat and sat down on the deck. Some *things* wiggled away from them in the darkness. A lone crab stood his ground, watching them. He must have sensed Gar's intentions, because he suddenly skittered sideways and disappeared right over the side.

Hashimoto sat down beside him, produced a tiny candle from his pocket, and lit it. The smoke was fragrant, driving away the stench of the tidal flats. He then opened a small cotton bag. It contained a small piece of warm fish and a handful of cooked rice wrapped in some kind of green leaf. Gar ate it all in about three bites. He then handed Gar another bottle of water, again with no cap. Gar could see that it was an old beer bottle, and he had a bad feeling about the quality of that water, but even so, it was wonderful to get it. Hashimoto then produced two cigarettes, lit them both, and handed one to Gar. He wasn't a smoker, but he became one that night, if only to suppress the rank air and drive off some of the larger mosquitoes. Hashimoto settled back on his haunches and gave Gar a look that said, *Okay, what the hell happened?*

Gar told him the story, from having to send the sub down without him to going over the side as the *Shinano* met her end east of Bungo Suido. Hashimoto listened in weary silence. He looked older and much thinner. When Gar was finished, he nodded several times and then fished for more cigarettes. Gar shook his head, so he lit one up for himself. In the candlelight he looked like one of those Buddha figures, weary, patient, and imperturbable.

"Goddamn army." He sighed. "It is very bad here. No food. Army take everything. Army make us go out, then take everything we catch. Army give us fuel, but it is not real fuel. We hide some fish in the boat. They know we do this, but they know we must eat or they will not eat. Village get one sack of rice each month. That is it. Alla farmers' food, fruit from trees, rice from field, alla the villages' food, go to army. Children die everywhere. No food. In Hiroshima City, also very bad."

Gar didn't know what to say. Having just consumed some of their meager rations, he actually felt a little guilty.

"Last night," Hashimoto continued, "army come. Officers very excited. All boats must go to sea. Go east, they say. Many submarines attack. Big ship go down. Many people in water. Find navy ships. Find people, bring them back here to village."

"That was *cold* water, Hashimoto-san," Gar said.

The old man nodded. "We knew. When winter comes, you have one hour, maybe two. Then you go to sleep and die."

"But you had to go out anyway."

He nodded again. "Army not asking. They *tell*. We gotta go."

He told Gar about a hodgepodge fleet of fishing boats all streaming out to sea in the middle of the night, some with army soldiers onboard with their radios. They searched until dawn, and actually picked up some survivors. The dead they left in the sea. There were many dead, and there was a huge oil slick bubbling up like some kind of underwater volcano. The fishermen had heard rumors that a great ship had left Kure under the cover of darkness, but the officers were crystal clear: No one was permitted to know or talk about this. Anyone talking would be shot.

He said they listened to Radio Tokyo every night in the village and heard reports of great victories in China and Southeast Asia, that the Americans were being thrown back to Australia and that the imperial armies were preparing to corner them there and destroy them. They said that the American navy had already been destroyed at Pearl Harbor, and later the remnants had all gone down at Midway. No one believed these reports. Fuel oil was desperately short; even the office buildings and hotels up in Hiroshima City had no heat. Rice was almost impossible to obtain, and people everywhere were trying to grow it in their yards, gardens, and even window boxes. A bridge had collapsed last winter due to ice, and there was no steel to rebuild it. When people went to the hospital, they often did not come back because there were no medicines or doctors. Then there were the B-29s.

Visible originally only as contrails high in the sky, they were now easily distinguished whenever they came over in daylight.

With the B-29s came fire, fire in the city, fire in even some of the smaller towns. They no longer dropped big bombs, which seemed to go off all over the place and only occasionally land on a factory or large building. The bombs now came in clouds, tiny things, six, seven pounds, and they spread some kind of jelly all over the place. The tiny bombs were then followed by slightly larger ones, and these lit the jelly on fire, and the combination then ignited the entire city. Just a few weeks ago there had been a terrible fire in the north. The news reports said that it had been extinguished quickly with little damage and not many casualties, but civilians fleeing Honshu told quite a different story, of an entire city burning, flaming figures running down the streets, and there being no air to breathe. Yes, it had been extinguished, but only because there was nothing left to burn.

The people of Honshu were very angry, Hashimoto said. It was one thing to bomb a ship or shoot down an airplane, quite another to set an entire city on fire. Gar told him the reason that he had been told: The Japanese army had dispersed war production throughout the country into the homes of workers in the city. There they made small parts, castings, and subassemblies. These were then sent to the factory where they were assembled into cannon shells, airplane parts, torpedoes, or heavier machinery. Hashimoto said he could understand that, but people on Honshu were killing the crews of any B-29s that parachuted into the countryside on sight.

Which brought them to Gar's situation.

"I cannot stay here, then," Gar said. "If the army finds me here, they'll shoot everybody in the village, won't they?"

Hashimoto nodded. "Yes. Two weeks ago, army officer found a family listening to American radio from China. They take men away, then burn house. People still inside."

"When do you go back to sea again?"

"In morning. Early."

"Can you trust your crew?"

He nodded again. "All family. Whole village, family. No one talk to army."

"They know you came back from Hawaii?"

"They know."

"Why *did* you come back, Hashimoto-san?" Gar asked.

"I am old," he said with a sigh. "Die soon. I am ashamed of what army has done to Nippon. Officers all crazy. They beat, sometimes *kill* soldiers for no reason. Soldiers very afraid. Officers carry swords, think they are samurai. Soldier makes mistake, officer cut off soldier's hand. This war destroy my country. I am ashamed. Angry. I will make revenge. Maybe get caught. Die then."

"Still have that thing?"

"I do," he said proudly. "The secret thing. Wait for paper rain, then go to Hiroshima City. Put it in gardens of Hiroshima Prefectural Industrial Promotion Hall. Then wait to see what happens."

"Is there a prisoner of war camp near here?"

"On Kyushu, there is big one. Many *gaijin* held there. Smaller one here, near Hiroshima City. We hear very bad stories in Hiroshima City. Many prisoners are slaves in the Kawasaki coal mine near Nagasaki. Many die."

"Has Hiroshima been bombed?"

"No. Radio Tokyo say no cities bombed, but we know that is not true. Railroad men come from the north, tell different story. No wanna go back."

"Okay," Gar said. "I think what we have to do is let me be captured again. Go out on the boat. Put me back in that hole, then come back in. You tell the army you found me floating on a box."

"They kill you."

"They will see I wear khaki. They will question me first. I will tell them who I am. They will think I am a valuable prisoner. That way they won't hurt you or your village."

Hashimoto considered that rationale. Gar sure as hell didn't want to be recaptured, but he also didn't want to bring death and destruction down on this little fishing village just because one of them had fished him out of the sea. He was pretty sure Hashimoto understood. He told Gar that it would be better if he stayed right here during the day tomorrow. He would then pretend to find Gar after dark while making a final inspection of the boat for the next day's fishing trip. He would call the guards at the nearest cross-roads. He would get the villagers to act excited over his big discovery. After that, he would wait for paper rain and do what he'd promised to do.

Gar considered trying to escape to sea. Perhaps steal a fishing boat at night and sail it through the minefields to the open ocean—but even if he escaped the Seto, then what? No food, no water, and 1,500 miles to the nearest American base. There'd be a high probability of being intercepted by Jap patrol boats, and then the village would still catch hell. It was obviously crucial to somebody important back in Pearl that Hashimoto did whatever the hell he was supposed to do with that thing. In turn, Hashimoto's chances were dependent on the village remaining on his side. Escape simply wasn't feasible, so he reluctantly agreed to what Hashimoto was proposing.

"One last thing, Hashimoto-san," Gar said. "Remember, put the secret thing where they told you, but don't stay there."

TWENTY-FOUR

Admiral Lockwood and Captain Forrester were discussing the planned move of the SubPac headquarters out to Guam when a messenger came in from the operations center.

"Op-immediate traffic, Admiral," he said, handing a message to Lockwood.

"Who's it from?" Forrester asked as Lockwood read the message.

"*Archer-fish*," the messenger said, and then he left the office.

"Who is claiming to have hit a carrier with six fish," Lockwood said. "Only to have the damned thing sail over the horizon as if nothing happened."

"That doesn't sound like Joe Enright," Forrester said. "If anything, he's too conservative with his reporting. And where'd they find a carrier?"

"Says it was an unidentified class, but definitely a flattop. Appeared to be very large, bigger than the *Shokaku*. He chased it for six hours and then got a shot. The thing never slowed down. Six steamers, and it kept going?"

"Bigger than *Shokaku*," Forrester said. "I wonder."

"The thing Gar Hammond went after? You're thinking they got her to sea?"

"It's possible. Hammond reported attacking the dry-dock caisson, but not the actual ship. That might have spooked the Japs to get her out of the Inland Sea and up to Yokohama or even Yokosuka. Somewhere that our boats couldn't go."

Lockwood put the message down. "They probably thought that the Inland Sea was somewhere our boats couldn't go."

Forrester shrugged. "We'll have to wait for ULTRA, see if there's chatter about losing a carrier."

"That's assuming we're still getting real traffic intercepts," Lockwood said. "After, well, you know."

Forrester nodded. "Gar Hammond giveth, and Gar Hammond taketh away," he said quietly.

Kyushu, Japan

By nine the next evening Gar was riding in the back of an army truck, arms bound, blindfolded, and escorted by two soldiers who'd looked like they were about twelve. Their rifles, with bayonets fixed, looked older and even taller than they were. The army officer who'd come to the village could barely contain his glee. He celebrated his accomplishment by whacking Gar across both shins with a baton, which brought Gar to his knees with what felt like two broken legs. Apparently he had been supposed to kneel the moment he saw the officer approaching. He knew that the longer he sat on that bench in the back of the truck, the harder it was going to be for him to get up and get out.

One of the village women had brought Gar a last meal and more fresh water. He had no idea of what he was eating, but he was still pretty hungry, and he knew that food was going to be in short supply wherever he was going. More than once he wondered if he'd made the right decision not to at least try to escape, but the reality was undeniable. If he got caught and was made to tell where he'd been, there would be a firing squad for the entire village, whose only crime had been to look the other way when a certain old man suddenly reappeared in their midst, acting as if he'd been there all along.

They drove for at least an hour, stopping at what sounded like several checkpoints along the way. Gar listened to much hissing and muttering at each stop. The officer who'd taken him into custody had come along for the ride to headquarters, or wherever they were going. When they finally stopped and shut down, Gar heard the canvas back of the truck pulled aside and then a lot of shouting in Japanese. He knew what they wanted, but he really couldn't move. His legs hurt like hell, and he was still blindfolded. Then he felt two sharp blades prodding him in the side and heard more shouting. He fell sideways, toward the back of the truck, rolled once, and then fell off the truck and onto the ground. Someone helpfully kicked him to his feet and prodded him in the direction they wanted him to go. When the blindfold finally came off he was in a cell of some kind, very small, with a single metal chair in the middle and nothing else. They prodded him into the chair, removed the ropes, and slammed the metal door. Gar actually appreciated being left alone for a few minutes while he massaged his burning arms and tried to stop the bleeding cuts in his side.

That lasted for five minutes, and then the door opened to reveal a middle-aged man in a civilian suit. He was carrying a metal folding chair. He was maybe five-six and had dark hair with graying temples and the face of a parish priest: a kind, calm, welcoming expression, and a look in his eyes that said, *Relax, nobody's going to hurt you, we're all going to be friends.* The two child-guards outside looked on with interest and bowed deeply as the older man stepped in and set up his chair. Then the new arrival produced a small black semiautomatic pistol. He checked to see that there was brass showing at the slide and then pressed it into Gar's forehead.

"Quickly, now," he said. "Name, rank, and serial number."

Gar made the required recitation.

"Commander," he said. "Did you say commander?"

"I did."

He withdrew the pistol. "Commander of what?"

"That is my rank. Commander, U.S. Navy."

"Commander of what ship?"

Gar recited his rank and serial number.

The Priest, as Gar visualized him, stared at Gar for a long

moment. His expression never changed. A sweet man, a kind man. Never hurt a flea.

"Commander of what ship, please?" His English was unaccented. Not *prease*, please.

Gar again recited his name, rank, and serial number, trying to maintain the pretense that the Japanese respected the Geneva Convention on the treatment of POWs, the one they'd never signed.

Gar's interrogator put the gun back into his jacket pocket and turned his head slightly. He nodded to one of the guards, who opened the cell door wide. Outside in the hallway an extremely gaunt and sick-looking Caucasian was kneeling on the concrete floor. His clothes were in tatters, and his eyes were swollen closed. Another, much older guard stood behind him with his own hands behind his back. The Priest said one word in Japanese, and the guard produced a pistol and shot the prisoner in the back of the head. He dropped to the floor without a sound and began to bleed copiously onto the concrete floor. The guard made a sound of disgust and shot him again. The two kids in uniform looked nauseated.

Nobody moved. A ribbon of blood had reached the drain in the floor outside and began to trickle audibly down into it. That was the only sound. The air stank of gunpowder.

"Commander of what ship, please?" Same placid expression. I've got all night and the world's supply of prisoners.

Gar heard the sounds of a metal door opening and someone else being dragged into the corridor outside his cell. Guards muttering in Japanese, grunting and pulling, and a third voice whimpering, "No, no, please," in English. A third guard dragged the dead prisoner out of Gar's sight, and a new one was forced to kneel in the mess on the floor. The guard with the pistol looked over at the Priest, waiting for the sign. The interrogator sat back, lit a cigarette, spit out a fleck of wet tobacco, and gave Gar a moment to consider his circumstances. So he did.

He was a prisoner of the Imperial Japanese Army, who, these days anyway, were the absolute masters of the ancient kingdom of Dai Nippon. The Japanese were a race of men who were the masters of the delicately intricate tea ceremony, the precision and discipline of Zen rock and sand gardens, single-stroke calligraphy, and the arrangement of fresh cherry blossoms. They lived in wooden houses with parchment windows, and they slept on flat mats with no heat in the winter. These same men were also the masters of the exquisite samurai sword and the perpetrators of the rape of Nanjing in 1937, where they used live Chinese civilians for recruit bayonet practice. They were the architects of the hell ship system, transporting POWs captured in Southeast Asia in the holds of merchant ships with the hatches bolted shut for the entire two-week journey to the copper mines of Honshu. If the ship happened to be torpedoed along the way, the Japs went into the lifeboats and listened as the POWs tried in vain to open the hatches before the ship finally sank.

They were an alien race, so alien that Americans couldn't even *begin* to appreciate how different the Japanese were in every respect. Death was supposed to mean nothing to them and everything to them. For any soldier, death in battle was the sublime objective. Death in captivity was the greatest dishonor they could imagine. Prisoners of war were therefore walking bags of offensive protoplasm, nothing more. POWs forfeited their humanity and all respect when they first raised their hands. Gar knew this Kempeitai officer would pull prisoners out of their cells and shoot every damned one of them until Gar decided to answer his question, and he'd do it without as much thought as he'd put into flicking that piece of wet tobacco off his lips.

Okay, he thought, I get the picture.

The only important thing that he knew and they apparently didn't was the immutable certainty that Japan was going to lose this war. There were forces assembling 8,000 miles away that were going to purge the earth of this bizarre race. There were half a *million* troops being trained for one mission and one mission only: to invade this tiny island country and kill every goddamned Japanese man, woman, and child who stood up in front of them without waving a white flag, which really meant they were going to have to kill them all.

He decided at that moment to answer any and all of this man's questions, because nothing that he learned from Gar would change what was coming.

"I was the commanding officer of the USS *Dragonfish*, an American submarine," he said.

The interrogator nodded pleasantly. Then he swung around in his chair and signaled for the guards to take the second prisoner away. Or so Gar thought. They grabbed the prisoner and pushed him down the corridor. As Gar sat back in his chair, relieved that he hadn't caused the death of another prisoner, two shots rang out, followed by laughter and shouts of fake annoyance at another mess in the hallway.

The interrogator looked at him as if to note his reaction, that infuriating smile still on his face. "Tomorrow," he said. "We will talk some more tomorrow. No. *You* will talk some more tomorrow."

He rose, folded up his chair, and left the cell. The two young guards, still looking unsettled at the murder of the two prisoners, were being handed wet mops as Gar's cell door was slammed shut.

The next morning they brought Gar a metal pitcher of water, a tin cup of tea, and some rice cakes. He was stiff and achy after a cold night curled up in a corner on the concrete floor. His shins had big red goose eggs on them, and he was very careful not to let anything touch them.

It wasn't much of a cell. A hole in the floor in the opposite corner served as the latrine. There was a single, foot-square window high up on the wall, which appeared to be open to the outside air. Twice during the night he'd heard locomotives huffing by the building, followed by the rattle of boxcars and squealing wheels. He'd also heard metal doors being opened and slammed shut throughout the night and wondered if this was some kind of transit station for POWs.

When the food came, one guard pointed a bayonet at him while the other deposited the pitcher, the tin cup, and the tiny wooden box on the chair. Then they withdrew, slamming the door as if trying to break it. Gar used a little bit of the water to wash his hands and face and then ate the food quickly, standing by the chair. He tried to warm his hands with the cup of tea before drinking some. It was very weak, and there were tiny stem fragments in the bottom. When he'd finished, he put the cup in the food box and put the box by the door. Then he sat down in the chair, facing the metal door, and waited. He stank of fish, mud, and general filth; in a land where they would have preferred to bathe hourly, he must have been a towering olfactory disturbance.

He awoke to the sound of keys in the door. He'd fallen back asleep without even realizing it. The door opened, and two different guards stepped in. These were not high school kids, Gar thought. These guys looked like battle-hardened infantry troops. They were not even armed. They motioned for him to stand up, and he did so, swaying a little on his badly bruised shins. One of them dropped a noose of rope around his neck, tightened it, and led him out of the cell. The other followed, leaving the cell door open. They went to the right, away from the scene of the butchery the evening before. At the end of the corridor they went outside into bright, gray light. They were walking across what looked like an army parade ground, surrounded by brick buildings of different sizes. Some were obviously barracks, the others offices or warehouses. A rail line ran behind the row of buildings on the end, not more than 100 yards from his cell house.

They walked across the parade ground, one guard in front, one behind, and Gar in the middle with his neck rope. He had the sense that if he had tripped and fallen, the guard in the lead would not have noticed. They went into one of the office buildings and up a flight of wooden stairs. So far, Gar had seen no one other than his two guards. The parade ground was deserted, and many of the buildings also looked empty. They took him to a room that held a long green-felt-covered table surrounded by several armchairs, with Japanese national and regimental flags mounted in one corner. Three water pitchers with glasses had been placed in front of the chairs on one side of the table. The guards nodded at one of the chairs on the opposite side of the table, and Gar sat down. The guard did not remove the noose. He dropped the other end of the rope on the floor, and then the two of them stepped behind him and went to parade rest. One of them made a quiet noise of disgust as he caught Gar's aroma; the other grunted agreement, and then they each took one step back. Gar tried to act unconcerned and closed his eyes. He had high hopes for a civilized interrogation; this didn't look like a place where they shot people on the carpet. On the other hand, he was sitting there with a hangman's noose around his neck.

He was just about to doze off again when a door behind him opened and he heard low voices. He'd learned by then not to look around or do anything without being told, so he just sat there. Two Japanese officers in greenish uniforms came in and went around to the other side of the table. Each carried a notebook and wore a holstered pistol. Accompanying them was his interrogator from the night before, dressed in an army uniform and still smiling as if he hadn't murdered any prisoners in at least, oh, eight hours. The naval officers sat down, and the one he'd been mentally calling the Priest cleared his throat and then rattled away in Japanese for a few minutes. Gar couldn't tell if he was in charge or just a briefer here. One of the naval officers looked to be much older and carried himself with the gravitas of a senior officer. The other one was paying close attention to the Priest, while the older one seemed a bit disinterested. Then Gar realized that the Priest was speaking to him.

"Tell us how you came to be here today," he instructed. Gar proceeded to do so, while the Priest did a simultaneous translation into Japanese. He told them about ordering the boat to dive without him, then being captured by the minesweepers and taken to Kure and eventually the *Shinano*. When he said the word *Shinano* the older officer came awake. He asked a question in a voice that sounded like he regularly gargled with sandpaper.

"He wants to know how *you* can know that name," the Priest said. "That name is a great secret."

"It was our mission to penetrate the minefields of Bungo Suido and sink that ship," Gar said. "Instead we had to attack her in dry dock. Later, after I was captured, I was aboard *Shinano* when she was torpedoed and sunk."

The Priest blinked and then gave him a long stare. The Captain, which is what Gar had decided to call the obviously senior officer, barked something.

"Think carefully," the Priest said. "No one here at this compound knows anything about a sinking. For your information, that is the official government line."

"You mean, *Shinano* wasn't sunk?"

"That ship was attacked at sea but shrugged off all attacks and has gone on to Yokosuka. Everyone knows that."

"What do you want me to say, then?" Gar asked. "Just so *you* know, I was the one who fired torpedoes at two destroyers, two ammunition barges, and then the dry-dock caisson wall at Kure. Once I was captured in the Hoyo Strait, a Kempeitai officer took me aboard the carrier for transport to Tokyo. The captain of the ship, Captain Abe, made me stand on the bridge so that I could see for myself that she was invulnerable. I was on the bridge when the four torpedoes hit, and an hour or so later I watched her sink, stern first, and take probably more than two thousand men with her."

The Priest hissed in annoyance and then spoke to the Captain, who had picked up on the name Abe. When the Priest was finished translating, the Captain spat out something that sounded to Gar a lot like the Japanese equivalent to "bullshit." The other naval officer looked very apprehensive, as if he shouldn't be hearing any of this. Then the Captain surprised him and spoke in English.

"Name of Kempeitai officer?"

"Yamashita," Gar said.

The Captain grunted and then said something in Japanese to the Priest, who hesitated and then replied. Whatever he said made the Captain look truly surprised.

"Why do you agree to talk to us?" the Captain asked.

"Because whatever you learn from me does not matter."

The Captain thought that one over. "Tell me something important. Something I do not know."

"Our submarines can penetrate your minefields because we can see the mines," Gar said.

"That is lie," the Captain scoffed.

"We came through Bungo Suido. Is it not mined?"

"You had chart. Someone betrayed us."

"Didn't need a chart," Gar said. "We can *see* the mines."

"How is this possible?"

"Sonar," Gar said.

"More stupid lies."

"Did a submarine fire torpedoes into the caisson where *Shinano* was berthed? Sink two destroyers? Explode the ammunition barges?"

More sucking in of air all around. The Priest had to translate some of the words.

"You are spy," the Captain concluded. "You have heard these things in one of the villages. In Kure, or Hiroshima City. None of this is true."

Gar sat back in his chair. If the Captain was going to label him a spy, he was a dead man.

"Have you been to Kure recently?" Gar asked. "Make a phone call. Tell them you wish to come down there and inspect the waterfront. See what they say."

The Priest had to translate again. The Captain glared at Gar for a moment, banged his palm down on the table, nodded, got up, and left the room. The other officer spoke up once the Captain was gone. He, too, had English.

"You must be much more careful," he said. "Whether or not the things you say are true, they are not permitted to be *spoken*, do you understand? Listen to the major."

Gar wasn't having it. "I understand," he said, "that the General Imperial Staff or whatever you call it is deluding itself. *Shinano has* been destroyed. The Kure naval base waterfront *is* a mess. The submarine that was waiting for *Shinano was* one of many. If you intend to kill me because I speak the truth, then I can't help that. But that won't change the truth."

The officer had no reply to that. Gar asked them how it was that they all were able to speak English. The Priest, whom he now knew was a major, smiled. "I am Kempeitai, foreign espionage division. These officers are naval intelligence. Of course we can speak English. Do all your naval intelligence officers not speak Japanese?"

The real answer to that was no—none that he had ever met, anyway. He shook his head.

"Then how can they ever catch Japanese spies?" he asked.

"They don't try," Gar said.

"Explain."

"If we think someone is a Japanese spy, we leave him alone. We let him report on the *true* situation. That there are now so many American warships there is not room for them all to anchor in one harbor. That new ships arrive every week. That large American airfields are being built on Guam and Tinian. That two American armies have invaded the Philippines. That—"

"Enough!" the Priest said. "This is propaganda."

At that moment a siren began wailing, and then a second one, more distant. The Priest made a face.

"B-29?" Gar asked.

The Priest shrugged, then nodded.

"This doesn't happen in America," Gar pointed out.

At that moment the Captain came back into the room and let fly with a torrent of rapid-fire Japanese. He seemed angrier with them than afraid of any impending air raid, if that's what it was. More sirens were going off now, and Gar could hear people stirring out in the hallway. The two guards stepped back into the room. One came up and removed the noose.

The major stood up, his face no longer quite so genial.

"You go now. Go with them. Keep silent!"

Gar turned around and followed one guard out the door while the other one fell in behind him. They didn't put the noose back on this time, and everyone seemed to be in just a bit of a hurry. They took him back outside and toward his cell house. What Gar had thought to be unoccupied office buildings were emptying out onto the parade field. It looked like the men were all falling into some kind of formation. He would have thought they'd be heading for bomb shelters, but it was apparent they had defiance on their minds. Gar listened for the rumble of a bomber formation but heard none, and there was nothing visible in that cold gray sky as they went into the cell house. They marched him right back into his cell, where the guard obligingly threw in the noose, in case Gar might yet change his mind and do the honorable thing. Then the door was slammed.

TWENTY-FIVE

After an hour or so the sirens went off again, sounding a steady tone for the all clear. Gar never did hear any airplanes. They brought some food and water toward evening, and a wet towel, which allowed him to wash off some of the accumulated filth. Sometime after that he heard a commotion out in the corridor. It sounded like all the cells were being opened up, and then his door opened and he was yanked out into a line of prisoners in the corridor. The man ahead of him was wearing a hood, and a short rope hung down to his waist from underneath it. One guard bound Gar's hands loosely with manila line and indicated that Gar should grab that man's rope. Then Gar's own noose, followed by a hood, was pulled down over Gar's head. A moment later, the man behind him took hold of his trailing rope. When the man ahead of him started walking, Gar followed suit to keep from choking him. Fortunately the man behind him also understood the game.

They were poked and prodded down the corridor and then outside, where rough hands kept them tripping down a set of stairs. Then more trudging, probably across that parade ground, until he heard the distinctive sounds of a steam locomotive idling somewhere ahead of them. They encountered a wooden ramp, where hands at the top guided them to the back walls of a boxcar and pushed them down into a seated position. Gar ended up in a corner, with another POW on his right. One of the guards shouted a series of commands, and then big doors rolled shut. Twenty minutes or so later, the steam engine started up with a jerk, and they were off, destination anybody's guess.

"Who are you?" the man on his right asked. Gar told him. The other man said he was army air force, Major Jimmy Franklin, pilot of a B-29 recce bird that had been taken down over Kyushu. He had a mild southern accent.

"I thought you guys flew so high they couldn't get at you," Gar said.

"We thought so, too," he said. "We were at thirty-five thousand feet, but they've got a new tactic. Guy gets in a fighter plane, on oxygen, we think, and flies out ahead and above us. They've done something to the engine, because at the last minute he inverts and then flies right into us. Took our left wing right off. Copilot and I got out; another fighter strafed him in his chute, missed me, and here I am, lucky fucking me. We're going to Tokyo, apparently."

"Why Tokyo?"

"We were briefed back at home base that senior officers are taken to Tokyo so the expert interrogators get a shot at them. You were a CO, so it's even more likely you're going."

Gar told him about his sessions with the Kempeitai and the naval intelligence types.

"You went beyond name, rank, and serial number?" Franklin asked. "You *talked* to them?"

He seemed genuinely surprised, even disapproving, so Gar explained his reasoning. "The Japanese here in Japan apparently have no idea of how bad the war's gone for them. I thought, hell, tell 'em, with a generous measure of bullshit, of course, and maybe open their eyes to the fact that they *can't* win. Maybe they'll give up. Plus that guy was going to shoot more prisoners until I gave him something."

A whiff of acrid coal smoke blew through the boxcar, making everyone cough. Having been around coal, Gar knew damned well that wasn't quality fuel they were burning.

"Yella bastards'll never give up," Franklin said. "We're gonna have to bomb 'em back to the Stone Age, and then invade. *I'm* not gonna give 'em shit, no matter what they do."

Gar was about to say that he might be wrong about that, having watched the Priest casually murder two POWs as an inspiration for him to talk.

"Is it true you can't really bomb Japan from China?" Gar asked.

"We can and we can't. No escorts can make it that far and back, so we go high. Half the time we can't see shit on the ground, but we have to drop our loads in order to be light enough to get back. Photo interpreters are sayin' we're not doing significant damage. The scuttlebutt is that we're all goin' to Tinian pretty soon. Then we'll get P-51s to come along. You really tell 'em how many subs are sitting offshore?"

"May have embellished it a bit, but, yes, I did. First time I was captured. That's why I ended up on that carrier—they were going to show me how invincible she was."

"What do you know about B-29s?"

"Big, go a long way, carry lotsa bombs. That's about it."

"Good," Franklin said. "Stick with that."

They stopped talking after that. Gar had the clear impression Franklin thought he was some kind of traitor for talking to the Japanese intelligence officers, but he still thought it didn't matter what they knew. If there were ten subs or even twenty operating off the Home Islands, the point was that they couldn't leave port without being hunted by an entire *pack* of submarines. The U.S. Navy's submarine noose was tightening every day. Eventually they'd quit leaving port, and it would be all over.

The train went around a long, squealing curve. That changed the relative wind, and soon they were all sucking coal smoke again. The hood actually helped. He finally fell asleep.

The train's whistle shrieking into the morning air woke everyone up. They were creeping along the tracks, the regular banging of the wheels on the track seams keeping noisy time. Gar thought he could smell the sea between occasional puffs of coal smoke. Then the air brakes clamped down and they shuddered to a stop. The doors rolled open, and there was the usual shouting in Japanese. When Gar felt his neighbor getting yanked to his feet he got ready to stand up, but nothing happened. He could feel and hear the rest of the prisoners being taken out of the boxcar. For a moment he wondered if he was being taken somewhere else, or for one of those one-way rides out to a swamp somewhere. Then he heard a familiar voice. It was the Priest.

"We go now," he said.

He stumbled getting up, his knees locking up after a long cold night on the boxcar's wooden floor. The major steadied him and then tugged on the neck rope. Gar followed, still hooded, and with his hands still bound in front of him by a short hank of manila. They went down the ramp, along what Gar assumed was the platform of a train station, and then into a building. The hood and rope came off once inside, and he was led to a small office in what looked like a train station. Outside he could see the column of hooded prisoners he'd been traveling with. The Priest sat him down in a wooden chair, told him to sit still, and then left the room. He came back with two cups of tea and handed one to Gar. By holding it with both hands he was able to get it to his lips. It was warm and had leaves in it, not stems. It was midafternoon, based on the sunlight.

"Not going to Tokyo?" Gar asked.

The major smiled at him, looking more than ever like a congenial rector at some parish church.

"Yes, we are. I will present you to Kempeitai senior interrogation staff. You have been cooperative, and you will be treated well. They are most interested in talking to you."

"What about them?" Gar asked, indicating the rest of the POWs.

"They are going to Tokyo as well, but they are going in coastal freighter. You will be traveling on destroyer."

Gar thought about that. Maybe some of his "mere propaganda" had gotten through. A coastal freighter, even if she stayed well inside, literally hugging the coast, was still going to be living dangerously. With the dearth of targets, the boats had been coming closer and closer inshore, looking for a score. A transiting destroyer, on the other hand, could go really fast, and thereby make it almost impossible for a boat to get set up for a killing shot. From Hiroshima

City to Tokyo Bay wouldn't take very long, and any sub spotting a destroyer going fast would assume there was something bigger in the offing right behind her.

"My own personal destroyer?"

He laughed. "No, Commander. This destroyer is going to Tokyo for far more important reasons. It happens to be the quickest method to get you there, that's all."

"And what will happen then?"

"That will depend on you, Commander. The things they want to know from you will be details about your submarines. You boasted that you can see mines underwater. They will want to know how you can do that."

"Why?" Gar asked.

"Why?" the Priest exclaimed. "Is that not obvious?"

"No, it's not. Japan is a collection of islands. You are using minefields as *defensive* measures. That makes perfect sense. If we know there is an enemy minefield ahead, we try to go around it, if possible, or we simply don't go there. If I could tell you exactly how this sonar works, what could you do about it? The answer is, nothing."

The priest thought about that for a moment, struggling for a reply.

"There's more," Gar said. "The most important things about a submarine are its teeth, yes? Its torpedoes. That's what you worry about. And yet it is *us* who want to copy *your* torpedoes, because they are the best in the world."

"We would arrange the mines in a different manner, perhaps," he said. "To confuse your sonar."

Gar shook his head. "Mines are mines. They are buoyant metal spheres. Filled with explosives and air. They are held between the bottom and the surface by mooring chains, so that they lurk at a prescribed depth from the surface. That's how they work, they just wait. If a ship or a submarine touches one, boom. That's all there is to it. You cannot make them invisible. It doesn't matter if you rearrange them—we can still see them."

"If we know the details of the sonar, we can perhaps jam it."

"Sorry, but you can't jam a sonar, except by using loud, explosive noises, and then your own sonars go blind as well. That is the point I've been trying to make all along here, Major. Japan is out of options. That carrier should have had fifteen destroyers around it. It had four. That tells the whole story, and that's why I've agreed to talk to your interrogators. They will absolutely *hate* what I have to say."

"You talk as if war is over."

"I think it is. Oh, not actually, not right now. Men will still die. Ships will still be sunk—perhaps like this destroyer we're going to ride. Cities will be bombed. More U.S. Marines will die on the beaches, and more Japanese soldiers will die in their caves. But on the grand scale, this war is as good as over. The Nazis have their backs to the wall in Berlin on not one but *two* fronts. We are all waiting for Japan to realize that she, too, will soon be surrounded and just stop."

"We will fight forever," the Priest declared. "We will *never* surrender. We will fight to last citizen. And if you come with your marines and your ships to invade these islands, everyone, old men, boys, women, *everyone*, will fight you to the death."

"We don't actually have to invade you, Major," Gar said softly. "Your people are beginning to starve now, and we're not even here, are we? But our machines are here. That's how this will end, Major. The Japanese people will indeed fight to the death—against machines. Against American technology. "

He shook his head in frustration. "I must not talk to you. You make me crazy!"

"I apologize, Major. If someone asks me a question, I tell them what I believe is the truth."

"If you say such things in Tokyo, they will beat you to pieces."

"For telling them the truth?"

"For having no *honor*!" he shouted.

Gar didn't know what to say to that, so he just thanked him for the tea. The major stomped out of the office, slamming the door. Gar closed his eyes. It was probably the last decent food or drink he was going to see for a while. Outside, the line of POWs had had their hoods taken off. Gar could see the air force major staring in at him through the window, an accusatory expression on his face. Gar didn't have to wonder much about what the major was thinking.

He could see now that his little crusade was not going to work. The Japanese weren't interested in the truth of their circumstances. They were only interested in maintaining the fiction that they were all samurai, devoted acolytes to the mystical Bushido code, and their warped sense of honor was not just everything to them—it was the *only* thing. They had to know that most of what had been their huge fleet was now being crushed in the black ocean depths of the Pacific. As for Gar, he was warm and nobody was whaling on him, for the moment, anyway. One hour at a time.

TWENTY-SIX

Two of those hours later they were driving through the perimeter gates of the Kure naval arsenal. The Kempeitai major and Gar sat in the back of a strange-looking black sedan with an enlisted driver and one guard up front. Gar was no longer hooded or handcuffed. He was sure they'd figured out that he would recognize the hopelessness of any escape attempt. How long would one khaki-clad, white-faced round-eye last in the Japanese countryside, where the locals were already butchering any fliers who managed to bail out of their B-29s?

Kure by day looked a lot like any U.S. naval shipyard or base. Sooty industrial buildings, giant yard cranes grinding along the narrow, cobblestoned streets, smokestacks streaming coal smoke, bright rail tracks in all the streets, and a throng of workers everywhere, wearing dirty uniforms and carrying canvas bags full of tools, parts, pipe, wiring or valves, or pulling welding gas cylinders on handcarts that looked like they'd been there from the days of sail. The car crawled through all the activity with the driver hitting a screechy horn every few seconds and the workers ignoring him with profound disinterest. When they got down to the waterfront, there were more cranes and small trucks tending to one large warship, a heavy cruiser whose entire bow was missing. She was parked inside a flooded dry dock, and Gar wondered if that was the dock he'd torpedoed. She was well inside the dock, her front end enveloped in a fountain of welding sparks. There were three destroyers nested alongside each other at the caisson end, but tellingly, there was no caisson. It was a dock, but no longer a dry dock.

Across the harbor was Etajima Island. The buildings of the Japanese Naval Academy shone dully in the waning winter sunlight. Out in the harbor was a large black battleship, riding to a buoy, her top hampers looking like the towers of a feudal castle. Gar had always hoped to see one—through his periscope. They drove down the sidewalls of the dock, passing underneath the big yard cranes that went rumbling by, their warning bells clanging a lookout for pedestrians and vehicles alike. There were clear signs of the Dragon's attack around the shipyard. There were craters in the streets, hurriedly filled in with sand, and holes in the window walls of the shops. One large yard crane had been burned out, and many piles of debris had been pushed up into corners.

They stopped at the nest of destroyers, where petty officers on the quarterdeck watched warily, waiting to see if there was going to be some ritual ceremony required for the new arrivals. The driver got out and opened the door for the major. The guard did the same for Gar, but with a lot less courtesy. As he was hauled out he heard a noise rising above the industrial hum of the metal shops, cranes, and power plants. It was a dull rumble of engines, and suddenly everyone, the crewmen on the destroyers, the shipyard workers, the guard and driver, and the major, was staring skyward. Gar looked up, too, and saw a complex pattern of contrails in the sky, turning light pink as the sun began to set. There appeared to be hundreds of them being generated by invisible sources against the darkening eastern sky. They were all headed in the direction of the Kure arsenal. Then the sirens started wailing. That's when Gar found out how many people were working at the arsenal, because the streets suddenly filled with shipyard workers, all running for the concrete Quonset-hut-shaped shelters located between the larger buildings. The major, in defiant contrast, folded his arms and sat down on a mooring bollard, obviously unafraid and ostensibly prepared to watch the show.

The three destroyers went to General Quarters as soon as the sirens sounded. Gar didn't know what to do. His guard looked like he really wanted to head for one of those shelters, but the major's nonchalant pose made that impossible. A large bang startled all three of them as the outboard destroyer let fly from its forward 5-inch mount. Gar was impressed at how fast they'd gone into action. The middle destroyer in the nest soon joined in, and Gar had to put fingers in his ears as the guns blammed away, pointing high, but probably not high enough, at the front of the advancing contrails. Gar could barely see black shell bursts high in the sky after thirty seconds or so, and finally the inboard destroyer went to work. Then came a mighty boom from out in the harbor. Gar turned around to see the battleship's main guns trained skyward and belching huge gouts of fire and smoke across the harbor. He knew battleship guns could throw 1-ton shells 20 miles, but he didn't know if that translated directly into altitude.

The contrails covered most of the sky as the bombers passed overhead, and for a moment Gar thought they were bound for Hiroshima and not bothering with Kure. He was wrong about that. The leading edge of the contrails had gone well past Kure when the first 1,000-pounders began to land about a mile east of them. He would have thought that a mile would make a difference, but the advancing wall of blast and fire erupting across the visible horizon was already shaking the concrete under his feet. The major didn't look so confident now, and Gar saw that their guard was no longer with them.

The major was visibly torn. Bushido required him to stand un-afraid and wholly unimpressed. The next stick of bombs landed somewhat closer, and his best efforts were faltering badly. Apparently, the B-29s, for that's what these planes had to be, dropped their entire load in less than a few seconds, and thus the bombs landed, all twenty of them, in less than a few seconds, pulverizing everything within 500 feet of the impact point. Gar noticed a steel ladder that led down to the water from the pier level in the flooded dry dock. It had a steel cage over it for safety. It probably went all the way to the bottom of the dry dock, which is where he would have preferred to be just then except that it was flooded with 42 feet of water. Still, standing out in the open on the pier was no longer an option. Gar ran for it, sure that the major was shouting some-thing at him, but he no longer cared. He hopped out onto the ladder and climbed down to the water, where he quickly submerged himself right up to his chin, leaned back against the cage, and closed his eyes.

By now the bombs were drowning out the sustained fire of the nested destroyers. Gar could no longer see where they were landing, but his head and ears were buffeted by blast waves as hundreds of large bombs fell into and all around the Kure arsenal. He finally ducked underwater when the pressure on his ears and face became too much.

He'd never felt so utterly helpless in his life. Even depth charges, whose terror he had barely come to master, were *nothing* compared to this unending, overwhelming, ear-crushing, chest-constricting, and utterly relentless barrage. It wasn't like the movies, where a few bombs went off and everyone was afraid. This was an *eternity* of stupendous, hammering power, with each God-like pulse seemingly aimed right at him.

He finally had to pop to the surface to breathe, then wished he hadn't. For the two seconds he pushed his face above the surface, the shock waves from the bombs burned the skin on his forehead and squeezed the fillings in his teeth. When he went back down he went *way* down, pushing himself on the rungs of that ladder to get deeper, as the *flash-flash-flash-flash* of the exploding bombs lit up the water in the dry dock with a continuous dull red glare. Gar felt a sudden compression in the water and heard an incredibly loud clanging noise, and then his face was whipped sideways by a shock wave. Only the cage kept him from being wiped off the ladder. He'd been holding his breath and was now out of air. He scrambled back up, his lungs bursting, and then the whole ladder was ripped off the concrete wall as another bomb went off. He'd been squeezing his eyes shut the whole time, but when he opened them he saw the propellers and rudders of the inboard, pier-side destroyer lurching toward him, and forward of that a dissolving red and white fireball under the water that boiled outward and upward, lancing his eardrums and flattening the skin of his face against his teeth as she blew up.

The cage that had been keeping him on the ladder now became

a deathtrap. His hands felt like they were welded to the railings until he finally realized that he was going deep into the flooded dry dock as the steel ladder, its pins blasted off, sank like a stone toward the floor.

He let go and pumped his arms and feet inside the cage, desperate for air, his vision turning red and his lungs screaming into his bleeding ears until he finally burst onto the surface, just in time to see the stern of that destroyer pointing skyward right over his head as her back half went down, her shattered hull glistening obscenely against a backdrop of the towering, glowing cloud of a magazine explosion farther forward. The other two destroyers had been shoved sideways out into the middle of the dry dock, their superstructures dismasted and deformed, and dozens of bodies were draped over their decks and lifelines. There was fuel oil everywhere, but fortunately it had not yet caught fire.

Gar was treading water and trying to breathe. The ladder was gone, and he was barely able to scrabble along the concrete walls of the dry dock, trying hard to get away from the subsiding carcass of the obliterated destroyer. He felt blood on both sides of his neck and could hear nothing at all. Every breath he took hurt his ribs, and there didn't seem to be enough oxygen in the air. His eyes felt as if they were hanging out on stalks, like some desperate crab. Large objects were still falling out of the sky and into the dock. For a moment, he wondered if he shouldn't just let go and slip back underwater.

This was just too goddamned hard.

But—it had stopped. The incessant body-slamming concussions had stopped.

It was over.

His forehead bumped up against an iron ring mounted on the seawall. He grabbed it with both hands, settled back into the cold water, hanging at arm's length, and closed his stinging eyes. His teeth hurt. His bones hurt. His *hair* hurt. His innards felt loose. His hands started to tremble, so he pushed one arm through the ring and just hung on by his elbow, which also hurt. He kept his face under the water, because it felt good.

It's winter here in Dai Nippon, Gar remembered. Water's cold. Cold enough to sting and hurt. Make you shiver uncontrollably. Then he realized that it wasn't doing that. Instead it was growing warmer, not colder. He vaguely remembered shivering his teeth out, but that seemed to be a long time ago. Now, it didn't matter so much. He was in the water and therefore safe from the apocalypse subsiding up above.

Hypothermia, his brain warned.

I know, I know, he told himself, but this is safer than being up there when they start coming out of their shelters and see what's happened. He wondered if he wasn't kidding himself. Which was going to be worse, he wondered: a crowd of hysterical shipyard workers seeing a round-eye climbing out of the dry dock, or what he would feel like when he actually saw the devastation wrought by *his* side, *his* air force, with just one bombing raid. Suddenly his old refrain, *Remember Pearl Harbor*, didn't seem to justify what had just happened here. Or maybe it did. He should perhaps ask the three thousand guys who died at Pearl what *that* felt like. Talk to all those guys on the *Arizona* who sat up in their racks on a Sunday morning just in time to see all the powder stored in the forward magazines coming at them in a wall of flame that flattened every bulkhead in the ship from bow to stern.

One raid. The first of many, as he had told the major, and now he knew firsthand what it was like to be on the receiving end of American firepower. The *Shinano* experience had been a little bit detached. When the torpedoes went off, they felt them but didn't truly experience them, not like, say, the carrier's engineers, locked down in their main spaces, when those four fish tore the main steam lines out of the overhead and scalded them all to death. When that destroyer in the dry dock went up in Gar's face, he got a firsthand taste of a ship kill, up close and much too personal.

You won't be fighting us, he remembered saying, one-on-one, samurai knights getting off their horses, taking off their fantastical headdresses, unlimbering their gleaming, multihued *katana*s to challenge the champion of the other side for the glory of the field. You will instead be cowering in your shelters, if you have shelters.

You will be trying not to shit yourself while unimaginable destruction rains down on everything you have ever known and loved,
everything familiar to you, your family, your workplace, your
home, your village, town, city, and all of it descending soundlessly
from a stratospheric composition of pinkish ice-crystal contrails
scribed across the skies of a winter's evening, and not for a few
minutes but for an eternity of overwhelming sound, pressure, heat,
bone-rattling concussion, and the certain knowledge that you will
never survive what is happening all around you.

Something small bounced off his head. He looked up.

The major was standing above him on the seawall. He appeared
to be entirely unhinged. He was wobbling on unreliable legs with
both hands clasping his bloody head. His uniform was shredded
from top to bottom, and his body looked as if he'd been flogged.
Blood trickled down from his eyes and ears. His mouth was moving while his hands clawed at his head and hair as if he were search-
ing for lice. Behind him the naval base was simply ablaze. Huge
clouds of smoke and dust pumped up into the lambent evening sky,
the smoke illuminated from within by intense fires. The major finally fell to his knees and tried to steady himself with one trembling hand. The other hand produced a pistol. His eyes were so
deformed Gar wondered if he could really see him, but he was obviously intent on shooting something. Somebody. Him.

Gar knew he should duck back underwater as the major raised
that pistol, even as Gar saw that his injured arm was unable to control the gun. Gar was in such a state that he decided not to bother
ducking. The major pointed the pistol in Gar's general direction
and began firing. Gar could feel but not hear the gun going off. He
could see the bullets scribing bright white bubble trails into the
water at odd angles. That seemed to be an important detail as this
half-mad, bomb-shocked Japanese officer tried to kill him. Gar
knew he should have been afraid, terrified, even. Instead, he realized that he sympathized with the deranged officer up above on the
pier.

The major stopped shooting when he realized he hadn't come
anywhere near Gar with his wild gunfire. He looked to his right,

where a small cluster of similarly stunned crewmen on the nearest destroyer—themselves still on their hands and knees, their faces bloody from concussion—were watching from the middle of the dock. Gar wasn't sure they even saw him down in the water, littered as it was with floating debris and oil. The major opened his mouth and tried to say something, but only produced bloody froth. He was weeping, so frustrated and concussed that he probably didn't even know he was crying. His mouth continued to move, and then he closed his eyes for a moment, bent over, and forcefully exhaled, seeming to shrink into himself. He then put the pistol into his mouth and fired one last time. His body dropped sideways into an awkward pile of bloody limbs and rags.

Gar stared for a second and then glanced left toward that destroyer. The men were standing now on her quarterdeck, some of them as blood-spattered as the major, at ragged attention and bowing deeply in respect for what the major had just done, apparently unaware that their ship was beginning to list to starboard.

They're not human, Gar thought. They're fucking monsters. They *approve*. Whatever are we going to do with these people?

TWENTY-SEVEN

Hours later he was back with the group of POWs at that tiny train station on the outskirts of Hiroshima City. He wasn't entirely sure how he got there, and his mind was already blocking out the images of utter destruction at Kure. The other prisoners had been gathered into a waiting room surrounded by armed guards, and the atmosphere had changed significantly. Each of the guards looked ready and all too willing to impale the nearest prisoner on his bayonet. It was getting dark, so they could no longer see much outside, but the red glow on the horizon from the fires at Kure remained undiminished.

Gar was booted into the room by a guard. His clothes, already ragged, were still wet and spotted with oil and blood from his damaged ears. Two guys picked him up and gently pulled him into the room, away from the nearest guards, who were prowling the perimeter of the group as if looking for potential culls. The room was warm because of the crowd, and Gar was grateful for it. He sat down. His brain still wasn't working well, not after the bombardment at Kure. He couldn't figure out why he was still alive. After the major did himself in, Gar remembered, he'd wondered how long before one of the watchers on that destroyer got a rifle and did the job correctly. By that point he wouldn't have minded.

The POWs slowly and surreptitiously pushed him all the way back into a corner of the waiting room. His traveling companion on the train, the army air force major, sat down next to him and asked what had happened. In halting words, Gar told him.

"They flatten the place?"

"Looked like it to me," Gar said. Then he realized he'd heard what the other man had said. He felt his sticky ears. He was no longer deaf.

"Big raid, then?"

"The sky was full of contrails. Looked like hundreds. Probably not that many, but big enough. They were long past Kure when the bombs started to go off."

Franklin nodded with satisfaction. "That means we're operational from Tinian. You see fighters?"

Gar shook his head. "I saw the end of the world," he said. "That was enough."

"Good," Franklin said. "About goddamned time. I saw you in that room with that Jap. Why were you getting special treatment?"

Gar told the major what had happened, and why.

"You're special, then?" Franklin asked. "'Cause you're willing to talk?"

"You're all wrong about that," Gar said. "That guy tried to kill me."

"Well, what the fuck were you doing talking to them?"

"Like I said, I was trying to convince them they've already lost the war. That there was no longer any point to resisting. That the whole industrial might of the United States was about to roll over them and squash 'em flat. That's what I was doing. Do it again, too. Because they are fucked. They just don't know it yet."

"Screw that noise," Franklin said. "You don't talk to the enemy. You *never* talk to the enemy. You do, you're a fucking collaborator."

"I guess you're entitled to your opinion," Gar said. "But collaborators help the enemy. When I tell 'em they're gonna lose this war, that's not helping."

Franklin shook his head and turned his face away from Gar in disgust. After about ten minutes, Gar asked the guy on the other side of him where he thought they were going.

"Doc thinks we're going to a coal mine on some hill right behind Hiroshima City."

Gar started laughing. They were being taken to a coal mine. His old man had been right after all.

Franklin gave Gar a funny look and moved away from him, as a train pulled into the station and stopped in a cloud of steam exhaust. The prisoners were herded into two boxcars. Gar had passed out again and was the last one to be rousted out of the waiting room. The first boxcar's doors were already shut, so he was driven at bayonet point to the second car and booted into a small group of British POWs. They picked him up and pulled him away from the sliding door, which had been about to break both his feet as the guards pushed it shut. Gar mumbled a quick thanks and then went back down to see his new best friend, oblivion.

They were brought into the camp in dump trucks just after sunset. There were twenty-two of them, eight officers, the rest troops. Gar was the only American in the group. The guards immediately lined them up in two facing ranks—officers on one side, enlisted on the other—then stood behind them with bayonets fixed, one guard for every two prisoners. Wooden telephone poles served as light standards, and yellowish floodlights illuminated the grounds of the camp. They could see what looked like a barracks in front of them, but no other prisoners were visible. By now Gar knew better than to do any obvious rubbernecking, but they could see that the prison perimeter walls were made of sheet metal panels attached to concrete posts. There were watchtowers at the corners and machine guns sticking out of them, pointed down onto the assembly area. Behind the barracks area were some large metal-sided buildings and what looked to Gar like the tip pile from a coal mine. A rail spur, filled with coal cars, came through the back walls of the compound.

In certain parts of the United States, coal was king. By mid-1945 in Japan, coal was king squared. It was so vital that POWs being used as slave labor in the mines worked right alongside regular Japanese coal miners, with the difference being that the miners were fed and the POWs were not. Uncle Charlie Lockwood's submarine war of attrition had reduced Japan's oil imports from their Greater Asia Co-Prosperity Sphere to almost nothing. They couldn't burn coal in their warships or airplanes, but just about everything

else requiring energy, such as merchant ships, power plants, facto-
ries, hospitals, and a good percentage of daily life, ran on coal or
even wood. Their coal-mining technology was somewhat primitive
compared to the States', and this was doubly so when diesel fuel
dried up. The POWs had become substitutes for powered mining
equipment.

There was what had to be an administration building to one side
of the open area out in front of the barracks, with covered porches
on three sides and a flagpole right in front. As they waited, a guard
pulled open the front door to the admin building and then saluted
an older Japanese officer as he came out. The officer stopped and
looked around the assembly area. This must be the commandant,
Gar thought, as the officer walked over to stand at one end of the
open space between their two ranks. He was wearing a short-
sleeved uniform shirt with badges of rank on its shoulder straps.
His trousers were bloused into shiny brown boots, and he wore
their version of a squared-off foraging cap. A Sam Browne belt rig
across his chest was attached to a large, holstered pistol on his right
hip, and an enormous sword dangled from his left. His face was one
enormous scowl as he roared out an order.

Nothing happened, and he sounded off again. None of the prisoners knew what he was saying, but the guards apparently did.
Two of them stepped forward, slid their rifle barrels over the nearest officer's shoulder, and pushed down, hard. Apparently some of
the officers had been POWs for a long time, because they immediately knelt down on the ground, then squatted backward onto their
heels, their hands flat on their thighs, and bowed their heads. The
rest of the officers did likewise. The enlisted remained standing.
The commandant, if that's what he was, walked down the line
looking at each officer the way an auctioneer might look at a steer.
Then he strolled back to the head of the two lines and asked the air
a question. One of the guards replied deferentially while pointing at
the officer line. The commandant nodded and then made a short
speech. Again no one understood until the last man on the officer
line, who Gar had been told was a doctor, said something softly.
The commandant stared down at him and spat out another order.

The doc spoke louder this time. "It's the honor speech. He wants to know if any of the officers want to kill themselves now to restore their honor. If you do, stand up."

None of them did.

The commandant gave each officer an inquisitive stare, then grunted. He then went to the doctor, and slapped him across the face as hard as he could. He repeated this welcoming gesture until each of the eight officers kneeling in the dirt had a bloody nose and a bright red palm print on his face. Gar didn't think his ears could ever ring again, but they did. The enlisted guys in the rank opposite pretended not to watch. Then the commandant went behind the rank of kneeling officers, unzipped his trousers, and proceeded to walk down the line, urinating on the back of every officer. He must have been drinking tea all goddamned morning, Gar thought, because he did a thorough job of it. Then he said something to the guards, who all laughed enthusiastically, and went back to his office.

The guards signaled for the prisoners to get up by prodding them with their bayonets, then marched the officer group over to a small building next to the barracks, where there were two large square cement tanks full of water. One of the guards rigged out a fire hose and hosed all the officers down, fore and aft, after which they were made to strip and take a second fire-hosing, with soap this time. Finally they were told to get into the square tanks and do another soap-down. They then scrubbed their clothes in the tanks and put them back on. The guards drained the tanks, washed them out, and let them refill. The POWs were marched back to the barracks and herded inside with much yelling and cursing in Japanese. The guards locked the doors and posted two sentinels out front.

The enlisted guys were already in the barracks, where it was apparent that the new arrivals weren't going to be the only occupants. There were two blocks of three-high bunk beds, one set occupied, the other empty. Filthy straw mats served as mattresses, and a block of wood as the pillow. A single sheet was rolled up at the end of each occupied rack. There were no signs of any personal possessions such as shoes, clothes, books, or anything else.

"Where is everyone?" one of the British officers asked.

"Probably down in the mine," one of the troops said. He also spoke with a British accent.

Gar wondered if he really was the only American here. Many of the Brits seemed to know each other, and he learned that they had all been shipped to Japan from the Dutch Indies on what they called a hell ship. Five hundred POWs left port; 240 made it alive to Japan. The rest died en route of starvation, malaria, pneumonia, dysentery, or just plain exhaustion and dehydration.

The doctor who'd been interpreting for the rest of them signaled Gar that he wanted to talk. "Alright then, Yank," he said, as they sat down together on one of the benches while some of the other officers gathered around. "Who might you be?"

TWENTY-EIGHT

Gar told them he was a U.S. Navy commander and erstwhile skipper of a submarine. The doctor asked his date of rank. Surprised, Gar told him.

"Right," he said. "Anyone beat that?"

The other officers were shaking their heads.

"You, sir," he announced to Gar, "are Senior One. Tonight when the rest of the chaps get back from the mines, we'll find out who *has* been Senior One and whether or not that still stands."

"Didn't feel very senior," Gar said, "when that guy was pissing down my back."

Some people smiled, but the doctor didn't.

"Look here," he said, "I'm Major Alex Morris. I'm a medical officer. M.O. We've learned this the hard way, believe you me. The only way we have survived has been to reconstitute our military organization and discipline. The senior officer in the camp, of whatever service or even regiment, becomes Senior One. We establish a chain of command, and we adhere to military discipline. We insist that the Japs deal with Senior One for all matters pertaining to the prisoners."

"And they tell you to fuck off and die, right?"

The major made a face at Gar's crude language. "No, surprisingly, they don't. One must of course observe the conventions. We bow, they don't bow back. We don't speak until spoken to. We never look them in the face, because, by surrendering, we have lost our faces."

"You used the word 'insist.'"

"Just a figure of speech, Commander. Thing is, most of the camp commandants have figured out that everything runs smoother if they pretend to recognize a military chain of command among the prisoners. With the exception of the occasional sadist, they don't want problems. They want *production,* because in their eyes, that's what prisoners are for—slave labor in coal mines here, copper mines in the north, railroad and bridge building in the far south. I mean, let's face it. A Japanese army officer assigned as a POW camp commandant is not likely to be held in high regard by the generals, is he. The last thing he needs is an 'incident,' a rebellion, a major escape, a drastic drop in production of whatever the hell, or some other problem that causes him to lose face with his higher command, because the consequences of 'problems' in the Japanese army is a quiet order to go find your short sword and use it."

"And you're saying this gives us leverage?"

"Not at all. We have no leverage, not one iota. At any time and on any given day, they could assemble the lot of us out front and tell the guard towers to open fire. You may not be aware of this, but it is common knowledge that Imperial HQ have given orders to all the camps that all prisoners of war are to be killed at the first sign of an invasion of the Home Islands."

"No, I did not know that," Gar said. "Nor do I think my bosses know that."

"Well, believe it, Commander. I wouldn't be surprised to learn tonight that even here they've been drilling for the occasion. This is a small camp, from the looks of it. Probably dedicated to the one mine, so perhaps the kill-all orders haven't reached here. Trust me, the larger camps are all firmly on notice."

"How long have you been a POW?"

"Since the fall of Singapore, I'm afraid."

"Jesus—that was, what, early '42?"

"February fifteenth, to be precise, and we will never, ever live it down."

Three years plus, Gar thought. That made his predicament seem trivial by comparison.

"What you must understand, especially if you become Senior One in this camp, is that we are all role-playing here. The Japanese officers are playing at being little gods. We are, in their eyes, vermin. They are being told that they are winning this war. We prisoners are supposedly evidence of that, and, as I mentioned before, we forfeited every scrap of our manly honor the day we put our hands in the air and our rifles on the ground."

"They are absolutely *not* winning this war," Gar said.

"Bravo," the doctor said, glancing out the window at the two guards. "And we are all *dying*, literally in some cases, to hear the latest news. But do not for one moment allow that notion to surface in front of even the lowliest Jappo out there. Understood? You get stroppy, we might all die."

Gar nodded. "Got it. I'm new to all this, and you guys obviously know how to play this game. I will do my utmost not to cause trouble, but someone's going to have to educate me on how to act around the Japs."

"Fear not, Commander," the doc said, indicating the guards outside with his chin. "You will receive daily instruction."

The resident POWs, some twenty men, came out of the coal mine a half hour later. They were indistinguishable from the coal they'd been working all day. The new prisoners watched as they passed through a barbed wire man-gate, where they were given a cursory search and then sent through a small fire-hose station, where a bored-looking guard hosed them down one by one. It was a small fire hose, maybe an inch in diameter, but the men were so weak they had to hold on to the wire to keep from being knocked down by the stream. Their soaking-wet clothes highlighted their skeletal frames, and about a third of them had to be helped by one of the others just to make it down the hill from the mine and into the barracks enclosure. Even after everything this new crew of Brits had endured on their long voyage from Southeast Asia, they looked to be in better shape than these poor bastards. The new prisoners moved away from the windows and clustered at the back of the barracks among the empty bunk beds.

The "residents" trooped in a silent single file up the steps between the two sneering guards and into the common room of the barracks. They went to the three tables grouped together in the middle of the room and sat down, side by side, on long wooden benches. They gave no indication that they'd seen the new people, and they looked to be so exhausted it was possible that they didn't even know others were there. Each man sat hunched over the wooden table, his forearms on the table, hands splayed out in front, head bowed, as if in communal prayer. Even from across the room Gar thought they smelled of near-death. Then one of them, an older-looking man in the first seat next to the doors, gave a quiet order.

"You lot back there," he said, in a fairly refined British accent. "Don't move."

Okay, so they did know there were new people, Gar thought. There were no lights on in the barracks, only the glow from some of the perimeter spots out along the metal fence. Then the front doors opened, and a tiny old man came into the room with a basket filled with rice balls. He set the basket on the table nearest to the door and scuttled back out. He returned carrying a galvanized 2-gallon oilcan with a long, flexible metal spout, which he also put on the table. Then he left, muttering to himself, and the guards pulled the doors shut behind him.

"Rations," the older man said. He picked up the basket, extracted one rice ball, and passed the basket down the table. Each man took one ball of rice and began to eat it, holding it in his blackened hands and nibbling the individual grains, chewing each grain slowly as if it hurt his teeth. Once everyone had finished his rice, two men got up and between them carried the oil can down the line, allowing each prisoner to have two audible gulps of whatever was in the can—water, Gar presumed. It was almost ritualistic, what they were doing, but it was clear they could all see that the resident prisoners' individual focus didn't go past the next moment. Rice. Eat. Water. Drink.

"*Benjo* detail," the older man said. Once again, two of the healthier-looking men got up and helped two very sick-looking men to the front door. The guards opened the doors and let the four of them out. The older man looked over at them. "Anyone needs the loo, now is the time," he said. About half of the new group started forward toward the doors, but the older man put up a hand. "In ranks, single file, heads down, hands flat at your sides, wait at the doors until they tell you to come out, and then go out one at a time. Do *not* look at them."

The new prisoners looked at each other and then formed the single line. They'd already found two piss-tubes in the back of the barracks; *benjo* detail was for more serious alimentary functions, especially for the men who were experiencing severe GI problems. The two men being helped out to the latrines were skeletal in the spotlights. Their skin was jaundiced and stretched across their cheekbones like parchment. Several of the others weren't in much better shape. Considering what they'd been through, and for how long, Gar realized that his captivity so far, beatings and bombings included, had probably been a cakewalk.

The original group of prisoners left the tables and hobbled to their racks. Major Morris took Gar over and introduced him to the older man, who turned out to be another army major, Willingham by name, an artilleryman from a Yorkshire regiment. Gar's rank as a navy commander was theoretically equivalent to a lieutenant colonel in the army, and thus he was now the senior officer in the camp. Theoretically.

"Congratulations," Willingham said with a weak smile. "Do you have the vaguest idea of what you're supposed to do?"

"None whatsoever," Gar said.

"Lovely," he said with a sigh. "What do you think, Dr. Morris?"

"I think we should leave things just as they are," Morris said immediately. "You are look older than the commander here, and the Jappos respect age more than some table of equivalent ranks."

"I agree wholeheartedly," Gar said before Willingham could say anything. "I know nothing about what to do here. I could get us all killed."

Willingham gave him a long stare. He was thin as a rail and weary beyond measure. His eyes were hollow and rheumy. There was coal dust in every seam of his face and hands. He looked to be in his seventies but was probably only a few years older than Gar was.

"Are you quite sure, Commander?" he asked. "As Senior One, you would have some protection from the more sadistic of the guards. As the lone American, well . . ."

"I understand, Major," Gar said. "For a little while they thought I was going to be useful to them. I was being taken to some place called Ofuna, near Tokyo, but after the Kure bombing, I think I got lost in the shuffle."

"Ofuna is the navy's POW center. It has a rather harsh reputation. You won't think so, but you're probably better off here."

"Even when the commandant uses us for a urinal?"

"That wasn't the commandant. That was the political officer, Lieutenant Colonel Kai. Kempeitai bastard. Fanatical like the whole lot of them. The commandant is Colonel Kashiwabara. Southerner. Has his family in Nagasaki. Not fanatical, which is probably why Kai was assigned."

"He looked ready to pull that sword and make all our heads roll."

"He is always ready to do that. Has Major Morris explained to you about the order to execute all the prisoners when the invasion begins?"

"He has."

"Do you have any idea of when an invasion might come?"

"Okinawa, any day now," Gar said. "The Philippines are back in human hands. Guam, Tinian, too. Your guys have most of Burma back in the British fold. The Home Islands, late this year, early next year."

"Okinawa could be considered a home territory," Morris said. All Gar could do was shrug. Okinawa was a thousand miles from Japan proper.

Senior One asked how Gar came to be captured, and he related what had happened to him since they were surprised near Bungo Suido. As they were talking, men began returning from the *benjo* detail, and a guard started yelling into the barracks. Senior One put up his hand and told Gar and Major Morris to get the new people into bunks.

"We'll talk more later," he said. "Sorry about no food. There's a water pipe in the back of the barracks. Don't let the guards see you using it."

"Why no food?" Gar asked.

"You haven't earned any," he said. "Yet."

Their day began at dawn. They'd be rousted out of their unheated barracks and given one golf ball of pasty white rice and two swallows of warm mystery fluid masquerading as either tea or soup—they could never tell which, but they consumed it religiously because that was going to be it until evening. The mine was bored into a high ridge that lay between them and the northeastern environs of Hiroshima City, which was just on the other side. Unbelievably, the guards would make them do morning calisthenics, if one could call it that. They were a squadron of wobbly skeletons going through the motions of flapping their arm and leg bones in the morning twilight while the guards did the real thing, constantly mocking the prisoners as they flailed weakly, trying not to fall into each other; the really sick ones lay back against the outside walls of the barracks, leaking at both ends. This was followed by the daily bowing ceremony, where they were forced to bow to a highly stylized picture of the emperor mounted in a boxy little shrine outside the commandant's office. Anyone not bowing "sincerely" would be hustled off to the punishment cells by two guards. They'd pass a stick between the prisoner's legs, jerk-lift him onto it, and trot across the grounds to the steel-sided building, making sure to keep their arms nice and rigid in the process. Earlier in the war officers had been exempted from slave labor, but things were very different now.

The POWs would then be marched, sometimes through snow, to the mine entrance, where everyone was searched. They never figured out what the Japs were looking for, but they were always searched, going in and coming back out. Then they'd crawl into enclosed transporter cars hooked together in a train, where six of them would be squeezed into a tiny compartment made for four Japanese, requiring them to bend their heads onto their knees. The train was parked on a slight incline leading down into the mine, so a guard would simply release the brakes and it would start moving down into the dark and the heat, eventually to the accompaniment of squealing brakes as it gathered speed. The tunnels were wide enough for two sets of tracks but only 5 feet from floor to ceiling. Once they got to the coal face, they'd crawl out and then lift the cars of the people-carrier from one track to the one alongside so that it could be pulled back up. The next train down would bring the regular mine workers and more guards.

The day consisted of using picks and shovels to gather up the coal that had been blasted by the all-Japanese night shift, prisoners not being trusted around explosives. They'd load individual coal skips, and then four of them would push the loaded, half-ton cars back out to the main chamber, where an engine would then take eleven at a time back out to the mine entrance. To Gar's surprise, most of the main tunnels in this mine were unsupported, which led to a lot of cave-ins, usually when they were blasting. The Japs were apparently used to that. The night shift would get trapped behind a rockfall. The prisoners and other Jap miners would clear it all out, and the night shift would come out looking none the worse for wear. It scared the hell out of the prisoners, of course.

There was little forced ventilation down there, so it was always hot and wet. During the winter, that was better than wet and cold, but by the end of July those of them who could still stand and work were on their last legs. Initially they'd been beaten for any infraction, real or imagined. As the summer wore on and the effective working numbers shrank, the Japs stopped doing that, probably because they realized why production was falling. Senior One's prediction about Gar being the lone American turned out to be spot on, as the Brits would say. It was bad enough for the Brits and the few Dutchmen in their group, but the guards made sure Gar knew how happy they were to have a Yank in the mix. A couple of times he was beaten senseless, only to wake up down in the mine, where he was expected to immediately get back to work. There were times he couldn't even stand up. The guards would then drag him over to the coal-skip rails at the head of the tunnel. He'd either move himself or be run over. He learned to just lie there, resting, until he felt the thrumming vibrations in the steel tracks that told him a train was coming down. Then and only then he'd crawl off the tracks. The guards would laugh, and money would change hands. The whole thing had been a bet.

TWENTY-NINE

At the end of his first month in the camp, Gar had a near-fatal confrontation with the guards at the face. He'd started work as usual but then realized four guards were watching him and talking something over, which sounded like they were working themselves up to a little fun with the American prisoner. The shortest one, who looked like a caricature of a Japanese soldier on an American propaganda poster, wandered over and demanded something in Japanese. The other POWs pretended not to notice, mostly to avoid a stick across their backs. Gar had no idea of what the man wanted, so he stood there, head down, not looking at the increasingly agitated soldier. One of the other guards came up behind him and whacked Gar's hands with his baton where they held the crude pick. Gar dropped the pick and folded his stinging hands into his stomach. The guards then indicated he should get back to work, but using his hands rather than a pick to claw down bits of coal from the seam.

Gar tried but made no headway. The coal wasn't very good quality, but he could not force any of it out of the seam. The guards laughed at him and "encouraged" him to try harder with their bamboo batons. He didn't know what to do, which was probably the whole point. The little soldier was the most aggressive; he kept badgering Gar with his stick and then with his boots until Gar snapped. Whirling in place, he landed a right cross to the soldier's face that almost snapped his neck and certainly broke his jaw. The soldier went flying across the workspace and lay still in a heap under one of the coal carts.

For one moment there was stunned silence, but then the remaining guards, all yelling at the top of their lungs, converged on Gar with their sticks. Gar rolled into a ball and then scuttled under a second coal cart to escape the beating. He wasn't thinking anymore, just reacting. Suddenly the beating stopped and hands were grabbing at his legs. He kicked back at them, but it was no use. He simply wasn't strong enough. When they pulled him out from under the coal car, one of the Jap sergeants was standing there with a pistol in his hand. Gar figured this was it and, at that juncture, almost didn't care. The other prisoners had stopped working when Gar had cold-cocked the little Jap.

The sergeant said something to Gar in Japanese. One of the Brits, who apparently understood, told Gar to stand up. He did so, slowly, alert for another bashing. The sergeant said something else, indicating with his pistol that Gar was to turn around and start marching. Gar couldn't figure out which way the sergeant wanted him to go, as there were four tunnels converging at the coal face, so he picked the main tunnel going back up to the mine entrance. The sergeant yelled at him and indicated he was going the wrong way. He then pointed his pistol down a side tunnel leading away and down from the coal face. Gar complied, stepping over the narrow-gauge tracks and their ties. The sergeant remained behind him, well out of range of any tricks Gar might try, as they crunched their way deeper into the tunnel. The lights strung overhead became more infrequent, but Gar had no illusions about getting away from the sergeant.

Finally they came to what looked like the end of the tunnel. Gar stopped up against the rock face, hands at his sides, waiting to see what would happen. He half-expected to hear the pistol and feel a bullet drilling through him, but then he felt a strong hand grab his hair from behind and an even stronger knee in his back, bending him backward like a bow. He windmilled his arms instinctively trying to stay upright as the sergeant pulled him backward to one side of the tunnel. He could smell the man's fishy breath as he leaned in close, his pistol barrel digging into Gar's neck. The sergeant said something in a low, incomprehensible growl, then at last jerked Gar to the right and kicked his feet out from under him. Gar felt himself dropping into darkness and then colliding with a steep slope of rock and gravel as he continued falling, accompanied now by a small avalanche of gravel and dust. After what seemed like an eternity, the slope began to flatten out until he was brought up short against a rock wall. His friendly avalanche proceeded to bury his lower legs before subsiding into silence and total darkness. Then the guard up at the top started shooting.

The tunnel did strange things to the sound of gunfire, but the bullets whacking into the surrounding dirt and howling off the rock walls as they ricocheted in the darkness sounded just like bullets. He felt a tug on the fabric of his right sleeve, and another one on his left leg, blunted by the fact that there was nearly a foot of dirt and gravel on top of his leg. Then he heard a yell from way up above and realized that something was coming down. Instinctively he jerked his feet out of the scree and slithered across the bottom of the hole until his face whacked into solid rock. A moment later something heavy arrived at the bottom in a second hail of loose rock, gravel, and coal dust, followed by the unmistakable sound of a bone snapping in the darkness. The snap was punctuated by a loud scream. Then silence.

Gar didn't know what had happened or what to do next. He couldn't see a thing, and every breath he took was full of dust. Then he realized his eyes were clamped shut. He opened them cautiously, still flattened against a solid rock wall. He had to blink several times to get the dust out of his stinging eyes. Then he thought he heard something. He listened carefully. Something was down there with him, moaning occasionally. He looked in the direction that he thought was up and discerned a grayish circle at the very top of the shaft. His eyes filled with tears as the coal dust irritated them, and his vision began to swim. He blinked rapidly until it cleared again. Then came another moan from somewhere in front of him. He finally figured out what had happened: Some part of the hole had caved in, and the sergeant had joined him at the bottom of the pit.

His first thought was to find that gun, assuming it had come down, too. The circle of gray light way up at the top did not extend to the bottom, so he could only feel his way on his hands and knees. He made small moves, trying not to make noise, although the more he listened, the more he became convinced that the sergeant was drifting in and out of consciousness. His fingers felt one of the sergeant's boots, and next to that was the pistol. He picked it up and pushed it back toward the pile of gravel that had broken his own fall, then backed up, in the direction of the far wall from which he'd come. His upper right arm was stinging. He felt the area. The fabric of his sleeve was sticky and wet. He knew he was lucky not to be dead, but now what the hell would he do? Then he realized the bottom of his pants was wet.

Pissed myself, he thought. Wonderful.

Except—he hadn't. As he felt around the bottom of the shaft, he realized there was water. There hadn't been any water there a few minutes ago. As he sat there, his befuddled brain trying to work it out, he realized that his fingertips were slowly being covered by water. The damned shaft was flooding. All those bullets had opened something up.

He sat back against the wall and tried to figure out what to do. After resting for five minutes with both eyes closed, he realized he could see better than before as his eyes adjusted to the darkness. He discovered the remains of a ladder going up one side of the shaft. Every third or fourth rung was missing, but the sides were still there, anchored into the rock with metal fasteners. He had no idea of how far up he'd have to climb, but he wasn't going to stay down at the bottom of this hole. He stuffed the gun into his pants pocket. He wondered if it was still loaded and chambered, but it hardly mattered; not knowing how to unload it, he just hoped for the best. If there was water seeping into the shaft, he *had* to get up that ladder.

It took him half an hour of climbing and resting to get to the top of the shaft. By the time he reached the lighted tunnel, he was having to wedge his left arm through the ladder attachment rings just to keep himself from falling back down into the shaft before attempting the next rung. The overhead light revealed what had happened. Fully half of the rim around the shaft had collapsed all the way back out into the middle of the tunnel. The gunfire had probably initiated the cave-in. There was room for Gar to crawl past the semicircular hole in the floor, but just barely. Finally he staggered back up to his feet.

He'd expected a crowd after all the shooting and then the noise of the cave-in, but there was no one there. He hadn't been down there that long—maybe an hour? There was only one way to go, and that was back to the work area in front of the coal face. He could dimly hear the sounds of machinery back down the tunnel. *Up* the tunnel, he realized when he started back, his breath wheezing as he made the climb. He pulled the pistol out of his pocket and checked it out while standing under one of the lights. It appeared to be either a 9 mm or .38 caliber. He popped the magazine and counted four rounds left. Plus one in the chamber, he calculated.

Carrying the gun in his right hand, he trudged back toward the work area, bent over as usual to keep from banging his head on the low ceiling. His right arm had stopped bleeding, and he was pretty sure it was a glancing wound, not a through-and-through. When he came around the corner into the coal-face work area, everyone, guards, civilian mine workers, and prisoners, froze in succession as they realized he was standing there with a pistol in his hand. The guards were armed only with batons; only the detail sergeant carried a gun. They were all staring at Gar as if Lazarus had just emerged from his grave, which was not all that far off the mark.

Gar had five rounds and there were five guards. He could shoot them all and then—what? Lead an escape to the mine entrance, where four machine-gun towers and the rest of the guards would be waiting?

He pointed the gun at the oldest of the guards, who quailed, dropping his baton and putting up his hands to ward off the expected bullet. Gar gestured with his other hand for the guard to come to him. The man stepped forward, his own hands still out in front of him, and started talking. Gar yelled at him to shut up. Then he gestured for the rest of the guards to come with him.

They looked at each other but didn't move until Gar lowered the gun to his side and gestured again. Then he turned around and started walking back. Gabbling among themselves, the five guards followed, accompanied by about a half-dozen prisoners.

When they got to the hole, Gar pointed down toward the bottom and then at the pistol. The guards were mystified, but then the older one understood. He pointed down into the hole and said what sounded like a name, his eyebrows rising in a question. Gar nodded and then picked up a rock and dropped it over the edge of the hole. Everyone could hear the splash down below. When he saw understanding on the face of the older guard, he handed him the pistol. For a moment he wondered if he'd really screwed up, but suddenly there was more urgent gabbling, and then they got to work. Gar sat down about 20 feet from the hole with the other prisoners and watched as the guards mounted a rescue effort. An hour later they brought the sergeant up in a makeshift litter made from a cargo net, assisted by everyone in the tunnel pulling on a long rope. The sergeant was in and out of consciousness, and his right leg showed clear evidence of a compound fracture.

One of the Brits came over after the rescue and shook his head.

"They'll either blame you for his injury," he said, "or the sergeant. Should be interesting, either way."

"Can't wait," Gar said. "I need to get this cleaned up, though. Before they shoot me."

In the event the camp commandant summoned Senior One and chewed him out for what Gar had done to the short guard. He then said that, because Gar had not left the sergeant down there to drown or killed him at the bottom of the shaft, he would not be punished further. Thereafter, the guards tended to leave Gar alone, and he wondered if that was a temporary thing or a sign that this horrible war was coming to an end. Lieutenant Colonel Kai had protested fiercely, but Gar thought the commandant was perhaps beginning to prepare for the future.

THIRTY

In mid-July three U.S. Army doctors were brought in from another POW camp. They'd been captured with Wainwright in the Bataan campaign and were now experts in how to serve time as a POW of the Japanese. They provided what little medical treatment they could. POWs sick with dysentery, asthma, influenza, malaria, and other assorted diseases were kept in what was euphemistically called sick bay, which was one end of the barracks screened off by hanging blankets. Anyone who died was taken to the camp crematorium. His ashes were buried in a well-like common grave that grew bigger and bigger as the summer dragged on. Each box of ashes had a small number tag, which the Japs nailed to a tree near the gravesite.

The bombing raids had intensified in July. The prisoners were usually down in the mine by daylight, so they never saw contrails, but their nights were filled with the sound of many rumbling engines passing high overhead, going north, and then coming back out again. There were rumors that the northern, more industrialized parts of Japan were getting hammered, but it may have been wishful thinking. There was no denying the nightly formations, though. The prisoners did wonder why they didn't bomb Hiroshima City; perhaps Kure had been the only militarily important target in the area. In the middle of July the Japs made them paint the letters POW on the roof of the barracks and their own buildings, probably figuring that that should fireproof the mining operation from the B-29s.

On the first day of August there was a major cave-in during the nighttime blasting work. The fittest prisoners were sent into the main tunnel the next morning to begin removing rubble, but the work was stopped at noon and everyone ordered back out. The fate of the miners trapped behind the rubble was not revealed. That night the Japs told them that they were going to be moved from this camp to one farther south, where the Kawasaki Company had a much bigger coal mine. Apparently "their" coal mine had flooded as a result of the cave-in, which meant it was finished as a productive asset. They were all aware that the general mood at the camp had changed markedly in July, with the Japs seeming not to care so much about what they were getting done in the mine. The guards acted dispirited, as if the real news from the front had finally begun to penetrate the propaganda screen. The POWs, on the other hand, sensing that the defeat of Japan was approaching in proportion to the number of planes coming overhead at night, became a tiny bit more confident and determined to live through the hell of being prisoners. One of the doctors who could speak Japanese and had been asked to treat the commandant for something or other told them that the commandant was getting worried about what would happen to him once the war was over. Everyone came up with ideas on that subject, although they rarely saw the actual commandant. Kai was another matter.

A week after the cave-in, they handed out cotton laundry bags, told the prisoners to gather up their meager possessions, and fall in on the square out in front of the barracks by 0730. Conveniently for the Japanese, this meant that they skipped any form of breakfast. As the prisoners were released from the barracks, they were surprised to find the parade ground littered with leaflets. The small scraps of paper were covered in kanji, the Japanese symbol language. It looked like they had blown across the ridge from Hiroshima City the day before. One of the prisoners went to pick up a leaflet and then quickly dropped it when the guards went ballistic. Apparently it was forbidden to even *notice* the leaflets, much less touch one. The prisoners couldn't read them anyway; they had a much more basic need for small pieces of paper.

Paper rain.

Gar remembered that paper rain had been Hashimoto's cue to go to Hiroshima City and turn the mysterious thing from OFF to ON. As they waited in crooked ranks, he wondered if the old man had managed it, or if he was even still alive. Based on the appearance of many civilian workers in the camp, food for the general population had become even scarcer than the last time he'd seen Hashimoto beneath the pier. The engineers driving the coal trains looked like skeletons, and they were all from the north. The people living along the shores of the Inland Sea could at least catch fish.

Their attention was distracted by the arrival of four army trucks that clattered into the yard in front of the barracks, their exhausts smelling like popcorn. The officer known as Kai came out and met with another officer from the truck convoy. The truck officer seemed bored with his mission, while Kai was full of himself, as usual, shouting and gesturing fiercely. The truck officer lit up a cigarette and waved a hand at all the assembled prisoners, as if to say, you want 'em loaded, you load 'em. This made Kai even madder, and there were more verbal fireworks, bringing the camp commandant to his office doorway to see what the problem was. He was just in time to see a magnesium flare ignite right above the camp. It was a really big magnesium flare, but strangely, it made no noise—no pop or bang, just the whitest light any of them had ever seen. They were all squinting through their fingers as they slowly realized that it had *not* gone off overhead but farther south, just over the ridge that stood between the camp and Hiroshima City.

The incredible light threw that ridge into stark relief, etching every rocky feature along the ridgeline into the glowing sky. Gar could see the black silhouettes of birds being wiped from the sky by some invisible hand, and then came a sudden and prolonged feeling of ear- and lung-squeezing noise, not a clap of thunder but rather a long crescendo of awful power, followed by an enormous rumbling cloud of burning gases, smoke, dust, and tiny bits of debris rising into the air, going much too fast, pumping straight up into the high atmosphere and filled with boiling red and yellow flame that lasted for what seemed an extraordinarily long time. Everyone, guards and prisoners alike, was transfixed by this apparition that got bigger and bigger as the seconds ticked by, violently shaking the ground like an earthquake and still rumbling as it billowed upward and finally began to expand at the top as the thermal column hit the icy air at 30,000 feet, the altitude at which the B-29s traveled. It was large enough that they wondered if it would reach them here in the camp when it collapsed.

One of the American army docs said it for all of them. "What the *fuck* is that?"

THIRTY-ONE

The drivers had shut down their trucks and climbed out to look, spellbound by the sight of that still-luminous cloud, which was now turning black at its base, as if whatever was underneath it were beginning to burn in earnest. The rumbling noise had subsided, but there was a great wind blowing *toward* the base of that cloud, strong enough to bend trees over and make most of the POWs hunch over or get down on the ground to keep from being blown up and over the ridge. A hail of dust and small rocks flailed their backs for a full minute, and the tin roof panels on the buildings chattered away like a chorus of snare drums.

It was clear the Japs didn't know what to do and were looking to the commandant for orders. That worthy was still standing on the porch of his office, mouth agape, as he watched that titanic cloud begin to curl at the top and assume an unsettling likeness to a poisonous mushroom in some God-sized vegetable garden. Whereas the commandant looked shocked, Lieutenant Colonel Kai looked even more furious, if that was possible. Everyone could hear the shrill ringing of a telephone inside the office over the shrieking wind, but the commandant was ignoring it as he stared upward at that hideous cloud.

Finally Major Willingham gestured that the prisoners should go back into the barracks. Everyone moved slowly, so as not to arouse the guards or Kai, and slunk back inside. The Jap guards did nothing to stop them, and eventually they all followed the prisoners into the barracks, looking over their shoulders at the monstrous

shape blotting out the sun to the south and west. They were visibly
shaken by what they'd just seen, and so were the prisoners. The
cloud reminded Gar of a picture he'd seen of Mount Etna going
off, and he wondered aloud if it would come back to earth and wipe
them all out.

There'd been neither air raid sirens nor the sounds they usually
heard when a large B-29 raid came in from the south, only that
eye-searing white light, blooming just out of their sightline behind
the ridge. Now that Gar thought about it, he could also see in his
mind's eye what looked like an expanding transparent sphere of
pure, multicolored energy racing out from the hidden center of the
white light. He'd seen something similar to that when they'd torpedoed what turned out to be a Jap ammo ship off Luzon. This thing,
whatever it was, had been many hundred times the force and scale
of that blast. One of the prisoners wondered aloud if those leaflets
had had anything to do with what had just happened. They could
see through the windows the contrast between a normal sunrise to
the east and the looming shadow of that enormous cloud to the
south and, increasingly, west of the camp as the high winds clawed
at the tops.

A guard sergeant burst through the door and shouted at the
other guards, who'd been hanging around in the common area of
the open-bay barracks as if wondering what to do next. Jap sergeants and officers never just issued orders—they always shouted
them as if they were perpetually furious at their subordinates, who
in turn jerked into quick bows and then hustled back outside. The
prisoners went to the windows and saw the commandant and
Lieutenant Colonel Kai engaged in a heated discussion on their office porch. An underling appeared in the office doorway with two
telephones in his hands, and the commandant threw some papers
down on the floor and grabbed the nearest phone. They could hear
emergency vehicles going by outside the fence in the direction of
Hiroshima City, where they could see a lower, more familiar black
cloud assembling. It looked to Gar as if the whole city might be on
fire behind the ridge, if all that smoke was any indication.

The sergeant came back into the barracks, glared at all of them, and then stepped back outside, where he locked the doors. Apparently their little outing to the other coal mine was off for the day. For the next few hours they heard many vehicles racing by the prison compound, some with sirens but most without. There was endless speculation about what had happened. According to some of the air force pilots, Hiroshima was a major ammunition assembly point. Perhaps a large ammo ship had exploded in the harbor, in turn setting off a warehouse or two. Most of them, though, felt that this was something new and very different. Ammo dump explosions often went on for hours, with trails of rockets and other munitions visible all over the place. This hadn't been like that at all. This had been a single colossal blast, so big that half the city had gone up into the air—and stayed there.

By late afternoon the vehicles were coming the other way, out of the city, over the ridge, and down past the POW camp. Now they were going much slower, and they were loaded with casualties, horrible ones. By evening there were columns of civilians walking among the crawling line of cars and trucks coming over the pass from Hiroshima City. Many of the walking wounded were so badly burned that their faces appeared to be dripping off their skulls like hot wax. Any of them who fell by the wayside were simply left. The prisoners had no idea of where the walking wounded were all going, but it was clear that the number of casualties in the city was in the thousands, not hundreds. After a while the gates to the compound were opened and some of the injured were diverted into the camp's central assembly area. They staggered in, the wounded helping the dying, dropping in rows and columns on the parade ground, while the guards watched in horror. The prisoners took care to remain inconspicuous as they stared out the dirty windows, standing to one side so as not to be too obvious. Gar saw one horrifically burned woman being given a cup of water, oblivious to the fact that it was pouring out of a hole in her throat as fast as she was drinking it.

Over the ridge there was still a vast cloud of smoke, bending to the west as the evening winds rose out of the Inland Sea and blew toward the Sea of Japan and distant Korea. The towering cloud had dissipated by then, but this new one indicated that everything that could still burn down in the city was burning. Another wave of emergency vehicles, with different markings, came down the road and went over the ridge, followed by a column of army trucks filled with soldiers.

At sunset the commandant and Kai were observed heading toward the barracks. The prisoners all scattered to their racks and away from the front windows. Kai unlocked the door and stood back to let the commandant in. Kashiwabara spoke some English and now shouted for all of them to get outside.

"You help," he demanded. "Outside. Now. You help."

Gar wasn't sure what they could do for the writhing mass of severely burned humanity on the ground, but out they came, dispersing through the huddled figures in the near darkness to do what they could. The first thing they noticed was the smell. A sweetish odor of overcooked meat permeated the enclosed prison compound, threaded with more elemental smells as people died where they lay on the grounds. The guards were making rounds with wooden buckets of water and small towels, and the prisoners' job became one of tending to individuals, wiping away burned flesh or administering sips of water. The burns were the most severe Gar had ever seen, revealing blue white bone in many cases every time they used a towel. Many of the victims could breathe only in a rapid-paced series of tiny puffs, and once they started doing that, they died before long. As the night wore on, the prisoners were detailed to carry bodies off the assembly area into a corner of the compound. They didn't need lights—there was a deep red glow in the sky coming from over the ridge as Hiroshima or whatever was left of it continued to burn through the night.

By dawn the area within the compound had settled into a profound silence. Gar realized that none of the two hundred or so wounded who'd been let into the prison camp were still alive. The prisoners were exhausted from their night's work. Most of them just lay down on the ground and tried to sleep. The guards did the same. The commandant had spent the entire night on the front porch of his headquarters building, just staring out into the dark-

ness. Kai hadn't been seen since they'd come to roust out the prisoners. Rumor had it that he'd gone into the city on the other side of
the ridge. There was no food that morning.

Major Willingham was afraid that there would now be a mass
execution of the prisoners. They all felt a terrible sense of forebod-
ing. When the Japs came to their senses, they'd want blood for
whatever had happened over the ridge. Then Gar heard air raid sirens starting up to the east of them, away from the city. Nobody
seemed to know what to do. None of the guards did anything at all,
so everyone just looked up into the dawn light and waited to see
what was coming next. Finally they could see two lone contrails
flying from east to west, very high over Hiroshima City, and then
south until they were out of sight. Photo-recce birds, no doubt,
Gar thought, coming to see what had happened to the city.

The prisoners spent the rest of the morning clearing away the
rest of the bodies, carrying them in litters down to the crematorium building beyond the mine entrance. They kept wondering if
there'd be rations, but the little old man never showed. As best they
could tell, there were none for the guards, either. The prisoners
straggled back to the barracks building in ones and twos, went in,
and hit their racks after getting some water from the communal
tap. Gar washed his hands and face and then dropped into his rack
still stinking of the night's work. They all did. He fell asleep immediately but was roused seconds later by a sudden shaking, and
instinctively waved his hand to swat away whoever was trying to
get him up.

"Get out, *out*, everybody out!" someone was yelling. Gar opened
his eyes to see everything not nailed down in the building dancing
in place as an earthquake rattled their side of the ridge, raising
whitish clouds of dust outside and shattering what few glass windows were still left in the barracks building. Gar could see the light
fixtures swaying back and forth at the end of their hanging poles,
and then some of them even came down, their bulbs exploding on
the floor, as some of the prisoners tried to crawl out of the shaking
building on their hands and knees.

Something in Gar's brain said, *Screw it*. He felt exactly the way he'd felt right after the bombing at Kure—overwhelmed, desperately hungry, despairing, surprisingly indifferent. He pulled the sheet over his head and just lay there, waiting for it all to stop, one way or the other, and he knew he wasn't the only one doing that. Eventually the shaking did end. A sudden warm breeze blew through the barracks, lifting the sheet off his face and blowing all the dust away. One end wall had cracked open, and all he could think of was that they finally had air-conditioning. He went back to sleep.

THIRTY-TWO

Two days later they were told that the entire group was definitely going to be moved to the prison camp servicing the Kawasaki coal mine. Once again they packed up their belongings in the cotton bags and mustered in front of the barracks at daybreak. Lieutenant Colonel Kai came out with his entire staff of six officers, and the prisoners immediately noticed something different—they were all wearing their swords. The English-speaking adjutant then directed that all the prisoners be separated into groups of five. They straggled out of ranks with their bags and congregated in small clumps in the assembly area. There was a larger contingent of troops in the area than usual, all toting rifles with fixed bayonets. Everyone was hungry. They'd received one meal yesterday consisting of some kind of soup laced with rice and what looked like bamboo shoots. This morning, however, there'd been only a single oilcan of bitter tea for all the prisoners.

Once the smaller groups had been separated, more soldiers showed up from the direction of the main gate. These were faces they hadn't seen before, and each soldier was bearing a rifle with bayonet affixed. They'd obviously been briefed in advance, because there was no yelling of orders this time. They spread out into the assembly area, forming a hollow square of inward-pointing bayonets, making it clear that no one was going to leave. When they were finished getting into position, there were two soldiers standing behind each prisoner.

Suddenly Gar became afraid. Kai's expression was unusually fierce, and he refused to look any of them in the face while all the additional soldiers formed that hollow square. The sun had just risen in a bright yellow sunrise that threw fantastical colors over the camp and the north-facing ridge rising between the camp and Hiroshima City. None of the usual Japanese workmen were present in the camp this morning. The guards in the towers were not visible, either, but their machine-gun barrels were.

Then Kai drew himself up to his full height and began giving a speech, his words and intonation rising in anger as he got into it. Most of the prisoners, of course, could not understand more than a word or two, but they watched warily as his officers began to spread out into a line abreast, all of them watching the prisoners intently. The soldiers forming the hollow square pushed in with their bayonets, compressing the little groups of five closer together. It looked rehearsed, and Gar remembered the doctor talking about the Japs practicing for the day of the kill-all order. Had the invasion begun? That enormous explosion across the ridge—had that been the opening gun for the final invasion?

Kai finished speaking. Gar saw the commandant appear on the porch of his admin building. He didn't look too happy. The adjutant nodded once to the sergeant in charge of the five-man group nearest Kai. Immediately one of the group, an Aussie, yelled in pain as two bayonets were jabbed into his lower back, forcing him to step out of the group in the direction of the lieutenant colonel. Senior One started to object but was quickly silenced by one of the bayonet-wielding soldiers standing behind him, who thumped him in the head with his rifle butt, knocking him to his knees.

As they watched in growing horror, the Aussie, an emaciated twenty-two-year-old man who looked fifty, was forced to kneel in front of Kai, who then drew his big sword in one swift and practiced motion. He began shouting again, like a man who had to work up the courage for what he was about to do. At one point all the soldiers in the compound started yelling *banzai*, and then Kai lifted that gleaming sword and brought it down in a vicious arc that partially severed the Aussie's head from his torso. A second stroke finished the job, and the headless body flopped down on the ground, bleeding profusely, but not for long.

A second prisoner was driven forward while Lieutenant Colonel Kai wiped his blade clean on the tattered clothes of the dead Aussie. This time the adjutant had his sword out. The prisoners began looking around for a way out of this, but that palisade of lowered bayonets made it clear that any kind of resistance was hopeless. Gar was ready to do something, *anything*. They might all die, but they'd go down fighting, and they might manage to take a few of these monsters with them. Then Gar felt a bayonet at the base of his own spine and froze.

Suddenly several of the soldiers cried out simultaneously. Everyone looked up and then to the south, where another tungsten white glow was blooming on the horizon, many miles away but no less impressive than what they'd seen two days before: that eye-searing white light painting the underbelly of a high cloud deck, followed by a luminous, multihued expanding sphere of energy lasting only a fragment of a second, and following that the towering cloud boiling up above the distant horizon, looking even bigger and wider than the one they'd seen before as it pushed quickly into the stratosphere. It took a half minute for that deep rumble to reach the compound. There was no blast of wind in either direction this time, but the titanic cloud looked like the arm of God, gripping the island to the south of them and shaking it to its core for what seemed like forever.

All of them, Japs and prisoners, were transfixed by the sight, and then the prisoners began looking sideways for a way out of the ring of steel knives surrounding them. Kai sheathed his sword and stepped backward into the courtyard to get a better view. He needn't have bothered, because that cloud was definitely bigger than the one that had risen over Hiroshima City, even though it had to be 40 or even 50 miles distant. Up on the porch, the commandant's hands rose to the sides of his face as he stared in absolute horror and started repeating the word "Nagasaki" in an anguished voice. Some of the soldiers behind them also repeated that word, but in a different tone, one that revealed deep fear.

As if on signal, they began to back away from the prisoners. A phone started ringing inside the commandant's office. An enlisted clerk inside answered it, listened for a few seconds, made a wailing sound, and then appeared in the door to give the commandant a message. Again that word, "Nagasaki," and they guessed that the clerk was telling the commandant that the city was no more, because he fell to his knees and began to weep ostentatiously, while the rest of his officers and soldiers began chattering excitedly. Gar kept watching Kai and the soldiers. Either they were all going to die right then and there, or the garrison was going to fall apart.

At that moment a small jeeplike vehicle arrived at the front gate and beeped its horn urgently. One of the guards handed his rifle to another soldier and ran to open the steel gates. The vehicle sped in and stopped in a screech of dust, and an older Japanese officer got out. A column of army trucks that had been following the jeep ground to a halt just outside the gates. The older officer, who was probably a full colonel or possibly even a brigadier, took one look around the assembly area, taking in the scene: the crumpled figure of the Commandant still on his knees up on the porch, Kai cleaning his sword again, and then the headless body lying in the dirt. When he spoke, it was in a much deeper tone of voice, filled with quiet authority, with none of the hysterical shouting of the camp's officers. They were all at attention now, their faces frozen as they listened to what he had to say. Then, as one, the officers all bowed, broke ranks, and started barking out orders to the guards themselves, who hopped to whatever they were being told to do. Gar kept watching the towers for movement, figuring they were going to finish what the officers had started on a mass-production basis. The colonel, if that's what he was, never so much as looked at the groups of prisoners. He did glance up one time toward the south, where the very tops of that towering cloud were just starting to feel the effects of the high-altitude winds. Now it looked even farther away than when the explosion first occurred. The colonel walked over to the commandant, helped him to his feet, and led him into the office building. The prisoners were left standing alone on the assembly ground, fearfully eyeing the machine-gun towers.

In fifteen minutes all the Japanese soldiers, including the clerks, were trotting down toward the main gates, carrying what looked like all their field gear. They started boarding the trucks waiting outside. Even the tower guards had climbed down and joined the exodus, much to the relief of the prisoners. A team of six soldiers went into the storehouse and dragged out burlap sacks of rice, which they hustled down to one of the trucks. One of the bags broke, and they just kicked it aside. The prisoners continued to stand there in their segregated groups. Nobody wanted to draw any attention to himself from anyone at all. Once the troops had boarded the trucks, the senior officer came out of the commandant's office building and approached the five-man groups.

"Senior One," he barked. Gar looked over at Willingham, who was still lying on his side, his hands cupping his bleeding head. Gar stepped forward, brought himself to attention, and saluted, taking care not to look him in the face.

"You stay here," the officer said. "Close gates. Stay here. You go outside, you die. Stay *here*."

Gar nodded once. He didn't quite bow, but he kept his head down, looking at the ground. He pressed his trembling palms into his sides, not wanting to show this officer how afraid he was. The officer nodded back at Gar in that sharp, up-and-down head motion they used. Then he turned and started walking toward his waiting jeep. At that moment a single shot was heard coming from inside the commandant's building. The colonel stopped, put his hands at *his* sides, bowed deeply once in the direction of the office, and then got into his jeep. The vehicle drove slowly down toward the gates and assumed its position in front of the column of trucks. Then the whole convoy simply drove away. As best the prisoners could tell, they were alone in the camp.

THIRTY-THREE

Gar asked two guys to go down and shut those gates before the local population figured out that they were unguarded. Whatever the hell had happened to Hiroshima City and now Nagasaki was apparently grounds for killing every POW within reach. For the next few hours they organized to secure the camp. Several men checked the buildings to make sure all the Japs had left. Two Brits helped Senior One into the barracks building. Gar and Dr. Morris went into the commandant's office, where they found exactly what they expected to find. Gar liberated the commandant's pistol and then set up a detail to get the Aussie and the commandant's body down to the crematorium building. The prisoners who went up the towers reported large crowds in the street outside the walls, but they were not agitated, just standing out there, staring at that enormous cloud on the southern horizon as it bent lazily off to the west, pursued now by much blacker smoke beneath. The guards had left the permanently mounted machine guns in the towers, but no ammo. Gar made a mental note to search for some.

They checked the three storehouses and found that the Japs had taken every scrap of food, leaving only that one broken 50-pound sack of rice behind in the dirt. They salvaged every grain of it, and a detail went into the cookhouse to get some water going. Within the hour each of them had finished an entire bowl of rice, their first real food in two days. Senior One then called a meeting with all the officers in the camp to reorganize themselves now that the Japs had pulled out. Willingham had been injured more severely than

Gar thought, but he was able to speak, and Gar didn't want to "relieve" him if that was avoidable. He was a Brit, and most of the inmates were also Brits.

Gar volunteered to put himself in charge of the organizing effort, subject to Senior One's approval. Willingham waved that off and asked Gar to simply take charge. Two British infantry majors took on perimeter security. They stationed men in the three towers, dressed from the waist up in what they hoped looked like Jap uniform gear. Their job was to man the machine guns and move the barrels around occasionally to make it look like the camp was still guarded. A second detail went up on the roof of the main barrack to repaint POW and add NEED FOOD on the roof in 20-foot-high letters. The "paint" was made by mixing lime from the crematorium with some used motor oil. In the meantime they all made copious use of the Japs' bathing facilities, although there was no fuel to heat water. Gar sent a team into the mine to see if there were any signs of life from the trapped night-shift miners. The team came back shaking their heads.

The recce flights began that afternoon, both over Hiroshima City and farther south. Senior One thought that the departure of the prison camp's staff meant that things finally might be coming to an end after those two gigantic explosions. Nobody wanted to voice the other possibility, that new guards were inbound. Two of the radiomen had managed to get the broadcast radio in the commandant's office up and running, although it wasn't very useful given that none of the POWs were fluent in Japanese. There was still a steady stream of people coming up over the ridge from Hiroshima City that evening and throughout the next five days. Those who could walk were all helping burn victims who could not, and after a while the prisoners stopped looking through the seams. Men, women, children of all ages, and even some household dogs trudged sorrowfully past the camp, headed generally north and away from whatever horrors lay just over the ridge.

On the fifth day after the Nagasaki explosion the rice ran out. Senior One met with his officer council again, and it was decided that they had to go out into the surrounding town to see if they could get food. As they were meeting, one of the radiomen stepped in and said that there was funereal music coming over the government radio and that the announcer sounded really excited. The tower guards reported that the town's residents were coming out into the streets outside the camp and that they appeared to be falling into ranks on the sidewalks. As they hurried to look through the cracks they could see hundreds of civilians standing along the streets, but not a single military uniform. There were loudspeakers wired up to telephone poles at the street corners, and the same music was coming out of them. The POWs speculated quietly; they wondered if there'd been another sun-bomb, as some of the guys were calling it. Hiroshima City, Nagasaki, and now perhaps one of the bigger cities in the north? Or were the Japanese simply expecting some other overwhelming event to land on them? Then they heard the sound of planes coming.

The people in the street were peering up into the sky apprehensively, but this didn't sound like the one of the big bomber formations. A moment later two U.S. Navy carrier planes came overhead at about 1,000 feet. Gar was pretty sure they were Corsairs. They weren't carrying any external weapons, and one pilot had his canopy rolled back. They flew over the town and the coal yards, circled back, and came down lower, over the POW camp. The civilians outside stayed right where they were, displaying amazing self-discipline. The lead fighter waggled his wings at the POW group as he came over at 500 feet, and all of them cheered reflexively. He'd obviously seen the letters on the roof, and Gar thought they might be safer now that the Japs outside had also seen the fighters. Then they both flew up and over the ridge, dropping out of sight as they headed toward downtown Hiroshima City on the other side. The good news was that there weren't any Jap planes pursuing them.

Once their engine noise subsided, they could hear the solemn music again. After a few minutes, it changed tone to something more like a fanfare, and then a different announcer came on. He spoke for a few minutes, then said something that made all the civilians outside come to attention and then bow their heads. Gar watched parents admonish their children to follow suit. The crowd went utterly quiet, so quiet that they could again hear those two fighters growling around beyond the ridge. Then a voice began intoning something in a high, singsong stream of Japanese. Everyone in the crowd bowed even lower, and most of them had their eyes shut. The POWs wondered what they were being told; whatever it was had to be pretty serious news, based on the way the people were reacting. When the weird singing voice finally stopped, the civilians straightened back up and began to disperse into their homes and shops. Everyone on the streets was visibly upset, with many people openly weeping.

The prisoners looked at each other with disbelief. Could it be? Could it possibly be? Was this goddamned war finally, *finally*, over?

Part III

THE SILENT SERVICE

THIRTY-FOUR

The chief of staff, now Rear Admiral Mike Forrester, welcomed Gar into the SubPac headquarters conference room. An aide Gar hadn't met before brought coffee and then withdrew.

"Well, Gar, how are you?" Forrester asked after they'd fixed their coffees.

Gar was hard-pressed to answer that as he stirred his coffee. His hands still shook a little, but that was getting better. He'd been driven over that morning to Pearl in a staff car. The top floors of the Pink Palace were still in the hands of ComSubPac, but Gar was currently the only resident. The marine guards and the concertina wire barriers were all gone, and the hotel was making preparations to close for a year's worth of major renovations, after which it would reopen as a true luxury resort. Gar had arrived back in Pearl on an army transport ship from Guam only three days ago, and even after all the downtime aboard the transport and the medical attention in Guam, he was still very tired. He knew he was one of the lucky ones, actually. Too many of the men who'd been POWs for as long as three years had not survived liberation, ground down by tropical diseases, slave labor in dank coal and copper mines, constant brutality at the hands of Japanese guards and officers, unending starvation, and the sheer hopelessness of their situation. One of the last things Gar had done at the coal mine camp was to collect all those tin medallions from the tree next to the camp crematorium.

He'd learned that the Japanese army general staff had indeed issued standing orders to kill all the prisoners throughout Japan at the first sign of an invasion on the part of the Americans and their allies. When the atom bombs forced them to surrender, they didn't know what to do, so they simply abandoned the camps and let the prisoners fend for themselves. Allied planes tried to supply the camps via parachuted food and medical supplies for the first two weeks until ships could arrive, but much of that material ended up strewn over surrounding countryside, where starving civilians naturally helped themselves. Even after nearly eight months of captivity, Gar was one of the stronger ones, although he'd lost 35 pounds and three of his teeth were in questionable shape.

The following thirty days became a blur—liberation from the camp, the first triage stations, then truck transport to a safe harbor, a voyage to Guam followed by medical treatment, SubPac debriefings, the restoration of service records, ID card, pay account, basic uniforms, and all of that, followed by passage back to Pearl. Gar was sure that most of them had gone back into the POW enduremode until the navy finally declared them relatively fit for limited duty.

It was in Guam where he finally learned the fate of *Dragonfish*. She'd made it out of the Inland Sea and back to Guam, where she'd received a hero's welcome, both for the penetration of Japan's inner waters and the damage done to *Shinano*. Joe Enright and his *Archerfish* claimed the kill, and with that one sinking, Enright became the third-highest-tonnage scorer of the Pacific War. What *Dragonfish* had managed to do at Kure had slowed her down on the run to Yokosuka, and that allowed Enright, whose persistence was legendary, to finally torpedo her. That was the good news. The bad news was that on the next patrol out to empire waters, *Dragonfish* had disappeared.

There was simply no information on what had happened. Gar was saddened beyond belief to hear it, while at the same time relieved that his getting caught on the bridge in a crash dive hadn't been the proximate cause of her loss. Then he felt guilty about feeling that way. The senior submarine captain who debriefed him in Guam, one of the division commanders, set him straight. "You didn't lose your ship, Gar. Your exec, Russ West, who took over as captain, lost his ship. What you did by closing that hatch while you were still topside was a heroic thing, and you're up for a Navy Cross for that and a second one for the attack on Kure. Other than that, it's fortunes of war, Gar. Fortunes of war. Think about it any other way, you'll go nuts."

Now, home, sort of. Home had changed a lot since V-J Day. The Palace was practically empty. The submarine piers sported two, count 'em, two submarines. The pack of carriers, cruisers, battle-wagons, and destroyers that used to crowd the 10-10 pier across the way was gone. The troop transports were all at sea, bringing GIs back from hellholes such as Okinawa, Iwo Jima, Saipan, Tinian, even Guadalcanal. The base streets were no longer humming with truck traffic, or any traffic, really. The shipyard across the lagoon was down to one shift. The O-club had closed for major renovations. All gone. Everybody had gone home. Except him, it seemed.

"Gar?"

"Sorry, Chief of Staff," Gar said. "How am I? I'm very, very tired, and I'm mostly sad, I think."

"Dragon?"

Gar nodded. "And what I went through as a POW. I knew war was a titanic waste of human life and material, but I saw things that beggared the imagination. Even so, I had it easier than a lot of other people, especially the Brits."

"I understand you were at a camp near Hiroshima? A coal mine?"

"Yes, sir. There was a ridge between the camp and the city, maybe two thousand feet high. That's the only reason we didn't have all our skin fried off, too."

"I've seen a picture," Forrester said. "The one the B-29 took."

"Didn't do it justice," Gar said. "That thing boiled up from behind that ridge and all we could think about was the end of the world, and here came Satan. When the liberation teams finally reached us, they took us to a ship anchored out in Hiroshima Bay. We went through the city in open trucks."

"How'd you get through all the debris?"

"There wasn't any. Just bare earth, bare streets, a couple of concrete buildings that looked like broken teeth, and no people. No birds, no dogs, nothing living down there, for as far as the eye could see. It was quiet as the tomb. There's a river that goes through the city. It was filled to the banks with the wreckage of cars, bridges, telephone poles, and probably under all that ten or twenty thousand people, based on the smell."

"Japs are claiming they lost sixty to seventy thousand people in one instant at Hiroshima."

Gar nodded. "We saw some of them going up. Nothing came back down. Nothing."

"Jesus."

"Well, I went through the war saying 'Remember Pearl Harbor' every time I killed a ship. I guess *they'll* remember it now."

"You're not alone in that sentiment," Forrester said. "We're still toting up our own butcher's bill, but it looks right now like we lost fifty-two boats in this goddamned war. That's three *thousand* five hundred people—one out of every five guys in the submarine force, killed."

"I didn't know that," Gar said. "I guess nobody wanted to tote it up while it was still going on."

The chief of staff sighed aloud. "I wept when the news came that they'd surrendered. Wept for joy, and then wept for all those ghost ships still on patrol, known but to God where or even why they went down. Uncle Charlie feels even worse than I do about it, and we were on the winning side!"

"Once we learned how, we hurt them, though, didn't we. Hurt 'em bad."

"That's absolutely correct," Forrester said. "We bled them white. The submarines more than anyone else destroyed their ability to wage war. We shortened the duration of the war. No one doubts that for a minute. But it cost us three and a half thousand of the best people the Fleet had to offer, officers, chiefs, and enlisted. Like you said, what a colossal waste."

Gar remembered thinking the same thing when he watched *Shinano* go down. "When's Admiral Lockwood getting back from Guam?" he asked.

"Early next week, assuming he can get a flight. Believe it or not, the logistics problem right now is bigger than it was during the actual hostilities. Thousands of people headed back stateside, most of the fleet boats headed for decom, commands and staffs being dissolved left and right. And of course, Emperor Doug MacArthur demanding everything and everyone so he can get set up as the regent in Tokyo. Washington's yelling at everybody, and we're jumping through our asses here."

Gar thought that the chief of staff's lament was just a bit surreal. These were all real problems, of course, involving real people. He himself was one of the problems. Still, compared to what the whole world had just gone through, starting with Hitler going into Poland way back in 1939? This was more a case of the big brass not knowing how to shut it down for a while. If they wanted to keep feeling important, than everything had to be a crisis. As for himself, the future was unclear. He'd eventually be assigned to some ship or station, but probably not in submarines, for the simple reason that almost all the fleet boats were going to be razor blades within the next two years. Only the newest boats would be kept, and not many of them. He voiced these observations to Forrester.

"You'll be assigned here temporarily," Forrester said. "BuPers is going crazy trying to deal with the demobilization while every naval officer who thinks he's got a career ahead of him is jockeying for this and that job. Three of our COs were sent to commands back in the States that no longer existed when they got there. What do you *think* you want to do?"

That last question slipped in casually, but Gar knew it was an important one. He was, in more than one sense, homeless. No family other than his aged mother, back in Pennsylvania, whose mind had seeped away just before the war. No wife, no family, and absolutely no desire to ever go back to sea in a submarine. He had five more years to go before he could retire on twenty years at half-pay and start a second career, doing—what? Coal mining, perhaps?

"Am I promotable?" Gar asked.

"Oh, hell yes, I'd expect you to make captain on the next list," Forrester said. "Your war patrols were successful, and your last mission was—extraordinary, to say the least. The real question is, what then? War College. Washington. An attaché job? Unless of course you want to stay with submarines?"

Gar shook his head.

"Right, I didn't think so. In a way our COs are hoist on their own petards here. The acme of a submariner's career is wartime command of a boat. After that, what compares?"

After what he had been through, Gar wanted to say, *anything* else compared most favorably. He'd achieved that bright shining zenith Forrester was talking about, with the net result that all his people were now asleep in the deep somewhere out in that vast Pacific Ocean. More ghosts.

The aide came back in, apologizing for disturbing their meeting. "This concerns Commander Hammond, Chief of Staff," he said. He handed Forrester a piece of official correspondence, glanced at Gar, and then left the office. Forrester fished out his reading glasses, perused it, and frowned.

"Well, isn't this is a fine kettle of fish," he said. He looked over at Gar. "This is from the CincPacFleet JAG's office. It says an army air force major who was a POW has accused you by name of collaborating with the Japanese, and that a court of inquiry will be convened to examine the merits of this accusation."

Gar was stunned, until he remembered his discussion in the boxcar with—what was his name? Something Franklin.

"*Collaborated?* What the hell does that mean?"

"I guess we're going to find out, Gar. Know any lawyers?"

I used to know one, he said to himself.

THIRTY-FIVE

At 1500 that afternoon he was sitting in the waiting room of the judge advocate general's offices at Pacific Fleet headquarters. The headquarters building was a leftover from the scary days right after Pearl Harbor—three stories of ugly, bare concrete, a bombproof bunker underneath, and most of its corridors on the outside of the building masquerading as lanai walkways. It was built on the edge of the dormant crater called Makalapa. Gar had never been in the headquarters building—lowly three-stripers serving in the fleet ordinarily did not have any business even visiting the five-star's head-shed.

"Commander?" the yeoman said. "Captain White can see you now. Right through there."

Gar went into the PacFleet JAG's office. Captain White was a severe looking four-striper with gray hair and piercing eyes behind steel-rimmed eyeglasses. Before the war every navy captain Gar had ever seen looked like that. Now most four-stripers were in their early forties, so this captain had probably been here since before the war. White pointed unceremoniously toward a chair in front of his desk.

"Commander Hammond," he said. "Let me set the stage here before you say anything at all. You have been designated as an interested party to a court of inquiry, to be convened here in Pearl Harbor, in order to determine if certain accusations made by another officer regarding your conduct as a POW are true. Is this what you've been told?"

"More or less," Gar said.

"Okay. I see here you've requested Lieutenant Commander De-Veers to represent you at a court of inquiry. Short answer: That will not be possible, and frankly, not advisable. She has been assigned to a long-term project while she waits for her discharge."

"Discharge?"

"All the WAVE officers were temporary commissions in the Reserves. They will now all be discharged and returned to civilian life."

"Why'd you say 'not advisable'?"

White looked down at the pile of papers on his desk for a moment. "Lieutenant Commander DeVeers has a problem, Commander. A problem that, in my opinion, has affected her performance of duty. I would not want her as my defense counsel, and neither would you. If she were to have anything to do with this court, it would be in the capacity as counsel for the court. But like I said—she's simply not available. In fact, I may have to do it myself."

"Counsel for the court—the prosecution, in other words?"

Captain White leaned back in his chair. "No. This isn't a court-martial. It's a court of inquiry. Two very different things. A court of inquiry means a board of three line officers—captains, in all probability, since you're a commander—chaired by the senior officer of the three. For admin purposes, the court will be convened by the 14th Naval District commandant. It's a temporary entity—it's convened for a specific case and then disbands once findings are made. The statute provides for a lawyer to be assigned to the court as counsel, since the members are all line officers. His job is to keep the court within bounds of proper legal procedure. To keep it fair, the 'interested party' gets one, too, assuming you want one. The whole point of a court of inquiry is to determine what further action, if any, needs to be taken in the matter."

"And that further action could involve a court-martial?"

"Indeed it could."

"So I *do* want a lawyer, right?"

"As I said, the court will have one, so I certainly would advise *you* to have one, and we will appoint one if you so request. You have rights in these proceedings. You get to confront your accuser, examine and cross-examine witnesses, if any, and introduce evidence. What you can't have is Sharon DeVeers."

Already have, Gar thought irreverently.

On the way out of the JAG's office he asked the yeoman for a staff directory and found Sharon's phone number. Once down at the front entrance he used an internal phone to call her. Her yeoman said she was busy, so he left a message asking her to meet him at the Pink Palace that evening, if possible. Being an orphan at the moment, he didn't have a phone number, other than the front desk of the hotel. He told the yeoman he'd check back and said to tell Lieutenant Commander DeVeers that this was a business, not a personal, call. Then he took a shuttle bus back to the sub base. He needed to find more permanent digs at the BOQ now that the Pink Palace was shutting down. SubPac was releasing the requisitioned rooms in ten days, as most of the force's submarines were already on their way to West Coast shipyards for demobilization. When it came to actual submarines, the sub base was becoming a ghost town.

He also needed to refill his seabag. He needed a complete set of uniforms and some civvies. He'd left the Dragon in a come-as-you-are exposure suit and work khakis. Unless they'd off-loaded his personal effects between getting back from the Kure operation and her last patrol, everything he owned went to the bottom with her, including his academy ring. Basically he had to reconstitute everything and, oh by the way, face a court of inquiry because of something he'd said to an army air force major in the back of a Jap boxcar. He still couldn't believe this was happening. Having survived all of the things that had happened to him over the past nine months, he now had to face an investigation by his own superiors while everybody else was headed stateside for Christmas.

Sharon showed up in the lobby at six thirty. She tried unsuccessfully to hide the shock she felt when she saw Gar. She looked none the worse for wear and still wore that waterfall of blond hair pulled across her forehead. Gar found himself wanting to touch it.

"Goddamn, Gar Hammond," she exclaimed. "You look like you got shot at and missed, shit at and hit."

"You look pretty good, too," he offered. They did a two-handed handshake and then just stood there for a moment. "My long lost, one true love," he said.

"Hell, yes," she replied, with that big grin. "Let's get a drink, before they dismantle the bar."

They spent the next two hours in a corner booth. The hotel wasn't exactly deserted, but it had the air of a place that was going to close pretty soon, and the staff obviously knew it. He told her his story, soup to nuts, and she listened intently. When he was finished, she asked why he had said this was business tonight. That's when he told her about the court.

"That's bullshit," she said. "A court of inquiry for a 'he said, she said' story? Bullshit. Total bullshit. I'll tell you what a court of inquiry is for: Would you believe I'm working on setting up yet another high-level investigation and inquiry into the December seventh attack on Pearl Harbor? And they want to take you to a court of inquiry?"

Total bullshit, indeed, he thought. Besides, who didn't know the answer to the question of who was responsible for the disaster that was Pearl Harbor? The fucking Japanese, that's who. "That's what they're telling me."

"For *collaborating* with the enemy?"

"I told this major that I talked to them. And I did talk to them, mostly to stop them from killing any more prisoners. They knew I'd been a CO, and they knew that I probably knew important stuff. That guy sat there and had a prisoner shot right in front of me when I did the name-rank-serial-number deal. Then they brought out another one—shot him, too, *after* I said I'd talk to them. They're not human—they're a bunch of medieval monsters from the tenth century."

"What did you tell this major that you gave up to the Japanese?"

"I told him I'd talked to them. That I delivered a whole lot of bullshit, exaggeration, lies, and some truths."

"Did you tell him *exactly* what you told them?"

"No."

"Did you tell him that you talked to them to save other prisoners' lives?"

"No. Well, maybe. I can't remember."

"Then here's the answer: You request an admiral's mast. You have that right when a court-martial is in the offing. Look, if a court of inquiry determines that whatever you did constituted collaborating with the enemy, you will be court-martialed and jailed until the end of time."

"How does an admiral's mast prevent that?"

"You were a CO—you did captain's mast, right?"

"Rarely, but yes."

"And if it actually came to bringing one of your crew before captain's mast, is it true to say that you could have, under navy regs, sent him to court-martial?"

"Yes, although we almost never did that."

"Listen to me, Gar Hammond—lady lawyer speaking now. You request an admiral's mast within *your* chain of command—that's ComSubPac. You have that right. You tell the truth about what you said to the Japs, and why, and everything that happened afterward. My view of collaborating with the enemy is a POW who trades information for better treatment, to the detriment of his fellow POWs. You didn't do that, and any flag officer in SubPac will recognize that. An army or army air force colonel might not understand that."

"You're saying this court of inquiry might not be navy?"

"Absolutely. You could be looking at three army colonels, who haven't the faintest idea of what it was like to be a submarine CO, or, for that matter, a POW. They're more than likely to be professional staff officers, and they'll have quaint notions like you only tell the enemy name, rank, and serial number, to the death, of course."

"To the death," he muttered. "Just like the Japs." He leaned back in the booth and closed his eyes. This was too hard. He thought he'd done well. He thought he'd so dismayed that Jap intel officer that he'd even shot himself.

"Look," she said. "You have to tell *your* story, the whole story.

You said you've been put in for two very high decorations. What I'm saying is that the same people who put you in for those decorations should be the ones who hear the whole story—what you told the Japs, *why* you talked, how they didn't believe any of it, what they did in the POW camp, what *you* did in the POW camp."

"Do I need a lawyer with me at mast?"

"No, although White will probably appoint one for the court if that goes through. Request admiral's mast within your own chain of command and just tell the truth. Go before Lockwood and tell him what happened. He's a straight shooter, and he knows what you guys went through. It's basic law: You're supposed to get a jury of your *peers*. Doesn't happen that way in civilian life, but you damned well *can* still get that in the navy. That's my professional advice."

"Whew," Gar said. "I feel like stripping down to swim shorts and clacks and going native at the back of the island."

"Gar, do you feel guilty about what you did out there in the Japanese prison camps?"

"Hell, no. Proud, if anything. I survived. I endured. That's what POWs try to do."

"Then do as I say."

"If it goes to court, can you represent me?"

She paused. "I'm not sure," she said finally. "Captain White makes those appointments, and he and I are not exactly on terrific terms."

"So he indicated," Gar replied.

"*What?*"

"He said that you had a problem and that he would not want you for his lawyer and neither would I."

"That *bastard*."

"He also said you were going to be sent back to the civilian world, along with all the other WAVES, now that the war was over."

"Yes, that's true," she said. "I'll be leaving here sometime next month." She frowned. "He actually said that? He wouldn't want me as his lawyer, and neither would you?"

"His words, not mine."

She sat back in her chair. "If it does go to a court, you, as an interested party, can request a specific individual to act as your counsel. In a court-martial, they *must* agree to that request if at all possible. In a court of inquiry, that's not always true. A court-martial can impose punishment. A court of inquiry is all about determining if there are grounds for a court-martial."

"In English, then, will you represent me if I ask?"

"Let's see what happens after you talk to Admiral Lockwood," she said. "Hopefully he will interject some adult supervision here and make this whole thing go away."

"New subject," he said. "Fancy having dinner with me?"

She took his hand. "Sorry, Gar. Previous engagement. Whole different social scene now that the war's over. Besides—"

"Yeah, I remember. Can't blame me for trying."

"I'd have been disappointed if you hadn't. Let me know what happens."

THIRTY-SIX

It took ten days. His request for an admiral's mast had upset the apple cart at CincPacFleet. It turned out that the whole court of inquiry idea had come from none other than Captain White. He wasn't pleased with Gar's request, but Forrester managed to convince him to let Gar take a shot at mast. Now, almost a month after getting back to paradise, Gar was waiting in Admiral Lockwood's outer office, wearing brand-new dress khakis, with a tie, even. Now that the boss was back from the advance headquarters out in Guam, the flow of staffers coming and going never abated. Gar got some strange looks from time to time; apparently they'd never seen a wartime sub CO sitting in the outer office awaiting mast. The faces were all new, and they seemed to be much younger than Gar remembered. Looking through the office windows, he was struck by how empty the finger piers looked. During the war there would have been a dozen or more boats out there, all beehives of activity. Now all he could see was palm trees. He'd moved to the sub base BOQ from the Pink Palace, and even the BOQ felt empty.

During the war. That was an expression that certainly would be coming into its own from now on. *Back in my day, sonny . . .* Gar smiled. The yeomen looked at him as if he were just a little bit nuts.

"The admiral will see you now, Commander," a voice announced.

Gar got up, put his brand-new brass hat on, took a deep breath, and went into the inner sanctum. He expected to see Admiral Lockwood standing tall behind a podium, with a sergeant at arms on one side and the chief of staff on the other. Instead, Uncle Charlie was in his shirtsleeves and speaking loudly on his phone, probably on an overseas trunk call. Admiral Forrester was fixing himself a cup of coffee at the sideboard, and indicating to Gar to get some. They both sat down while waiting for Admiral Lockwood to finish. When he did hang up it was with a mild curse.

"We're going to rue the day we let the goddamned Joint Chiefs of Staff have a vote on submarine policy, you mark my words," he said to Forrester. Then he turned to Gar with a smile. "Gar Hammond, welcome back to the land of the living. What's all this BS about an admiral's mast and a court of inquiry? Who'd you piss off this time?"

Gar shook his head, aware that his uniform shirt didn't fit very well at the collar. They apparently didn't make neck sizes for ex-POWs. "Wish I knew, Admiral. Not my idea of a homecoming."

"As I told you earlier, Admiral," Forrester said, "this hairball originated up at Makalapa. The CincPacFleet JAG received an allegation from the 5th Air Force headquarters over on Hickam that Commander Hammond collaborated while a POW. Connie White decided a court of inquiry was in order."

"Oh, hell," the admiral said. "Connie White's an old woman. Older than I am. A court is the only thing he knows. Gar, I've read your initial debriefing, the one taken out in Guam. That focused on operational stuff, your last patrol as skipper of *Dragonfish*, up to the point where you ordered the boat down while you were still on the bridge. Now I'd like to hear the whole story, from that moment on, and I've got as long as it takes. Just tell me what happened, and then we'll address legal issues, if any, and for what it's worth, I don't think right now that there are any. And if it's any comfort, I was very glad to see your name on the repat list. I only wish the Dragon were still alive so I could send you back to her. Now, relax, take your damned hat off, and tell your story. Please."

Gar took a sip of flag mess coffee, put down his cup, sat back in the big upholstered chair, and closed his eyes. "Call me Ishmael," he began, and heard Uncle Charlie chuckle.

"We thought we were just about home free," he said. "Ready for Bungo Suido. Didn't figure on wooden-hulled minesweepers."

An hour later, he opened his eyes and came back to Lockwood's office, a part of his mind prepared to find that they'd gone home for the day a few hours ago. They hadn't. Gar had been back in Japan, of course, remembering things he wanted to forget, while knowing that that would never be possible. He hadn't told them everything, choosing to skim over some of the details about his interaction with the Jap intel board and Charlie Chan. It took him a moment to focus on the room and the two flag officers sitting there, looking at him. Forrester deferred to his boss.

"That's a pretty amazing odyssey, Gar," Lockwood said. "And as to collaboration, it sounds to me more like a case of your screwing with their minds than giving aid and comfort to the enemy. Did you believe that the Priest, as you called him, would keep shooting prisoners until you answered his questions?"

"I certainly did. I think the fact that he had a second one shot *after* I agreed to talk to him proves that."

"And when you appeared before that board of three intel types, when you told the colonel to call the Kure arsenal and ask if they'd had a good night—do you think they believed the things you were telling them?"

"The colonel did not, clearly, although he did go to make a phone call—or at least that's what it looked like. One of the others indicated that what they knew about their situation and what they could say out loud were two very different things. I don't think, on balance, that I was telling them anything they didn't already know. They just couldn't admit it."

"Do you think that's why the major killed himself there on the dry dock after the bombing raid on Kure?"

"After first trying to kill me?" Gar reminded him. "Yes. He'd just been through what was probably his first real bombing. I have to tell you, being depth-charged was always frightening—you never knew when one was going to bang down onto the forward hatch and then blow you all to kingdom come. The difference between that and a bombing raid is that you *do* know, especially if you're out in the open. I was nearly flattened by the first bomb, and that one landed a half mile away. Then they came closer. I think he shot himself because he knew in his heart that this was the future, and that everything the top brass in Japan had been putting out was a lie. They were done. *Finished.* So was he. To tell the truth, while those bombs were falling, I just wanted to die. It would have been preferable to what I was going through."

The admiral sighed, looked at his watch, and got up from his desk. "Lemme think about all this, Gar," he said. "See if we can find a way to stomp out this little brushfire without causing even bigger problems."

"Thank you, sir," Gar said, also rising. "After everything that's happened, I'm not sure what to do at this stage."

Gar walked back to his BOQ room wondering if going to see the admiral had been a good idea or a big mistake. Lockwood had been friendly and concerned, but strangely, at the very end, non-committal. There'd been no protestations of this all being total BS, no "just let me think about it." Forrester hadn't said a word, and that worried him. The chief of staff had been friendly enough, but Gar could never be sure where he stood with Forrester. He wanted to call Sharon and get a reading from her, but even she'd been a little standoffish about further contact, unless it came to a court, and even then, there was doubt. He thought about going to get some chow but decided he wasn't hungry, perhaps for the first time in weeks. He went up to his BOQ room, lay down on the single bed, and tried not to think about what was coming.

Two days later, Gar found himself once again waiting in Admiral Lockwood's outer office. His appointment was with Admiral Forrester, who made him wait fifteen minutes while he dealt with a small parade of staff officers coming in and out of his office.

"Commander?" a yeoman said, indicating he could go in.

When he went into the office, he found Forrester seated behind his desk and another officer, a lieutenant junior grade, standing to one side. The jay-gee was tall and thin and looked to Gar like he was maybe sixteen years old. There were no dolphins on his shirt, either.

"Come in, Commander," Forrester said. "Take a seat. This is

Lieutenant Falcone, from the CincPacFleet JAG office. Mister Falcone, this is Commander Hammond."

They shook hands, and then both sat down. The fact that Forrester was calling him Commander and not Gar did not bode well.

"Commander Hammond, the court of inquiry is going to proceed. I know that's not what you wanted, and, frankly, not what we wanted, either."

"This is Admiral Lockwood's decision?" Gar asked.

Forrester frowned, clearly not liking Gar's insinuation that only Lockwood could make that decision.

"The admiral has considered the matter," he said. "And he spoke to Vice Admiral Rennsalear, who's moved up to chief of staff at PacFleet. The thinking is that you would be better served going before the court than if ComSubPac were to be seen interfering and perhaps papering over these allegations. Admiral Lockwood feels that you have more than a good case to refute the allegations, and that being cleared by the court is a much better outcome."

"Not going before a court of inquiry would be an even better outcome," Gar said. "Besides, I did ask for an admiral's mast. He can certainly make a decision at mast, can't he?"

"Yes, he could, but as I said, the thinking is—"

"The thinking is that if the submarine force's reputation as the all-powerful Silent Service is to be impugned, better it come from some court of inquiry than from Uncle Charlie."

Forrester stared at him. "Commander, watch yourself," he said. "I know you've been through a lot, but there are limits to the amount of insolence I'll tolerate, sir."

"Especially now that the war's over, right, Admiral?" Gar asked, standing up and picking up his hat. "Peacetime is back with a vengeance, isn't it. Okay, why not? I'm glad to finally know who my real friends are."

With that he strode out of the office before Forrester could say anything. When he reached the headquarters parking lot, he heard someone calling his name. He turned around to see the young lieutenant hurrying after him. That's when it penetrated that Falcone was a JAG officer.

"Commander," Falcone said, "I'm supposed to be your counsel, sir."

"Lucky you," Gar said.

"Sir, may I have a word? Or better yet, can I buy you a beer?"

"Do I look like I need a drink at eleven in the morning, Lieutenant?"

Falcone blinked. "Yes, sir."

Gar laughed. "Sold," he said. "Assuming the sub base O-club is still in business. The rest of the submarine establishment seems to have folded its tents."

They found a corner table and ordered sandwiches and a beer each. Gar asked Falcone when he had been appointed.

"This morning, sir," Falcone said. "They told me to get down here to the sub base for a meeting with the chief of staff."

"So there's definitely going to be a court of inquiry."

"Oh, yes, sir. Monday, starting at 0900, at the 14th Naval District headquarters building."

"That gives us, what, three days to prepare my defense?"

Falcone hesitated. "Sir, defense is the wrong word here."

"Not from where I'm sitting, Lieutenant."

"I know, sir. You've been accused of a serious infraction, collaboration with the enemy in time of war. But you've not been charged. There's a big difference."

"Sounds like lawyer talk."

"It is. Lawyers have to be specific, sir. If you were *charged*, then by now you'd have been arrested and confined. We'd be looking at a general court-martial, with a prosecutor, who's called the trial counsel, a defense attorney, who's called the defense counsel, and the members of the court, who are the jury. The prosecutor would be presenting evidence against you, and I'd be trying to poke holes in that or present some kind of evidence to the contrary."

"Isn't that what's going to happen Monday?"

"No, sir. Captain White, our senior JAG, will introduce the allegations made against you, and, if they can find him, they'll get Major Franklin to testify as to what he heard you say."

"And if they can't find him?"

"Then they'll just read the allegations out in the courtroom. Couldn't do that in a court-martial, but this is an inquiry into the facts, not a trial."

"I've been told all this, Lieutenant," Gar said. "But from my perspective, it sure looks like a trial. Lawyers on both sides. Senior member equals judge and jury, assisted by two more line officers. Evidence against me and for me. If the court of inquiry finds that there's sufficient reason to go to court-martial, that's as good as a conviction. And after that I go to the brig."

Falcone looked uncomfortable.

"What?" Gar asked.

"After that, sir, I regret to inform you that you could go to a firing squad," Falcone said. "Collaboration with the enemy in time of war is a capital offense."

Gar sat back in his chair. Welcome the fuck home, sailor. First a Navy Cross and now a firing squad? He should have taken his chances with that damned hatch. All those ghosts down in Bungo Suido would have been more sympathetic than any of these CYA staffies back here in Pearl. A capital offense. No wonder Lockwood and Forrester had run for cover. That wasn't like Lockwood, so Gar figured this was Forrester's recommendation.

"So what do we do now, Mister Falcone?"

"We begin by you telling me your side of this story, Commander, but not here. In my office conference room up at PacFleet, where I can record it, and then transcribe it."

"How long have you been out of law school?" Gar asked.

"Harvard, '43," Falcone said.

"Well, that's a good start," Gar said. "I think."

THIRTY-SEVEN

They did the transcription that afternoon. It took longer than it had in front of Lockwood because Lieutenant Falcone asked questions. A bulky RCA tape recorder went through two reels of tape in the process, while a stenographer sat in one corner typing silently into a desk-sized Ireland stenotype device that produced a continuous roll of paper. Gar was tired by the time they quit at five, both from the telling and the remembering. Lieutenant Falcone was obviously aware of this. He suggested that Gar go get some rest, and that they'd meet again Saturday afternoon to discuss strategy.

The following afternoon, Falcone surprised Gar with his first suggestion.

"We'll ask for an immediate recess," he said.

"Really?"

"Yes, sir. I'm going to ask for an immediate recess so that the members of the court can read the record of what you've been through. I'll suggest to them that this will better prepare them to ask questions. It will also spare you the emotional labor of reliving your experiences by having to give three hours of testimony."

"You think they'll do that?"

"I certainly would. The only risk is that they will be much better prepared to ask questions, but from what I've heard and read, you've done nothing wrong."

"A group of senior line officers might think differently," Gar said. "I wish I could get a POW or two on this board. By the way, do we know who *is* going to be on the board?"

"Court, not board, sir. And no, we don't. Probably won't even be submariners. This isn't about your conduct as the CO of a boat. This is about your conduct as a POW. I expect they'll be captains, with a really senior captain in charge. If it's any consolation, they won't know what this is about until it convenes."

Gar smiled. "You may have gone to Harvard, Lieutenant, but I guarantee they'll all know exactly what this is about by opening day. Pearl's a small place, really, and there's not much a captain, USN, *doesn't* know about what's happening in the harbor."

"That was probably true during the war, sir, but these days most of the faces around Makalapa are brand-new. I'm actually one of the few JAG officers who was here in early '44 and who's still here."

"You know Sharon DeVeers?" Gar asked.

"Yes, sir, and she's leaving soon, too. All the WAVES are going back to civilian life, from what I hear."

"I wanted her as my attorney for this thing," Gar said, "but Captain White said no. Said she had a problem, and that I'd be better off with someone else."

Falcone stared down at the conference table and said nothing.

"Do you know what that problem might be?" Gar asked.

"Lieutenant Commander DeVeers is a pretty sharp lawyer," Falcone said. "She was a state court judge back in '41."

"And?"

"I guess you should ask her, Commander," Falcone said. "It's not my place to—"

"Booze, isn't it?" Gar asked. "She's a hard-core alkie."

Falcone blinked, then nodded.

"She's damned good-looking, so I don't guess that anyone senior up there cared when it came to liberty time. But if she showed up the next morning looking like the wreck of the *Hesperus* . . ."

Falcone nodded again.

"Let me speculate some more. She's made some enemies up there, possibly by declining certain invitations in favor of other invitations. Or by surprising the shit out of opposing counsel who were focusing on her legs while she was focusing on their case."

Falcone raised a hand. "Guilty," he said. "She's good, real good."

"When she's sober."

"Yes, sir, when she's sober."

"May I ask a favor?"

"Sir?"

"Will you talk to her, tell her what you intend to do, see what she thinks?"

"Does she know this case?"

"She does. I met with her after White told me no. And you should know, we'd met before, socially, back before I left for my last patrol."

Falcone gave Gar a speculative look. "Socially," he said.

"Yeah, Lieutenant, socially. It's what she's *really* good at."

Falcone blushed. "I'll talk to her, sir, if that's what you want."

"Yeah, that's what I want. What the hell, having been a judge, she may have an angle we haven't thought of."

"Anything's possible, sir."

On Monday, Gar arrived at the 14th Naval District headquarters building at eight thirty. He was dressed in service dress khakis, complete with tie. Except for his single appearance in Lockwood's office, he hadn't worn this dress uniform since leaving Pearl on the Dragon's special mission to the Inland Sea. The one he had on now was his original uniform. Before departing on her final patrol, *Dragonfish* had put all of Gar's personal effects in a seabag and handed it in to the SubPac admin in Guam, who'd sent it on to Pearl, where headquarters maintained a locker for the personal effects of the missing in action. He'd even retrieved his Naval Academy ring, which he'd presumed had gone to the bottom with the Dragon. The uniform fit him like a beach towel. Lieutenant Falcone told him to wear it anyway—it would accentuate his much-diminished physical appearance.

Falcone met him at the main entrance, and together they went to the courtroom on the second floor. It was a large room that looked more like a classroom than a court. There were the obligatory green-felt-covered tables, one for the witnesses and counsel, and a second for the JAG officer who would act as counsel to the court of inquiry. One long table was set up along the wall for the members of the court. Gar saw that there were three places set up on the long table, each with its own silver water carafe, glass, yellow legal pad, and two navy-issue pens. There was no witness box and no PA system. Overhead two large fans were listlessly stirring the humid Hawaiian air. There was one row of chairs against the back wall, which Gar assumed was for spectators.

Gar took a seat at the witness table while Falcone put a copy of the transcribed debriefing at each member's place, plus one for the court's counsel.

"Think they'll grant the recess?" Gar asked.

"I prebriefed Captain White," Falcone said. "He's going to be court counsel. He thought it was a good idea and said he would so advise the court."

"So did they find my good buddy Major Franklin?"

"He's in a hospital in Oakland. He has a case of what they call black lung, whatever that is, complicated by pneumonia. He's in bad shape. The docs don't really expect him to make it."

"Black lung is what you get from breathing coal dust down in a mine," Gar said. "Most of us tried to wrap something over our nose and face when we were down there. Sometimes the guards wouldn't allow it."

Captain White came in at nine and informed them that the court would not convene this morning. He personally was going to take the transcripts to the president and each of the members, and they would convene formally once the members said they were ready. This arrangement saved everyone concerned the process of convening and then immediately adjourning.

"Commander Hammond," White said. "You sure about this? I understand that you agreed to it?"

"I did. Why wouldn't I—it's my testimony."

"Yes, it is. Let me ask you—does this transcript describe your interaction with the Japanese interrogators?"

"Peripherally," Lieutenant Falcone said. "We figured that's where the questions would focus, and we'd let Commander Hammond expand at that time."

White thought about that for a moment. "You understand, Commander Hammond, that my role as court counsel is not to act like a prosecutor. The president and the members will ask the questions. My job is to referee—to make sure neither they nor you venture too far afield, and also to answer questions of law."

"What's your point, Captain?" Gar asked.

"The central issue here is whether or not you gave the Japs anything more than name, rank, and serial number. Do you admit doing that in this transcript?"

"I guess I do," Gar said. "I didn't given them anything of real value, but—"

White held up his hand. "Say no more, Commander. Let's save it for the hearing. But as a point of law, you've admitted that you did what has been alleged. The president has the right to terminate the hearing based on that alone and then proceed directly to findings."

Gar hadn't known that. He looked at Falcone, who shrugged. "You've never denied it, sir," he said. "Because it's the truth. The truth is supposedly what we're here for. I see the central issues differently from Captain White. I see two issues, actually. One, were you justified in doing what you did. I think that's self-evident. Two, did you do damage to the American cause, and I think, once they read your testimony and discuss it, you did not."

"You better hope so, Lieutenant," Captain White said. "May I have the transcripts, please?"

"They're right there, sir, on the table."

After a day of waiting, Gar thought he was beginning to go crazy. He was deeply angry that he was being accused of treacherous conduct. If he'd made it back before the war ended, this would never have happened. Now that the war was over and the huge military establishment that had been needed to win it was being dismantled, it was a totally different ball game. Careers were at stake, with whole commands at risk of simply going away, and the legacy of senior flags at risk as investigations like this one ground through their paces. Gar knew that the submarine force had made something of a religion out of their Silent Service trademark. They didn't brag, but they made sure the statistics were in plain view.

The silent, invisible menace presented by American submarines was one of the least-kept secrets of what they were already calling World War II. Admirals like Lockwood and Forrester were juggling two hot potatoes: how much of the submarine force would survive the massive demobilization, and how much of the force's image would survive the inevitable explorations by historians over issues such as the torpedoes, the fact that the submarine force suffered the heaviest losses of any ship type in the navy, the sub captains who broke under the strain of command, and incidents like this one, where one of their skippers, honored as a hero for choosing to stay on the bridge during an emergency dive, was accused of aiding the enemy. Gar knew from years of experience that the submarine service wanted above all to solve its own problems in-house. So why had Lockwood acquiesced to this court of inquiry?

Lieutenant Falcone called the following morning, as Gar was getting ready to go back over to the naval district headquarters. The opening day's session had been postponed for one more day. Apparently the members wanted more time to read, study, and prepare questions for the actual hearing. Great, he thought. Another day of stewing in the BOQ. Falcone, however, had a plan. He had provided each member with a legal yeoman, whose job it was to type up any notes or questions being made by the members regarding the transcript. Those same yeomen worked for him. He had arranged for them to show him what they were putting together, and he wanted Gar to be on call that afternoon so they could begin to assess the questions and prepare answers.

"Is that kosher?" Gar asked.

"Sure," Falcone said. "If we wanted to, we could request a formal copy of all their questions, and then ask for our own continuance to get ready. This way we can get going."

"What's the hurry?"

"I think the longer this court takes, the more likely it's going to metamorphose into a much bigger deal." His voice became oracular. "Mr. President, grave matters of principle are at stake here."

"So maybe telegraphing my testimony was not such a good idea?"

"Do you think you did anything wrong?" Falcone asked.

"No, I did not."

"That's your best defense, Commander. Tell the truth. It's a pretty amazing story. You did the best you could. You saved some prisoners' lives. You saved your ship by staying topside in an emergency dive. Besides, they have to be careful, too."

"How so?"

"If they decide to recommend prosecution for you on the basis of some by-the-book-with-no-exceptions rule, they send a message to the entire fleet that anyone who becomes a POW is instantly in a no-win situation."

"You think these captains will consider that?"

"If they don't, rest assured I'll be raising it. Oh, by the way, Lieutenant Commander DeVeers wants to see you if you have time. She suggests you meet her for lunch at the Cannon Club on Fort DeRussy."

"If I have time?" Gar repeated. "I have nothing but time. Or maybe not."

"Great," Falcone said. "I'll tell her you'll be there at noon, then. I should have some stuff to talk about by three."

Gar had never made it to Fort DeRussy during his time in Hawaii. During the war it had been a staging area for the transshipment of thousands of GIs to meat-grinder islands of the western Pacific. It had also been an army coastal artillery site, complete with a battery of two 14-inch naval rifles lurking inside massive concrete bunkers high on the slopes. The officers' open mess, nicknamed the Cannon Club, had one of the best views on the island of Oahu, overlooking Waikiki Beach and a lot of Honolulu.

Sharon showed up at ten after twelve, looking smart in her WAVE lieutenant commander's uniform. Gar felt almost shabby in his ill-fitting khakis, but she pretended not to notice. They got a table inside, as the day was humid.

Gar ordered a cold beer, Sharon a gin and tonic. Once they had their drinks, he offered her a salud. She returned the gesture. Her hairdo was perfect, and she was, if anything, looking even sexier than the last time he'd spent time with her.

"Good to be back?" she asked with a rakish smile.

"Oh, hell, yes. Got a wonderful welcome, a medal, maybe two, and a court of inquiry, all in the same week. *Great* to be back."

"Tony Falcone told me about the transcripts. Good move, that. I haven't read them, of course, but I think they should make quick work of this business."

"I hope so," he said. "Although Captain White had a different opinion on what's possible. He seemed to have a very literal point of view on my talking to the Japs."

"Tony told me about that, too," she said. "Captain White is sixty years old; he spent the whole war up at Makalapa, overseeing the drudgery of military law. All the interesting stuff was done by reservists who came in for the duration, specialists, say, in international law, or law of the sea. He has to retire at sixty-two, and he's just hanging on for dear life."

"He told me he was going to be a referee, as opposed to a prosecutor. True?"

"Um."

"Um?"

"Well, that's what he *should* be doing, keeping the line officers on the court on the legal straight and narrow. But unless the president of the court has done this before, he'll depend on Captain White for procedural matters—what questions to ask, how far he can go with an issue, and what the other members can ask."

"And?"

"And he's a golfing buddy of Captain, now Rear Admiral, Forrester. He's the guy who advised Admiral Lockwood to let this go to the court. You two have history?"

Suspicions confirmed, Gar thought. "A little bit," he said, then remembered his last office visit with Forrester. "Maybe more than a little bit now, I guess. How do you know this?"

"It's a small island, Gar. When you requested admiral's mast, Forrester asked White for a JAG opinion. White asked one of the procedural law specialists to research it. He had a golf date, so he gave it to me, since I'm leaving in a few weeks and have no active cases, and therefore nothing to do, essentially."

"And?"

"I of course recommended the admiral's mast route. For some reason White did not agree, and guess how that all came out?"

The waiter showed up, and they focused on ordering lunch. Once he left, Gar went back to the matter at hand.

"I get the feeling that the outcome of this case is being driven by factors way above my pay grade," he said. "What do you think?"

"You're the submariner, Gar," she said. "Dues-paying member of the Silent Service, in more ways than one. During the war, you guys were untouchable, unless it was really bad, like the *Awa Maru* case. Now that the war's over, there may be just a wee bit of resentment against the Silent Service in the upper echelons. The Royal Hawaiian Hotel. The best chow in the navy. The relief crews who took over the subs when you guys came back from patrol. The aviators and the surface ship–drivers weren't treated like that."

"Damn, Sharon, you know too much."

"Despite the fact that I'm a full-blown alkie, hunh?"

Gat stared at her. His term. *Shit!* Falcone running his mouth?

She sighed. "Truth is, I am just that. I am an alcoholic. I *love* my booze. I want another G and T, and now would be nice. I wasn't exactly straight with you when I told you how I came to be in the navy. I was a state court judge, but I lost that position due to a car crash. The crash was my fault. I was drunk. I thank God every day that no one was seriously hurt, but the chief judge told me in no uncertain terms that I needed to find new pastures. I chose the navy. Still want me to represent you, Commander?"

"Can you function sober?"

"I can," she said. "Of course, that's just my opinion, and alcoholics are reliably confident that they can handle their problem. But it's an addiction. I crave the booze. Right now I'm sober, even after one G and T. My mind is clear. I could stand up in court right now and be effective. The whole time, I'm counting the minutes to happy hour."

"Wow."

"That's how it is with this particular monkey, Gar."

"What are you going to do when you get back to civilian life?"

She stared down at the plate for a long moment. "I have no fucking idea."

"Well," he said, with his first grin of the day. "Welcome to the club."

THIRTY-EIGHT

"Gentlemen, let's get started, please. Will the interested party please stand to be sworn. Captain White?"

Captain White stood and swore Gar in. Gar acknowledged his duty to tell the truth and sat back down.

The court's president, Captain Martell, gathered up the pages of his copy of the transcript. There were two other members of the court, both captains. Captain Hooper had just been detached from duty as commanding officer of a heavy cruiser. Captain Wilson was currently commanding officer of an escort carrier. Gar listened to their names and promptly forgot both of them. He was more tired than he realized.

"Commander Hammond, I want to thank you for your deposition. I think this will save us a lot of time. It's a remarkable story." The members nodded their heads in obvious agreement.

"We're here because another officer, a Major Franklin of the army air forces, has alleged that you collaborated with the enemy while a prisoner of war in Japan. "

"Why isn't he here?" Captain Hooper asked. "If he's going to make an accusation like that, doesn't Commander Hammond have the right to hear it face-to-face?"

Captain White intervened. "In a trial, yes. This is not a trial, so the allegation stands. It's an allegation, not charges and specs."

"Commander Hammond," Martell said. "Do you feel it's unfair that your accuser is not here in court?"

"I understand he's gravely ill in an Oakland military hospital,"

Gar said. "The only reason I'd want him here would be to hear his definition of collaboration."

"I can help with that," Captain White said, reaching for a piece of paper. "He said, specifically, that *you* said you talked to them. Something more than name, rank, and serial number."

"Commander Hammond?"

"I did say that. We were in a locked boxcar, on the way to some prison camp. But I did say that."

"Did you tell him what you talked to them about?"

"No, sir. He seemed upset, and we stopped talking. He said he'd never give them shit. His words."

"We noticed when we met last night that your deposition speaks to being taken to interrogation, but not what transpired there. Can we assume you'll clarify that here?"

"Yes, of course."

"With the clear implication that you shouldn't be giving them—anything, either?" Captain White asked.

"Objection," Lieutenant Falcone said.

White gave him an annoyed look. "Mister Falcone, this is not a trial, therefore you may not—"

"I agree, this is not a trial," Falcone interrupted. "It's a court of inquiry, which means your role in these proceedings is to speak to matters of law and procedure, not ask questions as if you were the prosecutor. Sir."

White's face went red. His expression forecast that there would be more to be said on this subject later, boss to subordinate.

"Moving right along," the president said, uncomfortably. "Commander Hammond, the first Jap officer who formally took you into custody—he did not interrogate you, did he?"

"No, sir," Gar said. "He already knew I was CO of a sub, and I think he knew that we were the ones who shot up the Kure base. He's the one who told me I would be taken to Ofuna, which I later learned is—was—their naval interrogation center."

"He did not question you?"

"No, sir. He said there would be specialists for that. Experts."

"Torturers, you mean," Captain Wilson said. "I've heard about Ofuna."

"Did you reveal anything to him or anyone else while in his custody?"

"Yes, sir, I did. I spoke to the CO of the carrier when he offered me a gun so I could shoot myself."

"He did *what*?"

"He said he was disgusted by the sight of a commanding officer being taken around the ship with a leash like a dog. Said I obviously knew nothing about the honor required of a commanding officer. He offered me his personal pistol so I could go out on the bridge wing and regain my honor. Words to that effect, anyway."

"And what did you do?"

"I told him we didn't do that. I also told him that there were some things I did know that he might find interesting. That in 1942, Japan was supreme in the western Pacific. Now, its armies were starving in Malaya, defeated in New Guinea, and expelled from the Solomon Islands, which even they called the Starvation Islands. Rabaul was lost. Tarawa was lost. Kwajalein was lost. Guam and Tinian were lost. The Philippines had been invaded. Okinawa had been bombed. In Japan, the flow of oil and food and rubber and tin and coal had been cut to ten percent of what they had coming in 1942.

"I told them that they had this one magnificent carrier, and that it was very impressive, but that it was one carrier. Admiral Halsey had forty-two big carriers and thirty-five smaller ones. He was coming with a fleet of five hundred ships. The American navy had more than ten thousand ships. Soon Japan itself would be lost. And finally, that he would run a gauntlet of American submarines if he even tried to get to Yokosuka."

"Where did you get those numbers?" the president asked.

"Made 'em up," Gar said. "And you know what he said? He said, nice try."

"He didn't believe you."

"Not at all, except maybe for all the island bases that were gone.

That pissed him off, I think. That's when I was sent below to pound oakum."

Captain Wilson raised his hand. "Commander Hammond, why did you try to save the life of the Jap officer who was your, what's the word, handler on the *Shinano*?"

"I needed him," Gar said. He told them of his efforts to free the other prisoners, and how Yamashita had actually helped him do it.

"Why the hell would he do that?"

"Because he was scared to death," Gar said. "The first torpedo hit way aft. She was settling by the stern. The swells were already starting to break over the fantail, and he could not swim. There were no life jackets, or lifeboats, that I could see. I was his only lifeline."

"Did you think that through, Commander? I mean, suppose you both made it. Wouldn't he just arrest you again and send you to Ofuna?"

"I suppose he would, Captain," Gar said. "But that beat being sucked down into the sea by a sinking aircraft carrier. I felt my job was to survive, whatever it took. And here, for better or for worse, I am."

"Tell us about your encounter with the fisherman, Hashimoto. You indicated that you knew him?"

Gar spent the next twenty minutes reviewing the history of Hashimoto's involvement in the mission. When he was finished, Captain Hooper had a question.

"You never figured out what Hashimoto's mission to Hiroshima was all about?"

"I still don't know. The paper rain business may have had something to do with the leaflets they dropped the day before."

Captain White stood up. "Mr. President, may I suggest a recess for lunch? It's nearly noon."

"Okay, we can do that," Captain Martell said. "Back in session at thirteen thirty."

As the court got up and headed for the doors, Captain White pointed a finger at Lieutenant Falcone. "I want to talk to you," he said.

"Yes, sir," Falcone replied.

When Gar didn't join the other officers to go to lunch, White said, "Alone, if you please."

"I don't please," Gar said. "He's my legal rep, and anything you have to say to him you can say in front of me."

"Commander Hammond, get out of the way, please."

"No," Gar said. "I'm beginning to think that you have an agenda here, Captain. And if you press this matter with Mister Falcone, I'll expand on that when we reconvene."

Captain White took a deep breath and then sighed. "Later for you, Mister," he said to Falcone, and then left the courtroom.

"Thanks, sir," Falcone said. "But he can't do anything to me. I'm a reservist, and I'll soon be back in the real world."

"He can do something to *me*, Lieutenant," Gar said. "Especially if he's in cahoots with the flags at SubPac. And something else—did you notice how Captain White shut the testimony off as soon as they started asking detailed questions about Hashimoto? I think there's a hidden agenda going on there, too."

"If you really feel that way, Commander," Falcone said, "I think I have a cure for that."

The court reconvened at 1345. Captain White had been late getting back, and Gar wondered where he'd been and to whom he'd been talking. They were all getting settled when Sharon DeVeers came into the room.

Captain White looked surprised and then asked what she was doing there.

"Commander Hammond has asked me to act as co-counsel for this hearing."

"I did not authorize that," White said.

"Do I not have the right to the counsel of my choice at this hearing?" Gar interjected.

"We have appointed you counsel, Commander, and—"

"Not the counsel I asked for, Captain. I'm happy with Mister Falcone, don't get me wrong, but he's new at this, and I'd like the experience that Lieutenant Commander DeVeers can bring."

White looked to Martell for help, but the president just shrugged. "I have no objection," he said. "What could it matter?"

"We have a full docket of work at PacFleet JAG," White said. "I cannot afford to dedicate two JAG officers to this hearing."

"I'm detaching in two weeks, Captain," Sharon said. "Per your orders, I have absolutely nothing on my plate right now, remember?"

Gar watched Captain White struggling for a reply. If he told the court why she had nothing on her plate, it would reflect badly on his office. He sat down and said nothing.

"Gentlemen, let's get going," Captain Martell said. "Commander Hammond, you indicated that you first went to a formal interrogation after the sinking of the *Shinano*. Was this another occasion where you 'talked' to the Japanese?"

"Yes, sir."

"Would you please elaborate on what you talked about?"

"They wanted to know where I'd come from, popping up in the Inland Sea like that. I told them we came through Bungo Suido and then we went to Kure and shot the place up before the carrier was sunk. They scoffed at the notion that anything had happened at Kure or that *Shinano* had been sunk."

"They denied it?"

"They were deluding themselves. I think the senior officer, the four-striper, knew that *Shinano* had been lost, but they were hard over on covering it up. I also told them that we could see their mines underwater."

"Was that wise, Commander?" one of the members asked. Gar noticed that their expressions all changed when he admitted telling the Japanese about their new capability.

"By that time I was very tired, Captain," Gar said. "I'd been captured, beaten, given very little food or water, then put on board a carrier, which then was torpedoed and sunk. That meant going back into the water, a second capture, more beatings, no food, and then a session with three professional intel officers. By then I *wanted* them to know that they were going to lose this war no matter what they did to me. That their minefields no longer protected them. That a submarine had managed to get into their version of the Chesapeake Bay and do some real damage—two destroyers blown in two, an enormous dry dock put out of commission, two ammunition barges blown up, with shells landing all over the yard—*and* get clean away. I was making the point that nothing they got out of me would make any difference because the end was coming and there wasn't a single damned thing they could do about it."

"How did they react?"

"The captain, the senior one, was scornful, said it was all lies. I challenged him to make a phone call, see how the cleanup was going down at Kure. He took me up on that, got up, left the room. When he came back he was really pissed off. In the meantime, one of the other officers told me to watch what I said, that some things were not allowed to even be mentioned."

"Then there was an air raid?"

"Air raid sirens; no raid. After that I was put on a train. That's where I spoke to Major Franklin. I had had another conversation with the interrogator I called the Priest. Same theme, really. You guys can't win this war. You'll be fighting our machines and not us. He finally just yelled at me, and then we went to Kure. They were going to put me on a tin can for transport to Yokohama."

"That's where he tried to kill you, after the bombing raid?"

"Correct."

"Why didn't you attempt to escape after he shot himself?" Martell asked.

"And go where? One shell-shocked American, wandering around the Kure shipyard right after the B-29s damn near leveled the place? Or wading through the bomb craters in the nearby rice paddies? I was in no shape to go anywhere. The destroyer I was supposed to ride to Yokohama took a bomb in her forward magazines while I was trying to hide between her and the sill wall."

"After that you were taken to the coal mine?"

"Yes."

"But you were a high-value prisoner—they just lost you?"

"I think they did," Gar said. "The people at Ofuna probably assumed I was killed at Kure. Once I was in a cattle car with other

POWs, I was just another round-eye. The Brits I eventually fell in with told me I was lucky to be there and not in Ofuna."

"How could they know that?"

"They'd been in captivity since February '42."

"Were you interrogated in the coal-mine camp?"

"No, sir."

"You were the only American, and they didn't single you out for special questioning?"

"That camp was dedicated to the production of coal and nothing else. I was singled out for special treatment. They'd yell at another POW if he did something wrong. I'd get hit with a shovel. The guards were not too bright. They were glad to be assigned at home and not starving on some hellish island, but coal was everything—even they knew that if they beat us down too much, they'd be hauling coal."

"Did anyone try to escape from this camp?"

"Not that I know of, sir. There really was nowhere to go. We were already starving, and most of the Brits were also seriously ill. No one had enough energy to even try."

"Gentlemen," the president said, "let's get back on track. Commander Hammond has been accused of collaborating with the enemy. Anyone have a question directly about that?"

Neither of the other two captains said anything.

"Lieutenant Commander DeVeers, Mister Falcone, you are allowed to bring witnesses to support Commander Hammond. Do you wish to do that?"

"Yes, sir," Sharon said. "I would like to have Vice Admiral Lockwood testify, please."

"Um, Commander, that's—"

"I believe he has information relevant to this accusation. The rules allowing the accused to present evidence on his behalf make no mention of rank."

"That would be highly unusual," Captain White offered. "Perhaps Commander Hammond's division commander, as his immediate superior in command, could be made available, but ComSubPac himself? That's reaching pretty high."

"Commander DeVeers, I tend to agree," Captain Martell said.

"Then deny my request, sir," Sharon said.

That gave Martell pause. If he decided not to let Gar call Admiral Lockwood, Gar's lawyers might claim he wasn't given a fair hearing.

"I'll take your request under advisement," he said finally. "I want to talk to the members about this."

Captain Hooper, the ex-cruiser skipper, raised his hand. "Nothing to talk about. I say bring him in."

Captain Martell looked to his left at Captain Wilson, who nodded agreement with Hooper. With the members obviously not going to support him, he conceded. "Okay," he said. "We'll call the admiral to testify. Captain White, can you arrange that for tomorrow, please?"

White nodded glumly.

Sharon leaned closer to Falcone. "We have some work to do, shipmate," she said.

THIRTY-NINE

Uncle Charlie did not look pleased when he entered the courtroom at 1000. Everyone stood up when he arrived, and he kept them standing while he went to the front of the room and took a chair. He was in dress khakis, and his golden three-star shoulder boards glinted in the morning light. Rear Admiral Forrester came in with him and took a seat in the spectator gallery at the back of the room, along with a captain from the CincPacFleet staff. Sharon told Gar that he was the public affairs officer.

"Admiral Lockwood," Martell began, "thank you for coming so quickly, sir. We know you're a busy man."

"Good," Lockwood said. He hadn't even looked at Gar and his attorneys. "Let's get on with it."

"Commander DeVeers, Mister Falcone, are you ready to proceed?"

"Yes, sir," Sharon said, standing to address the admiral. She introduced herself as Gar's co-counsel and then asked the admiral if he had had a chance to read the transcript of Gar's testimony. Lockwood said he had. Sharon picked up a piece of paper, on which she had a list of questions.

"Admiral, did the submarine force train its officers on the matter of surviving a Japanese prisoner of war camp? I'm talking formal training, not just people discussing it."

Lockwood had to think for a few moments. "Formal training? Syllabus, trained instructors, practicals? No, we did not. Everyone knew the drill—name, rank, and serial number—but no, there was no formal, schoolhouse training on that."

"There a reason for that, Admiral?"

"Yes," he said. "If one of our boats tangled with a Jap warship and lost, there were usually no survivors, so formal training didn't seem cost-effective."

"Cost-effective?"

"Not worth establishing a formal course at sub school or out in the fleet. Like I said, everyone knew the basic rule."

"The basic rule being driven by the Geneva Convention on the treatment of prisoners of war?"

"Correct."

"Were you aware that the Japanese never ratified the convention?"

"Yes, we all were aware of that. I thought that was a great incentive never to be captured."

"Would it be true to say, then, Admiral, that Commander Hammond, who *did* become a prisoner of the Japanese, had no formal training or guidance as to what he could say if the Japanese applied force majeure?"

"I think he knew what *not* to say—that he should try to reveal as little as possible that could be useful to the Japanese."

"But if they began to kill fellow POWs in front of him and told him that they'd keep doing that until he talked, would that in your opinion constitute sufficient reason to go ahead and talk to them, beyond name, rank, and serial number?"

Again Lockwood paused. He appeared to be choosing his words very carefully. "I think each individual would have to decide when enough was enough."

"But it is true that you, as commander of all submarines in the Pacific, never specifically issued guidance to your officers, even along the lines you just mentioned, i.e., when enough was enough, as to what they were supposed to do when faced with overwhelming force?"

"Yes, technically, that's correct. Look, miss, you haven't walked

in their shoes, or mine. We did not dwell on matters of POW be-
havior. It was, I think, simply understood. You resist doing any harm
if they capture you, as best you can."

"Do no harm, sir?"

"Yes. Do no harm. It was also understood that your chances of
being captured were nil—we lost fifty-two boats and over thirty-
five hundred submariners, and we had very few submariner POWs.
So there it is."

Sharon studied her list for a moment before continuing.
"Commander Hammond has testified that when he did give them
information, it was to discourage them more than benefit them,
tactically speaking."

"Such as?"

"He told them that we could 'see' their mines underwater, that
we could penetrate their minefields with impunity."

Lockwood seemed surprised. "That's a significant revelation, I
think."

"Could you elaborate, Admiral? How would that benefit the
enemy?"

"Well, toward the end they were using their minefields princi-
pally as defensive measures, specifically against submarines. Now
they'd know that their defenses had been weakened."

"And what could they do about that, sir? I'm talking about the
minefields—what could they do differently to counter the fact that
we had a sonar that could 'see' the individual mines?"

"I don't know, double the size of their minefields? Triple the
size? That sonar wasn't perfect, and it was no cakewalk to get
through a minefield even with the FM sonar."

"As Commander Hammond did."

"As Commander Hammond did. That was a major accomplishment, and what *Dragonfish* did at Kure was an equally major accomplishment. Captain Enright told me that the only reason he got a
shot at *Shinano* was that she wasn't making full speed. The Japs
must have been beside themselves when they realized what had attacked their naval arsenal. But I think it would have been even
scarier if they could not figure out how that boat got through."

Gar began writing something on his pad of paper.

"So in your opinion," Sharon continued, "he *did* collaborate with the enemy? I'm talking technically here, putting aside his reason for talking, to stop the murder of any more prisoners. Do you feel that he did harm to the American war effort?"

"It didn't help."

"Did any more submarines attempt to penetrate Japanese minefields after *Dragonfish*?"

"Yes."

"Did they get through?"

"Most of them did."

"Did you detect any changes in the way the Japanese deployed their minefields after the *Dragonfish* mission?"

"I'd have to research that. I don't think we did."

"So what harm ensued from Commander Hammond's revelations?"

The admiral said nothing.

"And morally?" Sharon continued. "Given his reason for agreeing to talk to their interrogators in the first place? That other prisoners would be shot until he did agree to talk to them?"

"I guess I still can't answer that, counselor. Each officer has to react to his own moral values, I suppose. I wasn't in a prison cell watching Jap guards murder prisoners. I was here, in Hawaii, safe and sound. I can tell you that those moral values you're harping on vary with rank. Sometimes we, or I, sent boats and crews on missions or into places where their chances of surviving weren't good at all, but where the potential for hurting the enemy seemed to justify the risk."

"To them, not you?"

Lockwood gave her a pained look but did not reply.

"Submarines were expendable, then?"

"Not in so many words, Miss DeVeers, but they existed to go on the offensive against Japan. Their mission was not to preserve the boat. It was to attack the enemy's shipping. If we had a boat go out on patrol and come home empty-handed, we usually replaced the skipper."

"And everyone understood that, correct?"

"After a while they did," Lockwood said.

"But some missions were extremely dangerous? Over and above the usual hazards of submarine operations?"

"Yes."

"Was *Dragonfish*'s mission into the Inland Sea one of those?"

"Yes, I suppose it was."

"Is it true that you had previously proscribed the Inland Sea as an operational area?"

"Yes."

Gar passed a note to Falcone. He read it, nodded, and handed it to Sharon. She glanced at it for a moment before resuming her questions.

"Was there more than one mission involved in *Dragonfish*'s Inland Sea operation?"

"Meaning?"

"Meaning Minoru Hashimoto, sir."

"Oh, that. That was some kind of a sideshow, in my opinion. We weren't told why PacFleet wanted him returned to Japan, nor were we encouraged to ask questions. Commander Hammond told me later that he thought it had something to do with the atomic bombing of Hiroshima."

"Did his instructions prioritize the elements of his mission?"

"The sealed instructions? I never saw them. Those came from Nimitz, CincPacFleet. We were focused on getting that carrier."

"Would you be surprised, then, to learn that the sealed orders told Commander Hammond to get Hashimoto ashore *before* he attempted any other elements of the Inland Sea mission?"

"I guess I would. Would you be surprised to learn that Commander Hammond initially refused to do the mission if he had to take a Jap on the boat with him? I watched Admiral Nimitz convince him otherwise, but, again, I viewed it as a sideshow. The mission was the *Shinano*. After that, it was to escape back to sea."

"Attack the carrier as best he could, and then escape?"

"Yes. And that's another thing—it seems to me Commander

Hammond had a couple of opportunities to escape, and for some reason decided not to try."

"But the reason Commander Hammond was captured a second time was that he felt he could not expose Hashimoto to the threat of capture or exposure by continuing to hide in the village. He basically instructed Hashimoto to 'catch' him again and hand him over to the authorities."

"If you say so."

"Commander Hammond says so, sir. And it was because the sealed orders made it clear that whatever Hashimoto was supposed to do, it was actually more important than the *Shinano*. Which brings me to my question: He basically allowed himself to be captured again. Did this act constitute, in your opinion, collaboration with the enemy?"

"He made his decisions and he had his reasons," Lockwood replied, angry now. "You're new to this navy business, miss. Decisions have consequences, especially in wartime. Earlier in the war we had a submarine division commander intentionally go down with a badly damaged sub when he could have escaped, rather than expose himself to the *possibility* of being captured and tortured and then giving up crucial intelligence information. No one required him to do that, which is why *he* got the Medal of Honor, and probably why Commander Hammond got a court of inquiry!"

"Was that what drove your decision, Admiral?"

"*What?*"

"The case of Captain Gilmore and the *Growler.* Is that what drove your decision to let the court of inquiry proceed after Commander Hammond had requested an admiral's mast to resolve this matter?"

Lockwood stood up, visibly furious. "Young lady, I do *not* have to justify any decision I make in the matter of an admiral's mast. Not to you, not to Hammond, not to anyone. Besides that, *I'm* not on trial here. Commander Hammond is. You're supposed to be finding out what *he* did and why."

"No one is on trial here, Admiral," Sharon said, smoothly. "But

I think you just hit the nail on the head: what he did and why. And I would add one more dimension to this inquiry: what real harm did he do. You brought up his 'failure' to escape. After the bombing at Kure he was picked up by some guards and thrown in with a bunch of British prisoners. Because of this, he did *not* get taken to Ofuna, where the real interrogators and torturers worked. Naval interrogators, experts in making naval people talk. He ended up in a coal mine, doing slave labor. Was this a better outcome them his ending up in Ofuna?"

Lockwood slowly sat back down. "I suppose it was," he said. "Are you saying that he did this on purpose? To avoid being sent to Ofuna?"

Gar had had enough. He stood up to face Lockwood. "I did not do that on purpose," he said. "The Jap officer I called the Priest had just finished emptying a pistol at me. I was floating at the edge of a flooded dry dock, having been pummeled by a few hundred thousand-pound bombs and the exploding magazine of a destroyer fifty feet away. I was deaf. I was in shock. My brain had been turned to mush. I thought maybe I had died. When I realized otherwise, I wanted to die. Then some guards hauled my bloody ass out of the water and threw me in a truck. They took me to the nearest POW detention facility and threw me into a railroad car. That's how I avoided Ofuna, Admiral. One more thing: That officer who'd tried to kill me in the water saved the last round for himself. He did that because I'd driven him crazy—he even said so. I didn't collaborate with that guy. I drove him to suicide."

"Commander Hammond," White interrupted, "you will have your chance to make a statement when the time comes. In the mean—"

"I believe the time *has* come, gentlemen," Gar said quietly. "I think this entire hearing happened for one reason and one reason only—someone is desperate to protect the image of the Pacific Fleet submarine force now that it's peacetime again."

"That's not true," Forrester shouted from the back of the room. Admiral Lockwood held up his index finger in Forrester's direction, indicating that he should be quiet.

Gar stepped around from behind the table and looked straight at Lockwood. "A collaborator," he said, "is a POW who does favors for the enemy in return for better treatment. To get food when the rest of the prisoners are being starved. To work in the office instead of at the bottom of a coal mine. To not be beaten on a daily basis. To get medicine if he needs it. A collaborator is someone who goes over to the other side. I did not do that.

"You seem to think that I could have escaped. I'm here to tell you that that was impossible. In Europe? Maybe. In Europe, the prisoners of war on both sides looked a lot like the enemy, didn't they. In Japan, all POWs looked like *gaijin*, foreign devils, white-faced, round-eyed, bad-smelling, and much too tall. The general population knew damned well that it was these foreign devils that were killing their sons and husbands on faraway islands, sinking their ships, cutting off their fuel, medicines, and food, and burning down entire cities. The fact that they started it didn't figure into how they felt at the local level. If an American flier parachuted into the countryside, he was cut to pieces with farm implements the moment he landed. Sorry, Admiral. There was no point to an escape."

He paused to gather his thoughts. "I did not collaborate with the enemy. Everything I told them, much of which was fantasy, made it clear that they were going to be invaded and destroyed, that there was no way out of what was coming. I told the captain of that carrier that his ship was doomed if he tried to make it to Yoko-suka, and it was. I could see it in their faces—they knew it, even if they couldn't speak it. You want proof that they knew it? They had a plan, a plan they practiced at all the camps. Know what that plan was, Admiral?"

Lockwood shook his head.

"They had a policy in place throughout the prison camp system: When the Allies finally invaded Japan itself, *all* the POWs through-out the empire were to be executed immediately. *All* the POWs. Did you know that, sir?"

"I think I read that somewhere," Lockwood said.

"I didn't read about it, Admiral: I was *there*. I experienced it.

Hell, I was next. We were all on the verge of being beheaded when the second bomb went off over Nagasaki. I think the only thing that saved us was the fact that the camp commandant's entire family lived in Nagasaki and he just lost it out on the parade ground when he saw that cloud. The next thing we knew, a column of army regulars showed up, and the camp officers were ordered to abandon the camp."

Gar took a deep breath. "There were no collaborators in the Jap prison camps, Admiral. There were only prisoners. Sick, starved, filthy, despondent, battered, and, in too many cases, dying prisoners. This inquiry that you and your chief of staff have allowed to happen is an outrage. The two of you have forgotten every*thing* and apparently every*one* you commanded during the war, and now you've reverted back to being the kind of navy that got caught with its pants down right here in Pearl Harbor."

"Commander Hammond," Martell said. "That's *enough*. I can't allow—"

"Wait," Lockwood said. He turned to Captain Martell. "By what authority did you convene this court?"

"Well, by yours, Admiral," Martel said, frowning. He waved a piece of paper. "ComSubPac. It's on your letterhead, sir. The naval district is just the admin."

Lockwood looked across the room at Forrester. "Mike, did you sign the convening order to proceed with this court of inquiry?"

"Yes, sir, I did," Forrester said. "After you and I talked, of course, and—"

"Does that mean I can retract that decision? Aren't I the convening authority within the submarine force?"

"Yes, sir, of course, but—"

"Captain Martell, since I started these proceedings, it seems to me I can stop them. I need some time to reconsider what I'm going to do about this allegation of collaboration. I believe I have two options: one, to proceed to a formal accusation and a general court-martial, or two, to dismiss the whole thing. In the meantime you and your members can stand down. I will be in touch. Mike, let's go. Commander Hammond, don't leave town."

With that admonition, Lockwood and Forrester left the courtroom. Gar and his attorneys stood there, none of them sure what to do next. Captain Martell picked up his cap and told the other two captains to come with him. Captain White glared at everybody and then stomped out of the court after the members. The only one left was the CincPacFleet public affairs officer, who was staring in astonishment at the departing captains. "Can anyone tell me what the hell just happened here?" he asked the nearly empty room.

Sharon smiled at the PAO. "Commander Hammond here," she said, "either just got himself off the hook or he did a lateral arabesque from the frying pan into the fire, if I can mix my metaphors, and all by speaking very convincingly and yet very much out of turn."

"Not for the first time, either," Gar said with a wry grin. "Anyway, what could go wrong now, hmm?"

FORTY

That afternoon Gar took a taxi downtown to Waikiki Beach. He rented a lawn chair and an umbrella and then found a beach huckster who could round up an ice bucket and a bottle of Scotch and make it appear beside his lawn chair right there on the beach. There were returning sailors and soldiers on the beach, along with a surprising number of young women. He wondered where they'd all been during the war. There it was, that phrase: during the war. Now that the war was over, he wondered how many men felt like he did, that there was a big-ass letdown gathering itself just over the horizon.

Earlier he'd gone to lunch at the O-club with his two lawyers. They talked about anything and everything except the proceedings at the court. Sharon kept smiling at him, but it was a sympathetic smile. She asked him what he was going to do for the rest of the day, and he said he was going down to the beach and get boiled. She thought that sounded like fun, but first the two of them faced the prospect of going back to headquarters for a séance with the indomitable Captain White. Lieutenant Falcone said he thought he'd go back to the BOQ and call in sick. Sharon said she was actually looking forward to it, as there were some things she wanted to say to the good captain.

The sun was warm, the breeze a comfort, and the Scotch was cold, but Gar's efforts to get drunk fizzled out. In his weakened condition it wouldn't take much whisky to make everything go away, but then he'd just end up sick and hungover. Besides, he had things to think about, like the future. Based on the general tenor of Uncle Charlie's remarks at the end of the court session, he didn't really expect a court-martial. That said, he knew he was finished in the navy. There'd certainly be no promotion now, and he'd probably get an assignment offer that would make it clear they wanted him to retire and simply go home. He didn't want to go back to coal country in Pennsylvania, but there was an empty house and fifteen very pretty acres waiting for him to just turn on the lights and move back in. His parents had been able to hold on to the place only because of Gar's Depression-era contributions, so he didn't think any of his relatives would care. He'd have to buy a car—did he have the money for that? There was so much about life back in the States that he didn't know. He could make a running surfaced attack on a Jap destroyer, but how was he going to get all the way back to Pennsylvania? Bus? Train? He thought about that and fell sound asleep.

He was startled awake by the sound of a beach chair scrunching down into the sand next to him. The sun was in his eyes as he woke up, but then he saw that it was Sharon standing in front of him, looking shapely indeed in a white bathing suit.

"You pass out or were you just napping?" she asked as she flipped a towel onto the chair and then sat down next to him.

He hefted the bottle of Scotch and saw that it was only one-quarter down. "I think I just fell asleep," he said. "Couldn't manage a proper drunk."

"Here," she said. "Let me help you with that."

He grinned and passed her the bottle and one of the glasses the beach man had brought him. "Ice in the bucket," he said.

"Straight's the way to do Scotch," she said. "Put water in it and you get a damn headache."

"Spoken like an expert," he said. "How'd it go with Captain White?"

"Oh, him. I went into his office, closed the door, took off my clothes down to my skivvies, and then screamed at the top of my lungs. His staffies came running in and I started crying hysterically and pointing at him. They were, how to put this—aghast?"

He laughed. "I'd like to have seen that," he said. "But really—did you two part friends?"

"We parted on a highly professional basis," she said. "Lawyer to lawyer. We spoke at length, as the expression goes, until I brought up Mrs. White."

"That sounds to me like a spider fight," he said. "But he'll be polite from now on?"

"Oh, yes, I do believe he will," she said. "And you were right about him and Forrester—they were trying hard to hang you out to dry. For the sake of the Service, as he so reverently put it, but I get the feeling there's still more to this, and I'm still not sure what it's about."

"Minoru Hashimoto, perhaps?" he said.

"Yeah, what was all that? Hashimoto didn't come up in our little tête-à-tête. Should he have?"

"Lockwood called it a sideshow, but the sealed orders were clear—Hashimoto first, then go raise hell if you can."

"The admiral said he never saw those sealed orders."

"I'll bet there's a copy up at CincPacFleet headquarters," Gar said. "The orders were signed out by Admiral Rennsalear."

"Christ, you're thin," she said, running her fingers over his rib cage. Her fingers lingered, but he was too tired to react.

"I'm positively fat compared to some to some of those guys," he said. "The Brits had been in captivity since early '42. They were walking cadavers. I heard that over a third of them died in Guam after liberation. *Fucking* Japs."

"Wait till you read what they found in eastern Germany and Poland," she said. "The Nazis were every bit as monstrous, only on a much bigger scale."

"I'm tired of all of it," he said. "Tired, tired, tired. And sad. We won. Whoopee. I can't even look out onto the ocean without wanting to just weep."

"Hey," she said. "I booked a room nearby. Why don't you and I go there right now and just, oh, I don't know, lie down? Hold each other? You can let go and I'll just keep you company. How's that sound?"

"Like heaven," he said, wiping his eyes. "I'm sorry."

"Don't be, sea dog," she said. "This whole thing has been a really big deal."

It's not over yet, either, he thought as they gathered up their towels. He could remember telling her how good he was at being a CO, and that he was something of a lone wolf. Well, there were two situations where you found a lone wolf: when he was a natural-born predator, and then again when the pack finally drove him out.

FORTY-ONE

The summons came at noon the following day. The BOQ front desk called him and told him that his presence was requested at SubPac headquarters at 1300, with his counsel. Gar had to assume SubPac had notified Captain White's office, since he did not have a telephone. He showered, shaved, and put on his service dress khakis. He didn't want to think about the previous night with Sharon. He'd ended up drinking too much, bawling like a baby, and then falling asleep. The good news was that she hadn't seemed to mind very much in the morning. He was pretty sure they hadn't made love. He liked to think he would have remembered that.

The yeomen in Admiral Lockwood's office were very polite when he arrived. Gar couldn't tell if that was because he was a condemned man and everybody already knew it, or they didn't want whatever he had rubbing off on them. Five minutes after he got there, Sharon and Falcone showed up. Sharon looked fine, but Falcone looked like he wanted to try out the *dive, dive* command and simply disappear. While they waited in the anteroom, two very serious-looking captains arrived and were ushered directly into Lockwood's office. The yeomen told them it would be just a few minutes more.

"Who are those guys?" Gar asked.

Sharon shook her head. "Not from PacFleet, that I know of," she said. "Never seen them before."

"Maybe they're executioners," Gar said.

"No," Sharon said with a straight face. "Executioners are always enlisted."

Gar chuckled. Falcone tried to smile but couldn't quite pull it off.

Lockwood's aide appeared in the doorway. "The admiral will see you all now," he said, indicating that they should go in.

Gar went first, followed by the two JAG officers. Lockwood was at his desk. Forrester was standing behind him with a folder. The two captains were sitting in armchairs to one side, looking at Gar as if sizing him up for a coffin.

"Reporting as ordered, Admiral," Gar said. He didn't salute, because the navy never saluted indoors.

"Very well, Commander," Lockwood said. Gar couldn't exactly read Lockwood's expression, but he sensed that it wasn't Uncle Charlie sitting there anymore. Rear Admiral Forrester spoke.

"Commander Hammond, I have been authorized by the chief of naval personnel to propose a course of action to settle, as it were, this allegation of unlawful conduct by a prisoner of war during wartime."

Gar blinked. Forrester was talking as if he weren't standing right there.

"You are talking about me, Admiral?" Gar asked. He saw Lockwood roll his eyes.

"Yes, I am," Forrester said. "The admiral has conferred with CincPacFleet, the chief of naval operations, and BuPers. They have agreed to the following . . . deal." Forrester's expression revealed his distaste at having to offer a deal. He took a deep breath before resuming. "There will be no court-martial. You will be allowed to retire immediately. You will be given five years' constructive service in recognition of your time as a POW, so you will retire on full twenty-year retired pay. You will retire in the rank of captain, on a tombstone basis. Your retired pay will be computed at the rank of commander. The court of inquiry will issue a formal statement that there were no grounds for the allegations and that the entire matter has been settled to the satisfaction of the command authorities. Do you understand so far?"

"I do, so far."

"Very well. That's the navy's offer. Here's what you have to agree to do, in writing and under a sworn oath. You will never, ever, mention, talk about, write about, or in any way reveal the nature of your last mission to Bungo Suido and the Inland Sea of Japan, especially your additional mission of putting a Japanese national ashore during that mission. Especially that."

"That's it?"

"That's it," Forrester said. Then he turned to the two captains. "Gentlemen," he said, "anything to add?"

The older of the two captains stared hard at Gar. "We are from the offices of Lieutenant General Groves, director of the Manhattan Project," he said. "Our main concern, and the sole reason that the proceedings against you have been terminated, relates to Minoru Hashimoto. I can't say this strongly enough: If you ever reveal what that was about, the United States government will find out and will smash you flatter than Hiroshima. Do I make myself clear?"

"Clear enough," Gar said.

The captain turned to the two JAG officers. "That goes for both of you, too. I'm serious, serious as a heart attack about this."

Sharon and Falcone said they understood.

"Commander Hammond, do you accept this offer?" Forrester asked.

Gar hesitated.

"He *does* accept this very generous offer," Sharon said. "He would be a fool not to, no matter what this Hashi-whazzit stuff is all about."

"I'm sorry, Commander," Forrester said. "I know you're his lawyer, but this has to come from him."

Gar was looking at Lockwood. There was one more thing he wanted, and he knew Lockwood knew what that was. The admiral stared back at him for a long moment. Then he spoke.

"You want an apology from me, don't you," he said.

"That is *not* part of the navy's offer," Forrester protested.

"Well, it should be," Lockwood said. "And I am sorry I put you through this, Gar. You were right about our dropping back into the peacetime mode of doing business. None of us knows what's coming next, so we all reverted to type, I'm afraid. But that's not the way I treated my COs during the war, and I shouldn't have cast you to the wolves just to protect our so-called Silent Service mystique."

"Thank you, sir. I appreciate your saying that, and of course I accept the deal. I know I'm lucky to get it."

"Then we're done here," Forrester said. "The terms of this agreement have been written down and will be signed by Commander Hammond and Vice Admiral Lockwood and then countersigned by the chief of naval personnel in Washington."

"And by his two lawyers here," the stone-faced captain said. "Who have forgotten everything they've heard here today except my warning."

Sharon had kept her hotel room at the beach, so they had a leisurely lunch out on the beachside verandah. They were both in uniform, he in khakis, she in whites. There were more civilians at the beach now. People wearing uniforms weren't yet in the minority, but Gar knew it was only a matter of time.

"Relieved?" she asked.

"Overwhelmingly so," he said. "Who'd a thought that one old man's piece of this would end up saving my bacon."

"I don't believe they'd have gone to court-martial," she said. "Your little speech there at the end hurt their feelings. Either way, I still think I could have torn them up."

"You were eager to try, too, weren't you?"

"Yup. I like a good court fight about as much as a good martini."

"Mister Falcone did not look like he was ready for a good court fight."

"Captain White broke his teeth when he tried to give me an ass-chewing, so I think Falcone took the brunt. He'll rebound—he's got a ticket from Harvard, and his future is going to be all about who he knows and where they all are now."

"And you? Who do you know?" he asked.

"Oh, my regulars. John Walker, James Beam, the Beefeater . . . What was that tombstone business?"

Gar laughed. "It's called a tombstone promotion. They usually do it when a captain retires. They retire him nominally in the rank of rear admiral so that when he dies his wife can put Admiral So-and-so on his tombstone."

"That was a hell of a deal," she said. "Do you actually know what that was all about?"

"Not anymore," he said. "But someday I'd like to go back and see if the old man made it alive out of the war. I did tell him to do what he was supposed to do and then to get the hell out of there."

"You witnessed Hiroshima, then?"

"Oh, yes. It's a whole new day after that firecracker. But back to my question. What're you going to do when they cut you loose? Where are you going to go?"

She shrugged. "I've saved some money these past few years," she said. "I'll find somewhere and start over. Not like I don't have a trade."

"I've saved a whole lot of money over these past four years," he said. "Especially after the Japs picked me up. I'll even be getting a retired paycheck somewhere along the line, and I have an actual house to go to back to in western Pennsylvania."

"And?"

"And, well, maybe we could join forces? You have to admit, we make a good team. I regularly get myself into trouble, and you seem to be pretty good at getting me out of it."

She smiled. "Is this a proposal, Commander?"

"It's a proposition, Commander. A proposal implies marriage, and as you know—"

"Right," she said. "Neither of us ever saw the need."

"There you go."

"I'll think it over," she said. "Some propositions need more time than others."

"In the meantime, can I buy the lady a drink?"

She frowned. "That's not going to change, Gar, at least not any-time soon. I know I have to do something about my boozing, but . . ."

"I understand, but I've always been told never to drink alone.

Look—the war's over, and the world has changed in so many ways I'm almost scared to face it. I've seen things, done things, lost too many friends and shipmates, and now they've put me on the beach and told me to go away. I'd be a really famous martyr if there weren't several thousand other people just like me headed back to the land of the free and the home of the badly bruised."

She reached across the table and gripped his hand, hard. "I may well turn out to be excess baggage, Gar. I wouldn't want to hold you back down the line."

"Back from what, Sharon?" He covered her hand with his. "For the past four years I've been looking at the world through a periscope, trying to kill people. This morning I was wondering how I'd get back to Pennsylvania from California, and I realized I didn't know how people do that back in the States these days. It'll never be a question of holding either one of us back—it'll be all about holding each other up, and learning how to live again."

She nodded. "I will think about it, kind sir. Sounds like we both have a couple of weeks." She sighed and looked out to sea. "In the meantime," she said. "How 'bout that drink?"

He laughed. "You're bad," he said. "Really bad. What are we going to do about you?"

She peered over at him through that waterfall hairdo. "We'll think of something," she said. "And if you're not going to buy me that drink I'll be forced to go back to my room, take off all my clothes, lie down, and—sulk."

"Sulk."

"Well what else could a girl do?"

"Like you said, we'll probably think of something."